One More Try

by

Paula Russell

Published by
Mabel and Stanley Publishing
March 2025

© All Rights Reserved

One More Try (Book 1)

Disclaimer

This is a work of fiction. Unless otherwise indicated, all the names, characters, businesses, places (and landscapes), events and incidents in this book are either completely from the author's imagination or used in a fictitious manner. Any resemblance to actual places, persons (living or dead) or events is purely coincidental.

One More Try (Book 1)

Iliana
Chapter 1

Iliana was lost in her own thoughts, enjoying the half hour scenic walk to her friend Elizabeth's house. She was thinking about her first day at school after she and her mum moved to the US. She was born in Scotland and had lived there happily for some time, that is, of course, until her dad had passed away suddenly just before her ninth Birthday. Her mum, Mary, wanted to return to her hometown of New Harrow, which was in the South of Florida, in between Sarasota and Fort Myers.

Iliana had been petrified about school and what would happen at the time but Elizabeth, she called her Liz now, had introduced herself straight away and she had spent the day with her and two of her friends. Since then, she and Liz had become very close, and Iliana spent a lot of time at her house whilst her mum was working; she was practically part of the family, sharing dinner, listening to music and talking for hours in Liz's bedroom.

Liz's parents owned a very large estate called Harrow Falls, named after the lovely beaches and unusual rocky ledges which were located close by. It was an amazing place where the family rented out holiday chalets and was very popular all year round. It was a family business that Liz's maternal grandfather had created and run until his death, just before Iliana moved here. Liz's mum ran the bookings and organised the different teams looking after the place like cleaning, repairs and maintenance, while her father did the repairs with the help of her four brothers, mostly her eldest brother Tom, who was eight years older than her. Tom had been helping his grandfather from a young age and had all the skills including plumbing, electrical and joinery. According to Liz he could pretty much fix anything.

Now that the girls were fifteen Liz had started dating some boys in their school; a few times Iliana had called

One More Try (Book 1)

round for her at a time they had agreed, and Liz had not been around. She hoped this didn't happen today as she was really looking forward to catching up with her and they had talked on the phone last night.

A smile appeared on her face as she approached the large two-story house and walked up the porch steps. The grand, midnight blue door had looked imposing on her first visit, but now its white frame almost seemed to reach out to her, welcoming and drawing her in. The matching tall, white-shuttered windows on either side of the door would often reveal a tantalising glimpse of the scene that typically awaited her inside; a collection of Liz's family - sometimes a few, sometimes all, depending on the time of day - chatting incessantly or arguing occasionally. Iliana noted the unfamiliar sound of quiet this time as she rang the doorbell, mere seconds passing before Liz's mother Patricia answered.

"Goodness me my lovely I've told you before you don't need to ring the bell or knock, just come in?"

"Oh thanks Mrs Anderson but that wouldn't feel polite to me." She gave her an affectionate smile.

"Okay then, but can you call me Trish please? I don't even think the people that work for me call me Mrs Anderson!" Iliana returned the smile and nodded. "Liz isn't back yet but she said she would be, do you want to wait inside?"

She stepped to the side and Iliana could see past the small hallway to the spacious, open plan living and kitchen area. She saw Liz's brother Robert sitting on one of the big corner sofas watching TV, he glanced back at her for a moment then away again.

"Oh, thanks but I'll just take a walk around outside and maybe take some pictures if that's okay?"

"Of course it's okay. You should let me see some of your pictures and perhaps we can use them in our brochure sometime?"

"Yeah sure. Thanks."

One More Try (Book 1)

Iliana walked around the back of the house through the grass playing area, past the large shed, which stored a lot of tools and equipment for maintaining the chalet business and headed beyond it towards the beach where she sat and enjoyed the beautiful scenery, as she'd done so many times before.

She pondered those first few years that she'd come here, playing with Liz on the grass she had just walked past. They would also sometimes play baseball with her brothers. Since there were five of them the addition of Iliana made the numbers even and she would always be in the opposite team to Liz with Tom looking after her and keeping her right as she never really understood the rules. Occasionally the older boys would get overly competitive and argue but it never came to any fights, and they all enjoyed themselves most of the time. As the boys got older, they gradually stopped playing baseball, Liz's younger brother Dan was still keen, but it wasn't the same with the three of them, so they gave up eventually.

Iliana thought Liz was so lucky to grow up here. Her mum had told her Scotland was a beautiful place too where they had lived before, but she didn't remember any of it unfortunately. She barely remembered her dad which was sad, she had one image of him in her head, but it was probably a photo that she had seen. She looked like him with her brown eyes, olive complexion and long nose. She smiled as she stood up and started to make her way back over to the house, she had waited for an hour now so Liz must have gotten held up somehow, she would just head home while it was still light.

As she walked around the back of the house, approaching the storage shed again, she spotted Liz's eldest brother Tom. He had his back to her, but she could see that he was busy. She watched for a while as he worked, he was very tall and a slim build. He had a black t-shirt on with dark grey combat shorts and a tool belt around his waist, this was his usual work gear. He was covered in wood shavings, she couldn't help but admire his broad shoulders and muscular arms as he was sanding, his toned legs, sun-kissed from working outside quite a bit like he was now.

He turned around and waved when he spotted her, so she walked over to see him. He stopped what he was doing and sat down for a break next to her on the wooden bench in their yard.

"Has she stood you up?" he asked with concern.

"Hmm, I probably just got the time, or day, wrong to be honest! It's fine I enjoyed the walk over here, it's good for me," Iliana replied, feeling suddenly very defensive about her best friend.

"Okay, if you say so. You guys used to be inseparable did you not?"

"We still are, it's just that she has boys interested in her and I don't. If I go with her, I end up being gooseberry which isn't much fun, so I stopped going along. It's not fun being the 'pal that tags along'!" Iliana felt bad as soon as she said this, it wasn't her friend that made her feel like that, it was the boys. "But then I guess that happens when you are best friends with the prettiest girl in school!" she added.

Tom took a drink of water from his bottle and seemed to think for a very long time. She glanced at him and was suddenly aware of what a very handsome young man he was, the girls at school talked about all of Liz's brothers but Tom, as the eldest, was always swooned over the most. He had very short brown hair and the deepest green eyes she had ever seen. He looked directly at her, "Why do you think she has boys interested in her then and you don't?"

"I didn't mean that ... I just ..."

"It's fine ... why though?" He was smiling at her.

"I don't know, because she is extremely pretty?" She frowned at him as she said it, but he was shaking his head.

"She is, of course, but you are too."

"Thanks, but I am not pretty, I am plain. But I am okay with plain as I am not a fan of being the centre of attention anyway."

One More Try (Book 1)

"You care and listen to people. Liz tells me that you are friends with all the kids at school, not just the popular ones, all of them, the clever ones, the odd ones, they all like you. But boys that age don't really bother about that, which is why they don't seem interested in you yet. When you are older you will meet guys who appreciate you for what you are and not the superficial ones chasing my sister just now. You wait and see."

"It doesn't really matter about the boys at school as I am not that bothered about any of them anyway, but thanks for the compliment, I think!" She was so relaxed talking with him that she found she smiled confidently without even realising it. "So, what are you making then?" she added, changing the subject.

"Oh this? It's nothing really, just a bit of leftover wood from repairing some furniture in the chalets, there's not much of it but I thought it could be useful for something at least. What do you think I could make out of it?"

"Hmm, not sure, there's a lot of it but small pieces." She pondered for a moment before adding, "Maybe a small jewellery box. It could even have little drawers. Or a chest type one?"

"That's a good idea, I might do that," he smiled.

They chatted for quite a bit of time about other things, families, the area, people, and what she wanted to do when she was older, she mentioned she liked the idea of teaching. Tom told her he thought she would be a good teacher as she had the right qualities for it which also made her smile.

They chatted for so long that before she knew it, it was starting to get dark, "Goodness me look at the time, I had better get home."

"Wow, yeah, I had better get cracking too, I have a date tonight. Can I give you a lift home?"

"Oh no it's okay, I enjoy the walk, besides I don't want you to be late for your date," she replied, not really meaning it.

One More Try (Book 1)

"Actually, it wasn't really a question. I am not about to let you walk home in the dark, I can drop you off now before I shower, or you can wait thirty minutes and I can drop you off on the way?"

"Okay, thanks. Now is good if that's okay as Mum might start to worry?"

"Of course, let's go!" and he jumped over the bench to get his car keys.

They walked around the yard to reach the cars parked in the driveway and she climbed in the passenger seat of his car. As she did so she caught sight of Robert who was watching them and smiling. Robert looked more like their father with his longer brown hair, round face and brown eyes and Tom towered over him.

"Oh yeah, what's this then? Is this who your date is with Tom? Didn't realise you liked them so young!"

"Go fuck yourself! Just being a gentleman, I guess you wouldn't understand that would you?" Tom snapped as he climbed into the driver seat, started the car, and sped away, leaving a sneering Robert behind them.

Iliana just chatted and made small talk with Tom in the car. A song came on the radio that she liked so she mentioned it and he turned up the sound. It was One More Try by George Michael, she loved the song so just listened to it for a while, taking in the words.

Tom smiled when he heard the word 'teacher' in the song, "Is that why you want to be a teacher then?"

Iliana laughed. She hadn't really thought about the words like that before.

"Well, I don't think it is meant literally, I always thought it was more that the person he is singing about is helping him learn life lessons rather than teaching in an academic sense?"

"Hmm, yeah good point." Tom raised his eyebrows as he spoke, and she thought he looked quite impressed.

As he pulled up outside her house, she saw her mum look out of the curtains, so she was glad she had gotten a lift.

One More Try (Book 1)

"Please tell me you won't walk home on your own in the dark anymore, it's not great you know?" he said, sounding concerned.

"Oh, I don't mind it, I like the sky at night, the moon and stars have always fascinated me."

"Well, it's not a good idea for a young girl to be walking on her own in the dark, just saying. Your mom sure wouldn't want it."

"Okay, okay, I get it, you're right. Thank you for the lift, I hope you enjoy your night tonight."

"Thanks. Anytime for the lift too." He smiled at her before she climbed out of the car.

She didn't hear him say anything more, but she looked back and gave him a wave which he returned with another smile.

Iliana found herself skipping around her house that night, her mum did notice and asked her what was going on, but she just said nothing. Liz called her later that night to apologise for not being there, apparently, she had been out on a date with Tony, who was a bit older and had his own car, but it had broken down, so they had to wait for his dad to collect them. Of course, Iliana said not to worry about it. Things had worked out quite well after all as she had had a very pleasant afternoon.

*

The next day at school Liz asked her a bit more about what happened. "So, I hear you spent some time with my eldest brother and got a lift home?" she said, raising a pretty eyebrow in Iliana's direction. She was about the same height as Iliana with long wavy dark hair, a dainty button nose, lovely big blue eyes and high cheek bones.

"Yeah, we chatted for a bit. It was dark before I knew it, so he gave me a lift home, no big deal." Iliana said casually with a shrug "Did he mention it?"

"No Robert told me. Just be careful Iliana, don't go falling for him as he gets in a lot of trouble from what I hear."

"What do you mean?"

"I hear Mom and Dad arguing about him a lot, he is hardly around but when he is, he is short of money, they think he is selling drugs, Dad calls him a waster," she frowned. "I know he can be charming though, so I don't want you getting hurt."

"He doesn't seem like a waster to me, we just talked but he has always been nice to me and seems like a really good guy. He is your brother, surely you don't believe that?"

"No. I don't believe it. He can be very sweet, especially to me as his only sister. But being the eldest of five must be hard so I don't have a go at him like some of the others do." Liz looked pensive as she replied.

"Well don't worry about me, I will be fine."

They didn't mention any more about it, but Iliana did wonder if there was more going on.

*

A few weeks later when Iliana was leaving school, she was walking out of the gates with her friends when she saw a lot of girls gathered in a group giggling and pointing at a familiar car across the street. She spotted Liz's younger brother, Dan, get into the car and noticed that the driver was Tom; his frown became a smile when he saw her, and he waved and gestured for her to come over.

As she crossed the street, she felt everyone watching her. It seemed like everything had gone silent in that moment as she approached the car. Tom was wearing a white shirt and blue striped tie; she was only used to seeing him in his work gear so tried hard not to stare.

"Hi gorgeous!" He greeted her with a smile.

"Hi," was all she could manage in reply, but she returned the smile.

"Do you know where Liz is? She is supposed to be here for me to pick her up as Mom has some photo shoot organised for us all."

"She ran out of class right on the bell, said she was meeting Tony."

"Oh man, what is she like. Do you know where he lives?"

"Yeah, it's not far. I can show you?"

"Hop in then, thanks."

She made her way towards the back of the car where Dan was, but he stopped her, "No you can come in the front, Liz can sit in the back when we get her."

Dan smiled at her, he was a year younger than she and Liz but was already much taller even at fourteen. As she walked around the car, she looked around at all the people, especially the girls, watching her. She wasn't keen on being the centre of attention, but this felt good, maybe it depended on where that attention was coming from? She climbed into the passenger seat and fastened her seatbelt. She noticed the girls were still watching Tom as they pulled away.

They drove the short journey to Tony's place in relative silence where Iliana retrieved a slightly dishevelled and embarrassed Liz. She was putting some makeup on and tidying herself as Iliana climbed out of the car and said her goodbyes.

She lay awake in bed later that night, pondering. *'Gorgeous.'* Had Tom really called her that?

Chapter 2

As Iliana and Liz approached their sixteenth birthdays, they remained very close and still managed to spend lots of time together at each other's houses, with the occasional sleepover and nights in listening to music. There were a few occasions where Iliana would bump into Tom while he was working, he would always say hi and ask how she was. She couldn't deny that the older she got the more her heart fluttered whenever she saw him, but she never told anyone.

At Liz's house one night, they had been drinking too much soda, so Iliana needed the bathroom during the night. Someone tried the door when she was in there, so she hurried up and when she came out Tom was waiting. He seemed very wobbly and was leaning against the wall, smiling as always.

"Hey, Iliana" he slurred his words, so Iliana sounded more like iillllieeeeeeeaana.

"Hi, are you okay?" she frowned and hesitated, "You're not drunk, or high or something, are you?"

He looked quite genuinely shocked, "High? You mean on drugs? Why would you think that?" His words were much clearer this time.

"Just something I heard, that's all."

"Probably from Robert or my father no doubt, it's not true." He stood up straighter. "Although it's true I have had a few beers, maybe a few too many, but the most I do is smoke a bit of weed occasionally, that's all. They seem to like to make everyone think I am a lot worse than that."

"I don't think you are worse than that. I was just curious, you know me," she smiled, feeling a lot more relaxed. "I had better get back to bed anyway, sorry to have kept you waiting." She moved to go past him.

"No problem, Illy, or Anna. What would you prefer your name be shortened to?" he said looking directly into her eyes as she walked past; there was only about a foot between them. She could see right into his green eyes, and she was ashamed to admit it made her feel slightly weak at the knees, even with the smell of alcohol on his breath.

"I haven't ever thought about it, no one has shortened my name strangely enough. So why don't you choose?"

He smiled.

"Okay, I will. Goodnight Illy," he whispered as he went into the bathroom and closed the door.

When she returned to Liz's room, she had trouble getting back to sleep as she couldn't stop thinking about staring into Tom's green eyes. She also couldn't help but overhear some arguing downstairs, it sounded like Tom and his dad, James, but she couldn't hear everything. She did hear James shouting about him using the house like a hotel and she thought she could hear his mum defending him but it was quite muffled in such a big house. It wasn't nice to hear, and she really felt for Tom. He seemed to do a lot around the place, helping with the business. She eventually drifted off to sleep, still dreaming about his green eyes.

Sunday mornings in Liz's house were always quite relaxed as everyone got out of bed at different times. Liz and Iliana typically got up quite late and got their own breakfast then Iliana's mum would pick her up or she would get a lift home from Trish.

This morning was different though as they could hear loud voices downstairs from about 10am.

"Is everything okay?" Iliana asked Liz as they stirred.

"Not sure, I will check," she frowned.

She put on her dressing gown and went downstairs. She was away for a good fifteen minutes but Iliana didn't hear any more arguing.

Liz came in the room with some breakfast items on a tray for them, "We'll just have some breakfast here today I think." She was muttering, her eyes focused on the tray.

"What's wrong Liz?" Iliana walked over to help her with the tray.

"Mum isn't talking to Dad as apparently Tom has now moved out."

13

One More Try (Book 1)

"What? I heard a bit of arguing last night but surely that's normal with family is it not?"

"Well, it happens a lot in this house, especially between Tom and Dad." Iliana reached over to give her friend a hug as her voice wobbled.

"Hey, it's okay. I am sure they will work it out. Shh, it's okay." They hugged for a few minutes until Liz composed herself.

"Let's eat," she mumbled, wiping her eyes and giving Iliana an extra pat on the back.

"Do you know where he has gone?"

"He is staying with a school friend for now but apparently, he has been looking for a while and has a place lined up. Our grandfather left us all money, so he is using it as a down payment on his own place."

"Wow, so it's not a temporary thing then?"

"No definitely not, I guess he is twenty-three so probably needs his own space anyway." Liz shrugged as she spoke. "Mom says he has an extra job working at the cash and carry as well, which I didn't know about. I think only Mom knew."

Iliana couldn't help but feel upset that she might not see as much of him, she felt quite selfish for even thinking it.

*

Iliana's birthday was in January, so she was one of the first in their group to turn sixteen. She had her closest friends over to the house for a sleepover, Liz of course, Victoria and Becca. They had pizza and soda then watched episodes of Cheers all night. She had a fabulous time.

The weekend after her birthday she had arranged a sleepover at Liz's house, her mum dropped her off just before 7pm as arranged but it was very quiet. She suspected the family weren't home yet from a day out or shopping trip. As she walked around the house, she heard a car come up the driveway and when she turned, she expected to see the big station wagon carrying Liz, Dan and her mum but it was Tom, on his own, in his car.

14

One More Try (Book 1)

She waited for him to park then spoke as he got out of the car. "Hi Tom, do you know where everyone is?"

"Illy, so glad you are here! I have something for you for your birthday."

"Oh, wow! Thanks. You didn't have to get me anything though?" she replied, secretly really pleased and intrigued.

"Oh, I didn't get anything. I made it, come on in then I'll get it for you. It's not wrapped or anything, sorry."

They made their way to the house together and he opened the door. "They are all out shopping, running a bit late."

"Oh okay."

"Mom phoned to remind me I was coming over to do some repairs and mentioned you were coming, then of course realised they would probably be late so I said I would come over early."

She made her way inside to the big living room and sat down on one of the sofas as Tom went back outside, presumably to his car. She looked around the large room and thought about all the good times she had spent here, sharing time with Liz's family, well most of them anyway. Tom occasionally, hardly ever their father or Robert, but their mum and Liz's other brothers, Dan and Brad.

Tom came back into the house looking quite coy which made her look twice as it was so unusual. He walked slowly and carried what looked like a box in his hands. He handed it to her, "Happy Birthday! I hope you like it."

She took it from him gently and looked down at her hands... it was a very small set of wooden drawers with tiny handles, there were two smaller drawers at the top and a bigger one on the bottom. It was about maybe six inches wide and a bit more in height. The two small drawer handles were in the shape of stars and the large one was a crescent moon shape.

"Oh, my goodness, it's amazing! You *made* this?" For me? she wanted to add but resisted.

"Well yes, do you remember it was your idea when I had some leftover wood a few years ago?" He was blushing and seemed quite modest about it, much to her surprise.

"Yes, I do remember. Of course. Did it take this long to make?" she responded cheekily.

"Ha no I just worked on it when I could and eventually thought it would be good to give to you for your special birthday."

"I LOVE it, thank you so much! "She reached out both arms around his shoulders to give him a hug but kept it very short so as not to embarrass him, or herself for that matter.

"You are very welcome, I'm glad you like it," he grinned.

"Did you carve the small handles too? They are amazing I love them! You are so talented."

"Thanks Illy. Can I get you a drink of soda?" He headed towards the large kitchen and opened the fridge. She noticed he grabbed a bottle of beer for himself.

"How about a beer?"

"Are you twenty-one?" he replied with a chuckle.

"Not quite, just a taste then?"

He walked over to her and stood in front of her, "I tell you what, if you try this and like the taste then you can have the rest of the bottle?" He was still laughing but not in a mocking way.

"Ah, you don't think I will like it?"

"Correct. I am almost 100% sure you will *not* like it. It takes years of practice to get used to it." He chuckled at his own joke, and she couldn't help but join in.

He leaned forward to offer her the bottle and she took it from him. She sniffed the top, it really didn't smell good, but she didn't want him to know that. She lifted the bottle to her lips and paused to look at him, still smiling with his intense green eyes fixed on her, just the way she liked it. She tipped the bottle and took a very small sip.

"Hmm, not bad." He raised his eyebrow slightly, waiting. "But not great, you can finish your beer after all." She laughed and handed the bottle back to him, a little sad the

One More Try (Book 1)

moment between them was over. "Maybe I should stick to the sodas for now, or wine, I might try that later."

He smiled and went back to the fridge to get her a soda. Iliana put the beautiful jewellery box carefully in her overnight bag and closed it. She wondered who else knew that he had made it for her.

Just at that moment Liz burst through the door with several shopping bags, followed by Dan and their mum, again with more shopping bags. They were all talking at the same time, so the once quiet room was back to its usual chaos; she continued to quietly relish the time she had just spent with Tom.

"So sorry we are late back Iliana, we got caught up as usual! I see my son has at least offered you a soda though, thanks Tom."

"You're welcome, you know me, always a gentleman," Tom responded with a smile while leaning down to put his arm around his mother. She kept smiling at him, she had lovely blue eyes, the same as Liz's and Dan's and long dark hair, although she always tied it back in a ponytail. There were a few light touches of grey at the edges on both sides but barely noticeable. She was now forty-three years old and still a very beautiful woman, despite a lot of hard work on their land running a chalet business and raising five children.

At that moment the phone rang, and Trish answered it.

"It's for you Tom."

Tom looked surprised but quickly made his way over to take the phone from his mum, still sipping at his beer. "Hello? Oh Hey, yeah just a minute." His voice softened a bit, and he took the cordless phone away upstairs with his beer.

"Bring that back when you are done with your phone call, please?" his mum shouted after him. He waved acknowledgement just before he disappeared around the corner on the stairs, still talking quietly and smiling. Iliana could feel her shoulders tense at the thought of him on the phone to a woman.

17

One More Try (Book 1)

The girls headed up to Liz's room to see what she had bought after asking Trish if she needed any help. As they headed up the stairs Iliana couldn't help but look for Tom, he was obviously in his old room as she could hear his voice as they walked past.

When they got to Liz's room, she placed her shopping bags on the bed then rummaged through them until she found a particular one. She held the handle with her forefinger and thumb as she held it out to Iliana, beaming. "Happy birthday best friend in all the world."

"Oh, you didn't have to get me anything, you already gave me a gift?"

"That was from Mom, this is from me, go ahead and open it."

Iliana carefully opened the bag, she could see material, a gorgeous colour of turquoise blue with a small pattern of white flowers. When she opened it, it was a v neck top which they had noticed in a shop a while ago when they were out at the mall.

"Oh, my goodness! It's the top I really liked, oh thank you, thank you so much!" she immediately took off her top and tried it on, it was a perfect fit.

"I love it! But you shouldn't have, it was too expensive!" she said, suddenly remembering how much it cost.

"Don't worry it was reduced and Mom said you deserve it for your special birthday."

"Oh, I don't know what to say, your family are all so good to me. I can't thank you enough."

"You don't have to thank us, you are pretty good to us too you know, always offering to help out around here. In fact," she pondered, "now that you are sixteen you should ask for a job to earn some extra pocket money… Why didn't I think of that before?" Iliana just nodded and couldn't stop smiling. "Here, let me cut the tags off. It really suits you that colour, brings out your lovely olive skin and big brown eyes. Also, your lovely cleavage, you should show a bit more of it, you are a young woman now!"

"Thanks, I didn't really think I had much of a cleavage but there it is," she chuckled, looking down at the small crease between her breasts, "well there you go!"

"The boys at school would be falling over themselves for you in that top," her friend said with affection.

"Meh, can't say as that would bother me too much, I don't really fancy any of them anyway. I prefer to have them as friends."

"What about Billy Garcia? He always goes out of his way to talk to you and hang out with you, do you not like him?"

"I do like him, he's great, but just as a friend. I guess I never really thought about him that way," Iliana replied thoughtfully. "I plan to go do teacher training after my SATs so will be moving away. I wouldn't want to have to leave a relationship."

"That's two years away, Iliana! Think of the fun, and *sex*, you could have in the two years between now and then!" she nudged her in the side laughing.

Iliana burst out laughing and prodded her friend back. "What? Well now I have a picture in my head of me having sex with him, thanks very much! I won't be able to look him in the eye on Monday at school." But the image in her head didn't seem real at all, it was comical almost, not to be offensive to Billy, she just didn't think of him like that, still it made her giggle.

Chapter 3

Iliana had asked Liz's parents about working that night at dinner and once they had agreed with her mum that it was okay, she started working from 10am until 3pm on Saturdays, cleaning and preparing the chalets for new arrivals. There were about twenty chalets so there was a team of girls, and they allocated the chalets to be cleaned first thing then got started right away. Everything had to be pristine in the rooms including all surfaces dusted, polished, cleaned, floors swept and hoovered. Clean linen was provided of course, and beds made, they even had to fold the toilet paper in a particular way. It was hard work, but she really enjoyed it and, of course, enjoyed the paycheck at the end of each week.

She would get dropped off for 10am by her mum, then typically walk home after finishing around 3pm, unless Liz was about then she would hang out for a bit and sometimes stay over.

Since she was interested in teaching, she also volunteered at the local Sunday school to help with the kids. It was hard work but only for two hours and it was valuable experience for her.

One Saturday while working she saw Liz's brother, Brad, who was six years older than she and Liz, and his girlfriend Jane leaving one of the chalets, still putting on shoes and arranging themselves. They didn't have their own place yet, but she was sure it wouldn't be long before they moved in together and got engaged, they had been going out since high school and were inseparable.

Another time, a few weeks later, she was almost done for the day and had just finished cleaning her second to last chalet. She was gathering up all her things onto the trolley including a huge bundle of dirty linen when she spotted Robert coming towards her, he was the nearest in age and probably the one Iliana felt the least close to. He appeared distant and almost devious in what he did, often winding up

One More Try (Book 1)

his brothers and sister and vying for attention from their parents. He was now nineteen though, so she really wasn't sure why. He was walking towards her with a toolbox in hand, looking directly at her as he swung it from side to side, grinning about something.

"Don't tell me you just cleaned number sixteen? I need to do a repair so it may be messy! You'll just have to do it again after!"

"Oh no, really?" she sighed. "Why didn't you tell the cleaning team there was a repair to be done, then we could have made sure we did that one last?"

"Oh, so now you are telling my folks how to run their business are you? When did you suddenly become an expert?" His tone was almost venomous, he really didn't like her at all, and it appeared she hadn't helped matters.

"No, you know I didn't mean it that way. It's not your parents' fault it's just about communication between their teams," she replied defensively as she was trying to move past him on the deck of the chalet whilst struggling with all her things.

"Whatever, you have no idea what you are talking about. Mom and Dad only employ you cos they feel sorry for you!" Again, with the tone, he had also made sure there wasn't enough room for her to get past so she would have to squeeze past him.

"Give me the key," he snapped, reaching out his hand in an already tight space. It also meant he was touching her breast which really didn't help the feeling of unease that she had.

"Don't you have your own set for repairs?" She instantly regretted saying this as his expression darkened. Before he could say any more, she went into her pocket, leaning back as far as she could so as not to touch him any more than she already was, and handed him the set of keys.

"Robert!" She heard a male voice shout and looked around to see Tom approaching them, she had never been so glad to see him. "What the fuck are you doing?" He looked furious.

"What do you mean, I need to repair this chalet as per Dad's instructions?" Robert replied defensively, his voice straining with false innocence. He immediately moved away from Iliana and attempted to search for the correct key.

"I think you know exactly what I mean? Also, if there is a repair needed then the cleaning team should have been informed as it will have to be cleaned again after."

"Oh, for fuck's sake," he rolled his eyes, "everyone's an expert now, eh?"

"No idea what you mean, it's just common sense," Tom stated, he had stopped at the bottom of the stairs and was looking up at them. Iliana felt even more awkward now as Robert looked indignant. She made her way down the ramp with her cart and gave Tom a look of thanks.

"I'll come back when you're done Robert, these things happen I guess."

Tom helped her with the cart as she made her way to the last chalet (well not the last anymore). "I've been looking for you, I need to go into town later to get something for Mom, do you want a lift home after your shift finishes? Liz isn't about so I didn't think you would be hanging around; this is hard work so you could get home sharp and relax?"

"That would be great, it's been a particularly tough day, and I will probably finish a bit after 3pm if I have to do that one again," she replied, nudging her head towards the chalet that Robert had gone in.

"Yeah, I'll speak to Mom about that, poor communication. I'll leave you to it, just come up to the house when you finish and we can head off, that okay?" He gave her his usual charming smile.

"Sounds great, thank you, again," she replied sincerely.

The thought of a lift home, from Tom as well, lifted her spirits a lot and before she knew it, she had finished both chalets, including the one that had been repaired, with no sign of Robert thankfully, and he had left the keys in the door for her.

Once she had finished, she called at the house for Tom. He had changed out of his work gear and was wearing a plain white t-shirt with jeans and sneakers; he looked particularly handsome for some reason, even more so than he usually did. He had well defined muscles and a very flat stomach which the white t-shirt seemed to accentuate. Her knees went weak sometimes when he called her Illy, as he was the only one that did so. Maybe she was just getting older and hornier as Liz kept saying to her.

"Was Robert hassling you earlier today?" he asked once they were in the car and on the way. He sounded concerned; his handsome brow furrowed as he spoke.

"No not really, he just creeped me out a bit as he didn't seem to want to let me past. I was probably just imagining it though." She immediately regretted saying that Liz (and Tom's) brother creeped her out and tried to make light of it.

"No, you weren't. It looked to me like he was trying to touch you. So, you were right to be creeped out, he can be like that sometimes. I'm so sorry!" He sounded very genuine, it made her heart melt.

"You don't have to be sorry, it's not your fault, anyway you rescued me. "She smiled and, again, tried to make light of it. She really didn't want to get in between siblings and cause any issues, or any *more* issues.

"Hmm." He frowned again.

"You guys don't really get on that well, do you?" she tried to continue the conversation.

"Not really, I've never really done anything to him, he just seems to have a chip on his shoulder. Of all my siblings he is the one I get on with the least, shame really but with such a big family I guess it happens. I'm also not always around and he seems to resent it when I am," he pondered. "Anyway, enough about him, how are you these days? Mom tells me you are helping at Sunday school?"

"Yes, I am. It's okay, its hard work as some of the kids are little shits if I am honest! But I guess if I am going to be a teacher then I have to get used to that," she laughed as she spoke.

He laughed too, "That's my girl, I thought for a minute you were going to tell me it was wonderful, and they were all angels, which would make me worry you weren't prepared for what was ahead."

"No, definitely living in the real world, me. You don't need to worry about that."

"Good, take it from me, the eldest of five, even kids in the same family can be little shits too. I have no idea why people want to have kids in the first place."

"Oh wow, so you don't want kids yourself, one day?"

"Probably not," he replied nonchalantly.

"Ah well, I am not sure yet, we'll see how the teaching goes I guess."

"Yeah, good plan," he shrugged.

They continued to chat until he dropped her off when she waved goodbye and thanked him for the lift.

*

As the summer months approached, she worked more, if her schoolwork allowed. After the incident with Robert, she made sure she was never around when he was about so that he couldn't offer her a lift home, not that he had offered her a lift before, but just in case.

One Saturday she finished late as there had been a lot to do on all the chalets that day, she knew Liz wasn't around and it was very quiet, so she was gathering her things and getting ready when she saw Tom, obviously just finishing his repairs too.

"Hey, you're finishing late today?" he said with his usual charming smile.

"Yeah it was a busy one today, I assume it was the same for you?"

"Yeah, although I started late cos I had trouble with my car so had to put it in the shop for repairs."

"Oh no, that's not good."

"Not good at all, there is no one around to give you a lift either, Mom is out and Dad has the van. Is your mom working?"

"Yes, she is. Never mind I can just walk, it's no big deal."

"No way, it's late Illy you are not walking on your own. Didn't we already have this conversation?" He didn't wait for an answer but continued, "I can walk you home. I am just hanging around anyway since I won't be driving home, or I can phone you a cab?"

"Won't you be heading back to yours anyway?"

"No, the shop is closer to here so I was going to stay and Mom said she would drop me off in the morning."

"But if you walk me home you will have to walk all the way back?"

"That's fine, it's good for me, don't worry about that. It keeps me fit. Just let me dump my toolbox and stuff. Do you need to get any water or anything from the house?"

"No I'm good, thanks."

She waited for him to come back, and they started walking towards the fields since it wasn't practical to walk along the road; besides, it would be quicker. She couldn't help but feel like there was something very special about walking with him. "So do you have a girlfriend these days then?" She tried to appear casual.

"Not really."

"But you are always saying you have a date are you not?" she probed.

"Just because I have a date, doesn't mean she's my girlfriend, nor does it mean it's with the same girl each time," he replied with a cheeky grin.

"Ah, I see," she really didn't.

"What about you, no boyfriend? No one at school that's snapped you up. I hear Billy Garcia is keen?"

"What? Has my friend been talking to you about my love life? Or lack of it I guess?" she feigned horror.

25

"Yeah, just a bit. But don't be mad she just wants you to be happy," he responded defensively.

"I am happy, why do I have to have a boyfriend to be happy?"

"Good point." He turned and smiled at her with a look of respect as they continued to walk.

"It must be great now that you are in your own place?" She continued the conversation.

"Yeah, it is. Although it has its drawbacks like having to cook and do my own washing but it's mostly good. It's great to have some independence for sure. I am still at the house a lot, helping of course as you have seen, juggling that and my other job is a challenge, but Mom needs the help and I have done it since I was a teenager so it's second nature now almost. I needed to get out of the house though …" he paused and looked off into the distance.

"I did hear arguing sometimes when I was staying over. Are you okay?"

"Yeah, it's normal with a big family, I guess. But Dad, well if you heard you know some of it, he was always at me, or at least it felt like that anyway. Remember the time you asked me if I was high?" He regarded her with such a serious expression it broke her heart.

At this point they had to climb over a fence, so Tom climbed first to help Iliana over, he made it look easy. She struggled a bit and slipped but he caught her arm and stopped her from falling.

"Thanks, climbing fences has never been my strong point," she said, brushing herself down and removing bits of fence. "Yeah, I am so sorry about the 'High' comment, I never believed it and neither did Liz if that makes you feel any better?"

"Thanks," he gave her a half smile. "I just don't understand it. But it's better I am out of the house for Mom's sake if nothing else, she was always defending me and arguing with Dad over it." Again he seemed to stop short. "My room is still there so I can stay over occasionally if I need to work late or anything I suppose, like tonight."

"I don't see your dad much at all when I am there, I get the impression he is hardly ever around as he is working all of the time?"

"Well, he is hardly ever around but I am not convinced it's because he is working all of the time."

"What do you mean? What else could he be doing?"

"I don't know, but when I see the things that need to be done around the place, I just wonder what he spends his time doing that's all. Maybe he is just slower as he is getting older." He smiled at her.

The walk to Iliana's house was only about half an hour but it seemed to go so quickly, as they approached her house, she found that she slowed down a bit. "Thanks for walking me home Tom, you are such a gentleman."

"Shh, don't tell anyone. Can't have people thinking I am a gentleman." He put his fingers to his lips and was laughing.

"Your secret is safe with me," she chuckled, "do you want to come in for a coffee or bathroom break?" She didn't want their time together to end and hoped she didn't sound desperate.

"No thank you."

"What about a beer? I am pretty sure Mum has some?"

"That's very tempting but I had better get back, thanks anyway."

"I feel awful that you have to walk back now too, I can call you a cab, my treat?"

"I have enjoyed the walk so it's no bother. Please promise me you won't walk home on your own if no one is around at ours to give you a lift though?"

"I am a big girl now you know?"

"Maybe, but there's also some big bad men out there and I don't like the thought of you walking on your own. Someone will always appear eventually at Harrow Falls if you wait a bit."

"Okay, I promise, thanks again. See you next time."

One More Try (Book 1)

"Yeah, take care."

    She wanted to acknowledge him in some way but wasn't sure if she should give him a hug or a peck on the cheek, but she didn't want to embarrass him or herself, so she just waved. He waved back and waited until she got her key out and opened the door before he walked off to make his way home. Her mum wasn't home, but she skipped around the house that night again. What was it about this guy that made her feel this way?

Chapter 4

Iliana's seventeenth Birthday was another great occasion, she celebrated with her mum and Liz and her mum gave her driving lessons. Once she got over the initial nerves, she found she liked driving and her mum was very patient with her; within a few months she had passed her driving test.

One Saturday in June Iliana didn't feel too well in the morning, she didn't think it would last as she had gotten her period, and she didn't want to let the cleaning team down, so she went to work anyway. She perked up a bit once she was there, but she certainly wasn't as fast as usual. By the time she was about to do her second to last chalet she was feeling exhausted, but she pushed on. After she left the chalet, she spotted Tom and he smiled and waved at her, as she continued though she felt surprisingly weak, she leaned against her trolley and was vaguely aware of Tom's voice in the distance but before she knew it everything went black!

When she came around, she was looking right into Tom's green eyes as he was lowering her onto something. It took her quite a while to realise she was in Liz's room.

"Hey, you're awake?" he whispered.

"What happened? I still have one more chalet to do." She tried to sit up.

"No way!" He gently put his arm across her shoulders to stop her sitting up. "Lie down and rest for a bit. You collapsed in a heap!"

"Did I? Wow I have never done that before."

"Mom is on her way. Don't worry about the last clean, I will go and let the team know. If needed, I can clean it."

"Thanks Tom." He smiled at her as they heard a soft knock on the door.

"Hey, how are you feeling?" Trish entered the room slowly, frowning with concern.

"I am fine, really I am."

"I will leave you ladies to it for a bit then." Tom got up and left the room abruptly.

"You had us worried young lady, you were as white as that sheet when Tom brought you in."

"What? He carried me in from outside?" Trish nodded "Oh, how embarrassing, at least I didn't wet myself I suppose!" She sighed and Trish laughed.

"Trust you to think of that first!" Trish was smiling but still seemed concerned.

"I am okay, honestly. I got my period this morning, so I was feeling a little bit off but nothing to worry about."

"Ah okay, I did bring up some pain killers for cramps just in case. Here you are," she got the pills out of her pocket and handed her a glass of water, "I've put the kettle on for a cup of tea as well, that always helps me and Liz."

"Thanks. I am sure I will be fine."

"Yes, I am sure you will, but I think some rest will do you good, you can just stay here tonight. I will phone your mom and the Sunday school to say that you are not well and won't be in tomorrow."

"I'll be fine by tomorrow."

"My advice would be to rest. I am sure your mom will agree when I call her?"

"Okay then, thanks." Iliana gave in as she knew it was hopeless.

"Let's get you out of your work clothes too, I'll get you something of Liz's." Trish got a t-shirt out of a drawer and handed it to Iliana then she helped her out of her t-shirt and work apron. Iliana put the clothes on then Trish tucked her in, as if she was nine years old again.

"Thanks," she said sincerely.

"You are welcome. Liz is due back for dinner so she can look after you too, she'll be worried."

Trish stood up just as there was a knock on the door, and they heard Tom's voice. "It's just me."

"Come in," Iliana replied. He pushed the door with his hip and entered the room with a cup of tea in one hand and a plate with a slice of toast in the other.

One More Try (Book 1)

"I noticed half a sandwich still in your cart, did you have any lunch?"

"I had one of my sandwiches but wasn't that hungry." He put the tea and toast down on the bedside table next to Iliana, this was essentially her bed when they had sleepovers so she, Liz, Trish, all just referred to it as her bed.

"Well, I am just off to make a few calls, back in a bit." Trish left the room. Iliana picked up the tea and took a sip as Tom sat back down on the edge of the bed.

"You make a good cuppa." She smiled at him for reassurance as he still seemed concerned.

"Well, it doesn't happen often so enjoy it while you can," he laughed as she took a bite of the toast. "You seem better already; you had us worried."

"It's fine really, just women's stuff, nothing to worry about."

"Ah, okay, not much I can help you with there then." He was still smiling, and she couldn't help but feel elated at the concern that he had shown for her. She finished her toast, surprised at how much she had needed it and immediately felt better as she had another sip of tea.

"Thank you."

"No problem." He stood up. "I will leave you to it then, hopefully you can get some rest and feel better in the morning."

"I feel better already."

"Yeah, you look better but best to be sure, I think. Take care Illy. I'll see you soon."

"Thanks again." She felt devastated that he was leaving so soon but guessed that he had better things to be doing on a Saturday night.

"No problem, I'd rather not make a habit of it though if you don't mind." That cheeky grin again, she loved to see it.

Once he had gone, she finished her tea and put her head on the pillow, she couldn't stop imagining Tom coming back in the room and climbing into bed next to her to snuggle.

One More Try (Book 1)

Her hormones were really playing games with her today, where did all that come from? Although it made her smile to herself and before she knew it, she woke up to the sound of Liz's voice. "Sorry did I wake you?"

"No, it's fine I was just dozing."

"You were out for the count young lady!"

"Ha, you sound like my Mum." Liz laughed, "and your Mum for that matter." Iliana laughed too.

"Everyone was worried, they said you were really pale, but you look nice and pink now."

"Yeah, I do feel better, how long was I asleep?"

"No idea."

"Well, it must have been about 2:30 when I collapsed as I only had one clean left. But I fell asleep just after Tom left, do you know when that was?"

"Ah, Mom said he left two hours ago."

"What? I can't believe I slept that long!"

"Well, you must have needed it. Do you want anything to eat?"

"No thanks. I am good. Tom made me tea and toast."

"What? He did? I don't think he has ever made any of us tea and toast, you should feel honoured. He must have been *really* worried about you." She laughed, clearly trying to lighten the mood.

"Yeah, must have been, your Mum looked worried too but really I am fine, just bad cramps."

"Yeah, Mom said. Some rest will do you good. I can keep you company. I'll get some magazines and we can look through them. Mom phoned your mom, and Sunday school, and it's all fine, she said she came up to tell you, but you were fast asleep, so she didn't want to wake you."

"That's so good of her, I will thank her in the morning."

They spent the rest of the evening in Liz's room chatting and looking through magazines. Liz made her some more tea and toast later and Iliana felt so much better. She had a good night's sleep and a relaxing morning the next day. Her Mum called around 11 to arrange to collect her, she couldn't

One More Try (Book 1)

help but feel a little disappointed that she didn't see Tom again to thank him.

*

Iliana didn't see Tom the next week but the Saturday after as she was just finishing up and putting her cart away, she saw him walking past the large storage shed.

"Tom!" she shouted, running out the door after him.

"Illy. Hey, how's it going?" He seemed in a hurry.

"Great thanks. I haven't had a chance to thank you properly for the other week when I wasn't well."

"Oh, that's no problem, you thanked me at the time." He smiled at her. "Actually, I could do with a bit of help just now if you are done for the day?"

"Yeah, sure what is it?"

"I think I have a cut on my back, but I can't reach it to put any dressings on it. I can shower to clean it but then can't do anything else and there's no one around."

He turned around and sure enough in the middle of his back between his shoulder blades there was a small rip in his black t shirt and a fair bit of blood.

"Oh yeah, I see it. There is a cut. Shall we go inside the house as I know where your Mum keeps the first aid things?"

"Yeah, that would be great, thanks." They both turned to walk towards the house.

"So, what happened then?"

"I was kneeling in one of the chalets and when I stood up, I scraped my back against the corner of a chest of drawers, it must have got chipped at some point as it was sharp. I've repaired it now."

"Ouch that would be sore."

He shrugged. "It's more annoying than anything as I can't reach it."

They entered the house, and Iliana went to fetch the first aid box Trish kept and had used on them all frequently when they were a lot younger, while Tom went into the downstairs bathroom. She brought the box into the bathroom and stopped in her tracks when she entered the room. The bathroom was one of the smaller ones in the house but still had a shower, toilet, sink with a mirror, and a chair in it. Tom was sitting in the chair which he had put in the middle of the room, he had his back to her and had taken his t-shirt off. Apart from the blood she was mesmerised by the muscle definition on his back and arms, he really was a very fit guy. He had a farmer's tan as he wore a t-shirt most of the time, but his shoulders and back were still bronze, just not as brown as his arms and the back of his neck. She had to mentally shake herself to concentrate on the wound. He turned his head to the side and looked around his shoulder when he realised she was there.

"How does it look?"

"Good!" That really wasn't what she had meant to say. "I mean it doesn't look too bad, it's about an inch wide and I don't think too deep, let me get it cleaned up and get a better look."

She got the cotton wool out and ran some lukewarm water in the sink to clean it, he didn't wince when she put the warm water on it, but she was being very gentle. She placed her left hand gently on his bare shoulder while she was washing with the other hand, his skin felt very warm. "I am just going to press a bit harder now to make sure it's clean. It might hurt, ready?"

"Yeah, go for it." He turned his head to the side and smiled at her as she pressed harder and gave it a good clean, but he didn't flinch. She used the cotton wool pads to dry the wound thoroughly then got out the steri strips.

"I think we need to use these strips to make sure the wound closes and heals properly."

He nodded gently. "Okay."

She washed her hands thoroughly with soap and hot water before touching the wound directly.

"Okay here goes."

She peeled off the steri strip and gently pushed the skin together with her fingers, she then applied the first strip with

the other hand and was pleased with herself as the skin met nicely and the strip stayed on. Once the first one was in place it would be easier after that, so she breathed a sigh of relief.
"Nursing isn't one of my skills I'm afraid, so I hope it's okay."
"I am sure it will be fine."
"You probably know quite a few nurses do you not, they could maybe have done a better job for you?" She wasn't sure why she asked that as she probably didn't want to know. She guessed she must be getting flustered being so close to him and touching his bare skin.
"Yeah, I know a few but none that I would want to call on if you know what I mean?" He chuckled.
"Hmm, yeah I can probably guess." She applied the next two strips either side of the first one and fought an overwhelming urge to gently kiss the back of his neck where his short brown hair met the tanned skin of his neck. She snapped herself out of it. "Okay that's you I think."
"Thanks Illy." He stood up and turned around to look at his back in the small mirror, she couldn't help but notice his muscular chest and six pack as he did so, but she was trying very hard not to stare.
"Looks great, you did a great job from what I can see." He turned back and smiled at her. "Do you need a lift home? I am heading off now anyway so can drop you off unless you're waiting for Liz?"
"No, she is out tonight. A lift would be great. Thanks."
"Great, I'll just go get another t-shirt."
Shame, she was kind of enjoying the view she thought to herself then wondered again what her hormones were doing to her. She chuckled to herself as she collected her bag and waited for him. He returned quickly with a clean black work t-shirt on, and they headed to his car.
"Any plans tonight then?" he asked her when they were fastening their seat belts in the car.

One More Try (Book 1)

"No. Sofa, TV and soda I think with Mum as she isn't working for a change. We don't get that much time together so it will be nice."

"That's good then."

"What about you, I take it you are out?"

"Yeah, out with the guys tonight. Probably a game of pool and some beers."

"Very good." She was secretly pleased he didn't have a date tonight but then even out with the guys he would still meet women. She envied the women his age who were out and about tonight. "I won't be able to go out here until after I return from college."

"Yeah, is it three or four years?"

"It's four so I will be 22 by then."

"No point in wishing time away. You will have a blast at college and meet new people. You might not even come back?"

"That's true." She felt a little sad at the thought of that. "I haven't decided exactly where I am going yet, and if I get accepted of course."

"You'll do well and be able to choose, I am sure of it." He smiled at her.

"Hopefully."

He dropped her off with his usual smile and wave and she skipped into the house to enjoy her evening with her mum.

*

As she approached her SATs, Iliana tried to balance her time between working at Liz's, volunteering at Sunday school, and studies. It was tough but she knew it would be worth it. Liz wanted to be a Lawyer but didn't seem to study that much, she was bright, and Iliana was sure she would do well.

The girls remained close and spent time together when they could. They both knew that after their SATs things would never be the same as so much would have to change, neither of them would have any idea just how much change was coming.

Chapter 5

For Iliana's eighteenth birthday she spent quality time with her Mum and Liz.

They went out to a nice restaurant then back to Iliana's house where they talked and laughed all night. Iliana's Mum allowed her and Liz to try some of her wine as a treat, so that they could raise a glass to Iliana's father, Andrew, who was Scottish and, in the UK, alcohol was permitted from age eighteen, so it seemed fitting.

The weekend after her birthday, Illiana stayed at Liz's for their own kind of celebrations, very similar to what they had done for her sixteenth. Although this time they went shopping together and bought some new clothes, tried them on and did each other's make up and nails.
During the night she had to go to the bathroom as she had drunk too much soda as usual. When she came out, she jumped as Tom was leaning against the wall smiling at her, again, it was like déjà vu from her sixteenth. Although this time he didn't seem drunk.
"Illy! So glad it's you, I have something for you for your birthday."
"Oh wow, thanks, you really didn't have to."
"What do you mean, it's your special birthday, it's tradition now for me to make you something is it not?" He grinned then ran back towards his old room mumbling, "Wait there I'll just be a second."
When he appeared a few moments later he had his right hand cupped over the other covering something small, she couldn't see what though. He reached out and then took away the top hand to reveal a silver chain, with a small carved wooden star and moon as a pendant. It was even more beautiful than the jewellery box and she gasped when she saw it.
"Oh, my goodness, it's beautiful, you made the pendant?"

"Yeah, it's the same as the handles on the jewellery box so piece of cake now." He shrugged.
"I love it!"
"Try it on, I wasn't sure what size chain to get." He frowned as he took it and undid the catch. "Turn around, I'll put it on for you if you want?"
"Yeah, that would be great, thanks."
She turned around and lifted her hair at the back, he loosened her dressing gown on her shoulders slightly so that he could see the back of her neck. She could feel his warm, gentle breaths on her neck which made her feel slightly light-headed. He fastened the necklace very carefully then replaced the dressing gown. "Ok, let's see?"
When she turned around, she glanced down, and the pendant was in a perfect position just below her collar bone. "It's perfect," she said, beaming.
"It is perfect."
He was focussed on the pendant and bent down a little, reaching out his hand just to straighten it a bit. As he did so he touched her skin ever so slightly and she could feel her body quiver at his touch, she really hoped it wasn't obvious to him. Her chest was rising dramatically as she struggled to keep her breathing under control. Suddenly she felt too warm in her dressing gown. He gazed up at her, their faces were within inches of each other, and she looked straight into his green eyes. He leaned forward very slowly, then put his hand under her jaw and gently kissed her on the lips. She froze, she really didn't know what to do, she hadn't kissed any one before so wasn't sure, although Liz had tried to tell her often enough. Time seemed to stand still. It felt amazing.
The kiss appeared to last a long time but still if felt too soon when he pulled away, he looked suddenly uncomfortable.
"Sorry, I shouldn't have done that." He ran his hand through his hair and shook his head. "Sorry Illy. Goodnight."

One More Try (Book 1)

Then he rushed away, just as quickly as he had earlier, she heard his bedroom door close.

She just stood there in shock for a few minutes, touching her necklace, her heart was pounding in her chest. What just happened? When she got back to Liz's room, she lay awake for a long time just reliving the moment in her head.

*

After that night Iliana could not stop thinking about the kiss they had shared, it was time she admitted to herself how she felt about this guy. He was a guy, not a boy, eight years older than her, and she didn't know if it was love she felt, or infatuation, or just a crush but she had to acknowledge it. She couldn't tell Liz how she felt, although it was highly likely that she knew anyway. She wore the necklace at home and told her Mum that Liz's family had given it to her (not really a lie) but at school she told people that her Mum had given it to her (well that was a lie). Several weeks went by, and she didn't see Tom, she couldn't help thinking it wasn't a coincidence.

*

One Saturday after Iliana finished work, Liz had invited her to stay as her parents were having a few friends round for drinks. She and Liz got ready in her room and had even sneaked in a glass of wine each. She was really looking forward to some time with her friend.

They went downstairs when they heard everyone arriving and said some polite hellos to the people gathered, there were about fifteen of them, mostly couples around their parents' age but the wine was flowing, and it was a good excuse for the girls to socialise and try a few drinks. After about thirty minutes Iliana heard the front door close and when she turned around her heart lifted as she saw Tom enter the room… until she saw that he was with a woman. She walked in behind him, and everyone turned around to look at her, she was stunning. She had waist length dark wavy hair and big blue eyes, she was tall and was wearing a close fitted black dress which showed off her amazing, shapely figure including an ample bosom. As they walked around the room Iliana couldn't help but notice the way he put his arm around her and rested his hand at the base of her back, where her flowing hair finished. Iliana always thought she felt plain next to Liz, but this woman made her look positively drab. She couldn't describe the sensation she was feeling, only that it felt like her heart had plummeted right down to her feet after the initial elation of seeing him. She wanted the ground to swallow her up so that she could just disappear.

Tom and his girlfriend said hello to people and made their way around the room. Liz and Iliana were busy in the kitchen trying to source another glass of wine without anyone noticing so she didn't see them approach.

"Liz, Iliana?" Tom seemed surprised to see them but continued. "This is Sarah." Liz turned around.

"Hi, nice to meet you, I am Tom's sister Liz, and this is my friend Iliana."

"Hey," Sarah responded without looking at either of them, she was glancing around the room looking slightly bored then she turned to Tom, "you didn't tell me the kids were here too?"

"They aren't 'kids' Sarah, they are eighteen." His cheeks flushed then he gently ushered her away towards more of their parents' friends.

Liz resumed her search, so Iliana waited and tried not to watch Tom and Sarah. Sarah was very pleasant to the other people Tom was introducing her to, flashing a lovely, charming smile and laughing at the occasional joke. Iliana wondered how it was possible to be so jealous of someone she had just met and hardly knew.

Thankfully they didn't stay long, Tom spoke to his mother and introduced them, then they left after about an hour. She and Liz eventually managed to smuggle a few more glasses of wine upstairs to Liz's room where they just chatted and listened to music, Iliana wanted to broach the subject of Sarah but wasn't sure how, she knew that Tom had a lot of women, but she had never seen any of them at their house before. Eventually the wine took over and she just blurted it out. "So, I take it you haven't met Sarah before then?"

"No, never. She seems like his usual type though."

"What do you mean?"

"Stunning, but a complete bitch! Calling us kids!" She shook her head and frowned.

"I've never met any of his girlfriends before, but I did think she was stunning, I guess the 'kids' comment was a bit of a put down. I hadn't really thought about it."

"You wouldn't though, you're too nice Iliana you just thought how beautiful she was. She would be more beautiful if she didn't scowl at us!" They both laughed.

"You are right of course," she shrugged, "what do we care what she thinks."

"Exactly, anyway we will likely never see her again. Not sure why he brought her, I haven't seen him for ages but next time I do I will ask him."

Iliana thought she might just know why he'd brought her along, she hoped she was wrong though.

Liz never mentioned any more about Sarah, so Iliana didn't ask. She didn't bump into Tom again, she kept her promise to him and didn't walk home alone though; sometimes she would get a lift from Trish or even Brad if he was there, or stay over if Liz was around. Tom was hardly ever about or if he was, he was often still busy when she was finished, or at least he would look busy if she caught a glimpse of him, in his work gear, with his toolbox.

A few weeks after that night the girls were all at their other school friend Vicky's party. She had a big sister who was supposed to stay behind and supervise but they had agreed that she would pretty much leave them to it. As they all headed over to Vicky's house, they could hear the very loud music as they walked along the street. Iliana normally looked for Billy at these parties so that she could talk to someone and not worry about being asked to go upstairs or be encouraged to drink too much. Her friends would take a bottle of wine between them all and not drink much more than that. Vicky was already very merry when they got there so they tried to make sure that one of them stayed with her so that she wasn't being led astray by some of the more unsavoury characters at their school. Tony was there too of course, and he was always keen to catch up with Liz. When Iliana dared go to the bathroom, she would walk past the bedrooms upstairs and hear things; noises of people enjoying themselves and each other she assumed.

 As the night went on, she started to feel tired and was ready to go home, it had been a particularly tough shift at work that day and she was still volunteering at Sunday school so had to get up early the following morning. Liz had mentioned that her Mum was picking them up at 11 so Iliana found she was counting down the minutes from 10:30. About ten minutes before they were due to be picked up, she heard a few girls giggling and saw that they were looking out of the living room window. There was a car parked on the street in front of the house, but she couldn't see it too well as it was away from the streetlight. She couldn't get close enough to have a look, but she could hear the girls saying something about Tom, this really woke her up and she made her way over to the window, she gently edged her way in to get a better look.

 "You'll know Iliana, isn't that Tom's car? Liz's extremely handsome and sexy eldest brother?" They all giggled.

 Iliana looked at the car again, it was too dark to see inside but she was in no doubt that it was his, she had been in it so many times and, although she wasn't too clued up on car makes and models, she knew the colour and shape very well, not to mention the registration; she could only see a bit of it, but it was definitely his.

 The girls were all still giggling. "Alicia's older sister said she dated him, and he is amazing in bed," one of the girls shouted, and they all giggled again.

One More Try (Book 1)

She found herself in a sudden panic about seeing him, so she rushed off to the bathroom to freshen up, worried that she looked like a drunken eighteen-year-old who was overly tired; although that's exactly what she was but never mind! She felt strangely protective of him, he was her friend, and they were talking about him in a way she really didn't like. Who was she kidding though? She really didn't think of him as just a friend anymore. She also couldn't help but wonder why he was here. Was this her chance to finally speak to him after what happened? Had he offered to pick them up so that he could talk to her? Unlikely, but she could at least hope. She splashed some water on her face and ran her fingers through her hair before looking in the mirror, she looked no different but would have to do. She made her way downstairs and heard the knock on the door as she did so. Billy was there and he gave her a look as if he knew what she was thinking. She just smiled at him. The girls were all scrambling to answer the door but when finally, someone managed to open it, Iliana could feel her heart thumping in her chest. She looked up as the door opened; she couldn't wait to see those green eyes and that smile, even if the other girls would all be swooning all over him. She felt herself smiling already in anticipation. Although that changed completely when she saw Robert standing in the doorway. They all greeted him anyway and asked him inside.

"We thought it was Tom, isn't that his car?" A few of the girls said.

Robert wasn't looking at them though, his brown eyes were focussed on Iliana. He wasn't unattractive, but he didn't appeal to Iliana at all, he was getting a lot of attention from the girls though and appeared to be enjoying it.

"Yeah, he said I could borrow it for tonight as he's not using it, and Mom's is in the shop."

"Hi Robert," she tried to sound happy to see him.

"Well done, Iliana," he replied.

"For what?"

One More Try (Book 1)

"Well done for at least trying to hide the disappointment on your face."
"I don't know what you mean." She was flustered and he knew it. Even Billy gave her a sympathetic smile. "I'll go see where Liz is, so we don't keep you waiting too long." She couldn't wait to get away, she eventually found Liz just coming out of the bathroom and when they went back downstairs Robert was talking with Billy.
"OK ladies let's go." Robert said with authority and a smile. They said their goodbyes and made their way to the car. Liz and Iliana were both stumbling a bit, and he just rolled his eyes.
"How come you have Tom's car?" Liz asked him, slurring her words only slightly.
"I think I have now explained this twenty times," he exaggerated with a sigh. "He said I could borrow it as he's not using it, and Mom's is in the shop."
"Oh OK, sorry." Liz giggled; she didn't sound that sorry. "In fairness I don't think I am one of the twenty people you have mentioned it to though."
"Much to the disappointment of all of your friends."
"Aw, Robert, I'm sure that's not true. We are grateful that you have come to pick us up aren't we Iliana?" Liz looked around at Iliana slumped in the back of the car, where she wasn't used to sitting.
"Of course we are Robert, thank you."
He managed a small smile at their tipsy state.
He dropped Iliana off first and Liz was already dozing in the front seat, the poor guy would likely have to carry her in the house when he got her home. "Thanks for the lift, Robert."
He shrugged. "No problem."
"No really, I mean it. I am sorry that you thought I looked disappointed, I really am."
"I know, don't worry about it, you weren't the only one. Goodnight, Iliana." She frowned as he pulled away, watching her as he did so.

Chapter 6

The time soon approached for the girls senior Prom so of course there was much talk about it at school. Iliana wasn't too bothered if she was honest but everyone else was, so she tried to join in the excitement. Liz had, of course, had several offers but Iliana and their two other close friends hadn't been asked yet. One day at lunch, Becca announced that she was going with Billy Garcia, much to everyone at the table's surprise. It was just the four of them as usual, but Liz looked straight at Iliana and so did Vicky, they had clearly all assumed that Billy would ask Iliana.

"Wow congratulations, great news Becca," Iliana said sincerely.

"Thanks, what about you girls have you decided what you are doing yet?"

"No, I think there are a group of people just going by themselves, but I am not that fussed to be honest. I am trying to work as much as I can to earn extra money for college and ..." she didn't say any more after that as it just sounded like she was making excuses.

"I'm not bothered either," Vicky agreed, "it would be a bit strange to go as a group of girls and just stand around watching all the couples all night."

"I am sure out of my four brothers we could find you both a date?" Liz said half joking but half serious from the look on her face.

"Oh wait, I didn't know we could pick one of your brothers?" Becca giggled, "I'll ditch Billy and pick Tom then." They all laughed.

"Well, he is probably out as he is a fair bit older and wouldn't come to a senior prom, Brad too I'm afraid as he and Jane are serious. So that leaves Robert or Dan?" Liz pondered.

"Ok I'll take Dan then, even although he is only sixteen, he's cute." Vicky piped up.

"He's seventeen now actually." Liz corrected her.

One More Try (Book 1)

"Even better then." Vicky grinned.

"Yeah, thanks Liz but borrowing one of your brothers appeals even less than going on my own!" Iliana said.

They all laughed again, thankfully they took her comment the way it was meant, and Liz wasn't offended. The thought of going with Robert did not thrill Iliana at all. They left the discussion there and headed to class when the bell went. As Iliana was walking down the corridor, she saw Billy Garcia walking towards her and smiled at him.

"Hey Iliana, how are you?"

"I am good, I hear you are going to Prom with Becca?"

"Yeah, she asked me earlier, is that ok?"

"Of course, why wouldn't it be?"

"Well, it's just ..." he looked like he wasn't sure if he should say what he planned to next. "I did think about asking you ... "

"Oh, did you? Well, I ..."

"I just didn't think you would say yes and then Becca asked me so ..."

"Yeah, sure that's fine, no worries."

"Would you have said Yes? Out of curiosity?"

"I don't know, maybe ... hadn't really thought about going to be honest ..." she felt a bit awkward, especially now that he was going with her friend.

"I figured there is only one person you would want to go to Prom with." He was watching her reaction.

"Who is that?"

"Liz's brother, Tom?"

"What? No, he is much older and wouldn't go to Prom." She could feel herself blushing so was quite sure that what she was saying wasn't making any difference.

"I see the way you look at him and talk about him."

"You have never seen me with him, I don't know what you mean?"

"I saw you get in his car once from school, ages ago now, but I notice the way you talk about him. Like most of the others I guess, he is a handsome guy. I also saw how

One More Try (Book 1)

disappointed you were that night at Vicky's when Robert came through the door and not him, after we all saw Tom's car." She flushed again.

"I didn't realise you noticed so many things Billy." Now she really felt awkward.

"Just be careful Iliana, will you promise me that?"

"Of course, I am Miss Careful I think you'll find." She tried to make light of it. He chuckled but didn't seem convinced.

"I'm serious, he has a reputation and is a lot older than us, I don't want you to get hurt."

"I won't, don't worry about me, honestly."

"Ok, best get to class, see you later?"

"Yeah, see you."

*

About a week later when Iliana was finished working at Harrow Falls, she was putting her cleaning cart away and checking supplies when she was aware of someone standing behind her, they were tall, so she had a feeling it was Tom but then turned around to see Dan standing smiling at her.

"Dan! How are you doing?"

"Good thanks, how about you? Need any help?"

"No thanks, I'm good; I'm done, just need to let the Team leader know we are short of bathroom cleaner. I haven't seen you around for a while. What's happening?"

"Well yeah since I passed my test, I've been out a lot with friends, it's great."

"Yeah, I heard, well done passing your test so quickly."

"Tom had taken me out a fair bit as well as a few lessons and Dad occasionally, so I did get extra practice."

"That's great. So, what do sixteen-year-old guys do when they are out in the car these days?"

"I'm seventeen now."

"Oh yes, so you are, sorry! So, what do seventeen-year-old guys do then?"

He smiled.

One More Try (Book 1)

"Oh, you know, just hanging out and stuff. Can I give you a lift home? Unless you plan on hanging out with Liz of course?"

"No, she's out so a lift would be great, thanks. I'll just get my things organised and have a quick chat with Trish if that's ok?"

"Of course."

Dan walked with her back to the house, he was tall and had short dark hair. He had a slim face with high cheek bones and deep blue eyes, a very similar colour to Liz's. After they had talked with Trish they headed to Dan's car. As she got in the passenger seat, she couldn't help but chuckle to herself, she had known Dan since he was seven and she was nine and here he was driving his own car.

"What's funny?" he said with a smile, putting his seatbelt on and starting the engine, he looked very comfortable.

"Nothing, it just feels strange, you're the youngest and I've known you since you were seven and now you are driving."

"Yeah, well I was going to say you'll get used to it but you're moving away, aren't you?"

"Yes, I accepted a place in Aqualta."

"Why so far away?"

"I just liked the place, and it made sense."

"Liz tells me you're not going to Prom?"

"Yeah, can't be bothered with it all to be honest."

"I can't believe no one asked you?"

"Aw that's sweet, maybe because I can't be bothered? A few of us were talking about just going as a group but I don't think I will."

"Would you go if you had someone to take you?"

"Well, it would depend on who that was I guess, I can't think of anyone that isn't already going."

"Would you go with me?"

She glanced at him to try and see if he was joking.

"Really? Are you asking me?"

One More Try (Book 1)

"Well only if you'll say yes, if not then no, I'm not asking you." Iliana laughed as he spoke. "We would have a good laugh so why not? It wouldn't be a date so don't worry about that …"

"Oh, I wasn't thinking ... it's just ... well ... are you sure?"

"Yeah, I can drive you. I'll probably have to take Liz and Tony too, but it'll be a laugh."

"Well ok then, that sounds great, thanks Dan."

He smiled at her again. They chatted for the rest of the journey, and he dropped her off at her Mum's house. She called Liz later and told her that she was now going to Prom with Dan, she suspected Liz had put him up to it but if she had, she didn't admit it.

*

On the night of Prom, Dan arrived right on time and opened the passenger door for her with a smile, she had to lift her plain long dress as she climbed in, the split showing a bit of leg as she did so. Liz and Tony were in the back and Liz beamed at her as she fastened her seat belt. Dan looked smart, and older than seventeen, with a grey suit on, crisp white shirt and dark blue tie. They put on some songs in the car on the way. Liz looked gorgeous in her dress as always, it was like Iliana's: long, slim-fitting, with a split up the side except it had thin straps where Iliana's had capped sleeves. Both were satin but Liz wore burgundy, and Iliana wore dark blue

When they walked into the packed hall they spotted their friends right away, standing next to the non-alcoholic punch. As they approached, she noticed several people, including their friend Vicky, pour something into her glass from a hip flask that she stashed in her purse.

They all chatted and danced and had a great time. There was a lot happening and she and Dan played a game where they tried to spot the next couple to have an argument or disappear somewhere for some quiet time, or even just make out on the dance floor.

One More Try (Book 1)

"Do you know that a lot of people, especially girls, plan to lose their virginity on prom night?" Dan mentioned casually as they were having a drink and a break from dancing.

"What? No! That's an urban myth started by guys who want girls to lose their virginity on prom night isn't it?"

"Ha maybe, can't remember where I heard it."

"Well either way, it wouldn't be me ... no way ..."

"You mean?"

"What? Yes, I am. Why did you think I wasn't?"

"I didn't, I guess. I just didn't think."

"Are you?" she asked.

He hesitated, "No, I'm not."

"Really? Who was it?"

"It doesn't matter, you don't know them."

"*Them*? You mean?"

"Yes, only two though."

Wow, Dan wasn't a virgin, and she was, not only that but he had been with two different girls, well there was a shock.

Towards the end of the evening the slow songs came on, Dan asked her if she wanted to dance to 'Everything I do, I do it for you...'. There were a lot of people making out while dancing, so she was a bit hesitant at first but then decided why not. He held her close, putting his arms around her waist and she put her arms around his neck. He just chatted to her while they danced and they had a good laugh, still checking out the strange looking couples around them. She giggled most of the way through the dance. After it was finished, they all made their way back to the car and Iliana and Liz directed Dan to the traditional after-Prom party.

As they arrived at the house, Iliana glanced around the room, averting her eyes from the people there who were clearly very drunk already. She and her friends all just found a corner and chatted, there were a few party games going on, but they didn't join in, she couldn't see herself staying there

very long. At one point she went to the bathroom and when she came out Dan was waiting.
"Sorry Dan, I didn't realise you were waiting."
"Oh, that's fine I haven't been waiting long, don't worry. Are you ok?"
"Yes, I'm fine, can't see me lasting much longer. How are you doing?"
"I'm fine, happy to go whenever you're ready though?"
"Ok well I'll see what Liz and Tony are up to."
"Ok, I didn't get a chance to tell you how great you look by the way."
"Oh thanks, you too, I've never seen you in a suit before."
He grinned. She left him to go into the bathroom and went to find Liz and Tony, they were in the kitchen trying the punch.
"How is it?"
"It's not great there is a lot of alcohol in it!" Liz was coughing. "Are you trying it?"
"No thanks, I'm set,"
Liz laughed. "Wise."
"Not sure I'm going to stay out much longer I am shattered. How are you guys?"
"Yeah, we're happy to head off soon too, where's Dan?"
"He's in the bathroom; he won't be long."
They left when Dan returned and when he dropped her off, she thanked him again, for everything and he smiled. She wanted to acknowledge him in some way before she got out of the car but couldn't think of a way to do it that wouldn't embarrass him or her: a hug, a peck on the cheek? So, she decided on just saying thank you and got out of the car.

One More Try (Book 1)

Chapter 7

As the end of summer approached it was time for Iliana to prepare for her biggest adventure. She was moving to Aqualta to attend teacher training, still in Florida but four hours away from New Harrow. She had gotten good scores for her SATs so received a few offers, but this was the one she was keen on. It was a bit further away, but she had been really impressed with the place when she and her Mum had gone to see it.

Brad was getting married in August and his Bachelor party was the day before Iliana was due to leave. She knew that, as best man, Tom would be there so she tried to figure out a way she could at least speak to him before she left for a long time. It would eat her up inside if she didn't at least confront him about their kiss. It turned out that she didn't have to try very hard as Liz suggested they get dressed up and crash the party to celebrate her last night in New Harrow.

The night of the bachelor party, they met up at Iliana's house as it was closer to town, and managed to talk her Mum into letting them have some wine. They got dressed up together and did their nails and make up. Liz looked gorgeous in a cropped t-shirt and a denim skirt just above the knee, her lovely big blue eyes and long, wavy, dark hair really did turn heads when she went anywhere. Iliana went for a light blue fitted top that showed a little bit of cleavage and same length denim skirt as Liz. She wore her shoulder length hair down and had tried to curl it a bit, she felt good, although maybe that was the wine and the company of her best friend. They linked arms and strutted along the sidewalk on the way to the bar.

"You look fabulous, did I tell you that?" Liz said.

"Thanks, so do you, it feels good to be out doesn't it?"

"Yeah, it does, I am gonna miss you when you're at college you know. You will be studying hard and it's so far away I doubt you will get much of a chance to come visit."

One More Try (Book 1)

"I know, I have no idea what to expect to be honest. It's a new chapter for both of us for sure. "

"Yeah true."

"Besides you are studying Law won't you be too busy studying to worry about seeing me?" Iliana laughed and prodded her friend knowing full well that she didn't study that much.

They entered the pool hall where the boys were starting off the bachelor party and looked around, it was a big place and was busy, but they spotted the group of around twenty guys right away. They got some wolf whistles when they walked in which gave them extra confidence as they approached the bar. Iliana could see Tom looking over out of the corner of her eye, but she didn't look his way, she thought she also saw the bartender nod in his direction, but she couldn't be sure. The bar was quite small given the size of the place, and there were lots of stools around it. The six pool tables were located behind where they were standing at the bar and on the other side there were several booth seats.

"Sorry ladies, you know I can't serve you, much as I would love to have your company tonight as you both look amazing!" the bartender said with a charming smile. He was wearing a short sleeved black shirt and trousers, and his name tag said Dave, he looked around mid-twenties so likely knew Tom.

"Oh really? Not even just a soda?" Liz leaned in closer… "disguised as something else?" She whispered to him, batting her eyelids, and flashing her lovely smile his way.

"Sorry Liz. Don't break my heart, you know I can't, I would lose my job and more importantly your eldest brother would kill me slowly and painfully."

"He drank when he was my age, that's so unfair! My friend here is moving away tomorrow to go to college, so we are having a send-off for her just the two of us!" This time she pouted.

He gave her a sympathetic look then got two tall glasses. He added lots of ice under the bar out of sight, then he poured out two coca colas. He put them on coasters on top of the bar and pushed them their way.

"There you go ladies, two cokes but after you finish them you have to leave, Okay?"

"Thanks Dave, you're a star!" Liz winked at him; she was so good at this. Iliana was impressed at her best friend's many talents! "How much?"

"On the house. So, you both don't hate me too much," he winked.

"Thanks." They both beamed and responded at the same time.

They sat on the stools at the bar and Iliana couldn't resist looking over to see what Tom was doing; he was playing a shot with his back to her as she looked over. He potted the ball then went round the table to play another shot, he was concentrating and looking very serious so didn't notice her staring. Some of the guys were playing pool and the others were standing around the tables drinking and talking, she spotted Brad in a small group chatting and laughing and Robert was in another group watching the game of pool. She noticed that the bartender went over to collect the empty glasses and said a few words to Tom as he did so. Tom had a short sleeved Hawaiian shirt on with smart trousers and shoes, just like the rest of the boys, so they were clearly planning on going clubbing later. Hawaiian shirts were clearly the theme! Tom still looked handsome in his loud shirt though, not many men could carry that off, but he did with ease. Her heart was pounding as it felt like so long since she had seen him and all it had done was make her want to see him more. She took a sip of her drink and realised that it wasn't just coke, her friend's charm had worked after all. She wasn't sure what it was but figured it was likely vodka as that was the easiest to disguise. She was enjoying it so just kept sipping, but she didn't want to drink it too quickly as they had to leave after that. Quite a few guys were looking over at Liz she noticed, but they just chatted together at the bar, sipping their vodkas. Hopefully she would at least get a chance to talk to Tom.

It didn't take long for two guys to come over to them, Iliana didn't know who they were, but they looked around early twenties, they were both tall, handsome guys, one had blonde hair and the other dark brown.

"Hi ladies, what brings you here then?" the blonde one said. He was standing next to Liz and looking at her as he spoke. The other stood next to Iliana and smiled at her.

"We are having a send-off for my friend here who is leaving for college tomorrow in Aqualta," Liz replied with a smile.

"Wow, so what does a 'send-off' involve then for two lovely ladies like yourselves?"

"Well, we haven't quite decided yet in all honesty, we are going to just go with the flow after this I think."

"Maybe we can help you out then, or tag along? My name is Gary, and this is Steve." he gestured towards his friend, the one next to Iliana.

Gary was doing all the talking but Steve was smiling at Iliana the whole time. They were both quite attractive, but she now couldn't see Tom as they were blocking her view, so she was a bit frustrated. She just kept sipping her drink which was going down far too well.

"Oh, I'm not sure, what are your plans?" Liz was so good at this, Iliana wouldn't know what to do or say to these guys.

"We'll have a few here then head off to a party down the road, you're both welcome to join us?"

"Sorry I am travelling tomorrow so I can't be too late," Iliana replied to let Liz know she really wasn't keen, although she got the impression Liz wasn't that keen either.

"That's a shame," Steve said.

"Yeah, we have been out for a while so we might just have this soft drink then head home," Liz said looking very innocent, sipping her drink.

One More Try (Book 1)

"Bit of a shame for you to head off home when the night is so young?" Gary said with a charming smile, this time he looked at both girls.

"Not as young as these ladies are I'm afraid, too young for both of you guys." Tom appeared behind them and spoke with an air of authority.

"Such a shame," Gary said. Iliana thought his smile was a little creepy as he spoke. Tom just glared at him. Dave the barman waved goodbye as Tom ushered the girls out, much to the dismay of a lot of the guys at the bar.

"Let's get you both a cab, yeah?"

"Oh, you're no fun!" Liz said as she stumbled on the sidewalk. "Oops!" she giggled, which set Iliana off too as they leaned on each other.

Just as Tom was about to say something else, a car pulled up next to them, "Need a lift, Elizabeth?" Tony said from the passenger's seat with a grin.

"Yes please," she replied and stumbled into the car. "Are you coming Iliana?"

"Yeah, come along Iliana we're off to a party?" Tony added.

"No thanks, I have to be up early in the morning. You go ahead though, thanks anyway. "

"It's OK Liz I'll make sure she gets a cab," Tom said.

"OK, if you're sure?"

"Yeah, go ahead," Iliana smiled at her. At least this way she could finally talk to Tom. Tony then sped away with Tom and Iliana watching.

She turned to look at him, feeling brave and wasting no time, "Can I talk to you?"

"What about?" He was still looking off into the distance where Liz had gone. "We need to get you a cab."

"I know but just hear me out first, please? I leave for Aqualta tomorrow," she said hoping her look was pleading but not knowing if she was pulling it off; she wasn't sure if the alcohol was helping or not.

"Ok then, what's up?"

"Have you been avoiding me lately?"

"Why would you say that?"

"Ever since you gave me this," she pointed to her necklace, "and kissed me, I haven't seen you around much at all."

"Ah, yes. I said sorry, didn't I? I should never have kissed you."

"You don't need to apologise, in fact that's why I wanted to talk to you. I am pretty sure that I have feelings for you, and I can't go away to college knowing that there is even a small chance that you feel the same way?"

He looked down at his feet, not a good sign. Then he glanced up at her, "I am sorry Illy, I truly am if I led you on in any way. You are too young for me, you are my baby sister's friend, and I have a lot of affection for you, but not in that way."

She sank back against the wall.

"I don't believe you," she screamed. "Why did you kiss me then?"

"A moment of weakness, I think, I don't know, please don't do this?"

"Do what? Make you admit you have feelings for me?"

"No, make me admit I don't." Ouch, that hurt. "Here let me get you a cab."

"NO! I can walk home from here you fuckwit, leave me alone!"

"Illy, come on, I've never heard you swear before, come on…"

Suddenly all the anger and frustration from the last months came rushing out of her…

"NO! You think I'm miss goody two shoes, never been kissed, or fucked. Well fuck you!"

"Right, that's it, I am done with this, is that what you want, a fuck? Well, why didn't you say so, come on!"

He led her around the back of the wall outside the bar, where the trash bins were. It all happened so quickly; it was like she had an outer body experience. He pulled up her skirt and pulled her panties aside then before she knew it, he was inside her, lifting her up against the wall. She wasn't being forced, she wanted it, she wanted him, but this wasn't how she had imagined it. He started thrusting into her and she tried not to think about how uncomfortable it was.

"Are you sure this is what you want?" he whispered after only a few seconds; their foreheads were touching so she touched his lips gently with hers before responding just as quietly.

"Yes." They kissed again until she was out of breath. "Yes, it is."

After a few minutes he let out a groan and stopped then staggered back shaking his head.

"Shit, Illy. What have I done? You should go, let me get you a cab."

He gently took her arm, and she stumbled with him back round to the front of the bar, as if in a trance. She was vaguely aware of him throwing something in the trash bins - likely the condom - as they walked, then a cab pulled up. She climbed into it with his help. She couldn't look at him as he gave the driver her address and some cash and the cab pulled away. As it drove her home, 'One More Try' came on the radio.

She felt like her world had just fallen apart.

*

One More Try (Book 1)

Tom
Chapter 8

Preparations were underway at Harrow Falls for Tom's parents thirtieth wedding anniversary, so the place was a hive of activity. His father had asked him if he would say a few words, which he had been quite touched about, until he and Brad were handed a piece of paper each which told them the exact words he wanted them to say.

It was a bit ironic as everyone knew their parents already had two children when they'd got married but they weren't allowed to say it was thirty years in the speech, just a 'special' anniversary.

He couldn't imagine his father ever being romantic enough to propose if he was honest, his mom did all the organising in the business, so he always wondered if she just organised it and he showed up! He smiled to himself at his joke as he walked across the yard to where all the tables were being laid out for the celebrations, looking for his mom. When he couldn't find her, he headed away from the yard and into the house where she appeared to be tidying in the kitchen with his sister.

They didn't see him, but he heard a name he hadn't heard for some time, Iliana, and he held back in the small hallway so he could listen, intrigued. He hadn't seen or heard anything about her since the night of Brad's bachelor party. He cringed at the thought of what he had done. He had tried to find out more about how she was and what she was up to but with no success. Liz hadn't heard anything from her either, which he knew bothered her, although he suspected she knew something had happened between them. His mom had only mentioned that Iliana's mom Mary, had gone to stay with her quite a few times over the years and had moved in with her to help her out. Iliana was apparently married with a family, but Tom's mom didn't know any more than that, someone was renting out Mary's house so that was the only reason they knew what little they did.

"..so I bumped into Mary last week in the store, as she was back to check some things in her house which she has been letting out. Apparently, Mary moved in a good few years ago, as we knew, because she seemed to be struggling with work and the child. It didn't take Mary long to find out that her husband was violent with her though, Iliana tried to hide it of course but Mary is not daft. It has taken her this long to persuade her that enough is enough. So, she has left him, and they are all coming back here next week. Iliana, Mary, and Iliana's son, I think he is five or six, but I can't remember for sure…" his mother said.

"Oh my god, really? Poor Iliana, what a nightmare for her. I guess some of that explains why she didn't get in touch."

"Oh Liz, you tried to reach out to her but, yes, that could explain it."

"Yeah," she sighed. "I did tell Mary to pass on my best but then when Mary moved out … I didn't even have an email address for her or anything. I also tried calling the college halls after that first year, but they said she had moved out and they didn't have any other information."

"Yeah, I know. It seems such a long time ago since we've seen her but I'm sure it's flown by for her, especially if she's been going through all that."

"Yeah, that's true. Is she teaching?"

"Yes, she is, she qualified for teaching then got married I think."

"Well, that's at least one thing, she was always so keen on it." There was a short pause, "I can't believe it."

"It's good she is coming tonight so you can see her then and hopefully get a chance to talk to her, not that this is an appropriate occasion, but her mom thought it would do her good to come back a little earlier first and get organised before Mary and her son come back tomorrow. We thought if she came here and was surrounded by people she loved, it

One More Try (Book 1)

would help her, especially you of course, Mary said she is very excited to see you."

"Yeah, me too, there's so much to catch up on. We won't focus on any of the bad stuff tonight."

Tom couldn't help but think back to the last time he had seen Iliana; he had gone over it so many times in his mind over the last eight years. She had looked stunning when she arrived at the bar with his sister, although the bar staff knew them so had signalled to Tom that they should leave, despite objections from some of the other guys in Brad's bachelor party group and at the bar. This just made him feel more protective of his sister and her friend of course. He was surprised at how jealous he had been when a guy was talking to Iliana if he was honest. But then he was the one that treated her so badly in the end. He cringed again; it was so tough to think back on it. The truth was that he had been avoiding her since they had kissed as he couldn't get his head around how he felt, he had tried to distract himself by dating Sarah but that didn't work at all. So, when she confronted him, he was torn, should he tell her he had feelings? She was still so young and was going away to teacher training for at least four years, if he had told her he had feelings would she still have done that? Was it fair given he was much older than her, should he let her go to college and meet someone her own age with more to offer her? He had no idea what came over him when she lost it, he did want her physically as she was very attractive, but he should never have taken her like that, then just to put her in a cab without another word? Maybe part of him had thought that if all she wanted was sex then she would leave happy, but he was quite sure that a quickie wasn't what she wanted. He cringed again at the memory. She hadn't been able to look at him when the cab was leaving; "No wonder," he'd thought to himself. When he had returned to the bar that night Robert had commented on how difficult it was to get a cab, he detected some sarcasm but ignored it. They had gone on to have a good night, but Tom was distracted to say the least after what had

One More Try (Book 1)

happened. When he awoke the next day, he hoped he had dreamt it, but the memory was all too real, (even after the beer and shots he'd had), for it to be a dream. He was sure that's why she hadn't been in touch with Liz since either, it just made him feel even more guilty when he heard how excited his sister was about seeing her. Having just heard that she has a husband who is violent towards her… it was all too much for him to take in. Would that still have happened if he had been honest with her?

    He had of course tried to get on with his life and put it all behind him; it became quite apparent that she did not intend to come back after a while. He dated women, enjoyed going out with his friends, worked hard, and found he had more and more to do at Harrow Falls so had to give up his extra job at the cash and carry. Brad and Jane got married and he was best man, it was a great occasion, and they were very happy. They had their first child, a son, a year after they were married and then a daughter two years later so there was always something going on with his family. Liz had met a guy who she seemed to be happy with, a fellow lawyer and a bit older than her; Tom thought he was maybe a year or two younger than him but couldn't remember exactly. Dan had become a police officer and last Tom heard he was dating a young lady at the law firm that Liz worked for. Robert even had a long-term partner, but they appeared to have a few ups and downs, not that Tom saw them very often.

    Tom had tried to talk to his parents about upgrading some of the chalets as they were starting to need more and more repairs and were looking increasingly out of date as each year went by. But his dad wasn't keen so that was the end of it. None of the women that Tom had dated really lasted long so he hadn't asked anyone along tonight, *thankfully*. It would be tricky to explain to a partner why he was so desperate to speak to Iliana and more specifically apologise to her. He did find that he was quite excited about seeing her again though. He shook himself out of the memory and his thoughts and walked into the kitchen at that point, keen to ask his mother and sister more questions of course. "Did I hear you correctly, is Iliana coming tonight?"

"Yes, you did hear correctly, were you listening at the door?" Liz responded with a chuckle.

"No, just caught the end." Liz gave him a 'yeah right' head tilt and look, he couldn't suppress his smile. "Haven't seen her for ages, quite a blast from the past. "

"Yeah exactly, it will be so good to see her after all this time and find out what she has been up to."

"So what time are the guests arriving then Mom?"

"Well food is served at 7:30 so people will start arriving from 7, except Iliana of course, she will be earlier. I said she could stay in one of the empty chalets since her mom's place isn't ready until tomorrow."

At that moment Liz let out a scream. "There she is, I see her across the yard!" She gestured out of the kitchen window onto the part of their yard which was next to the large driveway and parking area. She ran outside. Tom went to the window and looked out; there she was indeed. She was wearing jeans and a close fitting plain white t shirt, she had her long hair tied back in a ponytail and was walking slowly so that she could stop and say hello to people she recognised, there were still a lot of people working here that she would have known. When she saw Liz, her face lit up and she ran towards her friend with open arms, dropping her overnight bag in the process, it was like a scene from a movie. They hugged for a long time and kept talking to each other all at the same time. Tom smiled; he wondered if she would be as happy to see him.

They walked towards the house arm in arm, still chatting, he was suddenly in a bit of a panic, should he go and get ready, so she didn't have to pretend in front of his family to be happy to see him? It would seem obvious if he did it now, but panic took over logic. "Ah well I will leave you ladies to catch up while I go get ready, I can catch up with Iliana later tonight." Then he went up the stairs as quickly as he could without looking like he was running. He paused once he had

One More Try (Book 1)

gone around the corner upstairs and leaned against the wall, his conflicting emotions urging him to run but also to linger, somehow eager to hear her voice.

" .. so happy to hear you are teaching, and you're going to be teaching right here in New Harrow? That's amazing!" Liz sounded ecstatic as they came through the door.

"Yeah, I really enjoy it, I won't be able to teach Zac's class of course but I was so lucky that a position came up just at the right time, it's great. But enough about me, how are you? Trish, it's so nice to see you …" she ran over to Liz's mom and hugged her before Liz could answer.

"It's so good to see you young lady, we have missed you so much you know? Not just Liz, me as well, you were always like my other daughter," Trish said, affectionately as she hugged her. "We don't have a lot of time to catch up just now as everyone is getting ready, here is your key for chalet sixteen so you can get ready too, will you join us tomorrow morning for breakfast though so we can chat properly? We would also love to meet your son at some point once he is settled of course. You, your son and your mom could all come over for dinner one-night next week maybe? Sorry, I am planning everything already and you are just here! It's just great to see you, you look very well …" she seemed to stop there and there was a silence in the room.

"So, Mum told you one of the reasons we are coming back then?"

"Yes, she did, I'm sorry. She wasn't gossiping it was out of concern as she knows how much we all love you," Tom heard his mum say, softly.

"It's ok, I understand. She worries, and rightly so in this case."

"Let's not talk about that tonight, eh? There are so many other things to catch up on. Everyone will be here, Brad is married now to Jane of course, and they have two children, Ethan who is seven and Helena who is five, they will be here. Liz of course, Tom, Robert and Dan will all be here! I have lost track of whose partners will be here, but we'll soon find out!" Trish enthused, seemingly in a rush to get all the details out.

"Oh wow, great, it will be so good to see everyone. Oh, that reminds me, I have a gift for you for your anniversary. Do you want it now or later? It's just a small thing."

"Oh, you didn't have to. If you want, I can take it now, should I wait for James to open it? No, I am sure he won't mind," she chuckled.

"Here you go."

"Thank you, oh my goodness," it sounded like his Mum opened the gift quickly.

"Where did you get this picture, all five of my babies at the same time?" his mom sounded so happy to see this picture, he was curious. Tom really wished he could see them but stayed where he was.

"I found it when clearing out some of Mum's things, I must have taken it on my old camera, remember I used to often take pictures of the beautiful scenery around here? Everyone looks so young so it must have been not long after I moved here in 1983."

"It's wonderful, one of the best gifts I will get I am sure of it, thank you so much."

He could hear his mom's footsteps, so he figured they were hugging again.

"OK time to get ready, see you all very soon."

He ran to his old room and closed the door quietly so they wouldn't know he had been listening.

Chapter 9

Tom managed to get ready in time to start greeting some of their parents' friends as they arrived, it felt like his responsibility as the eldest. He was wearing a dark grey suit with a white shirt and his only tie, which was unusual for him, but he wanted to make the effort for his mom. He had his father's speech in his trouser pocket for later too, he was determined that tonight would go as planned for his parents, particularly his mom as she always put so much effort into everything she did, she deserved to celebrate herself tonight and relax.

He went out to the yard where the tables were set, there were only ten tables as it was just their closest friends and family, but it was all looking perfect, just as his mom wanted it. White tablecloths and chair covers with a large blue silk bow on each of them. Crystal glasses and the best crockery and cutlery on the tables. It was just a buffet, but this was how she wanted it.

As he walked past the tables, he noticed that his mom had even put down place names, so she had decided where everyone was sitting, it made him smile at his mom's attention to detail. Then he had a thought, where would he be sitting? He walked around looking for his place and found it right in between Iliana and Liz. He wondered what Iliana would think of that. Now he wished he had seen her earlier to break the ice a bit, maybe he should go to her chalet and talk to her now? But then he realised he wasn't supposed to know which chalet she was in.

This thought was, however, just a bit too late as the guests were starting to arrive. He walked to the edge of the tables to greet them and help everyone find their seats.

Within about ten minutes most people had arrived, and Tom felt exhausted already, talking with everyone and making polite conversation. When he turned around to look and see who may be missing, he noticed that Iliana had already taken her seat. She must have entered from the other side while he was greeting other guests. She was chatting to his sister and her partner, not that John appeared to get a word in between those two, poor guy. There weren't many others missing at all, so he decided to take his seat as his parents were coming out of the house arm in arm. He had never seen his dad even remotely romantic with his mom, so it was nice to see him gazing at her and smiling.

As he approached the table, he realised he wasn't just nervous about the speech. He noticed Iliana glance at his empty seat then catch sight of him coming towards her. She looked right at him and at that moment he wasn't sure exactly what would be the correct greeting for someone you had treated so badly eight years ago, so he just smiled at her. He couldn't take his eyes off her though as he pulled out his chair to sit down. "Illy, it's great to see you, how are you?"

"I am very well thanks Tom, how are you? "she smiled. So far, no sign that she was mad at him at all, maybe eight years was long enough to forgive, or forget these things?

She was wearing a light blue dress, with thin straps and a cowl neck which showed off her tanned shoulders, and wait a minute, she was wearing the necklace he had made her! He couldn't believe it, was that a good sign? It had to be. She looked amazing.

"I am good thanks, a little nervous cos I have to make a speech, but I should be more relaxed after that," he replied trying to force a laugh.

"I am sure you'll do great."

After five minutes his dad gestured to him about the speech, so he stood up and tapped his wine glass. He'd memorised the words he had been given but had the cards in front of him anyway just in case. The speech went well, everyone laughed and awed at the correct moments then Brad said his bit and they did a toast at the end to their parents and many happy years together. After the speeches everyone made their way to the buffet and formed an orderly, polite queue. He hung back a bit and stayed in his seat, hoping for a chance to speak to Iliana. As she went to

One More Try (Book 1)

stand up, he tapped her gently on her arm, she turned around to look at him and smiled.

"Can I talk to you at some point, maybe tonight but if not, tomorrow please?" he asked, feeling a little worried that if she was putting on a show for his parents (and sister) this might tip her over the edge and she would lose it with him, like she had done eight years ago.

"Does anyone ever say no to that question?" she responded with a smile.

He chuckled. "I guess they do, sometimes, I would understand if you didn't?"

"Ah, I see. I think we should talk, but I'm not sure tonight is the best time. Let's arrange something for tomorrow, Trish offered me breakfast in the morning so we could maybe catch up after that? Mum doesn't get back until later in the afternoon, so I have some time."

"That would be great. Shall we get some food?"

He motioned towards the buffet then put out his arm to indicate ladies first. She smiled, nodded, then headed that way, so he followed. She looked stunning, the dress was loose material but fitted around her slim waist and it was just above knee length so not too long but not too short either. It showed off her shapely tanned legs nicely, finished off with high heel strappy sandals. Her straight brown hair was quite a bit longer now and it had soft curls at the end which bobbed around on her shoulders when she walked. He couldn't help but watch her as they walked to the buffet.

"So, your girlfriend couldn't make it tonight then?" She was looking at the food she was putting on her plate and not at him, but she had a smirk on her face, so he knew she was fishing for information, and he found he was delighted that she wanted to know.

"Na, you know me, no one special right now, so it's just me tonight. What about you, anyone special in your life? I hear you have a son?"

The words were out before he could think about it, but then in theory he didn't know much or anything about the time she had been away, she didn't know he had been listening in on conversations and found out more today than he had in all this time.

"Ah, so you haven't spoken to your Mum or your sister recently then?" she said, looking directly at him.

"No, they have been completely focused on tonight, why?"

"Well let's just say there is only one special person in my life just now and that is my son. We can catch up on some of the rest another time, does that sound ok?"

"Of course, let's eat."

They sat down at the table and proceeded to chat to Liz and John after they had eaten.

Their parents had hired a band to play for some of the evening at least, and people were up dancing occasionally, including Liz and John. Dan was on his own so asked Iliana for a dance, and they chatted away. As the evening went on Tom was able to talk to Iliana a bit more. She talked about her teaching and asked Tom what he was up to these days.

"Oh, this and that, Dad is not getting any younger, so I help a lot more around here, pretty much full time now. Mom still organises things of course but I do a lot more of the physical labour stuff now." He paused to sip his beer. "Would you like to dance?" he asked, feeling brave.

"Yeah sure."

He tried to hide his surprise as they got up and made their way to the dance floor. The music was from their parents' choice of songs so not exactly a pop tune, but he put one hand around her waist and held out the other so that she could take it; she placed her hand carefully on his shoulder and looked directly at him. She had the most amazing brown eyes, he just wanted to lean down and kiss her so much, but he held back and just contented himself with holding her close instead. He couldn't bear the thought of someone hurting her, well someone else hurting her would be more accurate, but physically hurting her too.

One More Try (Book 1)

They returned to their seats after the dance, and she went to mingle with the other guests while he went to get more drinks and check in with his mom. Everything was going well, and his parents were enjoying themselves, so all was good. His brother Robert was his usual obnoxious self, his partner Lisa had had too much wine and Brad's kids were climbing trees in their best clothes and generally doing what they weren't supposed to. Everything was normal.

After the band, Liz had organised to play some CDs they had made up between them featuring songs throughout the years that their parents had been together. As these occasions go it was a great night, but the more time he spent with Iliana the more eager he was to talk to her and set things right. Not that things weren't right between them, in fact they were great, he still felt there was a connection there for sure. But was that just wishful thinking? Was she just being polite?

Some of the guests started to leave around 11 so things quietened down a bit although the music played on, the Anderson siblings were each tasked with changing CDs at the appropriate time so that the guests didn't feel they had to leave at any point, well not too early anyway. At one point, Tom heard the start of One More Try, Iliana's favourite song from what seemed like such a long time ago, he looked around to see if she was about and caught her eye right away. She smiled a shy smile at him, he nodded towards the makeshift dance floor, and she made her way towards him. She put her arms around his neck first, so he placed his arms around her waist once again and pulled her close. "Do you remember this song?"

"Of course, I do, although …"

"What?" He pulled back a little to look at her.

"Well … it's just that the last time I heard it was in the cab going home after Brad's bachelor party," she whispered resting her head on his shoulder.

"Oh no ... oh no. I am so sorry Illy, I have been wracked with guilt ever since then, honestly, that's why I wanted to talk to you." He leaned further in and held her tighter.

"It's not all your fault Tom, I was being such a bitch. It seems so long ago now, let's not dwell on it yeah?" She lifted her head to look at him. They were so close again and he was finding it difficult not to just lean forward slightly and kiss her.

"Ok, I just wanted you to know that's all," he continued looking into her eyes.

"Thanks, it means a lot." She smiled and put her head on his shoulder again.

By the time they had finished their dance a lot more guests had left. He looked around for his parents and asked if there was anything he could do, but it was all under control. Tom overheard Iliana say goodnight to Liz, so he tried to subtly make his way over to her.

"I'll walk you to your chalet, if that's ok?"

"Of course," she smiled. They walked together slowly. He didn't want the evening to end. "It was a nice night. I am so glad I was able to be here."

"It was a good night, I think Mom really enjoyed it too, and Dad, although it's hard to tell with him," he laughed.

He stopped when they reached the chalet and turned to her, there was no one else around. "I am really glad you were here too Illy."

He lifted his hand and cupped her face gently, losing himself in her brown eyes. She closed her eyes, and he just couldn't resist any longer, he slowly leaned in to kiss her, as he had wanted to do all evening. The kiss seemed to last a long time, just as he wanted. She put her arms around him and pulled him close as they kissed, he didn't want it to end.

When they pulled away, she smiled, "No apology this time?"

He touched her necklace, remembering their first kiss and then cringed when he remembered their second kiss. Both of which he had apologised for.

One More Try (Book 1)

"No, I have wanted to kiss you all night if I am honest."

She smiled at him and touched his face gently; she looked as if she was going to say something else then stopped herself and lowered her hand. "Well, I am quite tired so I will call it a night, we can catch up tomorrow before I head off though?"

"Yes of course, goodnight, Illy. See you tomorrow."

He waited until she opened the door and went inside the chalet, she gave him a small wave as she did so, then he headed back over to the house. His head was buzzing after the events of the evening, he hadn't had the chance to apologise to her properly but at least he had said something, and she didn't seem to be angry with him at all. If anything, she was a lot more chilled out and confident than the young woman he remembered. It sounded like she had been through a lot though, so maybe that was part of it. The house was very quiet when he got back, not surprisingly as he was the only one staying over, he grabbed himself a beer and chilled out on the sofa for a bit before going to bed, his mind still working overtime with thoughts of holding and kissing Iliana, well if he wasn't sure how he felt before, it was clear now.

Chapter 10

Tom awoke the next morning to the familiar sound of his mom preparing breakfast in the kitchen. He cleaned his teeth, washed his face, and dressed quickly into work clothes so that he could get downstairs in time. But, as he walked down the stairs his heart sank as he noticed his mom was already loading the dishwasher; he must have missed Iliana.

"Morning Mom, I was hoping to catch Illy before she left. Have I missed her?" He tried to hide the disappointment in his voice.

"She has literally just left, son, she and Liz walked out together so they are likely still chatting, you might catch her if you hurry?"

He ran out of the door and looked in the driveway, her car was still there but Liz's wasn't so she must have headed back to the chalet to get her things. He ran over and knocked on the door. She opened it right away. "Hi Tom, I was worried I had missed you?"

"Yeah, I didn't realise the time, do you need to get going? If so, we can catch up another time?"

"I am just going to Mum's to clean the place before she and Zac arrive back, so I have a bit of time, do you want to come in?"

"Yes, thanks."

He walked into the chalet that his parents rented out to holidaymakers, the same chalet that Iliana had cleaned when she was sixteen to eighteen years old. They hadn't changed much in décor, but they were clean and comfortable, and people liked the place so much they ended up coming back often.

"I can only offer you packet coffee I'm afraid?"

"It's ok I'll get something at the house later, thanks anyway."

She sat on the small sofa, and he sat next to her. "So where do we start?"

One More Try (Book 1)

"Brad's bachelor party," he replied emphatically. "I know you said it wasn't all me, but I still want to let you know how sorry I am, your first time should be special, and I was a complete fuckwit to you! I should have known better. All these years I have wanted to talk to you; to make it up to you somehow ..." he swallowed a big lump in his throat.

"It's ok, I just wanted you to know that I don't blame you, that's all. I was very aware of what was happening, and I wanted it too."

"I know, but I bet you didn't want it like that." He didn't pause as it was a rhetorical question. "Also, I wasn't being completely honest with you, and I think you knew that. I guess I just didn't think it would do you any good to say that I felt something too, I wasn't even sure what I felt, so trying to put it into words for you would have been hard. I'm so sorry that I didn't at least try."

She smiled at him. "It's ok, I understand. Who knows what would have happened if you had? As I said, let's not dwell on it."

"How do you feel now? Will you give me a chance to make it up to you? One more try?"

"I don't know Tom, I just need some time to get organised, I..."

"I know, you have your son to think of."

"Yes, we need to find a place. I am starting a new job, Zac a new school. There's a lot going on just now."

"I know. I just wanted you to know that's all. I best get on anyway."

"Oh, ok then, see you soon." She watched as he stood up.

He headed out the door without looking back feeling just as disappointed as before, but really what had he expected? Did he think she was going to run into his arms and declare her love for him, again! What an idiot he was. He went back into the house and poured himself a coffee, lost in his thoughts.

"Did you catch her then?' his mom enquired as she came back into the room.

"Yeah, I did, thanks Mom."

"You don't sound very happy Tom, is everything ok? You guys looked close last night, is that what's wrong?"

"Nothing's wrong Mom don't worry. It's all good." He forced a smile.

"Ok then, I'll get you something to eat."

"Thanks."

*

With his toolbox in hand, Tom took the porch steps of Iliana's mom's house two at a time then knocked on the door. Iliana answered looking flustered.

"Tom, thanks so much for coming so quickly, I'm so sorry to call you at Harrow Falls while you're working. I think there's a leak".

"Ok, I'll take a look don't worry".

He followed Iliana down the narrow hallway into an open plan kitchen and living area with two bedrooms and a bathroom down the other end of the hall. It was very drab looking; she had been away for quite some time, and it didn't look like the tenants had looked after it much. He looked under the sink in the kitchen area and found the leak right away. "It's ok it's easy to fix, don't worry. I can stop the leak, but we just need to make sure that the cupboards and floorboards dry out ok. It looks like it's been that way for a while. Your tenants obviously didn't notice it."

"Not surprising given the state of this place, I've been cleaning all morning and look at it, it's still a dump!"

She flopped down on the sofa with a big sigh.

"It's not a dump Illy, you can see where you have cleaned you've done a great job. If you want, I can come and help after I have finished today, my repairs won't take much longer, maybe an hour or two tops? When are your mom and son due back?"

"Not until tomorrow, he had a party today that he

wanted to go to, and Mum can't say no to him, so they are staying another day."

"Ok so we have more time, I can go and finish up then come back and help?"

"That's so good of you Tom, thank you."

"It's no bother. I'll leave you my cell number so you can reach me if you need me next time too instead of calling Harrow Falls."

"Ok great." She smiled at him as she handed him a pen and paper.

"See you in a bit, I can bring extra cleaning supplies as well?"

"Yeah, that would be helpful, thanks again."

He drove back to his parent's place and quickly finished his repairs. He politely declined his mom's offer of lunch so that he could return as quickly as possible. He arrived back mid-afternoon, and Iliana was still working hard, the place looked better, but she hadn't touched the bathroom or spare room yet, so Tom got started there. They worked for a few hours until he made her have a seat on the sofa as she looked exhausted. "Have you had anything to eat?"

"No, I'm fine your Mum made me a huge breakfast. I just want to get it all done; we are nearly finished Tom thanks to you."

"Yeah, not long now, I just have to vacuum the spare room and then I'm finished."

"Yeah, I am nearly done too."

"What's your plans for dinner? If you don't have any we could eat out if you want or at my place? I'll need a shower first no matter what, so will have to head back to mine anyway." He grimaced as he sniffed under his arms.

"Good point, me too. Dinner out sounds nice as there's nothing here and I don't want to make a mess after cleaning it all, but it's my treat since you helped me with all this."

"Ok so let's get finished, do you want to shower here or head back to mine?"

"Hmm if it's ok with you I'll shower at yours, I am sick of this place for today."

They finished up and Iliana grabbed a change of clothes before they drove to Tom's place. She had never been there before, so he showed her where everything was before she went to get cleaned up. He tried not to think about her naked in the shower as he tidied the place up a bit.

"I'm afraid I only have the dress I wore last night, a few t shirts and jeans to wear just now," she said as she came out of the shower in t shirt and jeans with a towel around her head.

"That's fine, we can just go to the Italian place in town, it's not fancy, just good portions, I skipped lunch so I am really hungry, you must be too?"

"Yeah, I am actually."

"Great, I won't be long, help yourself to a drink if you want?" He had a very quick shower and changed into t-shirt and jeans, when he came back into the living room Iliana was sitting on his sofa just looking around.

"Don't suppose you have a hair dryer, do you?"

"Ah, no, sorry, didn't think of that!"

"No worries, it will dry on its own. Will just take a bit longer." She shook her head a bit to loosen her wet hair and smiled at him.

"Did you not want a drink?"

"No thanks, I am too hungry, if I have a drink now, I'll be falling all over the place."

"Hmm yeah good point, let's just get going. It's early enough that we should be able to get a table. I'll drive."

They arrived at Patty's restaurant, located right next to Benny's pool hall where Brad's Bachelor party had been. Tom thought to himself that this may not have been such a good plan, but his stomach was now calling the shots and Iliana never said anything.

Tom waited until they were seated at their table and had ordered a drink and some food, "So, what have you been up to for the last eight years then? I just remembered you asked me if I had spoken to my mom or sister last night?"

"Yeah, I just wondered, that's all. I know my Mum told yours a few things about the time I've been away, but I wasn't sure exactly what yet. I spoke to them both this morning though."

"Ah, ok, that doesn't enlighten me at all but never mind."

"Well, one of the reasons we are coming back is because I split up with my partner."

"Oh right, partner? Not your husband though?"

"No not husband, thankfully."

"Are you ok about it? Is your son OK about it?"

"I am fine, Zac is fine too. it was my decision to end it, I …"

"It's ok, you don't have to talk about it if you don't want to, I'm sorry."

"It's ok, I do want to tell you, it's just …" she frowned, "I don't know where to start."

"So don't then, it can wait, I didn't mean to press, honestly." He took a sip of his soft drink. "Zac's a great name, I'd like to meet him sometime when he is settled?"

"Yeah, that would be good, he's a great kid." She smiled as she thought of Zac.

Their food arrived and they ate as if they hadn't in weeks, then finished their drinks and Iliana insisted on paying. As they left the restaurant Iliana said, "it's still quite early, do you want to get a drink next door?" Tom nearly fell over as he thought that was the last thing she would want to do.

"Really?"

"Yeah, why not? A trip down memory lane."

"Ok then, I can have one beer I guess since I had a soft drink with dinner."

They entered the pool hall and Dave waved at Tom as they did so.

"Tom, how's it going?" Dave said in his usual cheerful manner.

"Not bad Dave thanks, this is Iliana."

One More Try (Book 1)

"Yeah of course, I remember you, weren't you off to college last I saw you?"

"Wow, good memory. Yes, I was."

"I'm a bartender, I never forget a pretty face."

"Just as charming as you were then too," Iliana chuckled.

They ordered a few drinks and sat at the bar, it did feel odd as they were almost sitting exactly where Iliana and Liz had sat on that fateful night. But Tom put that out of his mind and soon relaxed a bit once they had their drinks. "It does seem strange being here, it hasn't changed a bit, has it?" She was looking around the place after a sip of her white wine.

"No, you're right, it hasn't changed at all!"

"I remember sitting here watching your butt as you played a game of pool!"

"Really?"

He laughed, "I don't remember an awful lot about it, I think I blocked a lot of it out in all honesty." He frowned and looked down at the ground. She reached out her hand to touch his gently.

"We've talked about this, it's fine." She was smiling at him as he glanced up at her again. "There is something about the last eight years that I need to tell you though and I have no idea how to. I'm sorry I froze earlier ..."

"It's ok Illy, honestly. There's no rush, I'm here for you whenever you want to talk but in your own time." He found himself gazing into her tearful eyes. "If it helps, I overheard Mom and Liz talking so I do know some of it, about your Ex anyway." She still had her hand on his and he squeezed it gently as reassurance.

"Well, that does help, a bit, but there's more ..." she looked down at their hands touching, "I am not sure if I should tell you here, but in a way it's kind of fitting I suppose." She shrugged a little as she wrestled with her memories.

"What is it Illy? You know you can talk to me?"

One More Try (Book 1)

She reached down for her purse and pulled out a small photo, about three inches by five.

"Alec, my ex, he isn't Zac's Dad." She was watching him intently as she spoke. "He was born in April 1993, so he is seven years old." Again, she was observing him.

"Jesus, what are you saying Illy? Are you saying what I think you're saying?" His heart was thumping in his chest.

"He is your son, Tom," she was nodding, "I discovered I was pregnant not long after I arrived in Aqualta. I carried on studying until I couldn't do it anymore, the college kept my place so I could pick my studies up the next year, then I met Alec."

Tom couldn't believe what he was hearing, he put down his beer, ran his hands through his hair and shook his head, was this really happening?

One More Try (Book 1)

Chapter 11

"What? I'm a dad?" Now it was his turn to observe her, her eyes were still filled with tears. She held out the photo to show him, so he took it from her. It was of a boy with short brown hair and green eyes, in a red and white striped tie and short sleeved white shirt smiling at the camera, with a few teeth missing. He looked just like Tom had when he was that age, no wonder she couldn't come back sooner, people would likely have guessed he was Tom's even if she hadn't said anything. He sat completely still for an age just staring at the picture. "Does he know?"

"Yes, well he knows Alec isn't his dad anyway. If you are ok with it, then we can tell him."

"Of course, I am ok with it, if you are, now I really can't wait to meet him, I was just being polite before."

She let out a nervous laugh.

"To be honest, I expected to come home and find you married with kids of your own."

"Really? You do know me, don't you?" He chuckled and she smiled.

"So, you are ok with it then? It's a lot to take in, I thought you would be mad!"

"Well, it is a lot to take in but why would I be mad?"

"I guess because I never told you."

"Well, I think we both know why that was though, I wouldn't blame you for that after what happened between us." He reluctantly reached out to hand her back the photo.

"You can keep that if you want it?"

"Thanks, I'd like that." He studied the photo again before putting it in his pocket. He reached out and held her hand gazing into her amazing brown eyes.

"Well, you have surprised me again, Tom, you never cease to amaze me!"

"I am glad to hear it, I don't like the idea of being predictable." He gave her his best charming smile and she laughed out loud.

One More Try (Book 1)

"So, you can meet him tomorrow if you want?"

"That would be great, I have stuff to do but I can be free late afternoon. I can just come around to Mary's if that suits you?"

"Yeah, that would be great." She looked pensive for a few seconds then continued, "…so, what you said this morning about one more try?"

"Yeah?"

"Does what I just told you change that?"

"No, of course not. It changes how I feel about meeting Zac, but not how I feel about you."

"How do you feel about me? You didn't quite say it?"

"I had thought that was pretty obvious, after last night and this morning, even Mom commented on how we were last night but if you want to hear me say it then fine." He took a deep breath, "I have feelings for you, and I would like to be more than your friend."

"Ok, good. I just need a bit of time to take it all in, is that OK?"

"Of course, Illy, I am not going anywhere so take all the time you need." He squeezed her hand again.

"Thanks." She sipped the last of her wine.

"It's been a long day, I'll drop you off at home if you want or you can stay at mine, in the spare room of course?"

"Thanks, I'll go home if that's ok as I have all my overnight stuff there?"

"OK."

They left the bar and waved goodbye to Dave as they did so, once they arrived at Mary's Iliana said "I hope you don't mind but I already told Liz about Zac. She promised not to say a word to anyone until you knew, I will give her a call and tell her that I have told you now."

"Yeah, I will probably go and see Mom after I drop you off, show her the picture, it's probably better I tell her face to face, I'll phone the others."

"Ok. Hopefully they won't judge me too much."

"Hey, of course they won't. Mom, Brad, and Dan won't judge either of us. Dad and Robert will judge me, but I can handle that. What did Liz say when you told her?"

"Not much, there's not much she can say really, she isn't the kind to judge. She said she can't wait to meet him, just like you did."

"Did she ask anything about what happened?"

"No, she didn't, don't worry, that's between us."

"Ok. So just call me tomorrow on my cell and let me know when you are ready for a visit, and I'll come over?"

"Yeah, I will. See you tomorrow then Tom." She got out of the car and gave him a small wave, much like she used to do.

When he arrived at Harrow Falls, he couldn't see his dad's car so that was a good sign, it would be much better to talk with his mom first. As he entered the house, he could hear his mom singing while emptying the dishwasher.

"Hi Tom, what a nice surprise." She greeted him while drying her hands on the towel. "I've already made dinner but if you're hungry I could make something quick?"

"No, I ate Mom, but thanks. Do you have a minute for a chat?"

"Yeah sure, of course, is everything ok?"

"Yeah, but you might want to sit down." He sat at the table and motioned for her to sit next to him.

"Well now you're worrying me, what is it?"

"I have to tell you something which you might not like very much," he said, feeling suddenly wary of how she might take the news. She was watching him with a furrowed brow and head tilted to the side. "There's something you should know before you meet Iliana's son, Zac," he continued, slowly. "She and I, well we … em, I don't really know how to say this now I have started. He is my son, your grandchild Mom." That wasn't really the way he had rehearsed it in the car but never mind.

She moved her head upright and her eyes went wide, mouth open. "He is what? Are you kidding me?" Was she

One More Try (Book 1)

annoyed or just shocked? He couldn't tell yet, normally he could read her quite well.

"No of course not, I wouldn't joke about something like that. He is my son, but I only just found out. I wanted to tell you before I tell the others."

"Well, that's not what I was expecting you to say I must admit, wow! I have another grandchild?" she seemed calm thankfully, so he let out his breath, not aware that he had been holding it in the first place.

"Are you ok?"

"Yes, I am fine, really, I am fine, just a bit of a shock that's all? Why didn't she tell you about it?"

"Well, that's my fault I'm afraid, it's a long story but the short version is that before she left, she tried to tell me how she felt, and I pushed her away. I was too scared and stupid, but I didn't know about the baby until today".

"And how do *you* feel about it son? "

"I am excited to be honest, strangely enough. I can't wait to meet him." He couldn't help but smile and she joined him.

"Are you guys an item now then?"

"Well, the ball's in Iliana's court there, I would like us to be but I don't want to rush her into anything."

"Of course, that makes sense, I take it you know about her Ex?"

"I don't know the details, but I know the gist of it, so that is why I don't want to rush her into it."

"That's good, I know you will both make the right decision so that's good," she smiled and stood up. "I suspected you cared for her that day when she wasn't well, and you made her tea and toast!"

"Really?"

"Yes, but I didn't know if it was platonic or not."

"It was platonic at that point. It wasn't until a lot later ..." he stopped there, as he wasn't sure if he should say any more, or what to say for that matter.

She reached over and gave him a hug "I have another grandchild!" she said with excitement.

He felt so relieved that she was ok with it. If he had his mom's support, he could handle anything else. The next thing to deal with was Liz, then Mary.

"Thanks Mom. I am meeting him tomorrow, I can't wait. Oh, I nearly forgot," he went into his pocket and got out the photo, "here he is."

"Oh my God. He is just like you were at that age," she smiled down at the picture.

"Yeah, that's what I thought, in fact I think you have an almost identical picture of me somewhere?"

"Yes, I think I do, I will look it out if you want?"

"No, it's OK Mom," he laughed, "Iliana might want to see it though, although I am sure she knows how much he is like me."

"Can I get you a coffee or anything?"

"No, I best get going, sorry, I need to phone my brothers and let them know. Liz already knows. I'll be up tomorrow for those jobs you need done then I will head off, hopefully early afternoon to meet him."

"You will let me know how it goes, won't you? I would love to meet him soon too of course, but no rush." Tom smiled at his mom telling him not to rush, he knew she didn't mean that at all!

"What about your father?"

"What about him?"

"Don't you want to tell him?"

"No not really, he will likely have something judgemental to say to me. You can tell him if you're ok with that?"

"Ok I will." She didn't disagree with him.

Tom grabbed a beer and put his feet up once he was home. He looked around and thought about changes he would have to make around the place now. He would remove some of his old stuff from the spare room and put it in the garage so it could be Zac's room, it would be more like starting fresh for Zac, he didn't know what else a seven-year-old needed or wanted in their room, but he could work on that. He would ask Iliana tomorrow. He then decided it was time to let his brothers know so he phoned Brad first.

"Hey Bro, how's it going?" Brad greeted him.

"Great, really great, you?"

"Yeah good."

"I won't keep you long. I just wanted to let you know what's happening with me. "

"Is it something to do with Iliana?"

"Yes, it is ..."

"You guys seemed really close last night, so it was just a guess."

"Yeah, well I am working on that but there is more that I wanted you to hear from me."

"Yeah?"

"Not sure if you know but she has a son, not just any son actually, he is my son, I just found out today and am meeting him tomorrow."

"What the fuck? Really?"

"Yeah."

"Wow, congratulations Bro. Are you ok about it?"

"Yes, I am actually, I can't wait, it's a new chapter for me for sure."

"Well, I am chuffed for you, can't wait to meet him. Wait until Ethan and Helena find out they have a cousin!"

"Yeah. Thanks Brad, we will catch up soon, Mom is keen to meet him soon too. Oh, and Brad?"

"Yeah?"

"Thanks for not asking any more about what happened between us."

"None of my business Bro, as long as you are happy, I am good."

"Thanks."

He called Robert after that.

"Hello."

"Robert, it's Tom."

"To what do I owe the pleasure?"

"I just wanted to let you know something, so you didn't hear it from anyone else," Robert didn't comment further so he carried on "I found out today that I have a son, with Iliana ..." he was interrupted as Robert started to laugh, which he really wasn't expecting, even from Robert. "Is something funny?"

"Yeah, looks like you're paying the price for your quickie next to the dumpster, eh?"

"What the fuck does that mean?"

"You know exactly what it means."

"Were you watching you pervert?"

"I *saw* you, that doesn't mean I watched you! I went outside to see why you were taking so long and got my answer right away."

"Right away? You had to walk around the back to look for us, you creep!" Tom hung up as he couldn't take any more, why did Robert always have to find an angle and wind him up?

He took a minute to calm down then phoned Dan but there was no answer. He would try and catch up with him later.

Chapter 12

Tom was pacing on Mary's porch waiting to meet his son. He had spent the morning working and trying not to worry until he received Iliana's call and couldn't quite believe what was about to happen.

"Hey, come on in. You all set?" She gave him a reassuring smile.

"A bit nervous if I am honest, but ready. Is your mom ok about me being here, everything?"

"Yeah, she is fine, don't worry."

When he entered the room Mary was sitting on the small sofa with her hands clasped at the front, there were boxes everywhere now, so the place looked smaller than it had yesterday. Mary looked just as he remembered her, not much older at all and she smiled at him. A small sigh of relief left him. Next to her on the sofa was Zac, he looked just as he did in the picture so it must have been recent, he was wearing a red t shirt with a soccer ball on it and plain grey shorts, with little sneakers. He stood up and walked towards him. Tom crouched down so that he was closer to Zac's height and smiled at him.

"Hi Zac, it's great to meet you."

"Hi." His brow creased as he spoke. "Are you my Dad?"

"Yes, I am."

"Should I call you Dad then?"

"You can call me Dad if you like, but if you prefer not to my name is Tom so you can call me that instead if you want to?" He looked at Iliana for some reassurance and she was nodding gently. Both women were watching them intently. Zac appeared to ponder for a few seconds.

"I think I'll call you Dad if that's okay." He leaned forward and put his arms around Tom's neck to hug him, so he reciprocated. He couldn't believe how good it felt to have this small person call him Dad and hug him, his arms around his shoulders felt tiny. He had never thought he would have kids, it had never really appealed, but there weren't words to describe how he was feeling right now. He would make sure that he was a good Dad to this little boy, help look after him, protect him, whatever it took. He had already missed the first seven years of his life but planned to make up for it big time. Zac pulled away first and stared at him.

"We have the same green eyes, Dad." Zac smiled as he spoke.

"Yeah, we do." He couldn't help but smile back, hearing the word Dad again was amazing. "What do you say we go do something together if it's okay with your mom? What sports do you like? I have a lot of catching up to do." He raised his eyebrows at Iliana as he spoke to seek permission.

"Yes, your Gran and I have a bit of unpacking to do so you guys could hang out for a bit, for sure." Iliana had a big smile on her face, and he thought he could see her eyes a little glazed too.

"Great, well that's settled. What would you like to do?" He crouched down again so he was at eye level.

"I like soccer, do you play?"

"I don't think I have played since twelfth Grade, but I may have some skills up my sleeve, shall we see?" He reached out his hand and Zac took it right away. They headed towards the kitchen and Tom stopped in front of Iliana. "Just shout if you need us yeah?"

"Of course." Her eyes were still glazed as she smiled.

They headed for the kitchen and out the back door which closed behind them.

"Do you have a soccer ball already out here?" Tom asked only just thinking about it now, he was too caught up in the moment to think of it before.

"Yeah, I have already been out with my ball, I have a goal as well see." Zac pointed towards the grass area of the garden where there was a small goal with three soccer balls. The garden wasn't huge, but it was just the right size for a boy this size to have a kick about. It was surrounded by a large hedge and some overgrown rose bushes so could have been slightly bigger if they were cut back, although at least it

One More Try (Book 1)

meant it was private, he made a mental note to ask about cutting back those bushes.

"Ah of course, how did I not notice the goal?"

Zac ran towards the goal and picked up the bright yellow ball, then came towards Tom, putting the ball at his feet.

"Ok, try and get the ball from me then Dad?"

They played football for quite a while and Iliana invited Tom to stay for dinner. When she took Zac away for his bath after dinner Tom was sitting in the living room having coffee with Mary.

"How are you then Mary?"

"I am well Tom, thanks. Can't do as much as I used to, but I am very lucky to have a wonderful daughter and grandson in my life. What about you? Quite a day for you?"

"Yes, I have never been better to be honest, today has been amazing."

"That's good."

"You must have been shocked when you found out Illy was pregnant?" He said the words before he thought it through, what was he thinking?

"I was, she didn't tell me you were his father for some time though."

"Yeah, I guess. Did she tell you anything about what happened?"

"No, and I don't need to know. She always had feelings for you I knew that much, she used to skip around the house when she came back from sleepovers or work if you had dropped her off. She thought I didn't notice but Moms notice everything." She smiled again. "I just didn't know how you felt, but Iliana assured me you didn't want to know so I didn't pry".

"She is a lot younger than me, and back then I don't think I knew how I felt either, not exactly."

Mary held up her hands "You don't need to explain, don't worry." She sipped her coffee and then smiled again. Iliana came into the living room at that point.

"Mum, do you want to say goodnight to Zac first? Then Tom can?"

Mary nodded then went into Iliana and Zac's room, "How are you doing Illy?"

"I am great, thanks Tom. Are you ok?"

"Never better; I'll get going after I have said goodnight to Zac."

"Your turn," Mary smiled at Tom as she came back into the living room.

Tom went into Iliana and Zac's room. He was tucked into the double bed, wearing a Spong Bob pyjama t-shirt which was one of the few cartoon characters Tom recognised. He looked tiny in the big double bed on his own.

"Good night, Zac. It was great meeting you today, hopefully we can play again soon." He sat down next to him on the bed.

"Yeah, that would be good," he said sleepily. "Can I tell you something Dad?"

"Of course, anything." Tom leaned in.

"I didn't like Alec very much, I'm glad you're my dad and not him."

"Oh, ok, well I never met him so can't really comment."

"Mummy never looked at him the way she looks at you." Tom felt like his heart would melt. "That's nice, your mom and I have known each other a long time."

"Yeah, I know, she said you made her the necklace that she wears all the time. It's her favourite thing."

"Yeah, I noticed she still wears it too, I am glad." Zac yawned. "Anyway, time for sleep. Goodnight son."

"Goodnight Dad." Zac smiled and then closed his eyes.

Tom went back into the living room to say goodnight to Iliana and Mary.

"I'll be off then."

"Ok, I'll walk you out." Iliana stood up and walked down the hall with him, she shivered a little in the night air as they left the house.

One More Try (Book 1)

"Zac is amazing, he is a lovely boy, you have done a wonderful job with him."

"I think he likes you too, I am so happy with how it went today but he has his moments don't be fooled."

"Yeah, I can't wait!" He reached out his arms and put them around her shoulders, "You look cold, I won't keep you. Thanks for today and tonight, it was great." He really wanted to ask when he would see them again but thought it best not to push. "Mom is really keen to meet Zac too so just have a think about it, no rush though."

"Yeah, that's right she mentioned Wednesday to me when we had breakfast, that was before she knew though. Do you think she'll still be keen?"

"Are you kidding me? She will be doing cartwheels! I hadn't realised you had made plans. We could just go for a visit if you want, it's up to you. Have a think about it?"

"I will but I think it will be fine, I'll call you tomorrow."

"OK great. Goodnight Illy." he reluctantly removed his arms from their very pleasant embrace.

"Goodnight." She put her own arms around her shoulders then waved at him as he got in the car and drove away with a huge smile on his face.

*

On Wednesday, he worked as usual then went to collect them after showering and changing. Even though it had only been a day since he had seen them, he found he couldn't wait. Iliana was wearing a dark red dress, which she looked amazing in, and Zac was wearing some kind of soccer strip with red and blue vertical stripes that Tom didn't recognise but he made a mental note to ask him about it later. Zac was carrying his football and took it in the back of the car with him. On the drive out he was asking questions about his grandparents and where they lived. It wasn't long before he was able to see Harrow Falls for himself of course and he was mesmerised.

"I used to spend a lot of time here when I was younger, it's such a beautiful place, I used to take a lot of pictures too."

I'll show them to you once I have found them," Iliana said to him as they drove up the long driveway.

"Yeah, it hasn't changed much in all that time," Tom added. "My grandfather built this place himself Zac, your Great Grandfather. He built up the business from nothing and ran it for several years before he died in 1982. You didn't meet him did you Illy?"

"No, I didn't, I arrived in 1983. Liz told me a lot about him though."

"He was an amazing man, I used to follow him around when I wasn't at school, he taught me everything I know." Iliana touched his arm gently as she could see he was feeling nostalgic. "I wanted to do some upgrades over the last few years but ..." Iliana glanced at him "... another time maybe," he whispered; he didn't want to mention the arguments in front of Zac. She just nodded in acknowledgement.

When they parked the car there were several others already there, he recognised Liz's, Brad's, and Robert's cars. No sign of his younger brother Dan's but he was likely working.

"Looks like you are getting to meet a lot of the family at once Zac, you ok about that little man?" Tom glanced at Iliana, and she nodded.

"Yeah, I guess", Zac responded with a frown, "who else will be there then?"

"Well, your cousins will be there for a start, Ethan is your age, and Helena is two years younger, at least you can play with them if the adults' chat is boring?" Zac nodded knowingly, as if he understood that adult chat was indeed boring but immediately grabbed Tom's hand as they walked towards the house. Tom gave it a gentle, reassuring squeeze as he reached out his other hand to open the front door.

When they walked in everyone stopped what they were doing and looked around, the two kids were sat at the table eating some kind of snack so just turned around in their seats. Robert wasn't with his partner, and neither was Liz. Tom's Mom immediately made her way over.

One More Try (Book 1)

"Hi Zac, I'm your other Granny, Tom's Mom. It's so good to meet you." She reached out a hand to him and crouched down. Zac still had a tight hold of Tom's hand but reached out his other little hand and shook Trish's.

"Pleased to meet you," he replied politely.

"And these are some of your Aunts and Uncles; Robert, Jane, Brad and Elizabeth." They all smiled and waved at Zac. He was leaning into Tom's leg now as if for protection.

"And of course, these are your cousins, Ethan and Helena, say Hi to your cousin Zac guys," she continued enthusiastically.

"Hi," they said in unison, looking extremely bored with having to do polite introductions.

"Hi," Zac responded. Ethan stood up and walked over to him.

"How old are you Zac?"

"I am seven, how old are you?"

"I am seven too, when is your Birthday, mine is July?"

Tom and the other adults just watched their interaction.

"Mine is April," replied Zac.

"Ah, you are three months older than me then. What sports do you play?"

"I play soccer mostly but some others, what about you?"

"Baseball, a bit of soccer but not much though."

"How about you teach me baseball and I teach you soccer then?" Zac said.

"Yeah, ok then, let's go."

The boys quickly ran towards the door.

"Sorry Mom, you can see him from the kitchen window at least, I suspected that might happen, you know what kids are like!" said Tom.

"It's fine," said Trish, as she approached the table to clear away the snack plates, "there's plenty of time. I am just glad I got to meet him. He is so like you, it's like turning back the clock twenty-five years for me!"

"Sorry for gate crashing Bro we were passing, and Mom mentioned you were dropping in so we couldn't miss the opportunity, the kids were really excited to meet their new cousin," Brad said with a big smile.

"It's fine don't worry, it's great for him to meet you all."

"We can't stop too long as Ethan has baseball practice and Helena has piano."

Chapter 13

Later, once Brad had left, Iliana and Trish relaxed on the sofas, whilst a much more relaxed Zac chatted excitedly to his Granny. Liz had followed Tom through to the kitchen:
"How are you doing then Tom?"
"Yeah good, thanks, you?"
"Good." She was nodding her head. "I won't stop long either I just couldn't wait to meet Zac."
"Yeah of course, it's no bother." He got the feeling she was fishing for something, but he wasn't sure what.
"He's a nice boy, he seems very attached to you already?"
"Do you think so?" Tom looked back at him chatting away to his mom and smiled, "I hope so."
"Definitely."
"What about his mom, do you think she is attached to me?" Liz looked surprised then gave him a sympathetic look.
"Hang in there big bro, I think you know the answer to that. She just needs time, she's been through ... "
"…A lot. I know, well I don't know the half of it yet, but I will. I have told her there is no rush."
"I know. You are just not used to having to wait that's all, you always get your own way right away?" She was teasing him and nudging him in the side. He laughed; she may have had a point.
"Did she tell you about us?"
"Yes, women talk. You should know that by now?"
"Yeah, I suppose."
"You know you could have talked to me?" she said with concern.
"What do you mean?"
"What happened, what you were going through, you could have talked to me about it?"
"Which bit? 'Oh, you know I slept with your best friend before she left for college' or 'you know I might have feelings for her'?" she smiled at him.
"Either or both, you could have talked to me about it."

One More Try (Book 1)

"I didn't know how I felt ..." he shrugged.

"Exactly why talking about it might have helped?"

"Yeah maybe. She is a lot younger than me." He paused, deep in thought, "I worried about what people would think. Specifically, what you would think?"

"I wouldn't think badly of you. You are my brother, and despite what you think, I know you are a good person and would never hurt anyone intentionally."

He felt quite emotional hearing Liz say these things, talking about feelings wasn't really something that he was used to doing, he didn't know many men that did. Too late to think of all this now though.

"Thanks, I appreciate it." She came closer to him and gave him a hug; he hugged her back. "I might need to take you up on the offer soon anyway."

"As I said, hang in there."

Tom noticed that Iliana was looking over at them with a slightly furrowed brow. After their hug, he and Liz made their way over to the sofas then Tom handed Zac the glass of water that had sent him into the kitchen in the first place.

"Thanks Dad." Tom sat down next to Iliana on the sofa.

"Well, I had better be off, it was great to meet you Zac, I will see you again soon?"

"Ok," Zac replied, "see you soon Aunt Liz." Liz grabbed her purse and said a general goodbye to everyone as she headed out the house.

"Do you guys want to stay for dinner?" Trish asked looking at Tom then Iliana.

"Sorry Trish, my Mum has got things prepared for tonight, we just thought it would be a quick visit."

"Oh, that's ok, Tom did mention a quick visit I just thought I would check ..." she avoided looking at them and Tom thought he would make a point of asking Iliana when they could all come over for dinner soon, but Iliana beat him to it.

One More Try (Book 1)

"We can definitely come over another night though, just let us know what suits you and we'll be here?" His mom's shoulders lifted immediately.

"Great, how about Friday then?" She didn't waste any time!

"Sounds great, that's settled." Iliana smiled at her as she stood up. "We best be getting back then; it was so great to see you." She hugged his mom then Zac did the same. Tom couldn't help thinking that although Zac looked like him, his personality was very similar to Iliana's.

During the drive home in the car, Iliana frowned as she gazed out the window.

"Was everything ok tonight? I saw Liz giving you a hug?" she said eventually.

"Yeah, it doesn't happen often, but she does hug me sometimes, we *are* family?" He laughed trying to make light of it, but Iliana wasn't fooled. "Ok. She just said that I could have talked to her that's all, about how I felt."

"Ah, ok. She said the same to me," she sighed.

"What did you say to her?"

"That I should have told her how I felt. As my best friend and your little sister, I should have told her, but I said I was worried about what she might think of me."

"Yeah, I said similar too. Wonder what would have happened if we had both talked to her?"

"Who knows!" She laughed and gave him a look as if she understood what he was thinking.

Zac then seized the opportunity to talk about how much fun he had had playing with Ethan which made both Iliana and Tom smile. Tom had worried at first, about him meeting almost everyone at once, but he figured it had all gone well in the end.

"See you again soon Zac. Looks like we are having dinner at Gran's house on Friday so I will see you then," he said as Iliana helped Zac out of the car.

"Ok, see you then Dad." He would never tire of hearing the word; he knew it would always make him smile. Iliana made a sign with her hand to her ear to say she would call him tomorrow, so he nodded and waved goodbye, still smiling.

*

The following day Tom had work to do in the morning then spent the rest of the day finishing off what was going to be Zac's room. It was late by the time he finished and sat down. He checked his cell phone to see if he had any missed calls but there were none. It was too late to try and call Iliana now, he opened a beer and sat down again, trying not to feel too disappointed. What was wrong with him? He was like a lovesick teenager, and he hadn't been one of those when he *was* a teenager, so he wasn't used to feeling like this. He put the TV on to see what reruns he could watch to distract him, when he thought he heard a knock at the door. When he opened the door, he got such a pleasant surprise.

"Illy! I was just thinking about giving you a call."

"Hi Tom, sorry to just drop by unannounced."

"That's ok, come in. I'm a mess though I am still in work clothes and have been tidying out the spare room, so I am all sweaty. I would have tidied up and had a shower if I had known you were coming." He pulled at the bottom of his tatty old black work t-shirt as he said it as if to emphasise the point. She looked at his getup and smiled but didn't say anything.

"Is everything ok? You look a little flustered?" She was in a plain blue v neck fitted t shirt and jeans with flat shoes and she had her purse over her shoulder.

"I am fine thanks, good in fact. I just wanted to see you." She frowned. They walked into the living room, and he went over to get his beer, Iliana remained standing.

"Yeah? You don't seem fine?" He paused but she still said nothing. "Have a seat. I just opened a beer; do you want anything? Or did you bring the car?" He held up his beer before taking another sip.

"I am good thanks."

One More Try (Book 1)

"You're worrying me now Illy." He put his beer down on the table and watched her. She put her purse on the floor and walked over until she was right in front of him then looked up. She reached out her hand and touched his face. He closed his eyes briefly at her touch. It felt so good.

"I've been doing a lot of thinking today."

He gazed searchingly into her eyes as she spoke. "And?" Surely, she didn't come here to let him down gently in person.

She stood there for what seemed like an age just gazing at him. She was still touching his face as she leaned forward slowly and kissed him on the lips. When she pulled away, she smiled at him then they kissed again, this time she was kissing him with so much passion he nearly fell over. She pulled his t-shirt over his head then gently touched his bare chest.

"Wait," he said, slightly out of breath from the kiss. He gently held her by the wrists and looked into her amazing brown eyes, which seemed to be even brighter than normal. "Are you sure you want to do this?"

She smiled, "You've said that to me before."

"I know… well, are you?"

"Oh yes, I have never been surer of anything in my life."

"Then let's do it properly this time. One more try." He took her by the hand and walked down the hall to his bedroom. He stopped next to the bed and faced her again. He pulled her t-shirt up over her head, then undid her bra at the back and gently pulled it over her arms.

"Expertly done," she laughed.

He had never wanted her more than at this moment.

They kissed again then she ran her fingers down his chest and abdomen, undid his shorts button and zip then pulled them down with his boxers so that he could step out of them. He undid her jeans and kneeled slowly, gently kissing her pert breasts and the soft skin on her stomach on the way down to remove her jeans, she removed her shoes then he pulled her jeans down with her panties so that she could step out of them.

He stood back up and cupped her face, "I so want this to be special for you Illy."

"It already is," she replied with a smile then gave him a long kiss.

He lifted her gently and placed her on the bed, he lay down and put one knee between her legs carefully to open them slightly more and continued gently kissing her skin, her neck, her shoulders, her collar bone, around the necklace before spending a lot more time on her beautiful breasts. He noticed some small round marks on her skin at the sides between her breasts and her waist but didn't stop or say anything. Eventually he couldn't wait any longer and her gasps of breath made him think she was the same, "Do we need to ...?" he whispered, not wanting to spoil the moment.

"No, it's ok," she replied, pulling him towards her. He entered her, and she arched her back and gasped as he did so. As he moved on top of her, she continued to moan and gasp, he had never been so aware of how a woman was feeling during sex and he had never cared so much about their orgasm, it was so intense; just when he thought he couldn't hold on any longer, Iliana let out a loud cry. He felt such a relief before he joined her. He gently lowered himself on top of her, gasping for air he managed to kiss her on the lips before placing his head on her chest. She put her arms around him.

They stayed this way for a few minutes, both getting their breath back. He lifted himself and moved to lay on his side next to her, still watching her, "Hopefully better than the first time."

"Oh yes." She was on her side now facing him, so he reached out his arm and held her close for a while. She glanced at him and smiled again then kissed him and rolled onto her front. He gently touched her shoulders then ran his fingers from there down her back and over her bottom, admiring her body.

One More Try (Book 1)

"You didn't even get to finish your beer, sorry," she said eventually.

"It's ok, you're worth it."

"We could have a drink now if you want?"

"Yeah, that would be nice, will you stay the night?"

"I'd like that, mum's with Zac," she replied.

He didn't think he could feel any happier at that moment. He gave her another kiss then got out of bed and put his boxers on. She got out of bed and put her panties and t-shirt on then they went through to the living room together.

He tried his beer which was surprisingly still cold, so he carried on drinking it. "Can I get you a white wine? I think I have some in the fridge."

"That would be great, if you have any?"

"Yep, there it is, no idea how long it's been there for of course but see what you think. I think one of the holidaymakers gave it to me as a thank you gift so maybe it's not been there that long."

He opened the wine and poured a glass then handed it to her, he watched as she took a sip.

"It's good, doesn't taste like vinegar so all good." She smiled as he sat down on the sofa next to her.

"I seem to have lost my t-shirt; do you remember where you threw it when you took it off earlier?" He grinned as he sat down next to her, looking around.

She giggled. "Ah no sorry, you said it was dirty anyway, I'm sure we'll find it. Besides, I like to see your chest, unless you're cold?"

"No, I'm not cold so it's fine, but why don't you do the same then?" He raised his eyebrows. Her smile faded and she looked down into her glass.

"That's different, boobs get in the way all the time and …"

"Sorry," he reached out his hand to touch hers, "is it to do with the marks on your sides?"

She nodded shyly.

"I was going to ask you about them but wasn't sure how. Are they what I think they are?"

"They are cigarette burns." She didn't say any more.

He gently turned her around so that he could see her face. "That's what I thought they were, we don't need to talk about it, not if you don't want to." He gently kissed her cheek.

"I do, but not yet, is that ok? Oh, and thank you for not mentioning them earlier, you know…?" she raised her eyebrows.

"I wouldn't have done that."

"Yeah, it might have put you off completely."

"No, nothing could have put me off at that point, I was a bit preoccupied..." he chuckled trying to lighten the mood. She laughed out loud, a lovely hearty laugh, which made him join her. "Can I ask you something?"

"Does anyone ever say no to that?" she replied with a cheeky grin.

"Good point, not that I know of," he laughed.

"Sure, what is it?"

"Now that I have the other room ready, would you and Zac like to come here and stay over tomorrow night, after we have dinner at Mom's? It's no problem if you don't want to, I just thought it would be good for us all to spend some time together, here, and for Zac to see his room, he can help me make it more his own too if he wants?" He realised at this point that he was rambling a bit hoping that she wouldn't say no. She was just smiling at him, a good sign he hoped.

"That would be nice, I think he would love it, he hasn't stopped talking about you all day."

"Really?"

"Oh yeah, he loved telling Mum all the details about his visit to your folks' place and meeting his Aunts, Uncles and cousins. She loved hearing about it too."

One More Try (Book 1)

"What about his mom though, you aren't just doing it for him are you? It means the two of us get to spend time together as well?"

"Of course, it's win, win really." She smiled at him and kissed him on the lips.

"Good, that sounds great."

"I see you have put his picture up," Iliana nodded towards the frame on the mantelpiece, "Zac will be happy to see it there."

"Oh yeah? Of course, I put it up where I can see it, it makes me smile every time I look at it. I can just hear his little voice calling me Dad. We'll need to get one for Mom too actually, do you have a spare? If not, I can get a copy made."

"I think I have a spare; I'll check tomorrow then we can take it around when we go for dinner."

"Great, she'll love that." Tom suddenly had a thought, "I keep meaning to ask you, you know you said Zac was born in April, you never said which day?"

"Oh yeah, I almost forgot, it's the twentieth."

"Really? Same as mine! Did you remember?"

"Yes, I did, although I couldn't be sure of the exact date, it's not like we ever really celebrated your birthday together, but I knew it was around then."

"Yeah, that's true."

"I feel a bit bad now as you always used to remember mine."

"Yeah, but it's easier for me to remember one birthday than for you to remember the five of us, I never bothered about the others, Mom always reminded me."

"Well, but you were always my favourite, you must have known that. Except for Liz of course, favourite of her brothers I should have said." she smiled, clearly trying to make sure she worded things correctly.

"I didn't know that actually, you were always great with everyone, so I didn't." He gave her a kiss then continued. "We'll have to tell him tomorrow; it was yesterday when he

105

told Ethan his birthday was April, it reminded me but then I forgot to ask you."

"Yeah, I am sure he will love it."

They finished their drinks and retired to bed where they snuggled together and fell asleep both feeling very content.

One More Try (Book 1)

Chapter 14

Tom, Iliana, and Zac were on their way to Harrow Falls in the car and Zac was chatting about his day. Tom told him that Auntie Liz would be there with her partner John and probably James, his grandfather, this time around, as he had missed him last time. "Did your mom tell you that we have something else in common, not just our green eyes?" Tom couldn't wait to ask him. Iliana just smiled from the front seat of the car.

"No, what is it?"

"Well, my birthday is the twentieth of April, when is yours?"

Zac's mouth fell wide open with genuine shock, "Same! Really? We have the same birthday?"

"Yes, we do, isn't that funny?"

"Yeah, we can celebrate together, you can invite your friends, and I can invite mine; it will be great fun."

Iliana just chuckled.

"As you get older you don't celebrate birthdays the same way Zac but that's a nice idea."

When they arrived Liz and John were already there, Zac wanted to give his Granny the picture that Iliana got for her himself so insisted on taking it inside with him.

"Oh, this is great, thanks so much Zac." Trish hugged him. "I will put it over here with all my other special pictures."

Tom and Iliana sat on the sofa next to Liz and John.

"What's that one Mom? I don't think I have seen it before?" Tom asked as she placed the frame down next to a picture he hadn't noticed before.

"Oh yes, this was a gift from Iliana, isn't it amazing, it's from a while ago and I think it is actually the only picture I have of all five of you together."

She carefully picked up the picture in the small frame as if it was a delicate ornament that could break. She walked over to the sofa and handed it to him. It was all five of them

One More Try (Book 1)

out in the yard, all doing different things, not posing but at least together, some looking at the camera some looking off in the distance including him, he must have been about seventeen or eighteen he thought, he looked so young.

"Wait a minute I thought you guys had a photo shoot when we were about fourteen, remember you came to pick up Liz from school Tom and she was at Tony's house? Oops, probably shouldn't have said that." Iliana asked.

"Don't worry about it, they all know what I was like, even John." Liz responded with a chuckle.

"No that didn't happen at all, Liz wasn't the only one that forgot so we were too late for the photo shoot in the end, I was so disappointed. We never got a chance to arrange it again, for one reason or another, you kids got older and busier, so it just didn't happen. I can't thank you enough Iliana, you have no idea how much this picture means to me," Trish said, "…to us."

"Oh well I am glad," Iliana replied sincerely. Tom carefully put the photo back in its place.

"Where's Dad?" Liz asked their mom.

"I have no idea, he said he would be here, we won't wait though, food's ready so let's eat."

Liz and Iliana got up automatically and went over to help. Tom made sure everyone had a drink, including Zac, and sat him at the table before they all joined him.

"This all looks great, thanks so much," Iliana said as they sat down to eat.

"It's great to have you all here. I don't get to entertain as much as I would like to these days."

"Oh Mom, you know we can come over and eat all your food anytime, just name the day?" Liz lightened the mood a bit and Trish gave a genuine smile to her daughter.

"I hear you are all staying at your dad's tonight, Zac, that's exciting?" Trish said to her grandson, changing the subject.

"Yeah, it is, I've never been before but Mummy has, she already had a sleepover at Dad's last night."

One More Try (Book 1)

Iliana almost choked on her wine as did Tom with his mouthful of food. Liz burst out laughing and couldn't seem to stop.

"Oh wow, that's great, how exciting for Mummy and Daddy!" Liz managed to get the words out after her fit of giggles. "I actually think you are blushing Tom; in all my years I have never seen that." This set her off again and now Iliana looked like she was struggling not to join in. John was smiling too along with Trish.

"OK, OK. Very funny," Tom smiled at Iliana.

"Why is that funny, I don't get it?" Zac pondered, looking around.

"Sleepovers for Mummy and Daddy are private Zac that's all," Iliana replied, still chuckling.

"Oh, it's ok you haven't said anything wrong don't worry Zac," Tom patted him on the shoulder.

"Exactly, I am really glad that your Mum and Dad are having sleepovers," Liz chimed in, "I have never seen either of them looking as happy, so it's all good."

She smiled at them both. Tom leaned over and gave Iliana a kiss on the lips. He wasn't normally one for public displays of affection but now that everyone knew anyway, he figured why not. Iliana didn't seem to mind either as she was still smiling, or laughing, he couldn't tell.

"Well said Liz," His mom agreed, winking at Iliana and Tom.

At this point James came through the front door.

"You're late!" Trish glared at him.

"Sorry, traffic was bad. What's all the hilarity?"

"Oh nothing, just having a nice family dinner that's all."

He grabbed himself a plate and got some food then sat down.

"This is your Grandson, Zac, James, won't you say hello?"

"Oh yeah. Hi Zac, nice to meet you."

"Nice to meet you too," Zac said politely as he was about to put more food in his mouth.

"Is Zac short for Zachary then?" James added. Zac looked at Iliana.

"No, it's just Zac," she replied, James just nodded and started to eat his food.

"Granny?"

"Yes Zac?"

"Did you know that my dad and I have the same birthday?"

"No, I didn't! Really? How lovely for you both!" Everyone was smiling although Tom noticed his dad didn't seem to be joining in.

"That's so special, your first child and your first grandchild born on the same day," Liz joined in.

"Isn't it?" their mom said chuckling to herself. James still hadn't said anything which Tom thought was a bit odd.

They enjoyed the rest of their meal; Zac was quite tired, so they decided to head off after the tidying was done. They thanked his mom for the meal and said goodbye to everyone. Tom drove them home to his place and pulled in the driveway. "Did you remember your pyjamas little man?"

"Yeah, I did. Spider-Man ones."

"Oh wow, can't wait to see them."

When they entered the house Tom showed Zac around, which didn't take long, but when he saw he had a room to himself he was really impressed. Tom had bought Sponge Bob bed covers for him after seeing him in the pyjamas the other night and an alarm clock with a soccer ball on it and he seemed really pleased with them. He also noticed that Tom had his picture on display, as Iliana had predicted, and was very happy about it.

"Does he sleep well then? I am always hearing stories from Jane about the kids not sleeping or getting up in the night?" Tom said to Iliana as they settled down on his sofa after a very tired Zac had his bath and they had tucked him in.

"He sleeps pretty well unless he's poorly or has a bad dream, I blame Spider-Man for that though."

One More Try (Book 1)

"You can't blame spiderman, he's the good guy?"

"Yeah, but he fights bad guys, even in the cartoons, and I am sure that's what gives him nightmares."

"Can't see it, but I'll watch some of them and let you know. Do you want some wine?"

"Thanks, that would be lovely, are you having anything?" she asked as he walked towards the kitchen.

"I'll have a beer with you, I wouldn't like you to drink alone."

He opened a beer for himself then poured a generous glass of wine and returned to the sofa. They spent the rest of the evening cuddled on the sofa chatting until they agreed it was time to call it a night.

*

The next morning Zac woke at 7am and came through to their bedroom.

"Time to get up Mummy," he announced as he pulled back the cover to climb into bed with them. Iliana must have known this might happen as she had insisted on putting on a vest and panties after their lovemaking the night before, now he understood why, he had thankfully put on boxers too.

"Did you sleep ok Zac?" she asked him as he snuggled in.

"Great, I love my new room, how did you sleep Mummy, you look a bit tired?" Tom got out of bed and put a t shirt on, trying to hide his smile, they had indeed not had that much sleep.

"If Mommy is still tired you and I can go through and get breakfast if you want little man Zee?" Tom walked around the bed and reached out his hand.

"Zee? No one's ever called me that before."

"Oh sorry, it just came out, no idea why, ask your mommy, I like to shorten people's names for some reason. But if you don't like it, I won't use it again?"

"No, it's fine. I like it, it makes me sound like a superhero," the little boy said cheerfully as he climbed out of bed and took Tom's hand.

One More Try (Book 1)

Tom couldn't help but laugh, "Yes, it kinda does, doesn't it?"

They went through to the kitchen to make breakfast and Iliana followed them, she said she didn't want to miss out on their first breakfast together as a family before they all got ready to leave.

Tom's day went quickly as was usual for a Saturday, there was always a lot going on due to changeover and any urgent maintenance issues needed to be dealt with before new holidaymakers arrived. He was finished around three though so had a coffee with his mom before heading home to get ready to go out with his friends. There were a few guys, including Dave the bartender, from school who he kept in touch with, and his brothers sometimes came out for a few to catch up, mostly Brad but occasionally Dan and very rarely Robert. On this occasion they met for a few games of pool as Dave was finishing at eight, at which point they would likely have some food. Brad couldn't make it along, but Dan was there for a few hours and had a game of pool with Tom. This was the first time Tom had seen him since he found out about Zac, so he wanted to make sure that he knew.

"So, sorry I missed your call the other night. I am guessing you were phoning to tell me about your son though?"

"Yeah, I was. I just wanted you to hear it from me first. How did you find out?"

"Mom told me, and I saw his picture. I thought it was you!" He was smiling.

"Yeah, he is very like me. I'm glad it was at least Mom that told you so that's good."

"Are you ok about it?"

"It's great, he's a great little boy, hopefully you'll get to meet him soon."

"Yeah, that would be good. Are you and Iliana an item now then? You looked close at Mom and Dad's Anniversary?"

"Yeah, we are."

Dan nodded. "Good, I'm happy for you. Not sure if I ever told you this but I had a bit of a crush on her when we were growing up. Obviously, she left when I was seventeen, so I got over it, but I always liked her. She would always take time to talk to me even when all you guys couldn't be bothered." He was smiling as he said it, but Tom knew that being the youngest of five must have been tough. With nine years difference between him and Dan he didn't really see that much of him when they were younger. They were close now though and had been for a long time, which he was glad about.

"No, you didn't mention it, I knew you took her to Prom of course. She has a way with people, so I am not surprised." Tom was smiling to himself. "Are you still seeing that girl who works in Liz's office?"

"Yeah, I am meeting her later actually, we have a good laugh."

"That's good."

They carried on their game and then Dan headed out to meet his girlfriend. When Dave finished, he joined the group for a beer, then they went for food and a few more drinks. Tom liked to walk home from a night in town so found himself thinking about Iliana on the way home, he went the long way so that he could walk past Mary's house and sent her a message on his cell asking if she was still up as he would be walking past soon. Within a few minutes he got a reply saying that she was still up and would look out for him. When he approached the house, he saw her looking out the window and then she came outside, wearing just a vest top and shorts with bare feet; she stood on the porch, thankfully it was a warm night. She was smiling at him as he walked down the driveway and approached her. She walked down the steps to meet him. He stopped at the bottom, so they were the same height and put his arms around her waist. Her vest top was quite loose, so he put his hands underneath to feel her bare skin.

"Hey."

"Hey, this is a nice surprise," she said, putting her arms around his neck and leaning close.

"I was just thinking about you." He gave her a long passionate kiss. "Are you cold?"

"Well not anymore," she laughed.

"I missed you."

"Yeah, me too, do you want to come in?"

"I don't want to wake anyone up."

"Yeah, I know and it's not like there's room for you to stay either, sorry."

"No need to be sorry, how about you stay tomorrow night?"

"That would be good although I am working Monday, getting the classroom ready for the kids going back to school."

"Where will Zac be?"

"Here with Mum."

"Oh."

"Do you want to see him? I ask my Mum to do a lot so it would be fine if you wanted to, I am sure she would be happy to have a rest?"

"I would love that, if you and Mary are ok with it?"

"Yes, I am sure it will be fine, I will bring my work things, and you can have a whole day together. We can come by tomorrow for dinner if that suits. I have work to do in the afternoon to get ready and check Zac has everything for school too so can't really do afternoon."

"Well, why don't I take Zac tomorrow afternoon so that you can get stuff done and we can have more time? Then you can join us for dinner and stay over?"

"Are you sure?"

"Yeah of course."

"Ok then. He will love that, thanks." She smiled at him.

"I can collect him after lunch if that works. I have a few things to do in the morning, but it won't take long."

"Yeah of course, that sounds great." He kissed her again; he really didn't want to leave but he knew he had to. "Well, I best get going and let you get inside."

"Ok." She held him tighter; he got the distinct impression she was the same which warmed his heart.

"See you tomorrow, goodnight, Illy."

"Goodnight." He reluctantly pulled away from her embrace and she waved at him as she turned to go in the door, he waited until she was inside, as she closed the door she smiled and waved again.

One More Try (Book 1)

Chapter 15

  Tom awoke Sunday with a spring in his step, which was unusual after a night out with the guys, he got ready to do some work but phoned Brad first for advice about the afternoon with Zac.
  "Hi Tom, Brad isn't around I'm afraid he is at Baseball with Ethan," Jane said when she answered the phone.
  "Ah ok, you might be able to help me then, I have Zac this afternoon and wondered where was good to take him?"
  "Well, it depends on what you want, if you just want a good play outside then Priory Park is great. There is a large grass area for playing sports but also swings, climbing frames and lots to play on."
  "That sounds perfect, yeah, we definitely want to be outdoors as he will want to do a bit of soccer, I am sure. Thanks Jane. I won't keep you ..."
  "Did Brad mention you guys coming over for a visit sometime soon?"
  "No but I haven't seen him since he met Zac on Wednesday."
  "We just wanted to invite you all over for the day next Saturday, Ethan is really keen to have Zac round for a play?"
  "Oh, that sounds great, I'm sure Zac would love that. I'll just check with Iliana to make sure she doesn't have any other plans and let you know."
  "Great. Are you guys together now then? When I asked Brad, he just said you were 'working on it' whatever that means," she laughed.
  "Yeah, we are together now but we weren't right away, she just needed a bit of time, but it's all good now."
  "Good, you sound happy so I am pleased for you, anyway we can catch up properly next Saturday when you come over."
  "Sounds great, thanks Jane." They hung up. Tom collected Zac from Mary's house and left Iliana to do her prep work for school. They drove to the park and Zac

looked impressed; it was exactly as Jane had described. He played on the swings and climbing frames for a while then they played soccer before sitting down for a well-earned water break.

"Is that Ethan?" Zac said as he was drinking his water, he pointed over in the distance where the cars were parked, there was a guy and a boy his age walking towards them.

"I think it might be, and Uncle Brad," Tom replied trying to see if he could be sure.

"Zac!" Ethan shouted as he got closer.

"Hey!" Zac immediately ran over to him, and they chatted.

"Can we play on the climbing frame for a bit?" Zac eventually asked.

"Yeah sure. Gives me a chance to have a rest," Tom replied laughing. Brad sat next to him.

"Yeah, me too. Jane said you would be here so we thought we would come and say Hi."

"Good idea, I never thought to suggest you guys come down, she said you were at Baseball?"

"Yeah, it finished about an hour ago, I took Ethan for lunch as Jane and Helena are out, somewhere, I can't remember where." He was looking over to see where the boys were, then continued, "so I hear you and Iliana are an item now then?"

"Yeah, I think I wore her down." They both laughed.

"Nah I think it was just a matter of time bro."

"You're just saying that because you are my brother?"

"No, I am not. You guys were so close the other night, and with the history as you call it. You have a kid too, it's madness really!"

"Yeah, I know, tell me about it. I still can't believe it sometimes, but he is amazing. He is so little, and he looks like me, but his personality is so like Illy, I just can't help but think that he will do great, and the world will be a better place with him in it."

One More Try (Book 1)

"Wow, Tom. You always claimed to be the least intelligent of all of us but sometimes you come out with some real pearls of wisdom."

"You think?"

"Fuck yeah! Now let's go play some soccer with our boys!"

They completely lost track of time until Tom looked at his watch and noticed it was 4:30, he couldn't believe the time as Iliana was coming around at 5 for dinner and he hadn't given her the spare keys yet. They had a quick drink and said goodbye to Ethan and Brad then headed home to his place. He managed to at least make a start on dinner before Iliana arrived. Zac was sitting on the sofa watching TV when she arrived, he ran to meet her and give her a hug. Tom was in the kitchen area busy doing prep, the open plan layout of his place meant that he could still chat with them while doing so.

"Hey, how was your day Zac? Did you have fun with Dad?" she asked him after giving him an extra-long hug.

"Yeah, it was great, we went to a really big park and played then Ethan arrived, and we all played soccer, it was Ethan and Uncle Brad against me and Dad, it finished 3-3 so a draw."

"Oh wow, a close game then, that sounds like fun. I bet you and Daddy make a great team."

"Yeah, he's pretty good actually." Zac looked very serious as he was nodding his head explaining to Iliana and assessing his dad's soccer abilities, she was just smiling along with him and occasionally looking at Tom. He was chuckling listening to him, so he kept catching her eye.

"Sounds like you all had a great time," she said once Zac was finished, she stood up and went over to give Tom a hug. "Your poor Dad will be tired out."

"Yeah, it's been a while, but it was great fun, don't worry about me," he said after their hug; he gave her a small kiss on the lips.

"Can I help with anything?"

"It's all under control, thanks. I just went for something simple, Chicken and Pasta with salad. Is that okay?"

"Yeah great, thanks. I could get used to this."

"Well simple is what I do I'm afraid so I'm sure you will get used to it! Oh, I nearly forgot Jane asked if we could all go up to see them on Saturday. Ethan is keen to have Zac over for a play?"

"Oh wow, that sounds great."

"Great, just wanted to make sure you didn't have other plans?"

"Yeah, no plans."

"Great, I'll tell her it's a 'Yes' then?"

"Sure," she smiled.

They ate dinner together and Zac continued to tell Iliana about his afternoon, they told him about the planned visit to Brad and Jane's the Saturday after and he was excited. After dinner they chilled out then Zac had a bath and Tom read him a story while Iliana insisted on tidying up. Zac was very tired so went to sleep quickly which left them time to catch up on the sofa together.

"I'm so glad it went well today," Tom said as he sat down and handed Iliana a cup of tea.

"Yeah? Of course, it would, he loves spending time with you."

"Yeah, I know but I just want things to get off to a good start. He's a good kid."

"He is, but, as I said before, he has his moments, as they all do. We just deal with them when they come up though, so if he does have a tantrum don't take it personally."

"Ok, I'll remember that hopefully."

"Just make sure you always have water and a snack handy, just in case."

"Ok. Thanks."

"I hate to do this but when I was looking through his school things, I noticed he needs some new t-shirts. Would you be able to get some tomorrow, I know you mentioned getting some things for his room so if you're at the mall anyway?"

"Yeah sure, just let me know exactly what you need, and we can get it."

"Great."

"I take it you'll want an early night if you are working tomorrow?"

"Yes, I probably should, not too early though. I want to make sure I get time with you too?" she snuggled into him.

"That sounds like a good idea to me. I hated leaving you like that last night. It was great to get your message." He gave her a kiss on the lips.

"Good. I wanted you to know I was thinking about you," she smiled. "I meant to ask you, remember when we were heading out to your folks house on Friday you mentioned that you wanted to do some upgrades but then stopped?"

"Oh yeah, it caused some pretty serious arguments with dad, and I suddenly realised I didn't want to mention it in front of Zac, sorry about that."

"Oh, it's ok I figured it was something like that. I just wondered what happened that's all, if you wanted to talk about it? I don't really know much about what you have been up to for the last eight years?"

"There's not a lot to tell really, I had to give up my other job at the cash and carry a long time ago as Mom needed more and more done so it was taking up a lot of my time, it seemed we were just repairing the same things all the time in the chalets so I suggested we do some extensive work and wrote out some plans which she was happy with but Dad didn't want to. He said we would lose too much money as we would effectively have to close for at least a month, but my suggestion was to work during the quiet winter season anyway and not even to upgrade them all at once.

"That seems reasonable to me?"

"Yeah, I know, but Mom gave up arguing with him. It infuriates me that she just gives in to him, especially since she's the one who owns the business, but what could I do, I have come between them enough I didn't want to make it worse."

"What do you mean you have come between them enough?" she frowned.

"Well, you know more than most what he's like with me, you were around the house enough to see some of it at least and you know why I moved out when I was twenty-two?"

"I didn't know the exact reasons, but I did hear arguments sometimes when I stayed over."

"Yeah well, he has always been tough on me, probably because I am the eldest, but some of it was hard to take." Tom couldn't say any more as the memories came back to him of some of the arguments and how upset his mom would get. He just stared into his cup of coffee for a bit, lost in his thoughts.

"I didn't realise it was that bad, I am sure Liz didn't either, she never really talked about it much and I never pressed."

"No, it's not the sort of thing that people want to dwell on really."

"I'm sorry I didn't mean to bring you down." She put down her tea and reached out to lift his chin.

"It's ok, as I said, you of all people understand it." He gave her a kiss.

"So, what else have you been up to then, any serious relationships?" She looked like she was trying to lighten the atmosphere and cheer him up.

"Not really, a few girlfriends here and there but nothing serious, or lasting." He smiled at her, then put down his coffee cup. "I thought about you a lot, wondered what you were up to. I would occasionally ask Liz if she had heard from you but then I stopped as I thought she might suspect something, and I knew she missed you."

"I know, I thought about contacting her so many times, but how would I explain Zac, it was so complicated, and it hurt me not to be in touch with her too."

"I know, and I'm sure she understands, as you said, 'what matters most is what we do now'." He gave her a long kiss.

"That is true," she straddled him on the sofa and grinned at him before leaning closer, "maybe we should have that early night after all."

One More Try (Book 1)

Chapter 16

The next day Iliana was up early, so they all got up at the same time and had breakfast together. After she left for work Tom and Zac chilled out with some TV then got changed and headed out to the mall. They had lunch when they arrived then walked around for quite a while, Zac chose a few more things for his room but Tom had no idea where to buy plain school t shirts. They eventually found them after asking an assistant in Macey's department store.

As they left the store Tom was trying to figure out which way to go to the exit where his car was parked when he noticed Zac was falling behind a little, he had a tight hold of his hand, petrified in case he lost him in the busy mall. When he looked back Zac was glaring at him.

"I want to go home." His eyes were filling with tears as he spoke.

"I know little man Zee that's where we are heading, I just need to figure out which exit we need to go out," Tom said softly while looking around for signs.

"But I want to go home now!" He stamped his feet. A few people stopped and stared at them.

"I know buddy that's what we're doing, come on with me and we'll find the exit together?"

"NO!" He was scowling now. "I don't want to, and *you* can't make me! I am staying here, and you can bring the car round."

"What? You know I can't do that buddy."

"Yes, you can, Mummy would. She does it all the time."

"Okay well I'll talk to Mommy about that when we get back but, in the meantime, I need you to take my hand and come with me."

"No! I said no, and I meant it." His lips were curled under now and his bottom lip was wobbling. Tom knew he was going to cry. What was he meant to do now? More people were looking at him, some with sympathy (obviously parents themselves), some shaking their heads. He wanted to run after the sympathetic ones, shake them by the shoulders and say '*help me*? *I am new at this, what do I do?*'

He took his hand anyway and started to gently pull, Zac kept his feet firmly on the ground so started to slide along the floor. More people gathered to watch them, this couldn't be going any worse!

"Help!" Zac shouted, okay well maybe it could be worse.

A substantial crowd had now congregated, someone stopped and asked Zac if he was okay, Tom confirmed, "It's okay I am his dad, he is just having one of those days. Thanks so much for your concern." He was so mortified. Iliana had said he had his moments; well this was likely one of them he supposed. That's when he remembered she had said to always bring a bottle of water and a snack with him.

"Hey, why don't we go get you a drink and a snack little man?"

Zac just looked at him suspiciously but didn't let go of his hand, which was a good sign. They walked towards the nearest mini mart and bought a bottle of still juice and a packet of biscuits. Within seconds of having a drink and a bite to eat Zac seemed to totally change his mood, he sat on the bench outside the shop swinging his little legs, quite happy. Tom let out a huge sigh of relief.

When Iliana returned home that evening Tom told her all about the episode at the mall. She laughed and said she had been there a few times. He was still shocked and not sure it was the same child but the fact she laughed made him feel like it was more normal than he realised. *This parenting malarkey is tough.*

Later, they had to get everything ready for Zac starting school, it was a big thing for a kid his age, so Tom was worried, but Iliana didn't seem to be. "Has the school changed much then?" he asked her while they were chilling on the sofa after Zac reluctantly went to bed.

"Not at all actually! Everything seems smaller than I remember it, suppose that's natural though as I was smaller then," she replied, while sipping her cup of tea.

"I hope he will be ok."

"He will be absolutely fine, I did it at almost the same age?" she said in her reassuring manner.

"Well making friends with the most popular girl in school on your first day helped you though, that's what you said to me once was it not?"

"Well, yes that is true, I was lucky, but he is a tough little boy, so I have every faith in him. Plus at least he knows someone in his class, his cousin Ethan?"

"Yeah true. Ethan will look out for him, just like Liz did for you."

She smiled and nodded.

The next day was a big one, so they had a reasonably early night themselves. Iliana was really looking forward to meeting her new class and she wanted to get to school early so Tom had agreed to drop Zac off at the required time. They went together to meet the Principal since Zac was new to the school and then he was shown to his classroom. Tom then left the school and headed for his car, on the way he tried to subtly see if he could see in the classrooms, he stopped before he looked in too many though. He was new to this parenting thing so didn't want to blow his son's street credibility (he wasn't even sure if they still called it that) on his first day if his classmates saw his dad peering in the window.

He couldn't help but notice though in the last classroom he checked that it was Iliana's, twelfth grade she was teaching he thought but couldn't quite remember. She was in front of the class talking and pointing at the chalkboard, as you would expect from a teacher, but she looked so relaxed and natural with it, she was in her element talking to the kids and smiling as she did so. She had mentioned that it had its challenges, but he couldn't help but admire her, it was all she had ever wanted to do from a very young age.

He bumped into his sister-in-law Jane on his way to the car. "Hi Tom, big day for Zac, eh?" she said in a very cheerful tone, possibly she had seen him trying to look in classrooms, hopefully not!

"Yes, he seems quite chilled about it though, unlike me."

"Oh, don't worry he will be fine, Ethan will look out for him, he said so this morning. He said he would keep a spare seat next to him so that Zac could sit there, isn't that sweet? I think they really hit it off even although they have only met a few times," she replied.

"That is good, thanks Jane. I can relax a bit more now."

"You're welcome, are we all set for this weekend then?"

"Yeah, that would be great, thanks again."

He made his way to the car already feeling much better, then headed to his parents' place to get some work done. He would make sure Zac told him every detail about his first day when he picked him up later.

When Tom arrived at school to collect Zac, he parked the car and thought he would just wait, he knew at that age that the kids made their own way out of the school and either home or to their parent's cars, so he sat and looked out for him.

There were lots of kids piling out of the school in groups talking and laughing, running, walking, and having a carry on. It seemed so long since he had been at this school, he could hardly remember what it was like but the more he thought about it the more he thought it had been pretty much just like this. Illy was right, the school itself hadn't changed that much in the eighteen years since he had been here.

He eventually spotted Zac walking out with Ethan, they were around the same height, walking side by side and chatting intensely about something. He got out of the car and waved over to Zac who spotted him right away and headed in his direction, Ethan was looking for his mom and looked like he spotted her quickly. He passed the car and said goodbye to Zac then hi to Tom as he headed for his mom's car.

One More Try (Book 1)

Tom got into the car and Zac got into the front passenger seat, since he no longer needed a booster seat (*whatever that was*) he could sit in the front according to Iliana.

"Well buddy, how did it go then, your first day at the new school?" Tom tried not to sound too excited, but it was tricky, he wanted to hear all about it.

"Good," Zac said, nodding to himself and looking out of the window.

Tom waited for more, but it didn't come. He wondered if he was like this when he was younger and just didn't remember or didn't think anything of it.

"Good? Is that it, just good?" Tom added trying to remain upbeat but still pressing for more information.

"Really good," Zac added. Well, that was that then.

They had dinner together that night before Iliana and Zac went back to Mary's. Tom found it really tough as the place seemed empty without them.

*

"Hey sleepy heads," Tom woke with a start at the sound of Iliana's voice. She was smiling down at him and Zac on the sofa, they had dozed off after their Friday afternoon at the park. Tom was lying across the length of the sofa and Zac was alongside him on the inside with his head on Tom's chest. Zac opened his eyes.

"Hey little man Zee, we fell asleep!" he laughed but Zac was still waking up and looking a bit dazed.

"Huh? Did we?"

"Yeah, you did," Iliana said with affection.

"Mummy." He got up and went to give her a hug.

"You tired me out little man, all that soccer is taking its toll on your old dad." They both laughed.

"You're not old."

"Thanks son, but I never used to sleep in the afternoon so I must be!"

Iliana chuckled along. "I'll get started with dinner."

They had dinner together and talked about their week. Zac stayed up a little bit later since he had had a nap earlier but once he was in bed Iliana and Tom chilled out on the sofa together with a drink each.

"I almost forgot, I thought it might be good if you had an extra set of keys for this place, just in case?" He handed her the keys.

"Yeah, I guess that makes sense." She put her wine down and found her purse, then bent down to put the keys in and came back to sit down. He noticed her necklace when she bent down and gazed at her sitting on the sofa with her wine.

"I love the fact you still wear the necklace I gave you; did I tell you that Zac mentioned it to me that first day I met him?"

"No, you didn't. What did he say?"

"He said that you told him his dad made it for you and that it was your favourite thing."

"Yeah, he asked me about it when he was about five, I think." She touched her necklace as she spoke. "I have no idea why I told him; I must have been feeling nostalgic at the time. Alec didn't know that you made it for me so I probably shouldn't have told him about it. I guess I just wanted him to have some connection with you. Does that sound silly?"

"No, it doesn't."

"He never said anything more about it though so he must have guessed that it wasn't something Alec would have liked. Occasionally he would just touch it when he was giving me a cuddle though." She smiled to herself.

"Did he ever ask why you weren't with his dad?"

"Yes, he did. When I told him about the necklace." She looked pensive at this point but didn't continue.

"What did you say?" he pressed.

"I just said that we hadn't kept in touch and that sometimes that happened with Mummies and Daddies. As I said, he was young, so I didn't see the point in saying any more. He accepted it and never asked again."

"Fair enough. So, what did you say the day I was coming over to visit?"

"I explained that his dad lived here and that he would like to meet him, he never really asked anymore which isn't like him but then he didn't have a lot of time between me telling him and you arriving, which was maybe a good thing." She gave a nervous laugh.

"Were you ever tempted to contact me?" He wondered if he should have asked that, but it was already out there before he thought about it.

"Not while I was in a relationship with Alec, but after I had him definitely." She stopped again, "but not for long, you said you didn't feel that way about me so I didn't think a baby would change that. It would only complicate things, and we were so far away anyway. Do you wish that I had told you?"

"In some ways but not in others. That doesn't sound right now I have said it out loud …"

"It's ok I think I know what you mean, we were both younger, maybe we both needed the time apart to think about things and realise a few other things?"

"That's exactly it. I couldn't have put it better. But that doesn't change what you had to go through, having a baby on your own, your relationship with Alec. I feel gutted that I wasn't there for you."

"I know you do." She reached over to him and put her arms around his neck to cuddle in, he held her close. "As I said before, it's in the past so what matters most is what we do now."

"That's true."

Chapter 17

Tom and Brad were tidying up after dinner at Brad and Jane's house. The kids were all playing outside while the ladies had a glass of wine.

"So, I guess everything is going well then bro? You and Iliana seem happy."

"Yeah, really good, it's been quite a few weeks but yeah, we are really great."

"Good, I'm glad. it's about time you settled down."

"You ok Bro?"

"Yeah fine, just ... it's nothing ..."

"Seriously, what's up?"

"I am probably just worrying over nothing, it's just that ..."

"What?"

"It's just that Jane always used to think I had a thing for Iliana. Which isn't true of course. I was just worried she might say something to her while they are alone, that's all." He watched Tom carefully.

"Well but even if you did," Tom said putting his hand up to stop Brad from trying to deny it again, since it really didn't matter, "you guys are well past that now, married eight years, two kids, great house, come on, stop worrying."

"Yeah, you're right. Although I never thought that little pep talk would come from you, big bro?"

"Yeah, that is true. I never thought I would be here like this after all this time," Tom couldn't help but smile and Brad joined him.

"Seriously I never realised how much she meant to you; I am happy for you both."

"I don't think I realised either." Tom patted his brother on the shoulder as they finished up the tidying, grabbed a beer and went outside where the ladies were sitting comfortably, laughing at something. Brads shoulders visibly dropped with relief at this sight. The kids were all playing together in the yard, so they all sat for a bit longer and chatted. When Tom went back in to get more drinks, Jane came with him.

"There's more wine in the fridge, I'll get it for you, and beers are on the bottom shelf," Jane said as she came in the kitchen behind him.

"Oh right, thanks."

"I thought you might need a hand."

"Great, thanks. Oh, and thanks for the recommendation the other day. Zac loved Priory Park, so we've been a few times already. It helped that Ethan came along of course, thanks for that too."

"You're welcome, Ethan loves having a cousin his own age, it means he can ditch his kid sister more often," she laughed.

"I think Helena decides when she is being ditched or not?"

"That is true, no idea where she gets that from." They both laughed at that.

"You and Iliana look happy together; I am so pleased for you both. I always thought there was a bit of a spark between you two, but I never said anything to Brad, I think he liked her at one point too, until me of course."

"Of course. When did you think there was a spark between us then, can you remember?"

"Hmm, let me think, it was when Iliana was working at your Folks' place, Brad and I used to steal time together and she nearly caught us once so she would be seventeen maybe?"

"Yeah, that's probably about right, although I don't think I realised."

"All these years I wondered why you didn't ever stay with a woman; you had plenty of offers but I have never seen you look at a woman the way you look at Iliana now."

He laughed.

"What's funny?"

"Zac said something similar to me about the way Iliana looks at me."

One More Try (Book 1)

"He's a bright boy, he's polite too. I am super impressed; you must be very proud?"

"I am but I can't take the credit, it's all Iliana so far. Hopefully that's gonna' change though, hopefully I can make up for the last seven years."

"I am sure you can, and you will Tom."

"Thanks Jane."

"Where are these drinks?" Brad joked as he came into the kitchen and went over to give Jane a kiss. "The service around here is awful. Are you ladies gossiping?"

"Yeah, we are." Jane gave him an affectionate hug.

They enjoyed the rest of their day with Brad and his family and left early evening. Zac fell asleep in the car after playing all day, so they took him straight to bed. Tom got them both a drink and they settled on the sofa.

"Today was great fun," Iliana said as he sat down next to her. "I like Jane and Brad a lot."

"Yeah, it was good, it's great that the kids all get along too."

"Yeah definitely."

"I really missed you guys this week; I know it seems strange as I have been here for so long on my own but when you go away it's like there's something missing in the house, two things actually. Do you think you could stay a night during the week as well, maybe Wednesdays?"

"Hmm, I would be ok with that. Shall we ask Zac what he thinks tomorrow?"

"Yeah, that sounds good, I'd like that." He snuggled in and put his arm around her so that they were closer as they sipped their drinks. "Can I ask you something?"

"No," she responded, then burst out laughing. "Sorry but I always wanted to do that, no one ever says no to that question."

"Yeah, you got me again, good one." He laughed too; she had a point.

"Shoot?"

"Do you ever hear from Alec?" He watched her closely, it wasn't really any of his business, but he was curious; apart from despising the guy he really did not want him anywhere near any of his new family.

"No, I haven't heard anything, don't worry. I think he got the message loud and clear." She stared into her glass, as if there was something interesting right down at the bottom.

"Good, I don't want to pry. I just worry, you know." He reached out and gently touched her arm.

"I know you worry, and I can't blame you. He wasn't always like that though; we were happy to start with. We met at teacher training college, after I had Zac, he was part of the group from the year after us, we got on well and eventually he asked me out, he knew I had a child. After he moved in with us, he started to resent the time I spent with Zac and that's when things changed, probably around a year after we started going out. He never hurt Zac, he hardly spent time with him either, but he didn't ever hurt him, you should know that."

"That doesn't make him a good guy Illy! Sorry, sorry!" He held up his hands as she looked at him with that 'I know' expression. "I guess I just don't understand it, that's all. If it started after a year, why did you stay so long?" Well, that was the 'take it slowly and don't ask too many difficult questions' theory out the window!

"If I am honest, I don't understand it either. I go over it in my mind a lot and can't seem to work it out. I have a few theories though. I think I just felt like I wouldn't manage without him, or that I couldn't do any better."

"He made you feel like that, it wasn't you. I didn't mean to imply anything, sorry!" He felt like he had to tread very carefully here.

"You didn't imply Tom, and you don't need to keep apologising. It's a fair question, and one I know my Mum wanted to ask me several times. I thought I could hide it from her, but she isn't daft. It seems strange now looking back on it all," she added still searching deep down in her

One More Try (Book 1)

wine glass. "It was like one day a switch just clicked in my head and I thought *this isn't right*. You are right, he did make me feel like that, but not just by hitting me, or burning me with his cigarette. He did it by his words, what he said to me, little put downs every now and then and subtle insults. I didn't see it at the time, but I can now. He made sure if any of my friends wanted to go out that there was something else more important, or that he couldn't be in to look after Zac, when my Mum was there that didn't matter so he would find another way... like comment on what I was wearing, anything to make me doubt myself. So, I would end up not going out, and basically losing any friends I had as they gave up asking me."

She was tearing up now, he put down his beer and leaned over, he took her glass away and put it on the small table next to the sofa. He reached out both arms and held her close, she wasn't sobbing or crying, just a single tear running down her face which he gently wiped away.

"What about the burns?"

"Oh yeah them," she closed her eyes for a second, "if we were making love and I was on top, he didn't like it if I closed my eyes, he thought that meant I was thinking of someone else. So, he burned me with his cigarette a few times and I stopped it."

"For fuck's sake, that's just awful!" He couldn't believe what he was hearing, he didn't think for a minute it would be anything like that. This guy was a piece of work. He held her closer.

"I know, I know, but again he made me feel like it was my fault because the truth is I was thinking of someone else, sometimes, well quite a bit if I am honest, I was thinking of you!" She pulled back and looked at him for a reaction, but he tried hard not to let anything show on his face, he just pulled her closer again.

"If he had treated you better then you wouldn't have been thinking of someone else though." Was it wrong that

One More Try (Book 1)

he was secretly pleased she was thinking of him? "Sorry Illy, I shouldn't have asked."

"It's ok, I wouldn't talk about it if I didn't want to don't worry. In some ways it's good to say it all out loud and offload it if you know what I mean?"

"Yeah, I think I do, you know you can always talk to me?"

"Yeah, I know, thanks Tom." She cuddled in.

"It's ok now, you're safe with me." He held her closer, and she leaned into him.

"I know."

"You're safe with me, forever," he added the last word with feeling.

"WHAT? Did you just say the 'f' word?" she grinned.

"Fuck! Yeah, I did, how did that happen?" He was laughing now, and she laughed with him. He was so glad he had managed to lighten the mood and cheer her up, he meant it though, and he hoped she understood that. They snuggled up on the sofa and chatted for the rest of the evening before agreeing it was time to call it a night.

One More Try (Book 1)

Chapter 18

Tom and Iliana had arranged a Friday date night, so Zac was staying at Mary's house, and Tom was sitting on his porch waiting for Iliana to get ready. When she stepped out of the front door he stood up, she looked amazing, she had another dress on with thin straps but this time dark red with a plain neck, it was fitted at the waist again and more fitted around her shapely legs. She had black shoes on, and she was holding a black purse. Her hair was loose around her shoulders just as it had been on the evening of his parent's anniversary dinner.

"Wow! You look stunning," was all he could manage to say with his mouth gaping open.

"You look pretty hot yourself," she said as she leaned in towards him and kissed him on the lips.

Tom was wearing a plain blue shirt and jeans and suddenly worried he was too casually dressed but she seemed ok with it. They got into the car for the ten-minute drive to the restaurant where the waiter showed them to their seats. They enjoyed their meal together and had a good chat about the last week. Iliana talked about the school, her class and how things were going. They would occasionally hold hands across the table during the meal, especially when talking about Zac. At one point a couple walked past their table and Tom noticed that they were looking at Iliana for longer than was polite.

"Iliana? Is that you?" said the woman.

"Oh my god, Becca? How lovely to see you." Iliana stood up and hugged her, "and Billy, wow you're still together," she added as she noticed the guy Becca was with.

"Yes, we are, I guess you are a little behind since you've been away."

"Yeah definitely! Tom, this is Becca and Billy who Liz and I knew at school."

"Nice to meet you both." Tom stood up to shake Billy's hand, he just nodded at Becca as he wasn't sure what the appropriate greeting was, a hug, a kiss, a handshake?

"Nice to meet you too Tom although we knew it was you, we heard so much about you back in the day from Liz and Iliana," Becca said looking lovingly at Billy.

"Ah I see."

"Anyway, we'll leave you to your meal. We'll have to have a catch up some time, we have two kids now. You guys could come over for a visit?"

"Yes, that sounds great, here's my number." Iliana quickly wrote down her number on a piece of paper from her purse and handed it to Becca, "So nice to see you both. See you later."

"Bye!" Becca waved as they moved away.

"So, Billy. Is that Billy Garcia?"

"Yes, it is. I didn't know they were still together, married, as I noticed they were wearing wedding rings."

"So, if I remember rightly Billy Garcia had a thing for you back in school. Didn't he?"

"No, Liz always said he did, but I don't think so. They look happy together, so I am glad for them both." Iliana said, sounding a little defensive but pulling it off quite well he thought. "They went to Prom together so things must have gone on from there."

"Hmm."

They enjoyed the rest of their meal, resuming the chat about the last week and Zac; Tom had one beer since he was driving, and Iliana had a few glasses of wine. When they left the restaurant Tom put his arm around Iliana's shoulders to keep her close and she put her arm around his waist. As they made their way across the parking lot they were talking and laughing when they heard someone call Tom's name. They both looked over in the direction of the call to see a familiar face, smiling and strutting towards them.

"Well, well, well. Nice to see you, Tom."

"Hi Sarah."

One More Try (Book 1)

She was still a very attractive woman but was scowling slightly. She wore a tight-fitting black dress and high heels with a matching handbag.

"I was going to say how are you doing but I can see that you are doing pretty well?" Sarah said, looking Iliana up and down. Thankfully Iliana wasn't intimidated at all, she stood tall and smiled at Sarah, still holding Tom's waist. "Well, I know you like to keep me waiting but don't keep me in suspense, who is your lovely companion tonight then?"

"This is Iliana, you have actually met her before a while ago at the house ..."

"Wow, so I thought she looked familiar, but I couldn't be sure, she is your little sisters' friend?" she interrupted.

"Yes, she is but she is also my girlfriend, and we have a son together. Not that it's any of your business, but just so that you're completely up to date." He felt Iliana squeeze his waist just a little bit tighter.

"Wow, you have a kid? I never thought that would happen, well congratulations to you both I guess. Anyway, I had best get to my dinner date. See you around." She swept away before he could say any more.

"Well, that was strange?" Iliana said as they carried on towards their car.

"Yeah, sorry about that. She can be a bit of a bitch I'm afraid."

"No need to apologise. It's not your fault, what did she mean that you like to keep her waiting?"

"Well, I'm afraid that is kinda' my fault. Things didn't really work out between us; I stopped calling her and she didn't like it very much."

"Ah I see, I thought you seemed close when I met her at the house, she is absolutely stunning too. I felt quite intimidated by her then."

"Yeah, she is attractive but not a very nice person I'm afraid and very hung up on those looks of hers, it's all she talks about. It's important to be able to hold a conversation with someone too." He pulled her close and she smiled up at him, hopefully getting his meaning. "You are every bit as attractive; as well as caring, funny and great fun to be with so there is absolutely no need to feel intimidated by someone like Sarah."

"You always did know how to say exactly the right thing to me Tom." She was still smiling at him as they reached the car and got in.

"Well, I'm glad you think that, but I never said anything to you that I didn't mean, excluding the Bachelor party of course." He frowned slightly at the memory as he put his seat belt on. He glanced over at her and she was still smiling at him, so he leaned over and gave her a kiss on the lips.

"I have to admit it felt good to hear you say I am your girlfriend, and we have a son together."

"I must admit it felt good to say it, I liked the extra squeeze you gave me." He gazed at her sitting in the car with her legs crossed, looking very happy and relaxed and couldn't resist leaning over for another kiss.

"Let's get home and you can show me just how much you appreciate me then." He raised his eyebrows, and she laughed.

They drove home and parked the car in the driveway. As they reached the porch, Tom suggested Iliana tried her set of keys to make sure they were okay, so she got them out of her purse. As she did so, he couldn't resist putting his hands around her waist and kissing her on her neck, she sighed as she opened the front door, he undid the zip at the back of her dress and moved his hands up to caress her breasts. He had been dying to kiss her and hold her all night and could hardly wait to get her inside the house.

*

"So, what did you used to say about me at school then?" he asked when they were chilling out on the sofa later.

"Ah I wondered if you would come back to that."

She was still flushed from the sex and wine, and he couldn't help but think she looked more beautiful than ever. "Just curious, you know," he shrugged.

"I didn't say that much to be honest; it was mostly the other girls asking Liz about you, you were seen as a bit of a sex symbol back then with all these hormonal teenage girls. Anyway, what about you, what made you think Billy had a thing for me? You must have been talking to your sister about it were you?"

"Ah you got me there, although to be fair Liz just mentioned it in passing one day, I think Mom was asking why you didn't have a boyfriend and Liz said Billy liked you, but you weren't fussed, that was all."

"It all seems so long ago don't you think? Then sometimes it seems like yesterday?" she added after a sip of wine, she was looking very pensive now.

"Yeah, I know what you mean, although I am quite a bit older, so I wasn't part of the same scene, but I remember you girls singing and dancing to Pat Benatar in Liz's room all the time." He was smiling to himself too now.

"Oh my god, yes, we did, didn't we. That was such good fun. OK so here's a question for you?" she had another sip of wine... "When do you think you started to notice me in *that* way then, when did you start to feel attracted to me?"

"Hmm let me think." He pondered for a moment. "It has to be your eighteenth birthday at the house, when I gave you the necklace, when I was making it, I suspected there was more to it because I so wanted you to like it, sounds strange I know but ...".

"It doesn't sound strange at all."

"I always liked you though, you must have known that. We would chat a lot when I was at the house if you were around?"

"Yeah, but chatting to someone doesn't always mean you are attracted to them."

"True, but as I said to you earlier, being able to hold a conversation is really important."

"Yeah."

He reached out for her and held her tight. He pulled back a bit so that he could look into her eyes.

One More Try (Book 1)

"I am so glad to have you and Zac in my life. I love you, Iliana."

"I love you too." She smiled and held his face, then gently kissed him on the lips. "You used my full name; you never do that?"

"It felt like the occasion deserved your full name, no idea why. But then I have never told anyone I love them before," he said with feeling.

"Wow, really? In all these years and all the women you have dated?"

"No, never. I never felt like it either, I liked some and obviously was attracted to them, but I never felt like I do when I am with you." He spoke quietly and looked away from her for a moment, then back again.

"Oh Tom, that's so special, and honest. I think I love you even more now." She held him tight.

"I wanted to tell you that first night you stayed here," he glanced at her to see if she reacted, "but I didn't want to scare you."

"It wouldn't have scared me." She gave him a kiss.

Chapter 19

The next two weeks followed the same pattern where they stayed over at Tom's on Wednesday then spent Friday to Sunday together. On Saturday night they all went out for a meal together as a family. Zac was tired so was in bed early which gave Tom and Iliana a chance to talk. It was a nice night, so they were sitting out the back having a drink.

"I've been thinking," he said, deliberately leaving a gap after for her to comment.

"Yeah? About what?" She raised an eyebrow.

"About everything but specifically I wondered if you guys would want to move in here, with me? Instead of having to live at your mom's and just spend Wednesdays and weekends here. I would like to make up for lost time and see Zac as much as possible and of course it means we can share more time too, if it's okay with you I mean, and you want to? I mean, there aren't many places available just now and it saves you unpacking all your things at your mom's before having to move again ...." he stopped talking at this point because he felt he was rambling on so that she couldn't say no.

"Well, I don't know, don't you think it's a bit soon? We wouldn't want to put you out or anything," she gazed at him searching for something in his face.

"You wouldn't be putting me out, and, for the reasons I just said, it would be great for me. I really miss both of you when you're not here."

"I guess we could, if you're sure? We are feeling a bit like we are under Mum's feet. She loves seeing Zac but it's not like we're far, we can still visit her for dinner regularly."

"Yeah, let's try it out then, we can speak with your mom tomorrow."

"Ok then."

Tom couldn't stop smiling. He nearly felt like doing a fist bump but refrained.

"We miss you too when we're not here you know?" she said.

"Do you? That's good. It's settled then, it's best for all of us." He leaned over and gave her a long kiss. "Can't wait to tell Zac, do you think he will be excited?"

"Oh yes, I think so, you can tell him if you want at breakfast?"

"We can tell him together."

The next day at breakfast Zac was munching on his cornflakes when they were all sitting at the table in Tom's open plan kitchen. "Zac, Mummy and Daddy were chatting last night, and we wondered ..." Iliana left it there and looked at Tom.

"Yeah, we wondered how you would feel about living here all the time instead of just Wednesdays and weekends?"

"Wow, really? That would be great, I could have my own room, and we can be a family all the time?"

"Yeah exactly."

"Well, that's settled then, we thought it would be good, but we just wanted to ask you what you thought too?" Iliana added.

Zac just smiled and carried on eating his cornflakes.

The rest of that week was spent moving Iliana and Zac's things into Tom's place, now theirs of course. Iliana still had the jewellery box that Tom made for her, and it took pride of place on her bedside table. He was surprised it still seemed in decent condition and commented on it when she placed it down.

"Wow, I recognise that! You still have it?"

"Oh yeah, you seem surprised?" She walked towards him with her arms out. They hugged and looked at it together.

"I suppose I am, firstly that you still wanted it and secondly that it looks the same and hasn't fallen to bits!"

She giggled. "Of course I would still want it, you made it for me. I didn't hate you the way you think after what happened. Besides, it's practical!" She hugged him and he held her tight.

One More Try (Book 1)

"Is that all of yours and Zac's things then?" Tom asked her as she then started putting more clothes away.

"Yes, I think so, I will check with Mum in case I left anything, but I'm pretty sure we got it all."

"I didn't see a bike; does he have one?"

"No. He doesn't." She paused while hanging up trousers and seemed pensive. "We lived in a small apartment, so it wasn't really practical."

"Fair enough, I wasn't being critical, I just wondered. Do you think he would be keen?"

"Yes, I do, he has asked a few times about it. Why?"

"Well, I have seven years of Birthdays and Christmas to make up for so I could get him one, but only if it was ok with you?" She smiled at him again but didn't respond. "It would mean a lot to me if I could teach him, in some ways it's great that I didn't miss it." He couldn't read what she was thinking as she had stopped what she was doing and was just watching him. He couldn't tell if she was trying not to smile, was smirking or annoyed.

"Well, when you put it like that, I guess it makes a lot of sense." This time she definitely smiled.

"Exactly, we can have him riding it in no time hopefully, we can use all the space at Mom's, that's how I learned."

She walked over to him and gave him a hug. "Great. I think he would love that."

Her voice wobbled so he pulled back so that he could look at her.

"Are you ok? Have I upset you?"

"No Tom, quite the opposite, you make me very happy." She leaned further in, "You will make him very happy too I am sure of it."

"Good. I must admit I am excited about it. I will take him to choose one at the weekend and he can help me build it."

"You can tell him first thing in the morning, he will be just as excited as you, I guarantee it. Do you remember how your dad taught you?"

One More Try (Book 1)

"My Grandfather taught me, not my dad."

"Really?"

"Yeah, my grandfather wanted to, and Dad was ok with it, I learned at five. Then I taught my brothers a good few years later when they were interested. .I used to go fetch things for Grandad all the time on my bike, so I think that was his plan all along." He chuckled at the memory of his grandfather, and she smiled at him.

"Well then you have a lot of experience, I am sure Zac will be riding his bike in no time."

The next day they awoke at the usual time for school and work. Zac got up and was pouring milk over his cornflakes when Tom came through to the kitchen and started to make coffee.

"Hey Dad."

"Hey little man." Tom waited for Iliana to come out of the bathroom before he said anything else, she gave him a look as if to ask if he had said anything yet, so he shook his head slightly to let her know

"I was talking with Mummy last night Zee." He paused to make sure Zac was listening, albeit with a mouthful of cereal.

"Yeah, what about?"

"I just wondered if she was ok with me teaching you how to ride a bike?"

"Well, that's a great idea Dad but there is one small problem with it," he frowned.

"Oh yeah what's that?"

"I don't have a bike."

"Well, we can sort that at the weekend if you want, I thought you might like to choose one yourself instead of me choosing it for you?"

"What, really? I am getting a bike this weekend?" he beamed.

"Well yes, if you want to that is?"

One More Try (Book 1)

"Yes, I do! Thank you!" Zac abandoned his cornflakes and ran towards him to give him a hug, although he did so with such force, Tom nearly fell over.

"Well, it is special circumstances, we have a lot of catching up to do so it's part of that, okay?"

"Okay, thanks Dad, and Mum."

Iliana looked on; her eyes decidedly misty!

One More Try (Book 1)

Chapter 20

The weeks and months that followed went by very quickly, Zac went to school and continued to become great friends with Ethan. He learned to ride his bike very quickly which pleased both him and Tom. He also went to Mary's house once a month so Tom and Iliana could have quality time together just the two of them, Iliana continued to enjoy teaching at the school, they visited family and friends as a group and generally had a good time. They had their ups and downs like any family, but things were going very well. Tom spent more and more time at his parents' business, but he could at least be flexible about working hours so could help pick up or drop Zac off at school. He even collected Helena and Ethan a few times to help his brother and sister-in-law.

When Thanksgiving was approaching, Tom's Mom asked if they wanted to all get together at Harrow Falls, it had been the tradition for some time and she was keen to see Zac on his first Thanksgiving there, although she respected their wishes if they wanted to spend it just the three of them. Iliana would not leave her mom alone though so they had a chat and agreed that the whole family plus Mary would all have Thanksgiving dinner together which really pleased his mom.

On the day, they all got a taxi so that everyone could enjoy a glass of wine or a few beers and were dropped off at midday. Iliana looked beautiful in one of her lovely dresses, more of an autumnal dress this time with short sleeves but a low neckline, dark blue was the colour today, and she looked amazing as always.

They were the first to arrive so could help with a little organising before Liz and John showed up shortly after. Next to arrive were Brad and his family, then Dan and lastly Robert and Lisa, who seemed tipsy already. Iliana had only met Lisa briefly at Tom's parents' anniversary dinner and hadn't seen much of her since. Tom wondered what Illiana would make of her and specifically her relationship with

One More Try (Book 1)

Robert. They were frequently arguing when Tom saw them, but he didn't know why, or any more than that.

Once everyone had arrived his mom was the perfect hostess, she offered everyone a drink of their choice including beer, wine (sparkling, red or white) or spirits, you name it, and she had it.

"Do you want a beer Tom, or what about you Iliana?"

"Thanks Trish, I don't drink beer, can't stand the taste. Someone once told me I would get used to it, but I never have," she gave Tom a sly smile as she said it. Tom remembered the moment when she tried her first taste of beer very well so smiled back knowingly.

"A beer would be great Mom, but I'll get it, and I can see what everyone else wants too. Don't worry, you have enough to do with the giant turkey!" Tom said.

"It's no different to what I am used to but thanks."

"I will ask the ladies Tom if you want to ask the guys," Liz piped up, eager to help as well.

"You know, apart from the years you've been away Iliana of course, I can't help but wonder why we have never all had Thanksgiving dinner together before now?" Trish said thoughtfully while they were all eating dinner, passing bowls around for everyone to help themselves.

"Yeah, I was just thinking the same," said Liz. "I think you always just spent Thanksgiving with your mom Iliana?"

"Well but Mary could have come as well, just as we have done today?" Trish responded.

"Yeah, I don't know why we never thought of that to be honest," Liz said.

"I don't know either, although I spent so much time here, maybe you all wanted a break from spending time with me." Iliana laughed as she said it.

Tom smiled at her. "Especially when I was working here too."

"Well, when you were working here maybe it was you that needed the break from this place!" His mom joined in the joke.

"Well, we are here now so that's all that matters, it's so lovely to spend time with a big family. Thank you so much for inviting me along to share Thanksgiving with you all," Mary joined in with a smile.

"Exactly Mary, now we share a grandchild we are family!"

"Very true," Mary beamed.

"It's certainly great to be able to meet you in person Iliana after hearing so much about you over the years," Lisa said, much to everyone's surprise, especially Robert's.

Iliana smiled at her. "Thanks Lisa, are you originally from here then?"

"No, I moved here five years ago, when I met Robert."

"How did you guys meet?"

"Oh, just the usual story you know, we got chatting in a bar downtown."

"Aw nice, what do you do for a living?"

"I am a psychiatric nurse."

"Oh wow, I bet that has some challenges?"

"Yes, it does, but probably not that much more than teaching," Lisa smiled.

Tom couldn't believe what he was seeing and hearing, he had never heard more than two words from Lisa, and he wasn't sure if he had ever seen her smile either, or at least not for a while. He noticed Robert filling her wine glass before she took a big drink and continued eating.

Everyone continued to eat and started to chat in smaller groups. The kids got restless quickly so went to watch a bit of tv over in the living room area while everyone finished their meal. The adults all then cleared the table and helped load the dishwasher. As Tom carried some plates over, he spotted Iliana sorting dishes ready for washing and couldn't resist putting his arm around her waist. "Hey gorgeous." She jumped a bit and laughed then put her arms around his neck. He put his other arm around her waist, and she gazed up at him.

"Hey handsome." She gave him a very gentle teasing kiss on the lips and then her best sexy smile.

"Get a room you two," Liz said with a chuckle as she went past them.

"What does that mean?" Zac chimed in from over on the sofa. "They have their own room back at our house, why would they need another one?" All the adults laughed at this.

"It's just what we say when people are kissing each other, it just means that we are telling them they should kiss in private that's all," Liz explained to him.

"Yeah, people kissing is yukky," Ethan said making a sound to indicate his point.

"I don't mind it; doesn't it mean they are happy?" Zac replied to him, they both still had their eyes fixed on the tv.

"That's very true Zac, it's nice to see people being happy so I for one am ok with it," Trish smiled at Tom and Iliana who were still embracing. "He is quite mature for a seven-year-old," she looked directly at Iliana this time when she spoke. "I remember a certain little girl being like that too. He may look like Tom but there is a lot of you there too."

"Definitely!" Iliana took the compliment with a smile and gave Tom another kiss before resuming her tidying.

Once everything was done the adults split themselves between the table and the sofas and the kids decided to play hide and seek so disappeared in the large house as they were warned not to go outside.

At one point Tom was looking around and quietly reflecting on what Mary had said about a big family occasion. Everyone was chatting and laughing, it really was a great family gathering, he couldn't remember feeling happier at Thanksgiving at all. He noticed his dad was speaking to Mary and they were laughing about something, they seemed very comfortable, so he wondered if they were acquainted other than through interaction due to Liz and Iliana's friendship in their younger years. He made a mental note to ask Iliana about it later as she was currently chatting with Lisa.

One More Try (Book 1)

*

Lisa and Robert were first to leave, then Dan, then Liz and John; ironically the people with children were last as the kids wanted to spend as much time as possible together. As they were starting to get tired, a cab was arranged at around ten o'clock. Tom and Iliana dropped Mary off at her place first, she was quiet in the back of the cab with Zac resting his head on her shoulder sleeping. "Are you ok Mum?"

"Yes, I am, never better actually. I am very lucky..." she had been looking out of the window but turned around to smile at Iliana sitting next to her who just nodded and reached out for her hand. Tom watched them in the mirror; it was such a lovely moment and one he would always cherish.

Once they had put a very tired Zac to bed they chilled out on the sofa with a tea and a coffee.

"So, you seemed to get on well with Lisa? I can't say I have ever seen her as chatty to be honest," Tom asked her.

"Yeah, I was surprised, given how Robert is towards me, but she seems nice."

"Yeah, she likes her wine though, from what I have seen."

"Don't we all?"

"You know what I mean, she knocks it back much faster than you and Liz combined!"

"Yeah, I know, but Robert's the one that fills her glass a lot I noticed."

"Yeah, I noticed that too."

"She said they have been trying for a family for three years now with no luck, they tried IVF once and it didn't work. I felt for her, that must be tough."

"Wow, I didn't know that. It's a shame; maybe why he is so grumpy as well."

"He has always been like that from what I remember."

"True, huge chip on his shoulder about something or other," Tom agreed. "Do you think Liz wants kids? She is great with her niece and nephews and was good at answering Zac's question about getting a room."

"Oh, that was so funny!" Iliana giggled. "She was quick to respond to that one, thankfully, as I hadn't a clue what to say!"

"No, me neither, I was looking to you for that one!" He laughed with her.

"I am not sure if she wants kids, she never said she didn't when we were younger, but you would know more than me recently at least, she is good with Zac and hasn't ever said it's not for her. Why do you ask?"

"Just wondering."

"Next time we are out on a girls' lunch I will try and suss it out for you," she said, smiling at him.

"Talking of getting a room, let's go to bed. I love seeing you in a dress as you look amazing, although you always look amazing anyway, but what I love most about your dresses is taking them off at the end of the night and taking time to appreciate what is underneath them."

"My charmer," she giggled as he picked her up and carried her through to their bedroom.

One More Try (Book 1)

Chapter 21

They spent Christmas at Mary's house just the four of them, then New Year just the three of them at their house.

In January they were planning to have the family round to celebrate Iliana's birthday. Robert made his usual excuses, and Dan was working, but everyone else could make it, so they were all set.

Her actual birthday was a Wednesday, and they had planned a meal out for all three of them. The night before her birthday when Zac was in bed and they were relaxing on the sofa, Tom went into his bedside drawer and put the little box that he had bought recently into his trouser pocket. He went into the living room and approached Iliana who was sitting on the sofa watching TV. He walked up to her and went down on one knee, he had thought about this so many times in his head but now that he was doing it, he was nervous, and excited, all at the same time.

He opened the box and gazed into her brown eyes; she was watching him intently now…

"Illy, this last five months have been amazing, we are a great family, and I am so happy. I hope you are too. I know that I don't always put the toilet seat back down, or squeeze the toothpaste the correct way, but will you do me the honour of marrying me?"

"Oh my God, Tom. YES, of course I will!" She threw her arms around him, knocking him over as he was balanced on one knee. They rolled about a bit together on the floor laughing, and he managed to find the box again with the ring in it; he had gone for a plain platinum single diamond ring.

She tried it on, but he had measured her fingers while she was sleeping so he knew it would fit.

"I *love* it! You made a great choice Tom."

"Thanks, I am glad you like it. There's no rush to get married but I have been wanting to ask you for a long time now, I was thinking of doing it tomorrow at the restaurant or at the weekend when the family are here, but I wanted it

One More Try (Book 1)

to be just us, in case you said No." He added a nervous laugh.

"Oh, how could you think I would say no? But yes, I think you did the right thing, best just us then we get to enjoy the moment again when we tell everyone," she beamed.

"True, good point!"

"I was thinking the other day about the night I came back for your parent's anniversary," Iliana changed the subject slightly and seemed pensive.

"Oh yeah, what were you thinking about it? It was a great night."

"It was really special."

"I'm glad, we have had lots of other special nights since then too though, so many."

"Yes, that is true." She held his hand. "That night was extra special to me because I was so worried about coming back, I never said anything at the time, but I worried about seeing everyone again, especially if you were married and I worried what your family would think of me when I told you about Zac. I wasn't planning on telling you right away, I wanted to see how things were between us first. I guess part of me wanted to know how you felt about me and not how you felt about having a son, if that makes sense?"

"It makes perfect sense, especially the way things were left between us. I tried to find out about how you were; when Liz didn't know I tried to ask around, but I never saw Mary, and no one had heard from you. That's why I wanted to make sure you knew at the party that I wanted to talk to you."

"I know, that meant a lot to me. As I said to you, my first surprise was that you weren't married with several kids, Mum was a bit out of touch with things around here so didn't know anything and I didn't like to ask too much either. After you had originally said you didn't think of me that way it was a surprise, a nice surprise, to reconnect so well." She gave him a look that said 'let me continue' as he

One More Try (Book 1)

opened his mouth to say something in his defence. "I know why you said it so don't worry, it's all water under the bridge now." He nodded acknowledgement and listened as she continued. "Anyway, when you walked me to the chalet and kissed me it felt amazing, I did wonder if I should invite you in." She stopped for a minute then looked away for a while. "You made me feel like I was the only person in the world that mattered, and it was exactly what I needed at that time."

"I'm not surprised after everything you have been through; I am so glad to hear that I made you feel that way Illy."

"You were amazing, even after that night when I wasn't sure what to do next, you were so patient and everything that I needed. I know that you said you worried over the years about how things were left between us, but I wanted you to know that you have more than made up for anything you feel you did wrong. I don't think I ever told you so that's why tonight, of all nights, when you asked me to marry you, I wanted to make sure you knew."

"Thank you. That means so much." He leaned towards her and gave her a kiss. "Is it your birthday yet?"

She looked at the time "Not quite. Why? You have already given me my gift?"

"That was only part of it, there's more ..."

"Oh really? Does it involve us both being naked?"

"You know me too well."

She giggled and stood up, so he followed her lead.

He kissed her again, "maybe an early present would be ok then ..."

She took her top off, smiled, and took his hand and led him through to the bedroom.

*

After they made love, they were lying in bed facing each other.

"I love you," she whispered then gave him a long passionate kiss.

One More Try (Book 1)

"I love you too. Why does no one ever tell you that sex just gets better the more you love someone?"

"It was pretty amazing, wasn't it?" she giggled. "I guess some things are just better when you find out for yourself."

"Very true."

They snuggled closer and fell asleep in each other's arms.

*

On the Saturday Brad and family were, not surprisingly, first to arrive for Iliana's birthday gathering, so that the kids could play, then Mary, then Tom's parents, Trish and James, and lastly Liz and John.

Iliana hadn't yet worn her engagement ring publicly; she had worn it only in the house until they announced the engagement; she waited until everyone arrived then went to put it on.

Tom waited for her to come back and held his arm out for her to stand next to him. He put his arm around her shoulder, and she put her arm around his waist, she looked into his eyes with a big smile on her face. She had a bit of her beautiful long brown hair stuck in her mouth, so he reached out with his other hand and gently removed it for her. "Ready?" he said smiling back.

"Yes, I am, let's do it."

When Tom turned around, he noticed his dad was watching them.

"Ok so we are all here now, can I get everyone's attention please?" Tom shouted so that he could be heard over the noise of everyone's catch-up chatter. "I'll keep this short; you all know I don't like speeches much. Thanks for coming around today to help us celebrate Iliana's birthday."

"Happy Birthday!" Everyone shouted.

"Not so fast, we'll do that later," he said holding up his hand. "We are actually having a double celebration today and we just wanted our family to be the first to know." He paused for a second as he watched Iliana smiling at him. "I asked Iliana to marry me, which, thankfully, she said yes to."

There was a collective gasp then Liz made a beeline for her best friend.

"Oh my God, that's wonderful news, congratulations!" She gave Iliana a huge hug then made her way over to Tom, by which point everyone else had done the same. Mary and James held back to let the queue go down. Mary was smiling at the scene and Tom's Dad was whispering in her ear; he also appeared to be smiling which Tom couldn't help thinking was very unusual. Their relationship had always been tricky but maybe his dad was happy for him despite their differences. Tom wondered again how well James and Mary knew each other; he had forgotten to ask after the last time he saw them chatting.

Liz gave Tom a big hug. "Congratulations bro, so happy for you both."

"Thanks Liz. I have wanted to ask her for a while," She smiled at him before moving to let others come along and say their congratulations.

Eventually Mary got to Iliana, and they had a very long hug, including a few tears.

"I am so happy for you," Mary said to her daughter, "I just wish your dad could have been here to see how happy you are."

"I know Mum, I know." They held each other for a long time.

Tom was watching them when he noticed his dad waiting behind Mary, he made his way around to shake hands with him, "Congratulations to you both."

"Thanks Dad."

He didn't get a chance to say anything else though as the shouts of, "*We'll need to go and get some champagne,*" Rang out from several people.

"On its way," he called back as he went to retrieve some chilled bubbles from their hiding place in the salad drawer. "It's sparkling wine but Illy prefers this anyway, so it'll have to do!"

"The happy couple!" Liz raised her glass as the room joined her in a toast.

"So, any thoughts on when?" Liz asked Iliana after a few glasses of wine.

"It's likely to be next year so plenty of time." She was a little flushed from the sparkling wine, but she hadn't stopped smiling.

Chapter 22

A few weeks after they announced their engagement, Iliana had arranged to go out for a girl's lunch with Liz. Tom and Zac had a leisurely day together, eating, watching TV, and playing soccer. Around 9pm, Tom was sitting on the sofa watching TV and having a beer when Iliana called him on his cell phone. "Hi, it's just me, how are you doing? I didn't realise how late it was; did I miss Zac?"

"Yes just, he is in bed and shattered after a day of teaching me how to play soccer!" Tom laughed.

"Aw, shame I missed him but sounds like you two have had a fun day at least?"

"Yes, we have, how about you? Good lunch with Liz?"

"It was great, although lunch is pushing it now that I see the time, we had lunch then went for cocktails then had more food, it was great." There was a short pause." I just wanted to hear your voice."

"Are you in a cab? If so, won't you hear my voice in like five minutes when you arrive home?" he laughed.

"True, but I couldn't wait, I wanted to hear it sooner than that." She sounded very tipsy but happy. "I love to hear your voice on the phone, it's so sexy."

"Really? You never said that before."

"I haven't had several cocktails before today!" she giggled again. "I can't tell you everything right away, I need to keep something back for these special moments."

At that point he heard the cab pull into the driveway.

"I hear you in the driveway now, so see you real soon!" He could hear her paying the cab driver, so she didn't reply. He opened the front door, still holding the phone to his ear just in case she remembered she had been on the phone. The cab door opened, and she stumbled out, he walked down the steps to see if she needed any help. "Do you still have your cell?"

"Oops." She turned around and waved to the cab driver before he could reverse out of the driveway and indicated that she needed to check the back of his cab for her phone. She opened the door and leaned in, with her lovely bottom sticking in the air as she rummaged around for it on the floor. She re-appeared smiling holding it up in the air, very pleased with herself. The cab driver just smiled and waved at her as he reversed out. Tom gave him a look of thanks and he just nodded, Tom was quite sure he had seen worse sights in his profession.

"Thanks, I would have been really annoyed if I had left it in there!" She was running, well stumbling towards him and grinning, still with her phone in the air.

"You're welcome." He made his way towards her, convinced she might topple over any minute.

She put her arms out and fell into him for a hug. "It's so good to see you."

"I saw you this morning and we just talked on the phone." He was trying so hard not to laugh; this was the first time he had seen her as tipsy as this.

"Oh yeah, that's true, still ..." they made their way into the house, Tom was trying to hold her up as they did so. He opened the door, and they went into the hallway.

"Do you remember our first date night when we made love right here in the hall?" she said as she stopped and leaned against the back of the door, smiling at him.

"Of course, I do, it was amazing, you are amazing."

"We are amazing!" she beamed.

"That's true Illy, very true." She slipped a bit, so he moved forward to catch her and held her by the hands, but she still managed to slip on the floor right between his legs and come out the other side; he had forgotten to put his feet together to stop that happening.

"Weeeee, that was fun, can we do it again?" she said giggling while lying on the floor.

"I don't think so, you'll wake Zac, and he will want a go too. Come on let's get you to bed."

He reached for her hands again, this time with his feet firmly together so that she didn't slip and pulled her upright.

One More Try (Book 1)

Then he bent down and lifted her over his shoulder so that he could carry her easily.

"Aw, I don't want to go to bed yet, I want to chat to my fiancé first."

"Don't worry we can chat when you're in bed."

"Unless you mean go to bed for sex of course, then I am game." She giggled again; he couldn't help but chuckle along with her. "I have a great view of your butt from here you know, I am kinda' enjoying it."

"My view isn't bad either," he chuckled gently patting her bottom. She wriggled a bit while he was moving down the hall. "Careful! This is a very narrow hallway, and I am really trying to keep you steady, if you move around too much..."

"Ow!" Too late, she banged her head on the doorframe as he was trying to manoeuvre around the corner.

So close. "Oh sorry, are you ok? I tried to warn you." He gently placed her on the bed in a sitting position, she rubbed her head but stayed put thankfully.

"I am fine, don't worry."

He got her pyjamas out from under her pillow and started to remove her shoes. She lay back, almost asleep already. He removed her jeans, put her pyjama shorts on, then removed her t shirt and bra; she smiled at him but still had her eyes closed as he gently put her pyjama top on.

"Ok, let's get you into bed," he said softly then she giggled again. He pulled back the covers and rolled her onto her side of the bed, making sure she was on her side in case she was sick, then replaced the covers and tucked her in. Her hair was over her face, so he gently swept it away, and it spread over the pillow behind her.

"I love you so much Tom, I think I always have," she sighed as he was fixing her hair. He kissed her on her forehead.

"I love you too." He went to the kitchen and poured a large glass of water then placed it on her bedside table, she was already fast asleep by this time and snoring quietly. He chuckled to himself again then went back to the living room sofa and his beer.

The next morning Tom awoke to the sound of Iliana gulping the glass of water that he had left for her.

She then made a groaning sound "Oh my head, did I bang it last night or something?"

"Yeah, on the doorframe when I was carrying you, not sure that will be the only reason it's sore though?" he chuckled.

"Hmm, yeah."

"I'll get you something for your sore head and more water." He jumped out of bed and went to the kitchen then returned with a few tablets and a re-filled glass.

"Thanks, you are too good to me." She managed a smile as she took the tablets and drank the water to wash them down.

"I have been there many times, happy to help. Remember I am out with the guys tonight too so you can do the same for me tomorrow morning?"

"Ok, if I can move by then I will," she groaned, and lay back down on the pillow. Zac was still asleep, so Tom climbed back into bed. He gently put his arm around Iliana's shoulder and snuggled into her; her back towards him. "Sorry about your head, I tried so hard, but you were giggling and moving around." He chuckled at the memory.

"It's not your fault, you were very sweet from what I remember, I don't think I have ever been that drunk."

"I don't think so either, but you were so funny."

"Hmm thanks, I blame Liz completely of course, she must be used to it, but I am not. It was great fun though we had a great time and great chat."

"Yeah? What was the chat then or is it a secret what you ladies talk about?"

"It's top secret," she laughed. "Well, we did talk about kids, you, and John of course, just stuff really."

"Me? What were you saying about me?"

"Just talk really, she said she has never seen you look happier." She turned to face him.

"Well, it's true. You knew that though, I told you?" He smiled at her.

"Yeah, I know but it's nice to hear it from my friend, that's all. She asked me how long I had feelings for you. I always suspected she knew but I told her the truth."

"Which is?"

"I always liked you, but I think my real feelings started about sixteen, I was worried she might think that was the only reason I hung out with her, which of course it wasn't, but she didn't thankfully."

"She's a good judge of character; she knew you were a good friend from day one I think."

Iliana smiled. "We talked about kids too, remember we wondered….?"

"…Oh yeah, does she want them and more importantly is she happy with John?"

"Yes, and yes, but she isn't ready yet, she wants more time."

"That's good, I am glad she is happy, she seems it." He paused then continued, "What about you, do you think you would want any more kids?" He thought he would just slip it in there while they were on the subject. "It might be nice to think about another kid before Zac gets a lot older, and me of course!"

"Yeah, definitely, I think I would like to have another baby, but not until I have completed at least a school year here, does that seem ok with you?"

"Yeah, that makes sense, there's no rush." He leaned over and kissed her on the lips.

"Mummy!" Zac ran in at that point and jumped on the bed.

"Hey little man, I hear you were playing soccer with Daddy again?"

"Yeah, I was, he is getting pretty good actually," Zac responded looking very serious.

One More Try (Book 1)

*

Tom was heading out to his favourite bar with Brad, Dan, and some of his friends from school. They were meeting at six o'clock, so he had an early dinner with Iliana and Zac before going out. When he arrived Brad was already there with Robert, which was a surprise. He joined them at the table then Brad went to get him a drink.

"Don't worry I won't stay long," Robert said.

"Stay as long as you want, it's fine with me," Tom replied trying his best to sound sincere. Robert still had nearly a full bottle of beer so Tom thought he would at least try and make it a pleasant experience. "Lisa seemed to get on well with Iliana, so that's good." Robert shrugged, so he continued. "I didn't realise you guys were trying for a family?" Robert's face changed at this, he looked angry, as usual, oh dear, well that pleasantness didn't last long!

"Yeah well, we can't all have an instant happy family like you I guess."

"For Fuck's sake Robert, are you capable of having a civil conversation with me at all? You make it sound like it's easy for me, I missed the first seven years of Zac's life, hardly ideal?"

"Yeah well, my heart bleeds for you." He looked like he might have regretted what he said for a fraction of a second, but it didn't last. Thankfully Brad returned with a beer for them both at that point.

"Cheers Bro," Brad raised his glass to them both.

"Cheers," Robert and Tom said at the same time.

At that point Dan arrived with a few others so they all sat around the table and arranged to get drinks.

"So, what's this I hear you are engaged now Tom, never thought I would see that day?" Tom's friend Dave said.

"Yeah, it's true, it was bound to happen one day though I guess. Just needed to find the right woman."

"She is quite a girl mate, happy for you both, congrats." Dave raised his glass.

One More Try (Book 1)

"Thanks." He raised his glass in return and then they all joined in.
Robert stood up abruptly to leave. "I have to shoot guys sorry, catch you all later."
They said their goodbyes and resumed their conversations.
Brad raised an eyebrow at Tom after Robert had left, "What is it with you two? "
"It's always been that way bro, no idea why. He has always resented me for some reason, he is always trying, and succeeding, to wind me up."
"Well, I do remember him winding everyone up when we were younger, he seems to have stopped it with the rest of us, but not you." Brad seemed pensive for a bit then continued, "Maybe it's to do with inheriting Harrow Falls?"
"Mom has never discussed Harrow Falls with us though?"
"Well exactly, but as the eldest surely the assumption is that you will take it over, especially since you have done the most over the years and we all have other careers? Except Robert of course, I am still not that sure what he does," he shrugged.
"Hmm. I don't know what he does either, it's a good point. He made a comment about an 'instant family' tonight as well. Iliana said they have been trying for a while with no success so it could be a combination of all those things."
"I didn't know they were trying for a family, that's tough, especially when surrounded by others with kids. Still no excuse for being such a dick though." Brad laughed this time, clearly trying to lighten the mood on their night out.
"Yeah," Tom agreed. They left the conversation there and carried on chatting with the other guys in the group.
A great night and several beers later, Tom was walking home and thinking about getting back to his lovely fiancé and son, he reflected on what Robert said about an 'instant

family', uncertain why it had bothered him so much. He got out his cell phone and called Iliana.

"Hey, just on my way home, was thinking about you."

"Aw that's nice, just like me last night?" she laughed.

"Yeah exactly, so are you going to carry me down the hall and put me to bed then?"

"Well, I can try but I think you would have more than a few bumps and bruises!"

"Yeah, fair enough, I will be ok with us both just going to bed then." He was trying to sound sexy but wasn't sure if it was working.

"That sounds like a good plan to me, are you walking?"

"Yeah, I was but I am running now, see you in about five minutes?"

"Ok, don't use up all your energy though, save some for when you get home?" she giggled.

"Oh, I will!"

He sprinted the last bit of the journey and burst through the front door to find Iliana sitting on the sofa, smiling at him. She stood up, walked over to him, and put her arms around his neck. "Wow that was quick, you're all out of breath," she laughed. "I am just in t-shirt and sweatpants I was thinking of changing but I didn't get a chance."

"You look beautiful there's no need to change." He leaned forward and gave her a kiss on the lips. "I missed you."

"But you saw me earlier and we just spoke on the phone," she mimicked what Tom had said to her last night.

"Touché my beautiful fiancé, you are much too smart for me!" He held her tight, "I love you so much."

"I love you too."

"You don't have to get dressed up or even be naked for me to want to tell you that, just wanted you to know, that's all."

"Oh Tom, how is it you always have a way of making me feel like the most important person, well adult person anyway, in the whole world?"

One More Try (Book 1)

"Well, that's easy, because to me you are."

Chapter 23

Just before Zac and Tom's birthday in April, Iliana returned home from a trip to the supermarket where she'd been buying some supplies that Tom and Zac weren't allowed to see. "I bumped into Robert at the supermarket," she announced as she entered the house.
"Yeah? What did he say?"
"He just said, 'I hear you are engaged now then?' But not in a nice congratulatory way. Sorry but he still creeps me out."
"You don't need to say sorry; he creeps me out too and I am his brother!"
She laughed. "Well, that does make me feel better. Thanks."
"What did you say to him?"
"I just said yes, we are engaged and I'm really happy, we are not sure yet when we will get married but will likely talk about it over the summer."
"Well, that's more than I would have said to him."
"What would you have said?"
"'Yes.'"
She burst out laughing. "Ok fair point, you guys don't exactly converse a lot, do you?" She was still giggling.
"Exactly."
"He just did his usual standing in my way so I couldn't get past; he always just stands and looks at me without talking so I end up talking non-stop to try and scare him away."
Now Tom burst out laughing. "You are too nice, just push past him."
"But that means making contact and I don't want that."
"Fair point. Do you want me to have a word with him? I hate the idea he is creeping you out?"
"No, it's fine don't worry, I barely see him, and he doesn't do it when we see him at your folk's place."
"Hmm, probably because he knows I would punch him."

One More Try (Book 1)

She nudged him. "No, you wouldn't. You can't hit your brother."

"Oh yes, I would. Without hesitation."

"Anyway, enough about him. Let's get dinner on then talk about nice things like planning yours and Zac's birthday."

They prepared dinner and once they were sitting and eating, Tom noticed that Zac seemed pensive.

"Everything ok Zac?"

"Yeah, I guess. I was wondering," he paused.

"Oh yeah, what were you wondering?"

"There's a boy at school called Charlie whose parents aren't together; they haven't ever been together, and he sees his dad every week. His mum has a boyfriend too, but he still sees his dad."

"Okay?"

"So, I was wondering why I didn't even get to meet you until I was seven?"

Tom and Iliana looked at each other, it was a fair question and one they should have realised would come up soon.

"Well, that's really Mummy's fault Zac, you see I didn't tell Daddy about you until we moved back here, in fact you met him the day after I told him."

"It's not all Mummy's fault Zac, it's quite hard to explain but your Mummy didn't think that I would want to know because I wasn't very nice to her …"

"Well, that's not quite true, I thought it would be quite complicated and also we were so far away…"

Zac was laughing; Tom and Iliana looked at each other puzzled, then back at Zac.

"What's so funny Zac?"

"It's just funny, you are both blaming yourself and making excuses for each other, it's sweet!"

"Oh, I guess we are," Iliana said looking at Tom who shrugged.

"You are too bright for your own good my boy," Tom said with an air of pride.

Zac just smiled. "I just wondered that's all, it's no big deal."

That night while they were in bed Tom was lying on his back with one arm behind his head and the other around Iliana after they had made love; he was deep in thought…

"Are you OK Tom, you seem pensive?"

"I am. Do you ever wonder about 'what if?"

"Hmm, do you mean about the choices we make in our lives?"

"Yes, exactly that."

"Then yes of course I do. Is this because of Zac's question?"

"Yeah, kind of, it's just made me think again." He paused for a second to get his thoughts together, "I don't know if you watched it, but I used to watch a TV show, I don't recall the name of it, it's British, about a crew of guys in space, it's a comedy and it used to make me laugh."

"No, I can't say that I have seen it. What's that got to do with it?"

"Well, there were one or two episodes where they talked about a 'parallel universe', one where the characters made different choices in the major turning points in their lives. Whether to stay back in school, stuff like that." He paused as he collected his thoughts.

"Ah ok, I always did wonder what would have happened if I had told you about Zac when he was born, is that the kind of thing you mean?"

"Yes exactly, and I always wondered what would have happened if I had at least tried to tell you that I had feelings for you before you left for college."

"Yeah, I know. Who knows what would have been different, maybe it would have been just the same, maybe we would have been at this exact moment anyway," she said now pensive herself.

One More Try (Book 1)

"Except talking about something else! "Maybe the parallel universes converge at some point though? Or more than one?"

"Well now you are getting all technical on me."

"Yeah, I just wonder…"

"We wouldn't have Zac though or at least not this version of him; if we were together and had kids later, would he have been different?"

"Wow now *you* are getting technical. It's a good point." He turned around to look at her, "Anyway, as you always said, no point in dwelling on the past, what matters is what we do now."

"Very true."

*

The Saturday after Tom and Zac's Birthday they had all arranged to go to Tom's parents place for a family celebration since it was the first time they could all celebrate their birthday together. They enjoyed some nice food and wine at the table and then the kids played in the living room area while the others tidied up. Iliana and Liz were starting to tidy up and Tom watched Iliana as she walked over to put some plates in the dishwasher, he was smiling to himself as he often did when he watched her, and she caught his eye briefly and smiled back. He was about to get up out of his seat to help her when he noticed Robert stand up and make his way over to the kitchen area too. All the plates were cleared but he went over to get a glass of water.

Tom noticed that when Iliana was bending down to put things in the dishwasher Robert squeezed past when he could have easily gone the other way around. Iliana appeared startled and stood up quickly looking around, so he had obviously brushed against her, quite deliberately. Tom could feel the anger surge inside him at the thought of what Iliana had said before. This was his own brother, what was he thinking creeping her out like that? Lisa was here too but typically, Robert had kept her wine glass topped up; perhaps this was a ploy by him to make sure she didn't notice his creeping around? Tom got up out of his chair and slowly walked over to the sink where Robert was now drinking his glass of water. He stood next to him for a few seconds then said, "If you do that again I will knock you through that window."

Robert jumped as he clearly hadn't realised Tom was there. "Do what?"

"You know exactly what? Don't treat me like an idiot!" Tom walked away to sit back at the table.

When he looked back over, Iliana had resumed her task of loading the dishwasher, so she didn't catch his eye, but Robert was staring at him. It was hard to read the expression on his face, he was just looking at Tom and frowning. He finished his water then rinsed the glass and put it away. As he walked away, he stole a quick glance in Iliana's direction and came back to the table to sit next to Lisa, who was giggling at something someone had said. Tom watched him sit down and made sure he made eye contact one more time. Robert looked away.

One More Try (Book 1)

Chapter 24

Before they knew it, the summer holidays were upon them, Iliana, being a teacher, was off for the holidays but Tom had to work, at least most of the time. He would occasionally take Zac with him to work as he seemed interested, and they did make sure they had a few days a week together as a family. They went out on their bikes a few times now that Zac was confident. Iliana also offered to look after Ethan and Helena a few days a week to help Jane and Brad.

Ethan's Birthday was in July, and he had asked if both his and Zac's family could all go to the beach for the day. Tom made sure he finished any work that needed to be done in the morning and asked his mom to let him know if there was anything urgent; she told him to take the afternoon off and have fun.

They took some beers and a packed lunch and some things to keep the kids occupied, like a soccer ball and a volleyball for in the water. Iliana got ready in the morning and helped Zac pack a bag. She was wearing a vest top and shorts, with flip flops and her bikini on underneath. Both Tom and Zac were beach-ready with a t-shirt and swimming shorts on. They got in the car and there was much excitement, Zac couldn't wait for them all to spend the day together and he was also due to stay over at Ethan's house as a special birthday treat.

When they arrived at the beach, Jane and Brad had already found a good spot and put their towels down so Iliana and Tom did the same. Jane had brought a whole load of things with her including two large cool boxes, lots more toys, and playing cards so they were pretty much settled for the day. Zac took his t-shirt off, so Iliana put sunscreen on him and then offered to do the same for Tom. He sat down on her towel, t-shirt off, so that he was in between her knees, watching the water.

One More Try (Book 1)

"Wow, I haven't noticed that tiny little scar before," she said as she was rubbing the cream on his back.

"What little scar?"

"In between your shoulder blades, it's really tiny, is that where you cut it, and I put the strips on for you?"

"Oh wow, yeah, I forgot about that; must be, as I haven't cut my back any other time. How long ago was that?"

"Hmm think I was seventeen at the time so ten years ago?"

"Wow yeah, can't say as I have ever had a chance to check it," he laughed.

"Yeah, I suppose, I had forgotten all about it; I'd meant to ask you about it." She paused for a moment; he couldn't see her but when he looked to the side, she looked like she was lost in thought, "I think that was the first time I realised I was attracted to you."

"Yeah?"

"Yes, I remember touching you and you were so warm, I also had an overwhelming urge to do something that I knew I shouldn't."

"Really? Now I'm intrigued? Is it something you can do in public? As in show me now?" he laughed, and she chuckled along.

"It's not rude don't worry." He felt her lean forward slightly and gently kiss the back of his neck just below his hairline, he felt a shiver as she did so.

"Whoa! Not sure how I would have reacted then but it's nice now." He turned around to look at her.

"I would never have done it then; I knew it was crossing the line, and you wouldn't have liked it."

"I wouldn't go that far; I would have been surprised that's all."

"I know. I have done it now so ticked that off my list." She smiled and leaned in to kiss him.

"Your Mum and Dad are always kissing," Ethan said to Zac as they walked past with their soccer ball.

"Yeah, I know," Zac replied.

"Do you need any cream on your back?" Tom asked her.
"Yes please," she turned around.
"Are you not taking off your vest?"
"I wasn't going to?"
"Oh right, it's hot and I just thought you had a bikini top underneath..."
"It is but ..."
"What is it?"
"I just don't want people to see the burn marks," she whispered.
"Oh Illy, I'm sorry, I never thought. But honestly, I doubt anyone will even notice them? They could be anything, and no one will be that close, except me of course."
She chuckled, "Do you think so?"
"Yes, I do, but whatever you are most comfortable with, it's up to you?"
"Ok, I'll take it off, Jane is in her bikini too and it is hot." She lifted her vest up over her head to reveal her bikini top. Then she took off her shorts to show the matching bikini bottoms. They were both plain, turquoise blue which showed off her olive skin nicely. Tom put some cream on her back and shoulders and made sure he covered the lower part of her back. He deliberately made his hands slip underneath her bikini top just to make her giggle and it worked.
"Eh, wait a minute, I already put cream there and it doesn't need to be all over since those bits aren't exposed to the sun," she laughed.
"I would hate for you to get sunburn!... Ok so who wants to play soccer then and who wants to go in the water?"
"Soccer, soccer," Ethan replied.
"Well, the birthday boy has spoken so soccer it is."
"Wait a minute," Iliana said, "I can't play soccer in a bikini."
"Yeah, me either," said Jane. "We can go in the water with Helena maybe if she doesn't want to play?"

"But I *do* want to play," Helena said.
"Looks like you ladies are chilling out on the beach then!"
And that is how the day continued, the boys playing soccer until it got too hot, the girls joining them for a cool down in the water….it was a great day and Iliana managed to take some pictures of them all including one of all three of them, that Jane took, which Tom couldn't wait to see.
Early evening seemed to come around quickly so they started to pack up.
"Are you guys coming back to our house too?" Ethan asked.
"I don't know what the plan is. I think we thought we would take Zac home first and get all the sand off him before he goes to yours for a sleepover?" Tom replied looking at Brad.
"Don't worry about the sand," laughed Brad. "How about pizza and beers back at our house?"
"Yay, family sleepover!" Zac shouted, finding a new burst of energy as he ran around in a circle on the beach.

*

When they'd finally managed to coax some very tired children into bed - despite their protests that they weren't even slightly tired! – the adults flopped down onto the sofas.
"Cheers guys, here's to a great day at the beach," Brad said raising his beer after he had made sure everyone had a drink. "Thanks for coming along."
"It's been great, thanks for having us," Iliana said.
"Ethan said it's his best birthday ever when I was making sure they were in bed," Jane added.
"Aw it's so nice when they appreciate things isn't it?" Iliana said.
"Yes definitely, it's not always the case so we enjoy it while we can. I keep meaning to ask if you guys are any closer to plans for your wedding?"
Iliana and Tom looked at each other, they had talked a few times but no major plans yet.

"We've talked about it but we're just not sure about the best time and also ..." she looked at Tom before continuing, "we'd like to have another baby at some point soon so ..."

He smiled at her.

"Oh wow, that's amazing," Jane said.

"So, we just thought do we have a baby first, if it happens of course, or do we get married first? It's tricky to get venues when you want them and if you want one soon it's almost impossible."

"I always wondered why our folks had both of us before getting married, did you not Tom?" Brad said looking pensive. "I mean a lot of people have one kid then get married, but two? Seems odd to me."

"Can't say I ever thought about it but now you mention it…" Tom agreed.

"Why don't you get married at your folks' place? It's a beautiful setting and you wouldn't have to book it, just caterers and someone qualified to marry you?" Jane suggested, Iliana looked at Tom and raised her eyebrows.

"Why didn't we think of that?" Iliana replied.

"I have no idea, it's a good plan," he said, wondering the same thing. "I can speak with Mom tomorrow if you want? She knows caterers too so would be able to find out about that ..."

"Why didn't we speak to you back in January Jane?" Iliana laughed, Jane smiled and took the compliment.

"We might even be able to get married next month or September. Are you ok with that?" Tom said to Iliana.

"Of course, I am, I think it sounds great."

He reached over on the sofa and gave her a hug.

"It's so exciting."

"It certainly is, I am available if you need any help too? It was a while ago I planned one, but I am sure not that much has changed," Jane said.

"Thanks, yes I definitely might need some help… sorry we..." she glanced at Tom and laughed.

One More Try (Book 1)

"Don't worry mate this is pretty much how it goes; all you need to do is show up and look smart," Brad laughed along.

"Can't wait I'll speak with Mom tomorrow, before we meet up at Mary's to tidy her garden."

They continued to chat for the remainder of the evening until around midnight when they all agreed it was time for bed, Jane and Brad showed Tom and Iliana to their spare room which was small but cosy. They got ready for bed and climbed in, exhausted after a great day. Iliana snuggled into Tom, and he put his arms around her. She looked up at him and they kissed, she smiled, she could always tell when he was keen for more than cuddling, apart from the obvious signs of course, she knew sometimes before he did. It was warm so they both were wearing the minimum; he was in his boxers, and she had panties and a vest on. He rolled on top of her, caressing her beautiful skin and lifting her vest up.

She groaned. "We can't do anything here, people might hear us," she whispered.

"It'll be fine, it really won't take that long, trust me, I've been watching you in a bikini all day," he said in between kisses and attempts to take her vest off.

She giggled quietly. "Well but the quicker we are, normally the noisier we are."

It was his turn to laugh now. This was indeed true; she had a point.

"Fair enough." He cuddled into her from behind and could feel himself gently nodding off.

He awoke a few hours later still on his side but facing into the wall, away from Iliana, he wasn't sure what woke him as the house was deftly quiet. He pulled the cover up slightly and heard Iliana's soft voice. "Are you awake?" she whispered.

"No," he whispered back only to hear her quiet giggle. She cuddled into his back, and he realised she had taken her vest off.

"It's very quiet now, maybe we will get away with it since everyone is obviously fast asleep?" She gently kissed the back of his neck, like she had done on the beach but with her bare breasts against his back it had a very different effect. He didn't say anything but turned around to look at her and kissed her passionately before she changed her mind. They peeled off their underwear very quickly and wasted no time. He had been correct in his earlier assumption that it wouldn't take him long and she was, thankfully, the same. They lay there out of breath afterwards and snuggled, he pulled the covers around them and they both fell back asleep right away, very content.

Tom didn't realise it at the time, but this would be a very cherished memory for him until the end of his days, as it turned out to be their last ever night together, the last time they made love and the end of the happiest year of his life.

One More Try (Book 1)

Chapter 25

Tom was on his way to meet Iliana at her mom's house to help with the garden, it was really overgrown since she had been renting the place out. Zac had been staying over at Mary's a few weekends ago and had run into one of the rose bushes while playing soccer, he was cut quite badly so that was the last straw for Iliana, and Tom.

He pulled into the driveway of Mary's house and noticed straight away that Iiana had left the side gate open for him. As he got out of the car and walked around to the trunk to get his ladder and tools, he caught sight of something on the ground just next to the gate. He ran towards it, his heart quickening, his breath catching in his throat as the truth of the shape on the ground began to present itself. As he started to run, he could feel a wave of panic begin to rise up through his body like a wave of despair that threatened to swallow him up. He took a sharp intake of breath as he crouched down beside the figure lying motionless on the ground. It was Iliana, and her chest was covered in blood.

"Illy, oh my god, what happened?" He got his cell out of his pocket; his hands were so shaky, but he quickly dialled 911. "Yes, ambulance please, it's my girlfriend, there's a lot of blood, please hurry. Yes 161 Maple Drive, please hurry!" Then he hung up.

"Illy can you hear me?" He leaned in close and put his hand down to try and stop the blood. She was grimacing but looked directly at him, he really didn't know what to do, she was trying to speak so he leaned in closer.

Her words came out in short gasps, "I have loved you … all of my life."

"I have loved you all your life too, Illy, please it's going to be ok, don't worry, the ambulance is on its way. I love you Illy, please …" he put his head right next to hers.

"Look after our son … one more try Tom." She seemed to be struggling so much now as her words were so slow and careful.

One More Try (Book 1)

"I will Illy, of course I will, *we* will, it's going to be fine, stay with me, talk to me please I know it's tough but keep talking to me please?" He lifted his head, suddenly aware that he was sobbing uncontrollably.

"What happened?"

"It was a……." was all she managed before she closed her eyes for the last time.

"Illy, NO, NO, NO!" He studied her, eyes closed and so still, he couldn't believe this was happening, it couldn't be true. He held her tightly, rocking back and forward, shaking his head in disbelief.

He was still holding onto her when he heard the sirens and the sound of cars pulling into the driveway and outside on the main road.

"This is the police Sir. Step away with your hands in the air so we can see them."

Police? He was expecting an ambulance, although it was already too late, he was no medical expert, but he knew. He stood up.

"Tom? What's going on?" It was his brother Dan.

"Dan?" He had to cover his eyes to shield them from the bright lights. He was moving away from Iliana as the ambulance crew ran over to her. He could see the paramedics shake their heads at the policemen to indicate that Iliana was already gone. At that moment he looked down at himself, covered in her blood from holding her.

"Shit Tom, what happened?" his brother said before he was led away, into the police car; he was too personally involved to be allowed near Tom at this point. The policeman then used his radio and asked for them to send another car.

"Sir, I need you to stay still for me. Keep your hands up?" he moved towards Tom and got his handcuffs out.

"She's my fiancé, what are you doing?" he could hear the panic in his own voice.

"You have the right to remain silent."

"But … what the …?"

One More Try (Book 1)

"Anything you say can and will be used against you in a court of law. You have the right to talk to a lawyer for advice before we ask you any questions. You have the right to have a lawyer with you during questioning. If you cannot afford a lawyer, one will be appointed for you before any questioning if you wish. If you decide to answer questions without a lawyer present, you have the right to stop answering at any time."

"Am I under arrest? Why am I handcuffed?"

"I'm afraid I must do this Sir as this is now a homicide. We just need to get you back to the station to answer a few questions. Do you have any weapons on you Sir?"

"No, of course not!"

"Are you ok if I just check please?"

"Of course."

He patted him down and then, satisfied, led him away. The ambulance crew had left Iliana as she was, presumably the coroner was on his way, and they weren't allowed to touch anything. Another police car pulled up within a few minutes and Tom was led to it by the same policeman. He could see his brother in the other car, looking at him with real concern on his face. Surely, he couldn't think Tom had hurt her?

The journey to the station went by in a blur. When they arrived at the police station he was led inside, still handcuffed, and had pictures taken. They took swabs before he was allowed to shower to wash off the blood and change into blue overalls. He felt like a prisoner, but no one would say anything to him about what was happening. He was offered a phone call so called his mom, he did consider calling Mary, but he wanted to know more before he did so and thought it wasn't fair for her to have to tell Zac, although he wasn't really thinking straight. There was no reply so either she was out, which was rare, or Dan had already called, and she was on her way.

Once changed, he was let into what looked like an interview room. There was a table with two chairs on either side. He waited for what seemed like an age on his own in the room and then two officers came in, the one who had brought him to the station and another older gentleman who he didn't recognise. They both sat down opposite him, their faces impassive.

"Ok Mr Anderson we just need to ask you a few questions following the death of your fiancé. Your brother has phoned your mother, and she is on the way, as is your lawyer," said the older policeman.

"So, we read you your rights, you can wait for your lawyer if you want but at this stage, we really just would like to know what happened?"

"OK. I arrived at her mother's place around 4:15 and found her lying on the ground round the back of the house, through the side gate which I noticed was open, she was supposed to be making a start on tidying the garden, preening the rose bushes, stuff like that, and I was going to help. She was covered in blood but still alive, so I phoned the ambulance. She was really struggling for breath but managed to say, 'it was a' and that was it." He could hear his words tumbling out, he almost didn't recognise the sound of his own voice.

"OK, so we didn't find any sign of a weapon at the scene, but the autopsy should tell us more about the instrument and confirm the cause of death. Had you two had an argument or anything that we should know about?"

"What? No! I was meeting her to help her, I told you. Surely, I am not a suspect here?"

"Well as I said at this stage Sir, we are just trying to find out what happened, we can't rule anything out. Did you happen to see anyone leaving as you arrived?"

"No of course not, I would have mentioned if I had," he replied trying not to sound defensive.

"OK and when was the last time you had sexual intercourse?"

"What?"

"In case there is any sexual assault, we need to ask this I'm afraid?"

"I think I'm going to be sick!"

They stood up quickly and opened the door as he was led into a toilet just opposite the interview room by an officer who had been waiting outside. He barely made it into the cubicle, still handcuffed and threw up. He managed to splash some water on his face and then was shown back to the interview room. When he stepped outside the toilet, he noticed Liz and his mom sitting in the hall waiting with another man he didn't recognise, they stood up as soon as they saw him.

"Tom?" Liz's eyes were very red, and her voice wobbled as she spoke.

"This way," The officer said.

"Wait, this is his lawyer!" She gestured to the tall man now standing next to her.

The officer indicated that he should follow them into the interview room. Tom's Mom frowned but sat back down with Liz.

"OK," the older officer proceeded once they were seated. "I see your lawyer is present now, do you need some time with your client?" Tom looked at his lawyer who shook his head.

"Why don't you do a recap and then we'll see if we need to confer?" His lawyer responded.

"OK, we have established that you found Ms McCoy struggling for breath and showing apparent stab wounds at approximately 4:15 ..."

"I didn't say stab wounds, I just said she was bleeding ..."

"OK, sorry." He scored something out on his pad of paper. "You phoned an ambulance, and she apparently said, 'it was A...' Correct?"

"Yes."

"And your last sexual intercourse was?"

"Last night, well this morning ..."

"What time approximately?"

"I've no idea, probably around 5 am."

"OK." He wrote again. "Is there anything else you can tell us that you think might be helpful Mr Anderson?"

"Her Ex-boyfriend used to hurt her, maybe he came back? He would likely know where her mother stayed. The autopsy will show the burn marks he made on her too. His name is Alec Johnson, he lives near her college in Aqualta. Iliana's Mom might have an address. Maybe that's what she meant by 'it was A'?"

"OK that's helpful, thank you. I'm afraid until we know more, we will be keeping you here a bit longer, no longer than 48 hours though. We need to process the scene and your car for evidence, so you won't be able to get that back for a while too."

"It won't be as long as 48 hours officer," His lawyer said. "You don't have any evidence from what you are saying, his car will have his and Ms McCoy's DNA all over it, so unless you find something very specific it won't help. The coroner's report shouldn't take long either, we don't exactly have a lot of homicides in New Harrow, do we?" They didn't respond. "We'll be in touch," He added.

"OK, thank you." They all stood up.

"Of course."

They all left the room, and Liz came over to Tom as he was being led back to his cell.

"Tom?" She leaned over to him to hug him, and he broke down, sobbing.

"I can't believe this is happening ...surely they don't think I did it?"

"No, I don't think they do, but they have to follow procedure."

"What about Zac?"

"Dan's there now. You'll see him tomorrow; We will make sure we get you out of here as soon as possible." She glanced at his lawyer who nodded. Tom realised he didn't even know the guy's name, but it didn't seem that important at this point. "Even with the details Mary gave us, it could take them a while to find Alec and get him here for questioning."

"Come on then, let's get you back …" The officer interrupted.

Tom put his head in his hands, or as much as he could with handcuffs on, "Thanks Liz."

"I still can't believe it either … I'll see you tomorrow."

They all turned to leave, and the officer led him away.

He was put in a small cell with a bed and sink and the handcuffs were taken off. He lay on the bed looking up at the ceiling, thinking of Zac and how upset he would be, then his mind drifted to Iliana, her smile, and the way she laughed, of just this morning when they were holding each other. He felt like his heart had been ripped out. He eventually drifted off into a very restless and disturbed sleep.

One More Try (Book 1)

Chapter 26

The next day Tom received a tasteless prison-style breakfast which he barely ate, followed by more long hours of waiting and wondering. They came to get him just before lunchtime saying his lawyer was here to see him. As he was led back up to the interview room, he noticed a man walking down the long corridor, following a policeman into another room. The man looked to be in his late twenties, average height with short blonde hair, blue eyes, and a thin face. The two men made eye contact as the policeman who had interviewed Tom walked towards him with some paperwork.

"This way please Mr Johnson," said the policeman guiding his charge towards the interview room.

"You must be Zac's Dad then?" said the blonde-haired man. His tone was disparaging, and Tom felt a surge of rage as the realisation that this must be Alec slowly dawned on him. An image of the marks on Iliana's body, the marks of which she had been so ashamed, and which had caused her so much pain in more ways than one, sprang vividly into mind. He lunged forward, still handcuffed, the rage within him bubbling over with a force that surprised even himself; he was very quickly pulled back by several police officers as he screamed at Iliana's abuser,

"You fuck, it was you, wasn't it? I've seen the marks you made on her you fucking monster. How could you?"

Alec didn't respond but just smirked before he and another officer entered the other room and closed the door.

"Tom, that's not going to help," his lawyer said as he walked towards him. They entered the interview room together and sat down, exactly as they had the previous day.

"OK Mr Anderson, you are free to go but you cannot leave the country, we are still processing your car," he looked at his lawyer as he said this, "I assume you have someone who can take you home?"

"Yes," He confirmed.

One More Try (Book 1)

When they left the building Liz was waiting for them in the car park. He learned that the lawyers name was Michael, and he worked at Liz's law firm. He thanked him then they parted ways. Tom sat in Liz's passenger seat, still in the blue overalls they gave him at the station.

"I don't know where to start Tom. Are you okay?"

"No, I don't know where to start either, it's like a bad dream and I'm hoping I will wake up soon. How is Zac?"

"He's not great, it will help him to see you. Dan did a great job with him, but he just wants you, understandably." Tom nodded.

"Dan looked worried, surely he doesn't think I did it?"

"No of course not. I spoke to him; he's just worried for you, and we're all upset about losing her."

"And Mary?"

"She's not much better, we're all in shock. She doesn't want to go back to her place, can't say as I blame her. When the police are finished with it, she wants to sell it. Mom said she can stay at Harrow Falls in the meantime, so I got some things for her."

"You went to the house?"

"Yes."

"Oh Liz, are *you* OK?"

"Yes, the police let me in the house to get some of her things but there's still tape up around the driveway. I didn't go near any of ... it ..."

"That's not what I meant, she's your best friend, was ..." he closed his eyes.

"I know, it's hard for everyone, but hardest for you and Zac, we're all in this together though Tom, we're here for each other."

"Yes, we are." They pulled into the driveway and Tom couldn't get out of the car fast enough. He ran up the porch stairs and in the front door.

"Dad!" Zac appeared and ran towards him, Tom bent down and held him tightly, "Dad, tell me it's not true? "

"Oh son, I wish I could, it's true, I'm so sorry, I still can't believe it myself." The tears tumbled down Tom's face.

"No! ..." he squeezed Tom tighter and shook his head, "did you see her?"

"Yes ... yes I did ..." They held onto each other for a long time in the hallway. Tom heard Liz come in behind them; they stood up and went into the living room. Mary was sitting on the sofa; she looked a lot older, seemingly aged in the few days since he had seen her when she'd arrived to look after Zac, the day after their wonderful day at the beach.

"Tom ..." was all she could say.

Tom just nodded; Zac was still holding onto him, "Mary ..."

"Your Mum has kindly offered to let me stay with her so if it's ok with you I'll get going just now, leave you guys to have some time ..." her words stuck in her throat.

"Ok ..." he wasn't finding words very easy at this point, "I understand ... of course."

Once Liz and Mary had left, Tom changed out of his custody clothes; this should have made him feel a little better, but he feared he would never feel truly better ever again. Zac had all sorts of questions. Did he know what happened? Would they ever find out? Why do bad things happen to good people? All good questions and none that Tom could answer. They were both exhausted and fell into bed early, emotionally drained and heartbroken. During the night Tom woke up as Zac appeared at his bedroom door, asking if he could stay with him. In the morning when he woke, Zac was lying on his back looking at the ceiling.

He looked at Tom and said, "I keep dreaming she is still here, then when I wake up, I remember ..." he started to sob.

"Me too, little man. I wish this was a dream and we could all wake up. I am here for you now, always." He held Zac tight and let him sob. How on earth was he going to make things better for this poor little guy?

*

They tried to get on with things and most importantly, Tom was trying to be there for Zac, who would often come through during the night for a hug. Tom didn't know if it was the wrong thing to do or not, but in all honesty, he needed Zac just as much as Zac needed Tom. The police were no further forward in finding out what had happened to Iliana. She had been stabbed with a two-pronged instrument, something like rose pruners, and Mary's were missing and never found. Alec had an alibi which was confirmed, so he had been eliminated as a suspect, and of course there wasn't any evidence against Tom just as his lawyer, and Liz, had always known.

Iliana's funeral was ten days after she died, and that morning was particularly tough. Zac had asked Tom why people had funerals while they were attempting to eat breakfast; they were both just pushing food around their plates. How could he encourage Zac to eat when it was the last thing he himself felt like doing?

"It's a good question," Tom responded, chewing his food, for a bit too long, afraid that the lump in his throat might not let him swallow. "It gives people who knew the person a chance to say goodbye, in their own way, I guess."

"What if I don't want to say goodbye, what if I am not ready Dad?"

"I know what you mean son, I am not ready either, but we don't have a choice in some things I'm afraid. She is gone, and although that makes us sad, as sad as we can ever imagine, it's not going to change." He could feel the lump again. Zac's bottom lip started to tremble, Tom jumped up from his seat and went over to him.

"Come here little man, I am sorry, I didn't mean to make you feel worse," he hugged him tight.

"You didn't, Dad. I don't think anything could make me feel worse right now," he squeezed Tom back.

"I know what you mean, we will use today to say goodbye in our own way shall we?" He looked at him, trying to smile. "Auntie Liz wants to say a few words at the service.

So that will help her say goodbye, but you can do what you want, you can hum a song, eat her favourite food, whatever you want?"

"I will find some folded over crisps then, she used to like it when I gave her them."

"Good plan." Tom patted him on the back, and they got up to finish getting ready.

The funeral car arrived with Mary already in it. Most of the journey went by in a bit of a blur, Tom couldn't help feeling like he was watching it on TV, that it wasn't happening to him at all. When they arrived at the service, he, Zac, and Mary sat at the front of the ornate church that had helped make Brad and Jane's Wedding such a beautiful occasion. Today was, of course, quite the opposite. Liz and the rest of his family sat in the row behind. There were a lot of people including old friends from the school.

The service was quite short, Tom wasn't really listening to what the minister said until he said that Iliana's friend Elizabeth wanted to say a few words. He looked up at his sister as she stepped up, her hands shaking, holding a piece of paper; her face was very drawn, and her eyes were puffy and red. She cleared her throat.

"I thought it was easiest to read a letter that I wrote to Iliana which helped me arrange my thoughts," she cleared her throat again.

"My Dear Iliana,

My best friend, the best friend a girl could ever hope for, it doesn't seem that long since you walked into the classroom for the first time and we became friends, now we are saying our goodbyes far too soon ..."

Liz's voice broke and she hung her head and closed her eyes as large tears fell down her face. Tom stood up and slowly walked over to her, he put his arm around her shoulders and pulled her close. He gently took the piece of paper from her hands, and she nodded. The minister asked if they were okay and Tom said very quietly, "I'll continue reading, do you want to stay here Liz?" she nodded.

Tom continued with his arm around her.

One More Try (Book 1)

"*You were always there for me, and any of our friends when we were young, you cared so much for everyone, and we all knew it. Nothing mattered more to you than your friends.*

You and I shared so many good times, we had the usual arguments of course that young girls do, but nothing was ever too much to overcome, we would talk for hours and hours on our many sleepovers, we would also sing and dance like crazy ladies as we would call it."

Tom couldn't help but pause at this bit, he wasn't sure whether to laugh or cry, but he continued,

"*You were part of my family and always will be, even before you were engaged to my brother, we all loved you.*" Tom looked over at his family, especially his mother who was nodding along with Mary, a small sad smile on her face.

"*I missed you so much when you went to teaching college, but we have made up for it over the last year since your return, only to lose you again now. I still can't believe it, but I wanted to take this opportunity to tell you how much you meant to me and how much I will miss you, since I don't think I told you enough when you were here.*

Rest in peace my lovely friend."

Tom cleared his throat. Liz had her head down and her eyes closed.

"I would just like to add a bit of my own if that's okay?" He looked at the minister who glanced at Mary. She nodded. Tom cleared his throat and looked around, the church was packed, and he scanned the faces watching him, he recognised some people from the school, Iliana's friends with their partners. Some other faces he didn't know too, he noticed Ethan and Helena, their tear-filled eyes staring back at him as they also struggled to accept the shock of the past couple of weeks. He closed his eyes for a second and looked up at the ceiling then forced himself to continue.

"As my sister said, Iliana was the kind of person that cared for everyone, nothing was too much for her. She was the most kind and generous person I have ever met. She used to describe herself as 'plain', she would say that if she

One More Try (Book 1)

entered a crowded room that no one would notice her, unlike her beautiful best friend," he looked at Liz who gave a half smile.

"My answer was always that, although she may have felt that was maybe the case, Iliana could work the room in a way no one else could, she would chat to people, find a common interest, and become their friend almost instantly, so if they didn't notice her enter the room they would almost certainly notice when she left it. For me that sums her up the best. She was a real people person and that's probably one of the reasons she loved teaching and was so very good at it." He paused as he struggled to find his composure and he looked around again, at all the people in the church. "She certainly taught me a lot, about friendship, love, family. Looking around at the amount of people here today to celebrate her life I am sure you all feel the same," he could feel tears rolling down his cheeks now and didn't think he could continue but he had said all he had to say. Liz gave him a gentle squeeze to let him know she was still there. He looked at the minister who nodded to them and they went to sit down, Liz gave Tom a small hug and he motioned for her to sit next to him. They played Iliana's favourite song, One More Try, at the end and Tom sat with his head down, listening. He closed his eyes, remembering dancing with her a year ago and holding her tight. Zac cuddled into him, and Liz touched his arm; he was thankful for their presence, but he felt broken.

One More Try (Book 1)

Chapter 27

After the service they thanked everyone for coming and there was a short reception at a hotel nearby. There were several people Tom recognised from the area and from school, including Billy and Becca that they'd met at the restaurant; it seemed a lifetime ago now. They had a polite exchange where he thanked them for coming and they expressed their sincere sympathies. Becca went to speak to someone else leaving just Tom and Billy...

"Can I ask you something?" Tom asked him.

"Does anyone ever say no to that question?" Billy responded, which made Tom smile for the first time in a while. "That's what Iliana used to say." Billy returned the smile. "Did you have a thing for her when you guys were at school? She always said you didn't, but I had a hunch and figured I may as well ask you?"

Billy looked around, presumably to make sure Becca wasn't within earshot. "Yes, I did, what can I say I am only human. She is, was, an amazing person. I wasn't the only one who liked her either, but I think she only ever had eyes for you. Although I am sure you know that now. I am truly sorry for your loss, I really am. The words that you said at the service were spot on about her."

"Thanks." Tom didn't know what else to say so he shook Billy's hand and let him go find Becca.

A few minutes later, Lisa came over to Tom to say that she and Robert were just leaving. Tom realised he hadn't really talked with Robert at all, but then that wasn't anything new.

"We are just going to get off now Tom, I just wanted to say how sorry I am... we are..."

"Thanks Lisa."

"I really liked what you said at the service too, I hadn't really thought about it before, but she was a very easy person to get on with. Robert has been strangely quiet too, for what it's worth, I don't think you were the only one that loved her."

"Yeah, everyone loved her, I know that."

"That's not what I meant," she gave him an apologetic smile and a look that said she maybe shouldn't have said anything.

"I'm sorry I don't get what you mean?"

"Robert used to talk about her a lot when we first met. I always suspected he had feelings for her, until I met her and then I knew."

"She always thought he hated her. He was never that nice to her really."

She gave a half smile then a shrug, "I best get going, see you." Then she headed towards the door where Robert was waiting. *Is that why Robert was always angry with him?*

He noticed Ethan, Helena and Zac at the buffet table but he didn't get a chance to check in with them as Jane came over to him...

"Tom, I hope you're ok with Ethan and Helena being here? We really didn't know what to do, they have both been too upset to be at school, so we were going to get my mom to look after them but they wanted to be here for Zac."

"Of course, it's fine, they have been great, and it's good for Zac to have company. He asked me this morning what was the point of a funeral."

"Oh Tom, that's so tough, what did you say?" She gently touched his arm.

"I said it's a way for people to say their goodbyes."

"Oh well done, that's a good answer, you did well."

"Well maybe, but then he said he wasn't ready to say goodbye, he keeps thinking she might come back. I guess he doesn't have the closure that I had, seeing her ..."

"Oh Tom, I can't tell you how sorry I am, we all are. We are here for you, anytime and for anything you need, you know that?" She gave him a hug and held him tight; he knew she meant it.

"Yes, I do Jane. Thank you."

One More Try (Book 1)

Liz came over to ask Tom if Zac was ok; she pointed to him at the buffet table with a small plate containing only crisps. Tom went over to him and placed his hand on his shoulder.

"It's not working Dad; I don't feel any better." Tom looked down at the plate of crisps and the little boy had picked out only folded over crisps and put them all in one bowl. "Ethan and Helena have been helping me."

"Oh son, well how about if you eat them, I am sure she would like that."

"Hmm, not sure, she always *used* to like them. I think you should have them since it's just us now."

Tom took the offered crisps reluctantly; it was tough to hear but these were the facts, it *was* just them now.

A tired looking Mary approached them both, "Tom, I was chatting with Zac, and we wondered if it would be ok for him to stay with me tonight, give you a night to yourself ..." she stopped there as the words hung in the air.

"Oh, well, I hadn't thought about it."

"We just thought you might want to have a few drinks that's all, and if I am honest, I could really use his company, just for tonight, would that be okay?"

"Of course it is Mary, no problem."

"I also wanted to say that I loved your speech, you made me very proud today with your kind words." She put her hand on his shoulder.

"Thanks Mary, that means a lot, I meant every word." He gave her a hug.

People started to leave, and Mary took Zac with her. Tom made sure everything was all in order then left once everyone had done the same. He wasn't sure what to do with himself but hadn't had the heart to turn Mary down. He went home and changed out of his suit then decided to go and see if several drinks would make him feel better. He headed to the pool hall in town and sat at the bar, not where he had sat with Iliana of course, the pain of her absence was too much to bear. Tom's friend Dave was behind the bar, fully aware of the day's event, he didn't say anything but handed him a bottle of beer and left him to it.

Tom was staring into the bottle when he felt a hand on his shoulder, he looked up to see his brother Brad indicating two more to the bartender.

"Make that three please?" he heard his sister's voice as she came up behind him and placed her coat on the barstool next to him. He couldn't help but notice that she had turned quite a few heads when she walked in, just as Iliana always said.

"Hey, you guys, you didn't have to ..." he felt that lump again and couldn't say any more.

"We couldn't let you drink on your own, today of all days Bro, we are here for you, always," Brad said.

He was a bundle of pent-up emotions, which were threatening to explode like the bubbles in the bottle of beer that he was holding, he glanced at them briefly in an attempt to hold it together and keep those feelings hidden deep down. Dan appeared behind Liz and Brad. He just gave Tom a small smile and patted him on the shoulder.

"Thanks guys," was all he could manage to say.

They all sat at the bar and talked quietly for the whole night, just reminiscing about old times. They talked a bit about Iliana, nothing too serious or sad; just making sure that she wasn't a taboo subject. When Tom awoke the next day with the hangover from hell, he realised that alcohol did *not* make him feel better, but his family did.

*

About a week after Iliana's funeral, Tom was getting dinner ready in the early evening while Zac was doing his homework at the table. He heard a knock at the door and answered it to a girl standing on the step, with an A5 sized padded envelope in her hand, she was quite young, probably late teens, and he had no idea who she was.

"Hi," he greeted her.

"Oh Hi. Sorry to bother you, are you Tom Anderson?"

"Yes, I am."

One More Try (Book 1)

"I work at the photo shop in town, these belong to Iliana," she looked down at the envelope. "She never had a chance to collect them, in fact she must have posted them to us on the day she died so we really didn't know what to do with them. Eventually we decided you might want them so I thought I would just drop them off to you ..." she shuffled her feet a bit as her voice trailed away.

"Oh, okay, thanks. I have no idea what's on them but thanks, that's really kind of you."

"We were so sorry to hear what happened, I hope that you and Zac are okay."

"Thanks."

The girl turned to leave with her head down and walked up the driveway. Tom walked back into the living room where Zac was doing his homework and checked the stove. He got out a pair of scissors and carefully opened the envelope. He looked through them one at a time, there were a lot of scenic photos, the ones that Iliana liked to take, and then right at the end there were the ones of them at the beach on Ethan's Birthday. She had taken quite a few of each so there were some of Brad, Jane, Ethan and Helena and then ones of Tom, Iliana and Zac. Tom had his arm around her waist to cover up her burn marks he remembered, and his other arm was around Zac. In the first one Iliana was smiling at Tom and not looking at the camera then in the others she was looking at the camera. They were all smiling and looking happy. He stood frozen for some time, looking at the last photo.

"Are you ok Dad?" Zac was looking up from his homework. Tom walked over to the table and sat down next to him. He slowly placed the last photo on the table in between them and they both looked at it in silence. "We should put it in a frame, maybe get a bigger copy of it first?" The tears in his eyes spilled over and he broke down; he hadn't really cried much since the day he had found her but seeing the photo of the last day they spent together and how happy they all were, was too much for him. Zac came over to him and held him tightly for a long time. "I miss her too," he whispered.

 Later that night Tom and Zac decided they needed another focus, so they agreed they would get a puppy and they set about finding the perfect little companion to heal their broken family.

*

 Zac was so happy; he chose a yellow labrador, a male puppy; he'd always loved the TV adverts with them in. They decided to call him Rocky. When he was old enough, they walked him together twice a day at least. It gave them some time together when the focus wasn't anything to do with what had to be done in the house, or what was missing in the house, they would just walk and talk and admire the scenery.

 Rocky would sleep at the end of Zac's bed every night as a puppy, when he was bigger, he would often just curl up on the rug next to him and occasionally keep Tom company too. He would join Tom at work and was always happy for any attention from Tom's Mom or from the holiday makers. When they were visiting family, Rocky would always come too and he enjoyed a long walk along the beach close to Tom 's parent's place.

 Tom and Zac cherished the photo of all three of them on the beach and would often talk of that day along with all the happy times they had spent in their year all together. It seemed way too short, but they had a lot of good memories which helped, if only a little, in some of the sad times. Tom would often get an image in his head of Iliana in a wedding dress, it was so vivid, but of course they had never made it there; he had no idea where such a vivid image had come from, it felt so real. He could visualise every detail; Iliana had her hair up with a few soft curls falling. She wore a two-piece strapless outfit, in soft white fabric decorated with some subtle sparkles that shone when she moved. The skirt was long and flowing and she was standing smiling at him, it was almost as if he had taken a photograph of that exact moment. It made him smile whenever he pictured it, a vision of what should have been.

One More Try (Book 1)

Chapter 28

Tom, Zac and Rocky were on their way to Harrow Falls. It had been five years since Iliana's death and there had been no further developments, so they were no wiser as to what happened to her. It was now a cold case, according to Dan, which Tom thought meant it was unlikely they would ever find out.

Tom's mom had asked all the immediate family, including Zac, to gather at the house as she had something that she wanted to discuss with them all. They all arrived at the house within ten minutes of each other and congregated around the large dinner table. Rocky took his usual spot over by the sofas and curled up for a sleep after a fuss from everyone present.

"Ok so you are probably all wondering what this is about. I wanted to get everyone together to talk about my plans for this place, I am not getting any younger, so I thought that sooner was better than later." Their Mom spoke once everyone was settled. Tom couldn't ignore the frown on his father's face.

"...My plans for my father's business, which I am the sole owner of," Trish continued, glancing around the table. "It's probably not that much of a surprise but I would like to pass it over to Tom then eventually Zac."

"What?" His dad was first to react. His mom held up her hand to stop James from saying any more.

"Please hear me out." The others all just sat in silence.

"There is a substantial amount of money saved up for each of you children which you will get upon my death, or before if you so wish, it's all in these documents," she handed out pieces of paper to Tom's four other siblings.

"Tom yours is different because of this place and because it will pass to Zac if and when you choose to do so. It's not immediate of course as we have to work out where your father and I will live." She handed him a larger pile of papers. "Liz already knows everything as she drew up the papers for me. Just so you all know."

"Mom, this is your home?" Tom spoke as the others just watched he and his parent's reactions.

"It *was* our family home, yes, as it was my fathers before, but it's nearly time, it's far too big for us now."

"But …"

"We could even just swap, your place would be perfect for us, and you don't need any help with the business as much anymore, but I can be here if or when you need me."

"Do I not get a say in this since I have put so much time and effort into it?" James was still frowning, and the others just looked at their mother.

"Tom has put in more time and effort into this place than anyone for quite some time now James. Surely you know that."

"I knew this would happen. That's what I said to Ili …" His eyes went wide.

"What? That's what you said to who?" Tom looked up from the bits of paper he had been reading over, he placed them back down on the table. Another image of Iliana popped into his head but this time it wasn't the vision of her in her wedding dress, it was an image of James and Iliana; they were arguing, and James was pushing her. Tom was shouting as he intervened and shoved his dad away from his beloved Illy. It was an angry exchange, and Tom shook his head trying to erase the unwelcome and unexplained scene from his head - he didn't understand where it had come from, but he knew it was something awful.

"Never mind. I knew it would happen." James looked away then stood up. Tom followed him and faced him, looking down at his father who stood several inches shorter than he.

"That's what you said to who?" His heart was thumping in his chest. He just knew he had been about to say Iliana. "Tell me you fucker! What did you do? Why were you discussing this with Iliana?" Tom lifted his hand and grabbed him by the throat, lifting him off the ground slightly.

"Tom, what are you doing?" Trish shouted and he heard Liz scream. His brothers got up quickly and ran around the table to try and stop him.

"He's our dad Tom, what are you doing?" Brad spoke.

Tom released his hand but didn't move. He stared at him, right into his eyes, there was something there, he could see it. Guilt. A terrifying truth began to reveal itself deep in Tom's gut. James choked a bit then glared at him.

"I am not your dad!"

Trish let out a sob.

"I think it's time we told them the truth Trish, don't you?" He held his head up high.

"What truth?" The siblings all spoke at once, except Robert. Their mother put her head down but didn't say anything.

"Mom? What's going on?" Tom said, but still, he didn't move and didn't take his eyes from James.

She looked up.

"I am sorry son, this isn't the way I wanted to tell you, or even if I wanted to tell you." She gave him a suppliant look then glared at her husband.

"Go on…" was all he could say, his heart was still thumping in his chest, Zac was just looking at his Granny.

"I'm afraid James is not your real father, despite what it says on your birth certificate." She took a breath then continued, "I was in a relationship …"

"HA! Is that what you called it?" James interrupted and she glared at him.

"Yes, a relationship with a man who was in the army, he got stationed somewhere in England, I can't recall where, and I never heard from him again. I found out I was pregnant with you after he left. I'm sorry son, I just didn't think there was any need to tell you." Again, she glared at James.

"Well, there you go, that explains a lot! Why you always picked on me, called me a waster, hit me!"

"WHAT? He hit you?" His mother sobbed again; she looked horrified.

"Yes, once or twice, when I was smaller probably about Zac's age, but it stopped when I grew bigger than him, you fucking coward!"

"James how could you?" Trish said as Liz went to her and put her arm around her mother.

"I always thought it was just cos I was the eldest and you were trying to toughen me up."

Liz, Brad, and Dan were looking at Tom with sympathy which made him feel worse.

"…And you told HIM!" he pointed to Robert, "your favourite, which also explains a lot."

"It doesn't make any difference to me," Liz spoke, her eyes filled with tears, "you are still my big brother."

"Yeah, me too," Brad and Dan said at the same time.

"Thanks guys." Tom could feel the lump in his throat, this was all too much for him and when he looked at Zac, he spoke the same words of comfort,

"I don't care either Dad, are you okay?"

"Yeah, I will be, son, don't worry," he took a deep breath then glared at James. "Now the rest of it, tell me what you did?"

James looked down at the ground but took a while to respond. Everyone just waited, the room was completely silent.

"I spoke to Iliana, I tried to warn her," he finally said.

"Warn her about what?" Tom could feel the anger surging through him, surely this couldn't be true, but he couldn't ignore his intuition.

"Warn her about you, you were never going to play the happy families for very long were you let's face it, we all knew that?" He looked around, seeking support, but no one gave him any back up, not even Robert.

"When was this?"

One More Try (Book 1)

"What?"

"When did you warn her? Was it just in passing at the supermarket or did you go and see her?"

James looked sheepish; he was backed into a corner in more ways than one. They were all watching him, even the dog who had gotten out of his bed after the commotion.

"The day she died," he still wouldn't look up. Tom was shaking.

"And?" More silence. "AND?"

"She got defensive and went at me with those stupid pruners and in the scuffle, she got hurt. I panicked and ran."

"And took the 'weapon' with you? Not that much of a panic if you thought ahead?" Tom reacted quickly.

"You fucking bastard," everyone stopped to look at Zac who had shouted at the top of his voice, tears were streaming down his bright red face.

"Do you even know what that word means boy?" James replied.

"Don't *YOU* dare talk to him like that!" Tom lunged forward this time with both hands and lifted him up by the throat again.

"Put him down Tom, it won't help," Brad said, touching him gently on the shoulder.

"You killed her! He killed my mother!" Zac was sobbing now; anger was the only thing stopping Tom from breaking down too. "Punch him, Dad."

"I know son, I know, Brad's right though, it doesn't change anything. Also, he just admitted to it in front of a policeman and a lawyer, so he is screwed."

"It was an accident," James whispered.

"Ok so manslaughter then, same difference to me, and to Iliana!" Tom shouted her name at the end.

"How could you Dad?" Liz was also sobbing.

The gaze of the whole room was fixed on James; Trish wore a look of stunned horror.

"Well, I guess we'll never know if I could play 'happy families'! You made sure of that." Tom walked over to Zac

205

and put his arm around his shoulders. "Come on son we're going. Rocky, here boy."

He turned around and picked up the papers from the table, "For the record I have never expected any part of this place, the work I have done around here over the years was for you Mom, to help you, and I learned a lot along the way thanks to my grandfather, not YOU!" he pointed to James. He turned around and left with Zac and Rocky.

As they closed the front door and made their way towards the car, they heard the door open again, "Tom wait, "I am so sorry Son, I never meant for you to find out like that."

His mom was still crying so he stopped and walked back to her. He gave her a hug. "It's not your fault Mom, I need to go and speak to Mary, I can't be around him just now, but I will speak to you later, okay?" She didn't respond. "Is Dan calling it in?"

"Yes, he is," she sobbed, so he held her again.

"I'll talk to you later, okay?"

"Okay," She turned to go back in the house, he could hear shouting as she opened the door, but he didn't stop, they carried on towards his car and got in.

"Are you ok Dad?"

"Not really, you?"

"No, not really." Zac looked out of the window as Tom started up the engine.

"We need to talk to your Granny; she will be devastated all over again."

"Yeah, I know. We will be there for her though."

"Yes, we will. You are much more mature than I was when I was thirteen." Zac gave him a half smile and a shrug.

"Mom used to say that to me too, quite a lot, not the thirteen bit of course, but she always said I was mature. I didn't know what it meant for quite a while though." He looked out of the window again, deep in thought, obviously thinking about Iliana. "You know I never told you this, but I knew Alec hurt her, even though I was young, I wasn't stupid. I didn't want her to know though, so I never said anything. But then it meant when I heard her crying, I couldn't go to her and comfort her, I just thought she wouldn't want me to see her like that for some reason. It was tough. I was so glad that she eventually realised what he was and left."

They pulled up outside of the small house Mary had moved to soon after Iliana's death.

"Oh son, that's just awful. You have been through far too much for someone your age. For what it's worth I think you did the right thing, she would have been devastated if she thought you knew." He reached out a hand to touch Zac's arm. "Guys like that are scum, they make women believe they can't do without them or that they aren't worth anything just to get what they want. I only met him once at the police station, but I couldn't contain the rage I felt when I saw him."

"I can imagine. Do you remember me telling you I didn't like him that first day we met?"

"Of course, I do, son. I should have realised then that you knew, I guess. That day is a special memory for me for several reasons."

"Yeah, me too Dad, me too," Zac smiled at him, and Tom could see tears in his eyes; he undid his seat belt and hugged his boy.

"Let's go talk to Granny, this will be tough as well."

Chapter 29

"What a lovely surprise you two, three, sorry!" Mary said with a big smile as she opened the door to her bungalow and looked at Tom, Zac and Rocky. "You should have said, I would have made something for you coming?"

"Yeah, sorry about that, it was a bit of a spur of the moment thing, it's just that we have to talk to you about something and it couldn't wait."

"Oh, that sounds serious. Come in, come in," she stepped aside to let them in then closed the door behind her. Zac gave her a hug, Tom noticed he held onto her for a bit longer than he normally did, especially for a teenager. This was going to be so tough for all of them.

"Is everything ok?" She'd clearly picked up on the sombre mood.

"Not really Mary, you had better sit down, shall we go through?"

"Oh yes of course, now you have me worried, has something happened? Is your mom ok?"

"Yes, she is fine, well ..." Mary sat down, and Zac sat next to her, Tom sat on the seat next to the window overlooking the small yard. "She will be," he paused searching for the words to start. He glanced at Zac who was frowning, clearly dreading what was coming. "I'm afraid we found out today what happened to Iliana, or some of it at least, I don't think we will ever get the whole story..."

"What? How?"

"We had a family meeting about Mom's business and it ..." he paused again, how could he put it? "Well let's just say it came out."

"Dad scared it out of him," Zac said, still frowning, Tom made a mental note to ask him about this statement.

"Maybe..."

"Please tell me what's going on, neither of you are making any sense?"

"OK. Apparently, D ... James went to see Iliana that day to warn her about me..."
"What day? What was there to warn her about?"
"The day she died, he told her that I wasn't going to play happy families for very long and that I would soon get bored of it ..."
"Oh no!" she put her head in her hands... "I should have known."
"What do you mean Mary, how could you know?"
"At your engagement he had a smirk on his face rather than a smile so I said to him that he must be pleased for you. I remember we held back while all the others were congratulating you. But he said that he would be really surprised if any wedding happened and said something about playing happy families. But I just ignored it, what does this have to do with Iliana's….," her voice trailed away as the penny began to drop. "I knew he was cynical about your relationship, but I never knew…Oh God! I just never thought…"
"Oh Mary, how could you know, how could anyone? I keep wondering, if I had only got there sooner that day ... but there's no point."
"There's more to it though, I'm afraid," she looked at them both.
"You knew we were at school together, yes?"
"No, I didn't."
"Well, we were. He was my Billy Garcia if that makes sense to you?"
"Yes, I think so," Tom nodded.
"No. It doesn't make sense to me," Zac said.
"He was a good friend at school, or I thought he was, but I didn't want to be anything more than friends and he did. I think I broke his heart. He once made a snarky comment about 'no one around here being good enough for me' as I had left and married a Scottish man, as you know, Iliana's Dad, Andrew. He was in the army, and we met when he was stationed over here."

"That sounds familiar. Did you know he wasn't my father?"

"No, I had my suspicions, but I didn't know for sure. It's not the sort of thing I would have asked your mom as she was passing the Turkey on Thanksgiving," she smiled at Zac in a bid to ease the tension.

"So, you said he went to warn her about you, although God knows what he thought that would achieve! What happened then?"

"Well, he said it was an accident, that she got defensive and went at him with the rose pruners then when he defended himself, she 'got hurt' as he put it."

"'She 'went' at him? She wouldn't have done that!"

"Yes, we know. Don't worry Mary, he is not getting away with it. Everyone was there when he admitted it. Dan is calling it in, so we'll see what happens. I'm quite sure he didn't go there with any intention to hurt her, but we'll see; there's no excuse for what he did – accident or not. I will try and talk to Liz later to see legally where he stands."

"None of it matters really," Zac piped up, "it doesn't change anything or bring her back."

"I know, that's true" Mary put her arm around him, and he cuddled into her for a bit.

"Are you ok Mary?"

"I will be fine. I guess it's some kind of closure; it doesn't change the pain of losing her. As you say we will never know exactly what happened, my poor girl." She put her head in her hands again and Zac put his arm around her shoulders. They all just sat in silence for a minute or two, then she lifted her head... "Anyway, as you say no point in dwelling." She took a tissue from her sleeve and wiped her nose. "Can I get you anything? Coffee Tom?" Zac looked at Tom, he didn't like the idea of just leaving after breaking that kind of news to her and he sensed Zac was the same.

"That would be nice Mary, thank you."

She got up to go through to the kitchen, Tom understood her need to do something practical as she processed the awful truth.

They stayed for quite a bit longer just chatting and enjoying their coffee and a biscuit before they headed home. They prepared some dinner and didn't say very much more about the day's events, both of them lost in their own thoughts. While they were eating, Tom remembered what Zac had said about him, scaring the truth out of James…

"Did you mean what you said earlier son? About me 'scaring' it out of James?"

"Hmm, not really, sort of. I didn't mean it in a bad way. I don't blame you at all. I did wonder how you seemed to know already though?"

"It's really strange, it's like I had an image in my head, of … well … things …" Zac frowned as Tom tried to explain, "… an image shall we say …" he shook his head, "I'm not explaining this very well." He ran his hand through his hair. "It was like I was on the outside watching things happen, but it wasn't what happened. Have you heard of déjà vu?"

"Yeah, I have, it's like something that's already happened, isn't it French?"

"Yes, I believe it is, French for 'already seen', I think. Anyway, that's what it was like, but of course it didn't happen so …" he frowned, remembering a conversation a long time ago with Iliana. "I had a conversation with your mother once, about the idea of a parallel universe. I got it from an old show I watched about some guys in space, we should watch it sometime if I can find it. Anyway, we talked about a parallel universe where things are different depending on choices we make."

"Hmm, ok so you think déjà vu is from these parallel universes then?"

"No, I hadn't but now I do! Could very well be." He pondered for a few moments about the images of Iliana in a wedding dress, a lot nicer than the other images.

One More Try (Book 1)

"What is it?" Zac was smiling at him; Tom hadn't realised, he was smiling to himself.

"Ah nothing, just some nice thoughts about your mom. Anyway, as you said, I guess we'll never know exactly what happened."

They finished their dinner and while Zac was tidying up and Tom was feeding Rocky, they heard a knock at the door; his mom was standing there looking very upset.

"Tom. Hi, so sorry to drop by like this."

"It's fine Mom, are you ok? Did something else happen?"

"No, nothing else," she stepped into the hallway and walked into the living room and kitchen area. "Hi Zac."

"Hi Gran," Zac got up and gave her a hug and she started to sob.

"Mom, it's okay," Tom put his arm around them both.

"It's not OK Tom, I am responsible for this whole mess, it's me."

"It's not, sit down, come on. Why don't you stay here tonight? You can have my room, and I'll take the sofa?"

"No, it's fine I will be fine."

"No, you won't Mom, you've had a shock, we all have. I'll get you a drink and you can stay with us tonight?"

"Ok, thanks son. I can't tell you how sorry I am about all of this."

She started to sob again so he sat next to her on the sofa and put his arm around her. "It's not your fault."

"Oh, but it is, I should never have settled. He talked me into putting his name on your birth certificate and then was nice to me. Before I knew it, I was expecting Brad. Of course, we got married and were happy for a bit but ..." she stopped and looked at them. "He was never around; always said he was working but then so many things needed to be done, and my father would wonder why. Eventually I confronted him, and he admitted that he was having affairs. He made me feel like it was my fault that he needed to go to other women, because I didn't give him enough attention. By this time, we had five children though. I should have left

One More Try (Book 1)

him but deep down I always believed there was good in him, it was just circumstances." She put her head in her hands. "I did ask him to leave a few times, but he said I needed him and that I wouldn't cope, and in some ways, I believed him."

"Mom, it's not your fault. I have heard these things before, that's what guys like that do, they manipulate you."

"But I should have made sure he left, I should have been strong and kicked him out. Why didn't you tell me he hit you?"

"I guess I didn't think it would do any good, you argued over me enough I didn't want to cause any more rows. Then he stopped ... I guess because I got big enough to hit back. Not that I did, or would have, until today."

"Oh son, I am so, so sorry it happened like that, I know I should probably have spoken to your f... James first but things haven't been great recently, of course now I know probably why, but I wanted other people there, in the hope that he would see it was the right thing to do, regardless of his feelings towards you ... "

"It's OK Mom, he might not have let slip about Illy if you hadn't done it that way, don't worry." She nodded.

"It's not your fault, we all have things we wish we had done differently." He stood up. "Have you eaten anything? I have some leftovers. I'll get you a glass of wine with it too and you can stay?"

"Ok then, thank you. You have always been so good to me Tom; you are a wonderful son. I am not sure if I ever told you that."

"It's ok Mom, you didn't need to." He smiled at her, and she smiled back.

While Tom gathered some food for his mom, Zac went over to sit next to her and gave her a hug. She held onto him for a long time. Tom put the plate of food and a glass of wine on the table then the three of them sat down. He had a beer to keep his mom company, and they tried to chat about other things and cheer her up. They played some cards later

213

and had a kind of relaxing evening together, trying not to think of the events of the day too much.

In the morning, they had coffee and breakfast, and his mom left early. Not long after she left Tom heard a knock at the door and, assuming she had forgotten something, he opened the door ready to make a cheeky comment…

"Robert?"

"I know I'm the last person you want to see but can I come in please?"

"Sure," he stepped back and walked down the hall into the living room. "Take a seat." Robert sat down on the sofa and Tom sat gingerly next to him.

"I just wanted to talk to you after the events of yesterday."

"Okay…"

"I don't know where to start." Robert took a deep breath; "I guess the best place to start is when we were growing up, I had a big thing for Iliana, which you have probably guessed by now anyway?"

"I didn't but Lisa did."

"Oh, right. Anyway, I really liked her, but she would barely look at me. I think I gave her the creeps."

"Only because you would try to touch her instead of just talking to her and being nice to her."

"Yeah, I know, I didn't realise I was being creepy, I think I knew all along that she only had eyes for you though. Anyway, I got quite upset one day when I saw you both walking off together. I assume you were walking her home?"

"Yeah, I did walk her home once I remember."

"Well Dad saw me and that's when he told me that you weren't his son. I know it's hard to take, but now I look back, I know he encouraged me to cause issues. Not that I am blaming him entirely, I had a huge chip on my shoulder and was insanely jealous, I realise that now," he stopped again, he seemed quite genuinely upset and Tom found that he felt sorry for him. "I just wanted to let you know how sorry I am, about all of it, but most of all I am sorry about what happened to Iliana. If I had known Dad was going to 'warn her' as he put it, I would have tried to stop him at least. I loved her and as much as it pained me to admit it, she was so happy with you and he took that away from her, and from you, and Zac." Tom was astounded by Robert's contrition but tried hard not to show it. "I didn't know he had done it; I promise you. I assumed, like everyone else, that it was her ex. I never spoke to you at the funeral because I was too upset, probably another reason Lisa suspected about my feelings too."

"Apology accepted."

"Really?" he looked genuinely shocked.

"Yeah really, there is no point dwelling on it now. That's what Iliana said to me, when I apologised for the 'quickie next to the dumpster' as you called it."

"Sorry about that, again, I was just jealous. I am sure that you more than made up for it as she was very happy."

"Yeah, I hope so, I think so." Tom looked down for a moment lost in his thoughts; "Anyway don't be too hard on yourself." He didn't say anything about his mom confirming his dad's affairs, there was no point.

"Thanks Tom, I appreciate it. There was one other thing I wanted to tell you in person as well. Since you knew ages ago and mentioned it to me…"

"Oh yeah what's that?"

"Lisa is pregnant, finally!"

"Wooa, congratulations! I am so happy for you both!" Tom couldn't believe how happy he felt for them, knowing how long they had been trying.

"Thanks, we tried IVF one last time and we both stopped drinking for a loooong time, or maybe it just felt like that," he laughed "But anyway, it happened. She is due in July."

"That's brilliant news, I am glad you told me."

"You're the first to know actually," Tom just smiled and nodded in acknowledgement; he was touched. "Well, I best get back, she has a huge list of chores for me to do." Robert

laughed and put out his hand to shake Tom's. Tom shook it then gave him a hug, "Thanks bro."
"See you later. "After he left Tom struggled to remember a time Robert had ever called him 'bro'.

One More Try (Book 1)

Iliana
Chapter 30

 Iliana was getting ready to prune the rose bushes in her mum's garden which were long overdue. She would change into old clothes, find the gardening gloves, then get started. Tom was arriving a little later with ladders and extra tools for the job, but she wanted to make a start to try and save some time.

 Her Mum had taken Zac to their place, not Tom's place anymore; it was theirs now and it felt great, she smiled to herself as she was getting ready, what a difference a year makes. She thought back to all those years she spent at Liz's and all the great times she'd had, including her time with Tom, falling in love with him at such a young age.

 The night of Tom's parent's anniversary seemed like much more than a year ago now when she had been so unsure of what she would find. She had thought Tom would be with someone like Sarah and have at least a few kids of their own. In other ways though, it seemed like yesterday when she had seen him walking towards her in his suit, he had really looked after himself over the years and was still the same tall, slim build that she remembered. Her heart had been thumping in her chest when he had sat down next to her and given her his usual charming smile. They had got on so well and she was so tempted to ask him back to her chalet that night, her feelings for him hadn't changed at all, in fact they were only stronger. Maybe it was because it was eight years later and she was a stronger person than she had been back then, she knew what she wanted but she was also worried about telling him about Zac. As it turned out he was still a perfect gentleman, and it all went so well. Zac adored his father from day one and she would never forget their first proper night together at his place when she had dropped in to see him. It was so special, but then they'd had quite a few special nights together since then. She smiled to herself. Now they were planning to get married and even thinking of trying for another baby, it was so exciting.

 She went outside and started to trim things back according to the instructions she had found on the internet, it really wasn't her thing,

One More Try (Book 1)

hence the reason it had taken so long. Tom would be better at it, but he was busy with the upkeep of his parents' business these days, there were more and more repairs and things to be done.

She had been working for about half an hour when she was relieved to hear a car pull up in the driveway round the front. It would be Tom; thankfully he was earlier than she had expected. She wondered if it would be easier to just take large hedge cutters to the unruly rose bushes, but she was pretty sure it wasn't good for them to do that, from what she had read anyway. She heard footsteps after the engine stopped and looked up expecting to see Tom appear at the side gate, to her surprise though it wasn't him, it was James.

"Hi James, this is a surprise, is everything okay?" her first thought was that something had happened.

"Don't worry, everything is fine, can I come in?" he said, looking through the gate, which was about six feet high to try and stop anyone climbing over and accessing her Mum's shed, not that there was anything too valuable in there.

"Of course, I'll open the gate." She walked over to the gate and undid the latch, "Come in." She was still puzzled as to why he was here, "I am just helping Mum by trimming the rose bushes in the garden, they are really overgrown as you can see." James looked over at the rose bushes briefly, but then he nodded as if he wasn't interested, why was he here?

"Yeah, I heard Zac got hurt the other day," he responded dismissively.

"Yeah, he did, he's ok at least but it's a wakeup call," she paused, waiting for him to say something a bit more caring about his grandson, but it never came. "So, is there anything I can do for you James? Much as I'd like to stop and chat … " she left it there as she had a tonne to do, and this was more words than he had said to her in all her time knowing him.

"No, I just wanted to talk to you that's all. To warn you ..."

"Warn me? Warn me about what?"

"About Tom of course. You really don't think this happy family game is going to last do you?" His face had changed now, not that it was that pleasant before, but now he was scowling at her. "He will *never change, he will dump you and your precious son as soon as he is bored, which won't be long."*

"You're wrong, you don't know your son as much as you think you do, you have barely ever spent any time with him from what I have seen."

"Ha! My son! In case you haven't guessed he isn't my son! I only have three sons; Trish was already pregnant when we got together."

Iliana couldn't hide her shock at this, did Tom know? Did anyone know? Surely someone would have told her by now, she had always felt like she was part of the family.

"What?"

"Yeah, he is a waster, just like his father. In the army or navy, I think, can't remember. Visited here for a short time, probably got lots of girls pregnant then fucked off back to where he came from. You could have had your choice of my boys but none of them were good, or bad, enough for you. Just like your mom, she ran off with an army guy too, no one here was good enough for her!"

"What? I really don't get what you're saying to me, you're starting to make me uncomfortable now too," she went to move away from him, but he grabbed her arm, tight, it hurt a lot.

"Robert had a big thing for you, Brad for a short time and Dan liked you too I think, but they soon got over it, Robert though, he had it bad for such a long time, still does as far as I know. Why couldn't you go for him and make him happy? No, you had to go fuck Tom and have a kid young so now you're stuck with him."

"Oh my God! What are you saying? That's not true, I love him, and he loves me," she could feel the tears coming on. "Does anyone else know Tom is not your son?"

"Yes, Robert does. I told him one day to make him feel better when he was crushed at seeing you two together. Tom will never inherit the family business, I'll make sure of that ..."

"I think Trish might have something to say about that, Tom has put in a lot of effort, still does."

"Ah well see there you go, is that part of it then? That Tom, and of course then your son, will inherit the business I have spent years building up and making a success?"

"No, I don't care about the business, Trish does though is what I meant. Wasn't it her father's? Isn't she the legal owner?" She tried to pull her arm away from his tight grip, but he just pulled tighter and grabbed her other arm. She swung her hand around so that the hand pruner was facing him. "Let me go," she shouted, still struggling.

"No, maybe if I get a piece of you then that will put Tom in his place."

"NO! LET ME GO!" She struggled again as he moved forward, and the hand pruner got turned around in her hand. She felt a searing pain and when she looked down, the blade had pierced her chest, a deep ruby flow seeping into the fabric of her green t shirt turning green to dark, dark red. She dropped the pruner on the ground.

"Shit!" James moved backwards, shaking his head, then seemed to bend down.

She was struggling for breath; he moved further away. "Stop, help me," she whispered, so softly that she didn't think he heard. He ran out the side gate which was still open, and she heard the car start up, no! She collapsed on the ground holding her chest, struggling so much to call for help; her thoughts kept coming and going, she drifted in and out of consciousness as if she was halfway to somewhere before hurtling back.

Suddenly she heard a sound, a voice, it was Tom! She tried to speak but could hardly find the breath, he was shouting something, but she struggled to focus.

One More Try (Book 1)

Tom
Chapter 31
(18 Years Later)

Dear Illy

I am writing this letter because my sister suggested it would help me to gather my thoughts together, I am not sure it will work but figured it was worth a try, One More Try to be precise, that was our song and our words, so it seems appropriate.

Now that I have started though, I am not sure I can find the words to describe what the last eighteen years have been like without you. We found out what happened to you five years after you were gone and I am still crushed by it to be honest, it was my fault, if I'd had a better relationship with who I thought was my father, then you might still be here with me, with us. But I have been told by several people, without whom I would likely have cracked I might add, namely my sister, your mom, my mom and our son, that there is no point thinking like that.

It pains me to think about it, but I did sometimes. He said it was an accident, and we guessed that's what your last words to me meant, but why was he there? I know you, I know that you wouldn't have struggled with him unless you felt threatened in some way, which I can't even think about, as I said, so I will leave it there. I said that you were safe with me forever and it was hard to take because you weren't, and it was because of me. Anyway, he got what he deserved, which wasn't punched through a wall by me (or your son) but prison, where he died. I am not sad about it, as he caused the 'accident' and left you to die, so there, I said it, well wrote it.

Anyway, it took Zac and I a while to get used to a world without you, your mom once said to me that losing someone close must be like losing a limb, sometimes your body fools you into thinking it is still there, and we were the same for a long time. The first occasions after were the hardest, Thanksgiving, Christmas, your birthday, Zac's and my birthday, as we would always think that this time last year you were still with us. Not that it got any easier of course. Your mom also said that she had to believe there was a heaven, that the thought of not seeing our loved ones ever again was just too hard to bear. The idea that we would meet again on some level kept us going and I totally get what she means. Zac and I would often talk about what would be the first thing we would each say to you when we see you, this changed for him as he got older of course but I always enjoyed these conversations because, given how young he was when you died, he remembered and knew so much about you that he always amazed me.

Talking of your mom, you should know she has been my rock for so long, Illy, I don't know what I would have done without her, she looked after Zac once a month for as long as she could and he cherishes his time with her, they are great friends, and she loves spending time with her great grandchildren. My Mom of course remains there for us too and she was instrumental in Zac's future, but we'll come back to that.

It took me so long to date another woman, I occasionally went out when Mary had Zac and even had sex but that's not what I am talking about. Companionship I guess, I think it was about ten years after you were gone, when our son sat me down and had a talk with me, imagine being lectured about companionship by your eighteen-year-old son! Well, yes that was me. Her name is Cassie, and she is actually Jane's best friend, we met at their wedding but she was with her boyfriend at the time, now her ex-husband. We enjoy spending time together, but I think she knows deep down that my heart will always belong to you.

I am glad though in some way that we didn't get married because I would not have wanted you and Zac to have the name Anderson, we would have had to change it after everything that happened.

Anyway, back to Zac, enough about me. After my stepdad confessed, I spoke with Mom about my real Dad, his name was David Chapman, and he was English, but she never heard from him again. Zac and I did some research on the internet and eventually found out that he was killed in action the year I was born, at least that explains that I suppose. I didn't feel it was appropriate to take his name since

One More Try (Book 1)

we never knew him (not his fault I know) but I decided to change my name to Mom's maiden name, Williams, that of my grandfather. Mom discussed the business with the whole family and informed them that she would be handing it over to me, and now to Zac, and everyone was happy about it. It was my grandfather's business, so it seemed appropriate.

Liz married her partner John, and they now have a son who is eight, remember we always wondered if she would have kids as she was always great with Zac? Well now she is a wonderful mother to Mason who we see regularly.

Robert and I settled our differences, he had it pretty bad for you it turns out, which I probably should have guessed, but we are friends now. He also has a daughter who is eleven, he and Lisa finally had the baby they wanted for so long and they are happy.

I became good friends with Billy Garcia too, we chatted at your funeral and then I saw him a few times out at the bar. We now meet regularly to play pool, watch a game, or just catch up.

Dan married his friend Olivia, and they plan to do some travelling when he retires, they never seemed keen on kids so why not I guess?

Zac became best friends with his cousin Ethan and great friends with Helena too, they were more like siblings to him really as we saw them regularly. We also got a dog to keep us busy after we lost you and he was very special, he lifted our spirits when we were down and was an amazing companion to both of us until he died three years ago, aged fifteen, he had a great life though and as I said he really helped us through some dark times.

Zac married his childhood sweetheart, Jesslyn and they now have two beautiful children, Benjamin Thomas (aged 4) and Charlotte Iliana (aged 2) with another one already on the way! I just love having them around, they do run rings around me but that's half the fun! The jewellery box that I made you now belongs to Jess, Zac's wife, we both wanted her to have it, and she cherishes it just like you did.

I still wear your star and moon necklace that I made you, not all the time but I wear it sometimes when I need cheering up. I don't think I could bear seeing anyone else wearing it to be honest. I think I will ask to be buried with it, although I could leave it to Zac's daughter, but he may have more so that wouldn't be fair, and I don't know that they would appreciate it as much as you did.

I would still love to have a look at a parallel universe or two just to see if there is one where you are still here, and we are all together. I guess we make choices in our lives and there are consequences to them, several choices and probably several consequences but some I think are major. I know I have always wondered what would have happened had I told you how I felt when you were eighteen. Zac wonders if he had told you he knew about Alec if you would have come back sooner. Mary thinks she should have handled her rejection of James better and picked up on what he said at our engagement and finally my mom thinks she should have kicked him out a long time ago. But who knows if any of these would have made a difference? We make our choices at the time and then we accept the consequences and move on with our lives, I think.

Zac and Jess run the family business and live in the house now, all the chalets, and the house, were modernised which Zac and I did together with some help from my brothers. There is now a restaurant on site, which we built and kitted out ourselves. It is managed by Helena. It works really well, Zac spent a lot of time there with me and Mom especially in the summer holidays, our busiest time, observing how things were done, fixed, organised, he is a natural at it and it's another reason Mom wanted to hand the business over to him, she is still around of course now in our old place, helping out and passing on her words of wisdom, I am glad she has seen things the way they are as it is going so well, she is very proud, and so am I.

That brings me to my last points, Illy, Zac is such a wonderful boy, now a man, and although I am still devastated by losing you, at least I still had him. He is an amazing person, he may look like me, but he is so like you in his personality, he is kind, loving, sensitive, sensible, responsible and so many more good things. People are drawn to him, just like people were drawn to you, although you were oblivious to it most of the time. You did such a wonderful job raising him for his first seven years and I hope that you agree I kept my promise to you to look after him after that and give him everything he needed in life. He is an amazing person, and I only hope that we have made you proud.

All my love, always
Tom

THE END ...
for this reality ...
but could things have been different?

One More Try (Book 1)

Iliana
Chapter 32

(July 1992 again)

She turned to look at him, feeling brave and wasting no time, "Can I talk to you?"

"What about?" He was still looking off into the distance where Liz had gone. "We need to get you a cab."

"I know but just hear me out first, please? I leave for Aqualta tomorrow," she said hoping she was giving him a pleading look but not knowing if she was pulling it off; she wasn't sure if the alcohol was helping or not.

"Ok then, what's up?"

"Have you been avoiding me lately?"

"Why would you say that?"

"Ever since you gave me this," she pointed to her necklace, "and kissed me, I haven't seen you around much at all."

"Ah, yes, sorry about that."

"Are you sorry for kissing me or avoiding me?" He didn't reply. She sighed, "Look, I am pretty sure that I have feelings for you, and I can't go away to college knowing that there is even a small chance that you feel the same way?" He looked down at his feet, not a good sign she thought. "Tom?"

"I'm not good at this Illy."

"Good at what?"

"Talking about how I feel."

"Try me, just be honest?"

"I do have feelings for you, but I am a lot older than you and you are going to college …"

"Oh Tom," she lunged towards him and held his face, then kissed him. He seemed really surprised at first but soon kissed her back. They were standing in the middle of the sidewalk having a full-on passionate kiss and she couldn't have felt any happier. When they stopped, she pulled back

One More Try (Book 1)

and gazed at him, "You have no idea how happy that makes me."

"Hmm, I feel pretty happy now too, funnily enough." He smiled at her. "I have been avoiding you and I am so sorry, I just didn't know what to do. I tried to distract myself …"

"With Sarah?"

"Well yes, but that didn't work. Then I spoke with Liz yesterday and she said that I had to tell you before you went away."

"What? You spoke to Liz? She never said anything?"

"That's because I specifically asked her not to, I thought it needed to come from me."

"Ah ok, I'll let her off then." Now Iliana felt a bit guilty for not telling her best friend about how she felt either. "But how did you know we would get a chance to talk?"

"Liz made sure Tony would come and offer her a lift around this time."

"Wow, you two are devious," she said, impressed. He grinned.

"I was pretty jealous when that guy was talking to you back there, while I am being honest."

"Really? I was getting annoyed at them coz they were blocking my view of you playing pool," he laughed a lot at that and put his arm around her. "How do you think I felt seeing you with Sarah? That was tough."

"I know, I'm sorry."

"It's okay."

"I thought I was doing us both a favour, but it didn't turn out that way." He touched her face tenderly.

"I know, I get it."

"So, what now?"

"Mum isn't home, you could give me a proper send off before I leave tomorrow?"

"That's not really what I meant."

"I know, worth a try though," she laughed, and he chuckled with her. "Seriously though, can you come back with me, just for an hour, you can tell the guys in there that I

One More Try (Book 1)

am falling all over the place, and you need to make sure I get home safely?" He seemed to think for a minute. "Please?"

"Ok, just give me a minute, if you see a cab stop it and ask them to wait for me, okay?"

"Yes, sure." He ran back inside so Iliana looked around to see if there were any cabs, but he was back so quickly there weren't any in sight. They only needed to wait another five minutes before Tom hailed the next cab and gave the driver her Mum's address. She held his hand as they sat in the back of the cab, and he smiled at her.

"Was anyone suspicious?"

"No, I don't think so."

One More Try came on the radio and he smiled at her and squeezed her hand. When they arrived at her house it was quiet and she led him by the hand into her bedroom, there was no point in wasting any time she thought, she had wanted this for a long time. She kissed him passionately and they fell onto the bed together, still kissing. She could feel his hands go under her t-shirt and touch her bare skin, he undid her bra with one flick of his fingers, and she giggled. He was caressing her bare breasts which felt amazing. She sat up and took her t-shirt off over her head, letting her loosened bra fall to the floor. She started to unbutton his ridiculous Hawaiian shirt, admiring his muscular chest with her hands.

"Wait," he frowned. "Are you really sure you want to do this now?"

"I've never been surer of anything in my life," she replied, then kissed him again as if to prove her point.

"Eh, is it your first time?" he whispered.

"Yes."

"I want this to be special for you Illy."

"It was special as soon as you told me how you felt."

He smiled.

She continued to remove his shirt then he stood up to remove his trousers and boxers while she took off her skirt and panties. He lay back down with her, and they kissed again, naked, skin on skin; it felt wonderful.

She was aware of him putting on a condom before he lay on top of her. He kissed her on the lips then gently moved down and kissed around her shoulders and neck; he caressed and kissed her breasts.

"Ready? Let me know if it's too sore, okay?"

"Ok, I'm ready," she could feel him enter her and it was in fact quite painful, but the closeness she felt meant that it was bearable. She enjoyed kissing and holding on to him, feeling his bare back as he was moving on top of her. It was such an intimate experience, and she felt so close to him. He let out a long groan and then lay on top of her, so she held him tight until he moved off and lay on his side next to her.

"Are you ok?"

"Yes, I am, it was really special," she turned onto her side so that she was facing him.

"Are you sure? I heard it can be sore, so I tried to be gentle. It will get better for you, I promise."

"It's ok, it was a bit sore but it's okay, it was intense and so intimate. I am not sure why I am surprised, I just felt so close to you, not just physically. I'm not explaining this very well!"

"Don't worry, I think I know what you mean. I was surprised too; it seems when you really care for someone it feels more intense," he pondered. "I didn't know that until now."

She smiled, "Oh wow, I don't think I could feel any happier right now." She leaned forward to kiss him.

"Yeah, me too." He held her tight, and they snuggled for a while.

"You had better watch your time? Not that I couldn't stay like this all night of course but ..."

"Yeah, you're right. As best man I had better get back, so sorry, I'd love to stay too."

"It's fine, that's what we agreed." He got up and started to put his clothes on. Iliana lay on the bed admiring him.

One More Try (Book 1)

"Well, I have to go tomorrow but maybe I could drop in and see you before I go? We can talk then; I am trying to get a car with the money that Mum put aside after we lost Dad so I will be able to drive home some weekends and not rely on her picking me up or trains and buses."

"I could drive you tomorrow if you want?"

"Oh, that's good of you but you have a bachelor party tonight so I wouldn't want you to not be able to relax and have a few drinks. Probably best not to do a long drive after a night out like that?"

"Yeah true. We'll have a think about it and chat tomorrow then." He had dressed now and went over and sat on the bed next to her. "What's your plans for the rest of the night then?"

"Oh, you know, just chill out. Make sure I have everything packed. Think about you," she giggled and he leaned down to give her a kiss. "Shall I call you a cab?"

"Yeah, good idea."

Once he had gone, she put on her pyjamas and checked her bags one last time, she had no idea what to expect at college and of course she was now regretting picking one so far away. It had seemed like a good choice at the time when she was feeling like she needed a change, but now it felt like a mistake.

The phone rang around 10pm and when she answered Liz was sounding very cheerful.

"Hey, just wanted to catch you make sure you got home okay?"

"Yes, I did, no thanks to you!"

"What do you mean, didn't Tom make sure you got a cab home?"

"Yeah, he did."

"And?"

"And what? He made sure I got a cab home." *This was fun.*

"Oh, okay, that's good then. I just wanted to make sure that's all, I won't keep you."

One More Try (Book 1)

"Ok, nothing else you want to chat about or tell me?"
"Iliana? Are you up to something?"
Iliana giggled. "Maybe."
"What happened, tell me everything? Well maybe not everything that might be a bit weird, maybe tell me the headlines not the full news report?" Liz was giggling now too.
"Well, he said he talked to you yesterday?"
"Yeah, I know; I so wanted to tell you, but he made me promise not to."
"I know it's ok, don't worry. I think he was right, it had to come from him."
"Yeah, and?"
"Well, I asked him if he had been avoiding me, and he admitted to it and said that he has feelings for me."
"Good."
"Can you tell me what happened yesterday then? How did he talk to you and what did he say?"
"Well to be honest I was in my room chilling out listening to music when he knocked on the door. He looked so serious I was wondering what was wrong with him, but he just asked if we could talk then sat down on your bed." Iliana chucked at the fact they still called it 'her' bed. "Then he asked how you were, which wasn't unusual as he often used to ask after you, especially after that time you weren't well. Anyway, I said you were good, then he asked when you were leaving. So of course, I told him Sunday and he seemed surprised. He then told me that he kissed you on your eighteenth Birthday. I was shocked but not because he kissed you just because you didn't tell me."
"I know I am so sorry; I was really torn as he seemed to regret it, he apologised and then avoided me after that so I didn't think I should tell you. "
"It's ok I understand, don't worry."
"So …"
"Ah yes, so then he said he was sorry and that he realised he was a lot older than you, but he cares for you. At which

point I explained that I wasn't shocked that it happened just that you didn't tell me, and he relaxed a bit. Then he asked me what I thought he should do, should he just leave it and 'let you get on with your life and meet someone your own age', his words not mine, or should he tell you how he felt?"

"Wow. I am so glad you told him to talk to me. I just wish he hadn't waited until yesterday to talk to you as I am now going so far away for the next four years."

"Oh, I know, I said that to him but just be grateful that he did talk to me, who knows what might have happened if he just bottled it up then let you go away?"

"Yeah, I dread to think."

"Best not dwell on that, if it's meant to be you guys can work it out?"

"Yeah, I agree. I am going to try and get a car, and I might even see if any of the other places that accepted me would take me now or after the first year. Will think it over."

"Ok, best let you get some sleep then, it's a long day for you tomorrow, goodnight."

"Night Liz, and thanks again."

"You're welcome bestest friend in all the world, love you."

"Love you too."

One More Try (Book 1)

Chapter 33

Iliana was waiting for her Mum to return from work so had two cups of tea ready when she arrived home.

"Hey Mum, how was work?"

"Oh, just the usual you know," she flopped down on the sofa and Iliana handed her the cup of tea after giving it a thirty second blast in the microwave.

"Thanks. Well don't you look cheerful, how was your night with Liz?"

"It was great Mum; we had a great time."

"Yeah? What did you get up to?"

"Well, we went for a few drinks then Liz met Tony, and her brother Tom saw me home."

"Oh ok, that's good, he is always such a gentleman."

"Yeah, he is." She paused as she wasn't sure how to say the rest. "We had a good talk actually."

"You did? What about?" her Mum had a smirk on her face but wasn't giving much away.

"About us, me and him."

"Okay," she said slowly. "There's a you and him? I knew you had feelings for him a Mum notices things. You used to skip around the house when he dropped you off from work or from sleepovers."

"Well, there is a me and him now, as I said we had a talk, and I told him I had feelings for him." She touched her necklace, "He gave me this for my eighteenth birthday. I'm sorry I never told you about it, but I wasn't sure what you would think. I suspected before that that I felt something for him but well now I know I do."

"Ok, and he feels the same?"

"Yes, he has feelings too but was worried to say anything as he is quite a bit older and worried what people would think, particularly Liz of course, and you."

"Well, he has always been a perfect gentleman to you, so I have no issue with it whatsoever."

One More Try (Book 1)

"Thanks Mum, I thought you would say that." She leaned forward and gave her a hug, "I am so happy but …"

"But what?"

"But I am now going off to college of course and chose one really far away."

"Oh, that can be sorted I am sure of it, you're not thinking of dropping out, are you?"

"No of course not."

"Ok good, then I am sure we can work something out. We should try and get you that car sooner rather than later though," her Mum sipped the last of her tea. "Okay I am off to bed, I'll see you in the morning, what time are we leaving again?"

"10am, but if it's ok can we drop by at Tom's place for a bit? I said I would drop in to say goodbye."

"Of course, why don't you drive over to see him early then come back and get me for around 10-10:30, we'll still have plenty of time? Give you both some time on your own to talk?"

"Ok then, if you're sure. He offered to drive me, but I didn't think that was a good idea the day after a bachelor party."

"Yes, good point. That was kind of him though."

"He is kind, I think I love him Mum, I didn't tell him that of course as I don't want to scare him away."

"Yes, give it time, there's no rush," she stood up and went to the bathroom to get ready for bed.

Iliana remained on the sofa still sipping her tea and thinking of Tom. She eventually decided to call it a night but lay awake in her bed, thinking of the events there earlier in the night; she could smell him and she pulled the sheets in tighter as if drawing him closer. She couldn't wait to hold him again. Just as she was drifting off to sleep, she heard a sound and sat straight up in bed. Was she imagining it? It had sounded like a tap on the window. She got out of bed and pulled the curtain back to look out of her window; she couldn't quite believe her eyes. It was Tom, waving at her from the side garden. She pointed to the front door, and he started to walk around.

She opened the door and ran onto the porch in her bare feet, pyjama vest and shorts.

"Hey, what a nice surprise?" she said going to the steps to meet him. He stopped at the bottom so that they were level in height.

"Hey, sorry if I woke you, your light was on so I figured you might still be awake?"

"I was awake, don't worry. I couldn't sleep, probably the tea I had when Mum got home," she laughed. He leaned forward and kissed her.

"Are you cold?"

"Well not now!"

"I just wanted to see you again. Before tomorrow. I've been thinking about you all night."

"Really? Me too." She had her arms around his neck, and he was holding her waist. She kissed him again.

"How was the bachelor party?"

"It was a good laugh, but we started early so we are all pretty wasted."

"Hmm you don't seem too bad, what time is it?"

"It's three in the morning."

"Is it? Oh, wow I didn't realise."

"Did anyone say anything about how long you were away?"

"No, they didn't actually, I think they were too drunk to notice." He laughed. "Can I ask you something?"

"Does anyone ever say no to that question?" she giggled.

"Hmm yeah good point, I don't think so."

"Shoot?"

"Will you come to Brad and Jane's wedding with me in a few weeks?"

"I would love to."

"Really? I am best man so you wouldn't be able to sit with me, but Liz will be there of course and it's not like you won't know anyone. I think I might even have to dance with a bridesmaid but just the first one, I'll have to check that again as I should know the etiquette as best man. Anyway, I wasn't sure if you would be able to get back for it?"

"I will make sure I am back for it. Don't worry." She looked into his eyes and then kissed him again, "I wish you could come in. We could carry on from where we left off."

"I know but I don't think that's a good idea, I wouldn't want to wake your mom or push my luck," he grinned.

"I told her about us tonight."

"Did you? What did she say? Did she send the police after me?" He was half laughing but seemed worried.

"She is happy for us, she said you have always been a perfect gentleman in fact, so she has no issue with it at all."

"Really? Oh, that's good, your mom is great."

"You worry too much."

"Yeah well, maybe, I know my dad will have something derogatory to say to me, I think Mom will be ok with it though."

"At the end of the day it doesn't matter what others think, it's about us and the people closest to us that care about what makes us happy."

"That's very true Illy." He held her tight. "I best get going. I'll see you tomorrow."

"See you tomorrow." She kissed him again; she really didn't want him to go. "I'll be around about nine then I'll go pick my Mum up for ten is that ok?"

"Yes, sounds good. Goodnight."

"Goodnight."

He pulled away reluctantly and turned around to give her a final wave as he made his way up the driveway. She went inside and back to bed, she drifted off quite quickly and before she knew it the time was 8am and she had to get up and get organised.

She packed her bags in the car then headed off for Tom's place. When she arrived in his driveway and parked next to his car, she noticed that the place seemed quiet. She knocked on the door and waited. She knocked again, maybe he was still asleep, the house layout was like her Mums so maybe she should go and throw a stone at the window like he had? Knowing her luck, she would shatter the window though, she chuckled to herself. Then he appeared in a t-shirt and shorts rubbing his short hair with a big smile on his face.

"Hey, come in." He stood back so that she could enter, and she walked behind him down the long narrow hallway.

"How are you feeling?"

"Not too bad actually, I think the hour break from drinking helped." He grinned at her, "Tea?"

"Yes please. You know how I like it."

"Hmm yes, I do. Have a seat it won't take long."

She sat down on the small sofa. She hadn't been in his place before but had often wondered what it was like. It was quite small but tidy, open plan like her Mum's. She watched him as he made a cup of tea.

"I spoke to Liz last night."

"Yeah, what did she say?"

"Not much I just told her that we had talked, although I had a little fun first and pretended like nothing had happened. She sounded disappointed bless her so I couldn't keep it going for long." She chuckled at the memory and how sweet her friend was. He laughed too.

"I told Brad too, hope that's ok? I wanted to ask him if it was ok to ask you to the wedding so I kinda' had to."

"Of course, it's ok. Was he surprised? What did he say?"

"At first, he didn't say much as he said he wasn't sure if I was just asking you as a friend. But then he asked if you were staying at the hotel and if so, were you booking your own room? At that point I told him we were together so I hoped you would be staying with me."

"I hope so too." She smiled at him.

"He said that Jane mentioned recently that she thought there was a connection between us, a 'spark' he called it, so he wasn't that surprised."

"Really?"

One More Try (Book 1)

"Yeah, she never mentioned it to me of course, but then why would she I suppose."
"Yeah, me neither."
"I'll tell Mom later today too."
"I am sure your Mum will be ok with it."
"Yeah, me too, probably not Dad but can't say as that bothers me too much."
"No, it doesn't really bother me either. I can't say that I have ever spent that much time with your dad at all. I don't feel close to him like I do with most of your family. Your Mum, Brad, and Dan but not your dad or Robert. I can't really explain why."
"Same for me to be honest."
He came over with the cup of tea and handed it to her then sat down next to her holding his cup with both hands. She sipped her tea and looked at him.
"Mum was worried that I might want to drop out of college when I told her about us?"
"Yeah, I worried a bit about that too, but not for long, you're too smart for that." He smiled at her.
"Charmer! But yes, I am too smart. I will see what I can do but worst-case scenario we are in a long-distance relationship. Does that put you off?"
"No. It doesn't. We'll work it out."
He put down his coffee and turned to face her. He lifted his hand and cupped her face, much like he had done when he gave her the necklace. He leaned in towards her and then they kissed for a long time. She couldn't believe she was leaving soon and knew that she would miss being this close to him. It was tough but if it was as special as she thought it was, they would get through it, together.

One More Try (Book 1)

Chapter 34

Iliana spoke to Tom the night before Brad and Jane's wedding, they had spoken on the phone almost every night since she had left but they hadn't seen each other yet so she couldn't wait to see him. She'd had to rely on Liz to buy her a dress to wear to the wedding as she didn't get the chance, Liz knew her size and what she liked so she trusted her implicitly.

"Oh my God Iliana that dress is amazing on you," Liz gushed after her Mum had dropped them off at the church with a smile and a wave. Liz looked stunning as usual in a burgundy fitted dress, matching shoes and purse. She had on a stylish hat which only a person with her beautiful features could wear. The outfit that Liz had chosen was perfect for Iliana, the dress had a cowl neckline, thin straps, and lots of different shades of blue diagonal stripes. She had also chosen a shoulder wrap and sandals in turquoise blue which matched one of the colours in the dress.

"Thanks, you look amazing too." They hugged.

They had managed to arrive right on time so made their way into the church. It was a big ornate building with beautiful stained-glass windows and several rows of wooden pews. Iliana and Liz were sitting on the right, the side of the groom, and sat in the front row, next to Liz's parents, Dan, and Robert. Iliana was hesitant but Liz and her Mum both motioned for her to sit with them, so she complied. She was glad really because it meant she had a great view of Tom and Brad, standing at the front together, both looking handsome in their suits. They were standing with their backs to the pews, close to each other and chatting quietly, occasionally she could see Brad's shoulders move up and down slightly, so Tom was clearly trying to make him laugh and ease his nerves. She watched them for a while and was smiling to herself. Tom looked so handsome in a dark grey suit, she just wanted to run up to him and put her arms around him but that would have to wait.

They heard the music change, and everyone turned around to look down the aisle for the bride, everyone except Iliana, she was still watching Tom as he slowly turned around. He glanced down the aisle for a second then looked at the front row and his eyes stopped when he saw her, she saw a huge smile appear on his face and she couldn't help but smile back at him. She couldn't describe how she felt, except to say that the moment felt magical. Even though they were in a large church filled with people, she felt like they were the only ones there for a split second. He must have felt it too because he winked at her, it was so subtle that she didn't think anyone else would notice, which just made it feel even more special.

"Oh my God Iliana, everyone is looking at the bride except you two, and my brother is mentally undressing you in a church for goodness' sake," Liz whispered to her with a chuckle.

Iliana couldn't help but join in, but she still couldn't take her eyes off Tom. When the bride arrived at her destination he had to turn around and resume his duties, but she was still beaming about the moment they had shared.

They watched the beautiful ceremony, and Tom did well as best man. He gave her another look and a cheeky smile when it was over; the bridal party all made their way out of the church first.

Since Liz and Iliana were in the first row, they were last out and there was a long line of people waiting to congratulate the bride and groom when they got outside. She was so happy for them but was desperate to see Tom. She waited in line patiently, but it took so long. Were these people not going to be here later for all their chat? In her head, she realised how unreasonable that sounded but she couldn't help it and she tried hard to hide her frustration. Liz noticed of course and was laughing at her as they stood in line together.

"There will be plenty of time to see Tom later."

"Yeah, yeah, very funny! Are you laughing at me?"

One More Try (Book 1)

"Just a bit, you are so desperate to see him, from the look of him at the ceremony he will be the same, it's so sweet."

"It's not sweet, it's torture. I haven't seen him for two weeks!" Iliana pouted, but she wasn't as good at it as Liz was so this made her laugh even more.

"I am just trying to distract you so that time will go faster."

"It's not working."

Finally, when she got to the Bride and Groom she hugged Jane, said she looked amazing and passed on her congratulations then moved on to Brad quite quickly, there were still people behind her as well, so she excused her haste as just being considerate.

"Congratulations Brad."

"Thanks Iliana, but don't worry about hanging around. Go see my brother as he has been desperate to see you since the start of the ceremony, well before that, but never mind." He smiled at her, and she felt like hugging him again.

"Thanks so much."

She quickly moved away from the line and looked around but couldn't see Tom. They were in a spacious courtyard next to the church with an amazing garden behind. It was a big space, and she wondered where he could have gone. He would be needed for photos soon so he couldn't have gone far. She was thinking about walking around the back of the church to the large garden when she felt someone tap her shoulder. She turned around to look straight into those green eyes that she loved so much.

"Looking for someone?" he smiled at her. She threw her arms around his neck and held on to him so tightly, he put his arms around her waist and pulled her closer.

"Oh Tom, it's so good to see you," their foreheads were touching.

"Here, come with me." He took her by the hand, and they walked around the back of the church, where she had been thinking of heading earlier. Although the garden was large, there was a small, secluded area next to a hedge and he led her there before he turned around to face her again. He put his arms around her waist and pulled her close, "You look so beautiful."

"Well, your sister picked out the outfit, glad you like it," she said as she gave him a twirl. He smiled as he watched her.

"Oh yeah." He moved forward again and kissed her gently on the lips, she kissed him back. She pulled back and they gazed at each other. They could hear voices, so it sounded like the bridal party were on their way for photos.

"We had best not get carried away?"

"Yeah. It's so tough but we will hopefully have time later?"

"Well, I do have some good news there, I managed to shuffle a few things, and I have next week off so that I can find a car. I am allowed to study from home for just that week."

"Really? That's the best news I have had all week." He gave her a hug, "I can help you look for a car, will chat with Mom later and arrange some time off."

"Great. Did you tell her about us?"

"Yes. I did, she wasn't surprised, she said she suspected something when I made you tea and toast that time you were ill." Iliana giggled. "And she is happy for us."

"I best let you get back to your duties then. Catch you later." She gave him a peck on the cheek, "Oh, I nearly forgot, can I get the room key so that I can put my bag in and freshen up please?"

"You look pretty fresh to me." He smiled as he got the key from his pants' pocket.

"Flattery will get you everywhere as you know." She took the key from him and gave him a flirty smile, then turned to leave and find Liz and Tony. Liz had kindly offered to take her bag out of the church, so she was going to go and find her and put her bag in the room. She couldn't resist one look back at Tom as she walked away, he was still standing there watching her and smiling.

One More Try (Book 1)

Fortunately, Liz was waiting for her outside the front of the church, and they made the short walk to the hotel. Liz checked in whilst Iliana called the elevator to take them to the second floor.

"So, Tom said he told your Mum, did she say anything to you about us?"

"Yes, he told her two weeks ago just after you left."

"Yes of course, he said that. Is she ok about it?"

"Iliana, why are you so worried about this?"

"I can't help it; he is the same, I think. To be honest there are only four people that I care about what they think. You, Mum, your Mum, and Tom. Although maybe Dan and Brad too, so six."

"Oh honey." She reached out for her and gave her a hug, "You are so sweet." She held her for a minute then pulled back to look at her. "That's exactly why all those people are happy for you both."

"Thank you."

"Bit of a bummer we can't have a drink, eh? Sucks being eighteen at a wedding."

"Well, I might have persuaded Mum to get us a bottle of wine, it's in my bag, shall we have a little drink before we go back down?"

"Oh yeah, now that's why you are my best friend, none of this mushy shit." They both laughed. Iliana dropped off her bag in Tom's room before they went to Liz and Tony's room, kicked their shoes off and opened the wine.

"That's more like it." She sat with her feet up and sipped at the wine, "Won't Tony wonder where you are?"

"Oh shit, yes he will," Liz sat up for a minute then looked at her wine longingly. "Ah he'll be fine; we won't be long, and he knows I am checking in. Terrible queues for these things." They both giggled.

They sat and enjoyed their glass of wine while downstairs the wedding party took some photos and others just hung around. Then they freshened up and headed down to join everyone again at which point the photos were, thankfully, nearly finished.

Everyone then made their way to the hotel, specifically the bar, where they waited before the evening meal, or wedding breakfast as it was apparently called. Iliana had never been to a wedding before, so this was all very new to her. She walked to the hotel hand in hand with Tom while the Bride and Groom got in their fancy car for some time alone before the meal.

"How are you doing?" she asked him as they walked along.

"Ok, a bit nervous about the speech but a beer will help with that."

"I am sure you'll do great," she smiled at him and squeezed his hand.

"Thanks. How are you doing?"

"Really good, it's a lovely occasion. I am so glad I can be here."

"I am glad too," he squeezed her hand back.

"Are the speeches before or after the meal? Oh, and did you check about the first dance?"

"They are after the meal unfortunately, and yes, I checked. I have to dance with the bridesmaid but just the first one. Sorry."

"You don't have to apologise, it's fine. We can make up for any lost time later!"

"That sounds like a good plan to me!"

Chapter 35

When they arrived at the bar Tom had to go and see to his many best man duties, so Iliana looked for Liz, as she did so she bumped into Trish.

"Iliana, so glad I bumped into you. You look lovely."

"Thanks Trish, so do you." She gave her a hug and Trish hugged her for a little bit longer.

"Everything ok?"

"Yes, everything is great, it's a lovely wedding."

"Yes, it is. But that's not what I meant."

"Oh okay, everything is great," she smiled at her. "I am so glad you are ok with it. I was a bit worried."

"No idea why you were worried about it, my lovely girl, I have never seen my boy so happy, or you for that matter, you are glowing." She gave her such a genuine smile that Iliana thought she might cry with happiness. "Or is that the wine that you and Liz had earlier?"

"Did she tell on us?"

"She didn't need to, she can't keep anything from her mom, neither can you for that matter."

"That's true."

"Anyway, best mingle, take care my lovely."

"Thanks, you too."

Iliana spotted Liz and Tony talking with Dan and Robert, so she walked over to them.

They had a few soft drinks then made their way into the function suite for the meal. Iliana was sitting next to Liz, Tony, and Dan thankfully, so they all had a good chat during the meal. Occasionally she would catch Tom's eye at the top table, and he would smile at her.

She smiled all the way through his speech and couldn't help admiring him. After the meal, Tom had to dance with the bridesmaid, Jane's friend Cassie. Iliana wasn't too worried about it though as he kept looking over at her and smiling. When everyone was invited to join them Liz and

One More Try (Book 1)

Tony got up to dance then Dan stood up and walked around the table.

"Do you want to dance Iliana?" He was smiling at her.

"Of course."

She stood up and felt guilty that she was relieved it wasn't Robert who had asked her as she had seen him looking over a few times. Dan was only seventeen but quite tall, he had dark hair and blue eyes, very similar to Liz. He was a handsome young man and looked great in his suit, just like when he took her to Prom. He was chatting to her and asking about college as they danced. She asked him why he hadn't brought anyone, but he just shrugged and said he didn't have a girlfriend just now.

After the first dance everyone took their seats again. The band started to play another song that Iliana didn't recognise, when she looked over at Tom, she saw that he was making his way towards her smiling.

"Hey, that's best man duties done for now. Can I get you a drink?"

"Yes, just whatever soft drinks they have, thanks."

"Ok won't be long."

She wondered where Liz was as she couldn't see her and had images of her and Tony finishing the wine in their room. She smiled to herself, that was fine by her as she didn't want to leave Tom again anyway. He didn't take long with the drinks and when he did, he had a bottle of beer in one hand and a tall glass of something in the other.

"I got you a white wine spritzer," he whispered quietly in her ear as he put the drink on the table. "I figured just the one won't do any harm, is that ok?"

"Yeah, sounds great, never tried one before what is it?"

"Just white wine with soda water but it looks like a soft drink at least, whereas a glass of white wine doesn't."

"Good thinking." She smiled at him as she picked up the glass and took a sip, "It's nice, thanks." She leaned over and gave him a peck on the cheek.

"You're welcome." He pulled up a seat next to her from the other table, "Did I mention how beautiful you look?"

"Yes, I think you did but a girl never tires of hearing it." He laughed.

"It was tough watching my baby brother dance with you."

"How do you think I felt? You were with a lovely young lady?"

"Yeah, you know I would have much rather been dancing with you?"

"Ditto!" she laughed.

"Well, we can have a drink then dance as much as we want now."

"Sounds good. I still have the room key in case you need it, I'll just keep it in my purse."

"Ok, sounds good. Wish we could go there now for a bit of alone time." He paused and gazed into her eyes, she felt like she could melt, he didn't really have to say any more.

"Yeah, that sounds nice, but a bit obvious don't you think?"

"Yeah, and knowing my luck I would be needed for something while we were away, although I don't think it would take very long if you get my meaning!" He kissed her softly on the lips.

"Hmm I think I do." She smiled at him. The band started to play another song, this time a slow one.

"Do you want to dance, at least then I can hold you?"

"Ok then."

They went onto the dance floor along with several other couples and he put his arms around her waist and pulled her close, she put her arms around his neck and leaned into him. She put her head on his shoulder and closed her eyes, it felt so good to be close to him. He had taken his suit jacket off by now and he was warm.

"I love the fact that you wear your necklace all the time," he whispered to her.

"Yeah?" She looked at him. "Of course I do, it's my favourite thing. I only take it off to shower. I will wear it until the day I die, in fact I might even ask to be buried in it," she chuckled.

"Oh no, don't say that. I just got the weirdest sensation, goosebumps all over me when you said that." He shook himself a little bit.

"Oh sorry, I didn't mean to freak you out."

"It's ok, it was just super weird that's all."

He held her tightly again and she put her head back on his shoulder. After the dance they returned to their seats, Tom went to check in with Brad and Jane while Iliana went to the toilet. When she left the toilets, she walked along the narrow corridor back to the function suite and as she turned the corner she bumped into Robert.

"Oh Hi."

"Hi Robert. How are you doing?" He was doing his usual and making it difficult for her to pass without her having to rub against him. *How could he be related to Liz and Tom?*

"Good thanks. Not as good as you it would seem though."

"What's that supposed to mean?"

"Well, it looks like you and Tom are finally an item since you are all over him?"

"Not sure what you mean by 'finally'? But yes, we are together." She ignored the 'all over him' comment.

"I think you know exactly what I mean, you have had your sights on him for quite some time now have you not?"

"No, I haven't. It's just been recently. He is a gentleman; you should try it sometime."

She pushed past him before he could say any more as she didn't want him to think he had rattled her. She wasn't sure it worked but *who cares*? She made her way back to her seat where Tom was waiting, he was talking with Liz and Dan and smiled as she approached. She was smiling back when she realised that she was passing Jane, the lovely Bride, so she stopped to say hello to her.

One More Try (Book 1)

"Jane, what a lovely wedding. Sorry I didn't stop long earlier ..."

"Oh, that's ok don't worry about it, we knew you were desperate to see Tom, he was the same about seeing you, it was quite sweet. I have never seen him like that about anyone. You both look so happy." She had a big genuine smile on her face.

"Oh thanks, we are. But it's your day. You look stunning."

"Thanks. It's been lovely but it just flies by, can't believe there's only a few hours left."

"Yeah, I bet, well I won't keep you, enjoy the rest of it."

"We will, thanks."

Iliana continued to make her way towards Tom.

"Are you ok?" he said as she approached her seat.

"Yeah, I am good thanks."

He nodded and carried on talking to Dan while Liz pushed her seat closer to Iliana.

"Hey, I wondered where you went. I take it you finished the wine?"

"Yeah sorry, hope that's ok?"

"Of course, we didn't leave that much. Makes up for leaving Tony on his own earlier."

"Yeah exactly. What's that you're drinking?" Liz wasn't daft; she spotted Iliana's spritzer right away.

"It's a white wine spritzer, just the one," Iliana giggled. "Maybe if you ask Tom nicely, he'll get you one?"

"Or you could ask him nicely for me? He's more likely to say yes to you?" she fluttered her eyelashes and Iliana laughed.

There was a short break in the music for a buffet, so they all got food and chatted while they ate. Iliana did manage to persuade Tom to get her and Liz a spritzer, so she was happy. When the band started up again Liz dragged Tom up for a dance, so Tony and Iliana joined them on the dance floor. It was great fun, and they all had a good time. Thankfully Iliana didn't bump into Robert again, but she did catch him looking at her a few times. She and Tom had a slow dance for the last song then everyone started to leave. Cabs home were called and there were a few people staying in the hotel including the bride and groom, Liz, Jane's Bridesmaid Cassie and of course Tom.

Once a lot of people had left the staff started to tidy up, so Brad and Jane retired for the night after more congratulations from everyone. Iliana couldn't wait to be alone with Tom, it had been a lovely day but a long one and she wanted some time with just him.

Liz and Tony decided to take the stairs, whilst Tom and Iliana rode the elevator with the others who were staying over. Tom took Iliana's hand as they stood, waiting patiently for the others to leave. She smiled at him and squeezed his hand. The others all got off on the first floor and that just left the two of them. As soon as the elevator doors closed, she turned to face him and kissed him, he returned the kiss with passion and lifted her off the floor. She wrapped her legs around his hips as he lifted her, and he ran his hands up her thigh stopping at her bottom. There was a ping as the doors opened at which point, they stopped kissing and looked outside the elevator, thankfully there was no one there. They giggled and ran out hand in hand, in a rush to get to the room. When they got to the door Iliana fumbled with her purse to get the key out. She could feel Tom undo her zip at the back of her dress and put his hands in to reach around and caress her breasts while gently kissing the back of her neck. She sighed in appreciation as she desperately tried to open the door quicker.

"I've been wanting to do this since I saw you in the church," he whispered.

"Me too. I have been thinking about little else for the last two weeks," she chuckled. She managed to get the door open, and they both burst into the room. She threw her purse on the chair, kicked off her sandals and turned around to Tom right away. He had already loosened his tie, so she started on his shirt buttons. At the same time, he took the thin straps of her dress and gently eased them off her shoulders so that her dress dropped to the floor which just left her in her panties.

"Ok now I am nearly naked, and you are still fully clothed. We have to remedy that now," she giggled and tried to speed up with the buttons, while he pulled his tie over his head. He discarded his shirt and kicked off his shoes as she pulled impatiently at his trouser zip. He stepped out of his trousers and boxers in one swift move before quickly removing his socks. They kissed and moved slowly towards the bed where she lay down on her back. He lay on top of her carefully and kissed her again. He kissed his way down past her breasts and over her stomach then he removed her panties.

"I just need to ..."

"It's ok I have started the pill," she moaned as he went to move away.

He let out a low groan and resumed kissing her before she felt him inside her for the second time. This time it wasn't painful at all, and she relaxed into it, once again enjoying the closeness and passion of being naked with him. She had been thinking about this moment for weeks and now that she was here, she couldn't believe how intense it was, again, even more so than last time. Each time they kissed and every time he moaned, she felt so much closer to him as if they were one body. Suddenly, she felt an amazing sensation take over her body in waves and she let out a loud noise that was somewhere between a wail, and a gasp. She really hadn't heard anything like it before and couldn't believe it had come from her. She was worried about what Tom would think but then she noticed it seemed to be making him move faster and groan more then, not long after, he let out a very loud and final groan, not that dissimilar to hers… except maybe the wailing part! He lay on top of her, they were both breathless, and she put her arms around him. He lifted himself up on his hands and kissed her on the lips then lay next to her on his side, smiling.

"Wow, that's what all the fuss is about then," she giggled.
"I told you it would get better for you."
"Oh yes, not that the last time wasn't special …"
"It's ok I know what you mean don't worry."
"It was amazing," she said lying on her side, still catching her breath, and smiling at him.
"You're amazing."
"We are amazing."
"True." He held her face and kissed her softly on the lips, "Very true."
"People keep telling me how happy you look these days."
"They do? Who?"
"Yes. Your Mum, Jane, Liz."
"Well, that's because it's true."
"I love you, Tom. Sorry if it seems too soon but if I'm honest I wanted to say it two weeks ago."
"Why didn't you then?" He was watching her, taking in her whole face, waiting for her response.
"I didn't want to scare you away."
He smiled. "You wouldn't have scared me away, you couldn't. It's not like we just met. I love you too."
He put his arms around her, and they snuggled together. Iliana thought to herself that this was by far the happiest she had ever felt. It just couldn't get any better than this. Tom put the covers around them and they fell asleep snuggled together, both feeling very content.

Chapter 36

Iliana sank down on the sofa after a leisurely morning at the hotel then lunch out with her Mum and Tom before looking at cars.

"I'm exhausted, it's hard work shopping for cars," she giggled. "Thanks so much for your help today, Tom, I don't think Mum and I would have managed without you."

"You're welcome. Glad I could help. I think you got a good deal so that's the most important thing."

"Are you hungry?"

"No, I am still stuffed after our lovely lunch. What about you?"

"Yeah, not hungry yet." He looked around his kitchen, "Do you want a drink to celebrate buying your new car?"

"Good idea, do you have any wine?"

"Yes, I got some just in case. I shouldn't encourage you of course but just one won't hurt I guess." He gave her his best cheeky smile.

"Have I mentioned how much I love you?"

"Not today you haven't."

"Hmm well I don't want you to get tired of hearing it, but today's been so amazing, I have enjoyed all of it. You were so sweet with my mum; she loves talking about Dad and you were just amazing." He walked over to her and handed her a small glass of white wine then sat down and turned to face her; he had a small bottle of beer in his hand.

"If I ever say or look like I'm tired of hearing it then please just shoot me then and there."

She laughed. "Ok then." She kissed him on the lips. "I spoke to your mum yesterday, she was sweet. I keep forgetting to ask if you spoke to your dad though?"

"Yeah, he cornered me at the wedding."

"Well, what did he say?"

"He had a go at me of course, I knew that's what he would do. But what a time to do it - at his other son's wedding!"

"What did he have a go at you about? You've never been anything but a gentleman to me?"

"He doesn't give a toss about that. He just saw an excuse to have a go at me."

"But what did he say, exactly?"

"It doesn't matter."

"I know it doesn't matter but I'd like to know. What if he has a go at me? Robert did?"

"What? When?"

"At the wedding, on my way back from the toilet I bumped into him."

"What did he say?"

"He said something about me being after you for a long time and that I finally got what I wanted, or something like that I can't remember."

"What the fuck is his problem?"

"There's no point getting wound up about him, that's what he wants. Let's just ignore it. You still haven't told me what your dad said?"

"Ok I will but one last thing? What did you say to Robert?"

"Oh, I just said that you have always been a perfect gentleman and that he should try it sometime, I think, something like that."

He chuckled. "I like that."

"Thanks. So, what did your dad say?"

He sighed. "He just said that I was too old for you."

"Really, that's all?"

"Pretty much."

"Why do I feel like there's something you're not telling me?"

"You're too smart, that's why. Honestly, I don't give a toss what he thinks but I guess part of me worries that other people will think the same."

"Tell me what he said Tom, please? Let's start our relationship the way we mean to carry on, with complete honesty?"

One More Try (Book 1)

"Well, when you put it like that." He looked down at his beer. "He said that people will say I have 'groomed' you …"

"You are fucking joking me?" She slammed her wine glass down and stood up abruptly. "Does he even know what that means?"

"I knew you wouldn't like it."

"No one who cares about you, or me, thinks that. What a monster he is." She clenched her fists.

"I rarely hear you swear Illy, honestly don't let him get to you."

"I am so angry, I only swear when I am angry, I feel like driving over there and having it out with him. He doesn't even know you, not really. He certainly doesn't know me, as the fucker is never around, even I can see that." She stomped her feet. He stood up and put his hands on her shoulders.

"Exactly, so why are you letting it get to you?"

"Are you telling me it didn't get to you too Tom?" She shook her head and continued as he didn't need to answer. "But you're right, I won't say anything. It just makes me so angry; you have always been my friend and such a gentleman, and his precious favourite Robert is the one who creeps me out and tries to rub against me or grope me at every opportunity."

"WHAT?"

"You've seen him, you know what he's like, it was no different last night at the wedding."

"I wish you had told me?"

"Why so that you could start a fight with one of your brothers at your other brother's wedding?"

"Hmm, well when you put it like that."

"I just pushed him out of the way."

"Good. You will let me know if it keeps happening though won't you? it was bad enough before but now it just feels …" he pondered…

"Personal?"

"Exactly."

One More Try (Book 1)

"Well, that's just it though, he is probably only doing it cos he knows I will tell you and that it will bother you. Let's just ignore it."

"I'll ignore that one but if it happens again, I'll have to have a chat with him."

She sat back down and picked up her wine. "Let's not let them ruin our time together."

"You're right," he sat down and joined her, he put his arm around her shoulder and used the other arm to hold his beer. "We have a lot to look forward to this week. It'll be great. What's your plan tomorrow then?"

She let out a deep breath and tried to calm down. "Well, I have studying to do, then collect the car of course. What's yours?"

"I spoke to Mom earlier, there's a bit to do in the morning, but not much so I can leave you to study first thing, then come back and collect you to pick up your car?"

"Sounds great." She gave him a kiss on the lips again. "We'll make this work Tom; I just know we will."

"Yeah. We will." He held her face and kissed her on the lips.

*

Two weeks after Brad and Jane's wedding, Iliana was driving home to see Tom on the Friday, they had spoken on the phone and were both really excited about it. She was finding it tough being away from him for two weeks at a time, but they spoke regularly, and she did have a lot of studying to do so in some ways it worked out okay; she knew he would be too much of a distraction for her if she were at home all the time. He was expecting her at about dinner time, but she had done all the work she needed to do and decided to skip the Friday morning class, saying she wasn't feeling too great. She liked to listen to music on a car journey, especially eighties music as it reminded her of dancing in Liz's room when they were younger. She was hoping to catch up with Liz this weekend as well, which was another reason she wanted to come back early and surprise

One More Try (Book 1)

Tom, so that they could maximise the time they spent together. She might stay until Monday, to get an extra morning of waking up next to him. She smiled to herself as she sang along to the tunes on the radio.

When she arrived at Tom's place, she used her set of keys to open the door. His house was always quite tidy, but it looked like he had made a special effort for this weekend. She went straight through to the bedroom to put her things away so that he didn't notice when he came in. She parked her car around the corner, away from the route he took home so that he wouldn't see it. She then walked the short distance back to his house and went into the kitchen to get something to eat, she still had a little bit of time before he was due back and had suddenly realised she was quite hungry. Taking great care to tidy everything away after her, she climbed into bed. She felt quite nervous about surprising him, but she wasn't exactly sure why. She snuggled under the covers, enjoying the smell of him on them; she hoped she wouldn't fall asleep before he got home. She snuggled for about another fifteen minutes before she heard a car pull into the driveway. She suddenly had a bit of a panic; would she jump out of bed when he came in to change or just lie there and hope he noticed her? She hadn't really thought this through, if she jumped out at him, he might get the fright of his life. She was just going to have to wing it and see what happened. She heard his key in the door as he walked into the house, whistling; it made her smile that he sounded happy. She heard him put his keys down on the kitchen counter then walk straight down the hall. She was lying completely hidden under the covers of his unmade bed. She heard the shower start up, oh dear...she *really* hadn't thought this through, she could be here for ages! She heard the phone ring, then footsteps as he ran down the hall to answer it.

"Hello?" followed by a short pause.

Iliana was suddenly panicking, what if it was another woman phoning him? They had only been going out for six weeks so what if some of his many former girlfriends called him when she wasn't around?

"Oh, hey Liz…"

'Phew!' she breathed out a sigh of relief.

"No, she's not back yet, I think she said around five as she had a class in the morning." Another pause while Liz was talking. "Yeah, I am sure that will be fine, she'd love to see you. I can't hog her for the whole time she is home as she'll want to see her Mum too, don't worry. I'll let her know you called and get her to call you back." Another shorter pause. "Ok, bye."

This was her chance she thought, to grab him before he went back into the shower. She heard his footsteps falter at the bedroom and, despite this not being quite the romantic gesture she had concocted in her mind, and because if she stayed under the covers much longer, she would soon become an unattractive sweaty mess, she threw the covers back and shouted, "Surprise!"

He was wet and was wearing a towel around his middle. He jumped as she threw back the covers, a huge grin quickly appearing on his face.

"Hey, I was just looking to see if your things were here cos I thought I saw your keys on the sofa when I answered the phone."

"Oh no! I forgot about my keys, I put everything else away, including parking around the corner and then forgot about my keys!" she put the palm of her hand against her forehead.

He smiled and walked towards her.

"It doesn't matter, you're here," he reached out to hold her and his towel fell to the floor. They kissed and fell onto the bed, rolling around in a messy heap.

"You're still wet!" she giggled.

"I know, sorry, does it bother you?"

"Not really, you're just slippery that's all," she kissed him again then rolled on top of him.

"I could get used to surprises like this," he said in between kisses.

"I haven't finished the surprise yet, just getting started."

Chapter 37

They lay in bed after their love making, both on their sides looking at each other.

"I've missed you," she whispered, giving him a gentle kiss on the lips.

"Me too."

"I'm hopeful that I can move to another college but it's not looking like I will be able to do it this academic year. So, I will finish at the end of June then I can start a new college closer by in September."

"That's good, in the meantime you can keep surprising me like that anytime." He chuckled, and she giggled along with him. They snuggled in bed for a bit, relaxing and chatting even though they had spoken on the phone almost every day. They both showered – Tom for the second time! – before getting dressed.

"Did you have any lunch?"

"Yeah, I grabbed something when I got back, I knew I would need the energy!"

He smiled at her remark.

"Did you eat?"

"Yeah, Mom made extra for me, that's what she does most of the time." He put the kettle on, "Fancy eating out tonight?"

"Yeah, that would be good, I brought a dress with me just in case."

"Oh, I nearly forgot, did you hear me on the phone to Liz?"

"Yeah, I did, I should give her a call."

"She just wanted to know if you could catch up with her at some point, something about Vicky and Becca but I didn't catch it all. I only answered the phone cos I thought it was you, then I was distracted by your keys!"

She smiled at the thought of him running down the hall thinking she was phoning him before she left, when she was sweating under his covers waiting for him.

One More Try (Book 1)

"Ok I'll phone her now." She picked up the phone and arranged to meet up with Liz, Vicky and Becca on Saturday for lunch.

Iliana changed before they went out for dinner while Tom waited in the living room. She put on a dress as she wanted to look nice; she didn't own that many dresses, but she liked wearing them. The dress was plain but quite fitted, it had short sleeves and a low neckline, so it showed off her necklace nicely and a little bit of cleavage, which is why she had brought it. She wore plain black shoes with a bit of a heel and a matching clutch bag. When she entered the living room area Tom stood up.

"Wow!" he paused for a second. "You look amazing in that."

"This old thing?" she smiled at him.

"You really do, should I have put something more formal on? The restaurant isn't fancy, but I feel like a scruff now," he looked down at his dark blue t-shirt and jeans.

"You look great to me, I just fancied wearing a dress that's all as I live in jeans as a student."

"Ok then, if you're sure." He reached over and gave her a kiss. "Let's go."

They went to Patty's restaurant, where they had taken Mary the day they bought Iliana's car, next to Benny's Pool Hall. As they got out of the car, they heard a female voice call Tom's name. Iliana walked around the car and saw Sarah walking towards them, she was smiling until she saw Iliana. She looked as stunning as ever, even in boots, jeans, and a fitted t-shirt; the t-shirt was quite low cut and showed off her lovely figure.

"Hi Sarah," Tom said.

"Well hello stranger." She was back to smiling now that she was standing in front of Tom.

He reached out his hand for Iliana, so she walked closer to him and took it; she smiled at Sarah to let her know she was not intimidated.

"Where have you been hiding then?"

"I've not been hiding anywhere. This is Iliana."

"Yes, I remember you," Sarah looked at her directly now, the smile changed to a smirk, as if she knew something Iliana didn't. She really didn't like this woman.

"Hi Sarah."

"Hi," Sarah glanced at Tom and Iliana's hands. "Well good luck with this one Iliana," Sarah nodded at Tom and started to walk towards the restaurant. "You'll need it."

"Thanks, but I don't think I will," Sarah shrugged off her comment. Tom gave her a half smile.

Sarah was shown to her table first, and thankfully their table was nowhere near, so they sat down and looked through the menu after the waiter took their drinks orders. Iliana wondered if she should just pretend that the exchange with Sarah didn't bother her and leave it, but she could see Tom occasionally peek at her over his menu.

"Is anything bothering you?" he eventually spoke up.

"No." She carried on looking at her menu holding it up so that he couldn't see her face.

"Really? Are you forgetting how long I have known you?"

Busted!

"Hmm, maybe," she couldn't help but smile at that, she knew she hadn't fooled him.

"Talk to me Illy? You said we should be honest remember?"

She lowered her menu to look at him. "Okay. I guess I should expect to bump into your ex-girlfriends since there are so many…" she paused as that wasn't quite how she meant to put it, he didn't react, so she continued… "But I wasn't prepared for her to wish me 'good luck' that's all."

"I know, I'm sorry. I can't control that I'm afraid."

"I know that you have a reputation so I should have expected it really, I just didn't. I feel stupid."

"You're not stupid. I have a reputation? Says who?"

"Just people."

"Ok, I'll rephrase that. Did someone say something to you?"
"Yes."
"Who?"
"Billy."
"Billy Garcia? The guy who wants you for himself?"
"No, he doesn't he is with Becca now. He was just being a friend."
"Yeah right. When was this?"
"Just before Prom. He just didn't want me to get hurt."
"We weren't together then?"
"I know, he is my friend, so he guessed that I liked you that's all."
"Ok." He just nodded and looked at his menu again.
She noticed the waiter was coming back over to take their order, so she did the same before they both ordered. The waiter took the menus away after that, so she didn't have anything to hide behind. "There isn't a lot I can do about what I have done in the past, 'my reputation' as you call it, I'm afraid. Come to think of it if I were just your friend, I would probably warn you against someone like me," he gave a half smile. "I also can't make any guarantees, but I can promise you one thing," she watched him and waited, "I will always be honest with you and tell you how things are. The way I feel right now nothing is going to change, in fact things are only getting stronger." She couldn't help but smile at him, she reached out her hand across the table and he took it. "But if that changes, I will tell you." He paused again, "Do you trust me?"
"Yes, I do." She didn't hesitate for a second. He smiled.
"Good. I am a lot older ..."
"So you keep saying ..."
"Well, it's true. Since I am a lot older, then I have more baggage and yes you might meet some of them in the street or parking lot sometimes," she burst out laughing at that.
"I like the fact you are referring to Sarah as baggage." He smiled.

"But I will also say that, because I am older, I am also clearer on what makes me happy. If anything, it should be me that's worried, a lot can change between ages eighteen and twenty-two. You might get fed up with me by the time you finish college for all I know, or before, and you'll run off with a younger man and I'll be left with only my baggage on my thirtieth birthday." He frowned.

"Oh Tom," she squeezed his hand. "That's just not going to happen."

"You can't guarantee it though, that's the point I'm trying to make. There are no guarantees in life."

"True. Point taken." She took a sip of her soft drink. "I guess I am just saying the same as you, the way I feel just now I don't see anything changing for me."

"Good. But if it does?"

"If it does then I will tell you."

"Great. Then we agree, let's not let Sarah ruin our night then."

"I'll drink to that." Iliana raised her glass of soda and Tom smiled then raised his in return.

Their food arrived and they enjoyed the rest of their meal. After dinner, when they reached the car, she leaned on the car boot whilst Tom was trying to find his keys in his jeans pocket. She was just looking down at the ground smiling to herself. When she looked up, he was watching her and smiling, with the keys in his hand. He leaned over and kissed her on the lips. He gently took a strand of her long hair away from her face as it had blown into her mouth after they kissed. Then he kissed her again, for longer. She touched his face gently as he pulled away and looked into his eyes, she really couldn't imagine anything changing the way she felt at this time.

"Let's get home," he said with another smile.

"Sounds good."

As Tom made his way to the driver's side of the car, Iliana noticed Sarah and her female friend on their way to her car; for some reason Iliana had assumed she was meeting

One More Try (Book 1)

a guy. Iliana hadn't even seen her go past or come out, so she must have been behind them. Sarah was watching them; she wasn't smiling this time. Iliana gave her the biggest smile she could manage then turned around and got in the passenger side of the car. She felt very smug for some reason, was it wrong that she was so happy at Sarah seeing their tender moment?

*

The next day Tom had some work to do, and Iliana was meeting Liz, Vicky, and Becca for lunch in town. They went to a different restaurant and Iliana wore jeans and a fitted t-shirt and, since she had a car, picked her friends up. Once they had ordered they chatted about everything that they had been up to in the last few weeks. They were all studying at different colleges, so chatted about that quite a bit. Becca was now dating Billy, so she talked about him a lot; Iliana was happy for them as they were well suited and seemed great together. Vicky was single and Liz was doing her usual 'shopping around' she called it, she still saw Tony every now and then, but they weren't exclusive.

"So enough about us, tell us about Tom?" Vicky said looking at Iliana.

"What do you mean?"

"Well, what's he like?"

"Eww do you mean in bed Vick? I don't want to hear that about my brother!" Liz said, horrified.

"Ah yes, sorry! I did mean that, but I didn't think sorry!"

"I'll go to the toilet," Liz gave a mock scowl then left the table.

"Well?" Vicky said once Liz had gone.

"Em ... it feels a bit strange talking about him like that, but he is amazing. Let's leave it there."

"Oh wow," she gushed. "All that experience I guess, he would be."

"Vicky! Stop that," Becca spoke up.

"Just saying. Those extra eight years ..."

"Okay, okay enough."

At this point Liz was heading back to the table, "Ok fine, so let's keep the talk away from sex, what's he like as a boyfriend then?"

"Why all the questions?"

"I was the same when Becca started dating Billy so don't worry. I gave up on Liz as there's too many."

"Hey!" Liz interrupted.

"Sorry hon, but you know what I mean," she shrugged.

"Yeah, I do, but still…" Liz giggled.

"Tom is a very handsome guy, lots of women would love to be in your position I am sure, I am just curious. Humour me?"

"Well but to me he isn't just a handsome guy," Iliana paused as they were hanging on her every word, "he is caring, sensitive and honest." She looked down at her glass. "I love him, and he loves me."

"You told him you love him already?" Becca spoke up again.

"Yes, because I do."

"And he said it back?"

"Yes, he did."

"Well, if you had seen them a few weeks ago at Brad's wedding you wouldn't be surprised by that," Liz smiled at her.

"Really? "Vicky swooned.

"Yes, they were very cosy. It was lovely to see them both so happy."

"Aw, that's so sweet."

Now they were all smiling at her.

"We are so happy for you."

They enjoyed a nice lunch and carried on talking about what they had been up to; guys, school and who was up to what since they had left. After their lunch, Iliana dropped her friends off and thought about going to see her Mum, she couldn't remember if she was working or not so decided to just head back to Tom's place since there was more chance of her Mum being free on Sunday. She entered the house

One More Try (Book 1)

and shouted hello, and he called back from the kitchen. When she walked in, he was in only his boxers and was making a coffee, his hair was wet so he must have been just out of the shower.

"Hey, good lunch?"

"Yeah, it was good to see them all."

"How was work this morning?"

"Yeah good, Mom was on good form, we had lunch and caught up. Not much else to report really. What were the girls saying?"

"Oh, this and that, just chat. We talked about college, boyfriends, you know the usual stuff?"

"You talk about your boyfriends? What kind of things?"

"Well just how things are going, you know?"

"No, I don't. Do you talk about details?"

"Yeah sometimes. Vicky did ask me what you were like in bed?"

"What?" He nearly spat out his coffee. "You talk about details like that?"

"Well yeah, it did feel a bit strange, Liz had to go to the bathroom."

"I'm not surprised." He sipped his coffee and watched her, "So, what did you say?"

"I didn't go into detail, I just said you were amazing."

He chuckled and put his coffee down.

"Didn't we establish that you were amazing too and in fact 'we' are amazing together?"

"Oh yeah, so we did," she giggled.

"Can't believe you talk about that kind of detail," he was shaking his head.

"Liz used to tell me all sorts of things that would make your hair curl."

"Yeah, really don't need to hear that about my sister," he put his hands over his ears.

"Ah yes sorry," she giggled again. "I actually think Vicky has a bit of a crush on you."

"I don't know her, sorry."

"She's pretty, you would probably remember her if you saw her. It doesn't matter, I told them that I love you though."

"Yeah?"

"Yeah. They just see you as this handsome stranger, but you are so much more than that to me."

"I'm glad." He leaned over and gave her a kiss, "What do you want to do tonight then?"

"I am happy to do anything. You do know if you wanted to go out with the guys one weekend I am here, that would be okay?"

"Yeah, I know that. I want to spend time with you when you're here though. The guys are happy catching up every now and again it doesn't have to be every week or even every two weeks really. Don't worry about that."

"Okay. I am happy chilling out on the sofa with you and watching TV. Maybe even a small glass of wine."

"Hmm, that sounds like a good plan to me." He put his arms around her.

One More Try (Book 1)

Chapter 38

One weekend in winter, the quiet season for the chalet business, Tom suggested that he drive to see Iliana on a Friday, and they stay in a hotel for a few nights. Iliana was really excited about this because as much as she loved driving, it would mean they would be able to be together for the maximum amount of time.

They agreed he would drive through early and wait for her at lunchtime on the Friday in the reception area of the halls of residence. She had classes in the morning and couldn't wait for them to finish, her bag was all packed and ready to go. She had told her roommate Clare about Tom's visit; she seemed nice and was happy to listen to Iliana talking about him quite a lot. She was a pretty girl, the same age as Iliana, with short blonde hair and blue eyes.

When the time came Iliana changed into a denim skirt and her favourite top, they were the ones she was wearing when she and Tom got together so putting them on always made her smile. She was skipping her way down the corridor and before she turned the corner to enter the reception area, she heard lots of giggling and chatting, she stopped when she heard her name.

"No wonder Iliana goes home so often if that's what's waiting for her?" they all giggled.

"I would be going home every weekend without fail if it were me." More giggling.

"He is sooooo dreamy, look at those muscles."

"I wouldn't have come here in the first place if I had *that* at home."

"No offence ..." Iliana waited as she knew when people said that it normally meant something offensive would follow, she braced herself but deep down she knew what was coming. "... but what is he doing with *her*? She's nice and all but a bit plain for someone like that." More giggling. She couldn't put it off any longer, she lifted her head high and walked around the corner, she thought she recognised some of the voices but couldn't be sure. As she passed the group of girls, she glanced over to see who was there, she noticed Clare right away as she looked over and caught her eye very briefly. Iliana could see Tom just ahead, not that far from where the girls were standing, he smiled as soon as he saw her. He was wearing a plain dark t-shirt and jeans and did look particularly handsome.

"Hi," Clare said to her as she walked past.
"Hi Clare. See you Monday."
"Yeah, see you, have a good weekend."
"Oh, I will, thanks. You too," she smiled as she walked away, trying to convey a confidence that wasn't there. She could feel them watching her as she approached Tom. Her heart melted as he had such a huge smile on his face and didn't take his eyes off her as she walked towards him.

"Hey, you look lovely," he put his arm out to take her backpack from her then put his other arm around her shoulder and gave her kiss on the lips.

"Thanks." They walked out of the door together still with Tom's arm around her.

"Shall we drop off your bag first then get some lunch?"
"Yeah, that sounds nice. I have done a bit of research on some places nearby that are quite good."
"Great." He smiled at her and kissed her again, "It's great to see you Illy."
"Yeah, you too, I missed you."
"Yeah, me too."
"Were you waiting long?"
"No just five minutes or so, not long."
"Did anyone say anything to you?"
"Yeah, a girl asked me if she could help and when I said I was waiting for my girlfriend she asked me who that was, so I told her. I explained you knew I was waiting though and then she went away."
"What did she look like?"
"Dark hair, quite small, why?"
"Just wondered that's all, not sure I know her."

He shrugged.

They reached the hotel, and Tom showed her where their room was as he had already checked in. They went inside the room and Tom handed her backpack to her with a smile. She returned the smile and put her things away quickly including her bathroom things. When she came out, he was sitting on the very big double bed looking out of the window.

"There's a nice big bath?" she giggled.

"Yeah, I saw that, we'll need to give it a try." He raised his eyebrows. She walked over to him, and he stood up. She reached up to hold him and he kissed her.

"Sorry I should have done that as soon as I saw you," she whispered as she snuggled into him.

"That's okay, it was quite crowded, and I wouldn't want to embarrass you in front of your student friends," he laughed but she didn't.

"You couldn't do that, don't worry about that."

"What do you mean, are you ok? Did I say something to offend you?"

"No, you didn't, not at all. Sorry, it's just ..."

"It's just what?" He had sat down on the end of the bed again and patted the area next to him. She sat down.

"I overheard some girls talking about us when I was coming down the corridor."

"Really? What were they saying?"

"Just that you were really handsome ..." He frowned as she spoke; he was quite modest. "And what were you doing with me? 'Nice but plain' I think they said."

"Oh Illy, you are worth more than a hundred of them."

"How do you know; you don't know them?"

"I know their kind. They are not worth bothering about."

"One of them was my roommate, I didn't know the others."

"Ah, well that's not nice but at least you can maybe talk to her. But why do you care?"

"It's what everyone must think I guess."

One More Try (Book 1)

"No, it's not, the people that know you do not think like that. Please tell me you won't let them get to you. It's their problem if they don't know you like I do, you are the most beautiful woman I know, in fact you're the most beautiful person I know!"

"Oh Tom, you always did know what to say to cheer me up."

"It's true," he reached out his hand to her and she took it.

"Please don't let those Barbie dolls ruin our weekend together?"

"I won't, sorry."

"You don't need to be sorry; they are the ones who should be. Now let's get some lunch, I am famished then we can plan our weekend, is there anything good on at the movies? I thought we could sit in the back row and kiss our way through a movie for a change?"

She giggled and gave him another kiss.

"You're the best, you know that?"

"Yes, but I never tire of hearing it."

They had an amazing weekend together; it was different to her weekends home because Tom didn't have to work, and Iliana didn't have to visit anyone else or drive for a change. They spent so much quality time together, eating, watching a movie, shopping, trying out the big bathtub together and generally having an amazing time. On their last night, Iliana awoke early in the morning, around 3am, she reached out to the other side of the bed for Tom and saw him lying on his side leaning on his elbow with his hand behind his head, he was awake and watching her.

"Hey, are you ok?"

"Yeah, I am good." He smiled at her and snuggled in, "Promise me you won't change?"

"What do you mean? There are no guarantees in life as you know?"

He grinned and nodded in recognition.

One More Try (Book 1)

"True, that's true." He seemed to think for a bit, "Just promise me you will always be you, never try and be anyone else."

She sat up.

"Well of course I will, where is this coming from?"

"Nowhere, I just wanted to say it, that's all. I just wish you knew how special you are, just as you are."

"Well, I hate to use a really mature expression here, but it takes one to know one."

He smiled at her, and she just snuggled up to him and held him tight.

"I love you, Tom; I think I always have."

"I love you too."

*

They checked out on Monday morning and Tom set off for his long drive home. He walked her to the halls of residence first and they had a long kiss goodbye outside. She couldn't bear the thought of not being with him for the next two weeks again, but she tried not to dwell on it after such an amazing weekend together. Iliana went straight up to her room, put her backpack away then went to her first class. When she returned to her room later that day, her roommate Clare was already back.

"Hey," Clare said to her as she came in the door.

"Hi."

"Good weekend?"

"Really good thanks, you?"

"Yeah, not bad, quite quiet, went for a few drinks with the girls Saturday, did some washing, you know exciting stuff." Clare smiled at her. Iliana struggled to play along knowing what she had heard on Friday. "Is everything ok Iliana? Did something happen with your boyfriend?"

Iliana laughed.

"No, everything was great, as I said," she paused as Clare was watching her, she looked quite genuinely concerned. "I overheard some of you talking about us on Friday on my way out to meet Tom."

"Oh," Clare frowned. "I'm sorry, some of what they were saying wasn't nice, I know that and I'm sorry. I should have stuck up for you."

"Really?"

"Yes, I only said that it's no wonder you go home as often as you do. That's all."

"Thanks. But don't worry, I wouldn't expect you to say anything, we haven't really known each other that long."

"I should have, I have known you long enough to know that you are a very genuine person and that you would probably do the same, so I should have said something. I'm sorry."

"Apology accepted, let's forget about it then," Iliana smiled at her.

"Thanks. What's your plans tonight?"

"No plans yet, you?"

"Yeah nothing, fancy doing something?"

"That would be good. How about a walk then a drink in the bar?"

"Sounds like a good plan to me, what else is there to do on a Monday after all?"

One More Try (Book 1)

Chapter 39

Iliana was sitting on the bench in her mum's garden, thinking. She had just completed her teacher training, and she smiled to herself as she looked back over the last four years of dating Tom. She had moved college after a year so was closer but still had to travel. She came home for holidays, worked for Trish, and managed to get a placement at the local school in her third year. Tom proposed to her on her twenty second birthday and then they talked about kids on his thirtieth birthday a few months later. He had raised the subject with her when they were relaxing on the sofa after his birthday celebrations. She recalled the conversation; he was sitting next to her sipping a beer.

"Have you given any thought to when you want to get married then?" he asked.

"Not really, I have applied for a temporary job at the school to cover someone on maternity leave, so after that definitely." She watched him, "What's your thoughts?"

"Well, I guess there's no rush ..." He seemed to pause, deep in thought, "Unless ..."

She turned to look at him.

"Unless what? Are you ok?"

"Yes, of course. It's just that, we haven't really talked about kids yet have we? Do you want to have them and if so, do you want to wait or have them quite soon?"

"That's true we haven't talked about it," she paused, wary of what to say next in case he ran for the hills. "I would definitely like to have kids, I know you weren't keen though, although that was some time ago, how do you feel now?"

"When did I say I wasn't keen?"

"It was ages ago, one time when you were giving me a lift home, I think I was maybe sixteen."

"Ah right, that was a while ago." He never said anymore, so she just gazed at him and waited, she didn't want to prompt him in any way. "That was before I knew what it was like to love someone, to really love someone, totally, utterly and completely," he smiled at her.

"Oh Tom, that's so special," she leaned forward and gave him a kiss.

"Also, I see what Brad has with his kids and I know that I would like that, I think you would make a great Mom too. I would rather we were married before we had kids, but I guess it doesn't really matter, it's just I know my parents weren't married when they had me."

"I'm okay with that too."

"Although I don't want to wait too long because I'm not getting any younger and I want to be able to run around and play with our kids."

"Oh, come on Tom you're not that old?" she chuckled.

"I know but still ..."

"You are a fit, healthy young man. In fact, you're my fit, healthy young man." She gave him a hug and he smiled at her. "I could stop taking the pill and then we take it from there, these things can take some time so it would be a shame to leave it until we are ready and then it takes years after that?"

"Okay that sounds good. We had better get practising then."

She smiled and shook herself out of the memory, trying to focus on what she should be doing now. She couldn't wait to see him to tell him the news. She was supposed to be preparing to start tidying up the garden, including cutting back the large rose bushes that were just getting too big for the small garden. She had put her old clothes on but instead of getting started, she had made a cup of tea and sat sipping it when she heard a car pull into the driveway. It was quite early for Tom but maybe he got finished quicker than he thought he would. She stood up and walked towards the gate.

"James?"

"Hi."

"This is a surprise, is everything ok?"

"Yes, everything's fine, can I come in?"

She hesitated; she had managed to put his comments about Tom to the back of her mind most of the time. But why was he here?

"Of course, come in," she opened the large iron gate, and he walked in, looking around. "So, what can I do for you then, I'd love to stop and chat, but I have a bit to do?"

He looked over at the bench.

"You have a cup of tea there?"

"Yes, just putting off starting to be honest." She gave a nervous laugh, "I'm just waiting for Tom as I need to talk to him first."

"Really?"

"Really. So, what can I do for you?" She was not about to confide in this man at all. Truth be told he was starting to make her a little bit nervous.

"Well, I just came here to warn you that's all."

"Warn me about what?"

"About Tom."

"What about Tom? Did something happen? Is he hurt?"

"No. Not like that. Come on you don't think he's going to keep this up for long, do you? Playing happy families and pretending to want to get married to you and have a family?"

"What are you talking about? We are getting married; it's going to happen, and we *will* have a family."

"Yeah right."

"You're one to talk anyway."

"What does that mean?"

"Well, I think you forget that I have known your family for a long time and if anyone is 'playing happy families' it's you!"

"How fucking dare you!"

"No, James. How fucking dare *you* talk to me about your eldest son that way! Don't you think you have done enough to him?"

"He's not my son, surely even you have worked that out by now?"

She stopped short.

"What?"

"He's not my son."

She just looked at him, momentarily speechless.

"Does he know?"

"No of course not."

"Does anyone know?"

"Robert does."

"How?"

"I told him one day to make him feel better when he was crushed at seeing you two together. He had a big thing for you, Brad and Dan liked you too I think but they soon got over it. Robert though, he had it bad for such a long time, still does as far as I know. Why couldn't you go for him and make him happy? No, you had to go for Tom and now he'll break your heart just like you broke Robert's!"

She was starting to feel quite queasy now, this was all too much.

"I think you had best go now James. You're starting to make me uncomfortable." She went to move away from him, but he grabbed her arm, tight, it hurt a lot.

"Let me go!" she shouted, struggling against him. "That hurts!"

"No, maybe if I get a piece of you then that will put Tom in his place."

"LET ME GO!" The events that happened next, happened so fast that she was barely aware of them. She pulled her arm hard in an attempt to get away from him then saw someone rushing towards her shouting, she fell over as there was a scuffle and lay on the ground for a few seconds before she managed to lift her head and look up to see Tom punching his dad, or who he thought was his dad, full on in the face.

"What the fuck are you doing?" Tom shouted, his face was bright red. Then he turned towards Iliana.

"Illy? Are you ok?" his voice was wobbling; he seemed so shaken.

One More Try (Book 1)

"I'm ok, it's fine." She tried to stand up, but she stumbled, Tom ran to her and held her by her waist to help her up. James was trying to stand up now and he caught her eye as she stood up. Tom noticed her watching James and looked in his direction, so he ran out of the gate. They heard the car start up, pull out of the driveway, and speed away. She started to sob.

"Illy, it's ok. I'm here, it's ok." He held her tight; his voice still wavering.

"You're early? I am so glad you are early!"

"Yeah, I know, I found a pregnancy test in the trash, so I wanted to get here early and talk to you about it."

"Oh really? Oops I didn't think of that. There goes the surprise!"

"I'm glad you didn't think of it," he shuddered, so she hugged him again.

"Are you ok about it?"

"Are you kidding me? It's the best news ever? Are you?"

"Yes, I am so excited Tom. I didn't think it would happen this soon but it's amazing. I was just waiting with a cup of tea to tell you; I didn't plan on doing anything in the garden."

She frowned, still trying to understand everything that happened.

"What happened?"

"We need to go and speak to your Mum Tom, right now."

"Well yeah of course we do, Dad just attacked you! But why?"

"It's better if we speak to your Mum first, I think."

They made their way to Tom's car; Tom helped her in then went around to the driver side and got in. They fastened their seatbelts, and he just glanced at her, he seemed confused but how could she tell him? In some ways he may feel relieved, but she knew it would be a shock and that the only person that should tell him was his Mum.

One More Try (Book 1)

The drive didn't take that long, Iliana spent the time crying and trying to control her emotions and Tom just pondered, he stopped asking her what happened. One more try came on the radio and Iliana smiled, he gave her a half smile.

"Our song."

"Yes, funny it's playing now, do you think this is our 'one more try'?"

"Maybe." He shrugged, "I have no idea what is going on, so I'll tell you in a bit."

They pulled into his parent's driveway and noticed a few other cars there. Brad, Liz, and Robert.

"Looks like a family reunion," Tom said with more than a hint of sarcasm.

"Oh no."

"It's fine, there's no secrets in this family so let's do it. I am not waiting." He looked angry, not angry, frustrated she thought, and certainly not with her. She gave him a hug.

"You have to trust me; do you trust me?"

"Yes, I do, implicitly."

"Good, let's go."

They entered the house together and walked into the main living area. Trish, Brad, Liz, and Robert were all sitting at the large dining table in the kitchen area chatting, so they walked over to them. Tom's Mum stood up.

"Tom. What's wrong?"

"Sit down Mom, we need to talk, all of us."

"Why what's happened?"

"Where's Dad?"

"I don't know he popped out to run an errand earlier, why?"

"'An errand'? Really?"

"What's going on?"

Tom looked at Iliana.

"Trish, I am so sorry to do this, but James paid me a visit earlier today when I was on my own at my Mum's." She

One More Try (Book 1)

stopped and looked at Tom who nodded encouragement for her to carry on, "Is there anything you want to tell us?"

Trish clasped her hands in front of her and looked around the table. Iliana felt so terrible, Trish knew exactly what she was referring to. Trish put her head down for a moment, the room was completely silent.

"Mom?" Tom 's voice wobbled; this was just heartbreaking.

"I am so sorry Tom, I really am, this ..." at that moment James walked through the front door and into the living area. Tom stood up and glared at him. James had the start of a black eye where Tom had punched him.

"What happened?" Trish said.

"He attacked Iliana, that's what happened so I punched him. Now someone tell me what the fuck is going on?"

Iliana stood up and put her arm around him.

"What?" Trish was shocked.

"It's time to tell them Trish," James said, she sobbed and put her head in her hands.

"I am sorry Tom, I really am." She glanced at him, but he didn't react, "This really isn't how I wanted to tell you, or if I wanted to tell you at all." She took a deep breath, the room was completely silent, "James is not your father, despite what it says on your birth certificate. I was in a relationship ..."

"HA! Is that what you called it?" James interrupted, and she glared at him.

"Yes, a relationship with a man who was in the army, he got stationed somewhere in England, I can't recall where, and I never heard from him again. I found out I was pregnant with you after he left. I'm sorry son, I just didn't think there was any need to tell you."

"Well, there you go, that explains a lot! Why you always picked on me, called me a waster, hit me."

"WHAT? He hit you?" his mother sobbed again; she looked horrified.

"Yes, once or twice, when I was smaller, but it stopped when I got to be the same size, then bigger than him, you fucking coward."

"James how could you?" Trish sobbed.

"I always thought it was just cos I was the eldest and you were trying to toughen me up."

Liz stood up and went over to her mother, she put her arm around her.

"How does that explain why you attacked Iliana?" Liz said, clearly upset herself.

James didn't say any more.

"He said he came to warn me about Tom, said that he wasn't going to play 'happy families' for long and that he would eventually get bored and leave me."

Everyone looked at James.

"Surely you don't all believe this act? He's a waster, just like his father."

Tom jumped up quickly and lunged at James; his brothers Brad and Robert stood up and ran towards him.

"I can't be the only one that doesn't believe it?" James looked around the room, but no one backed him up, not even Robert.

Brad and Robert managed to just get to Tom before he grabbed a hold of James, but they struggled to hold him back.

"Tom, stop, it won't help, it won't. Stop," Brad whispered.

"She's pregnant, he attacked a pregnant woman, look at the marks on her arms for fuck's sake," he was struggling so hard.

It broke Iliana's heart to see him like this. Everyone looked at her. She rolled up her sleeve to show the mark James had left when he'd grabbed her arm. It was all the way around her wrist and starting to bruise already. Liz gasped.

"Dad? Why would you do such a thing?"

Trish sobbed again, "Get out! I am done with you; this is the last straw! I should have done this a long time ago; I cannot believe you hit him and now you attack his pregnant girlfriend."

"I didn't know she was pregnant ..."

"Like that makes it ok?" "GET OUT!"

He turned around and left. Brad and Robert let go of Tom. Everyone just looked around the room. Iliana had no idea what to say, she suddenly felt very ill and ran off to the downstairs bathroom to vomit.

Chapter 40

Iliana splashed some water on her face in the bathroom and looked in the mirror, she looked quite pale and the mark on her wrist was getting darker by the minute it seemed. She sat down in the small chair and closed her eyes, trying to compose herself. Even Robert had seemed genuinely shocked at what had happened. When she returned everyone turned around to look at her.

"Are you ok Illy?" Tom rushed towards her and put his arm around her.

"Yes, I'm fine, thanks."

"I'll get you a glass of water," Trish said as she approached the large table where everyone was gathered again.

"Thanks." She sat down and looked around, Tom sat next to her and still had a worried look on his face.

"I didn't even get a chance to congratulate you," Trish said with a soft smile as she handed her the water.

Iliana smiled back at her, "That's okay, there was a lot going on."

"I'm really happy for you both." She looked at Tom who wasn't making eye contact. "Tom," she reached out and put a hand on his shoulder, "I am so sorry, son, I really am."

He looked at her, his face still impassive.

"I wish you had told me he hit you. I ... "

"I didn't want to cause any more bother between you, I figured I had done enough of that ..."

"Oh son, it was never you and I should have known. I should have thrown him out a long time ago ...," She looked away for a moment, pondering, "After I found out about all the other women. He just made me believe that I needed him I suppose ..."

"Oh Mom," Liz stood up and walked over to her mother. She reached out her arms and held her while she wept quietly. "What other women?"

One More Try (Book 1)

"It doesn't matter now. I just ... deep down I thought there was still some good in him ..."

Tom reached out his hand for Iliana who was on his other side. She took his hand and gave him a reassuring smile.

"Are you ok Tom?" He nodded. She stood up and put her arms around his broad shoulders. He leaned into her so that his head was next to her tummy, where their unborn child was growing. He closed his eyes and held her round her hips. No one spoke for quite a while. Liz led Trish over to her seat and helped her sit down.

"I just popped in for a cup of coffee!" Brad said with a frown. Everyone smiled at this, and it lightened the mood ever so slightly, enough for them all to relax a bit.

"Do you know what son that's a good idea, I'll put on the kettle, and we can all have a cup of coffee?"

"Ok Mom but I'll do it," Liz said standing up, "I know what everyone likes. Does everyone want coffee? Tea for you Iliana?"

"Yes please," they all replied at once. Liz glanced at Tom, and he nodded, still holding onto Iliana. He looked up at her and smiled so she let go of him and sat down again, suddenly wary that she was a bit queasy again.

"You look pale again Iliana do you want me to make you something?" Liz frowned as she spoke.

"I'm fine, just needed a seat."

"I'll make you some toast, that will help."

"Yes, that would be great. Thanks."

"Sure, no problem," Liz busied herself making the tea, coffee, and toast.

"Do you want us to stay here tonight, Mom?" Tom said.

"No, it's ok son, don't worry ..."

"I'll stay," Robert interrupted, looking directly at Tom.

"Are you sure?" Tom replied.

"Yes, you take Iliana home and make sure she is ok. I can stay here and help Mom."

One More Try (Book 1)

Iliana was quite shocked by this caring gesture; she had never seen this side of him before.

"Thanks Robert, that would be great."

If Tom was as shocked, he didn't show it.

"So do you know when you are due then?" Liz piped up, clearly trying to focus on nicer things.

"I think it will be April or May but I'm not sure, I haven't even been to the doctor yet, obviously it's early so we wouldn't normally tell quite as many people at this stage." She glanced around the table and gave a small smile, "I hadn't even told Tom properly yet, he found out by mistake." She took his hand.

"Oh, honey I am so sorry."

"It's not your fault Mom don't worry, let's just move on," Tom spoke in a soft voice but was firm.

"We won't say anything to anyone else so don't worry," Liz smiled at her as did the others.

"Thanks. Obviously, you can tell Jane, Brad."

Brad nodded.

They finished their tea and coffee and talked quietly about day-to-day things.

"OK I think we'll head off now then. We can get together again soon and chat if you want, or we can just put this all behind us. Mom will need support though so we can talk about that." They all agreed. "I'll be over at the usual time tomorrow, Mom. We can see what needs to be done and I will change the lock."

"Ok Tom, thanks."

As they were walking down the driveway towards Tom's car, they heard a male voice shout Tom's name so turned back to see who it was. Robert was standing there looking at them both.

"Can I talk to you both quickly before you go?"

Iliana looked at Tom who shrugged.

"Sure, I guess."

"I just want to say I'm sorry, to you both, that's all."

"It's not your fault," Tom looked puzzled.

One More Try (Book 1)

"Not about that, about everything. When we were growing up."

"I'm a bit lost Robert you'll have to be more specific."

"You probably guessed but I had a huge crush on you," he looked at Iliana now, she didn't react since James had already told her.

"I thought you hated me; you were always so ..."

"Creepy?" he interrupted. She shrugged. "I know, I had a huge chip on my shoulder, I knew you liked Tom, and it really got to me. I'm not blaming Dad entirely, but he did encourage it, and he did tell me that you weren't his son." Tom's eyes went wide but he didn't say any more. "I really am sorry Iliana for creeping you out, I just wanted to be close to you."

"Oh Robert, you could have just tried talking to me?"

"Well, I know that now; of course, you would never have loved me but at least we could have been friends?"

"We still can." He smiled, a very genuine smile, she thought he seemed so much nicer when he wasn't scowling. "Apology accepted."

"Really?"

"Yes really."

She shocked herself by moving towards him with her arms out and offering him a hug. He was so taken aback it took him a while to put his arms around her shoulder and he didn't hold her for long, he was watching Tom carefully the whole time.

"Thanks. I met someone a few months ago and she has helped me realise a few things, her name is Lisa, maybe I can bring her to your wedding, if I'm invited?"

"That would be good," Tom replied with a smile.

"So, do you accept my apology too?"

"I do, not sure I am ready for a hug yet," he smiled and looked at Iliana, "but we'll work on that." Robert stepped forward to shake his hand instead which Tom did with a smile.

"Thanks guys, that means a lot, I best get back inside and let you go. Take care."

"You too, thanks for staying with Mom, remember to let us know if you need anything or get any hassle?"

"Will do, thanks bro."

Iliana thought to herself that was the only time she had heard Robert call Tom 'bro' which was especially poignant given the events of today. She suddenly felt like the day might end on a much nicer note than it had looked like it might have done earlier. She took Tom's hand and smiled at him before they got in the car. He just sat for a bit and sighed. She didn't want to keep asking him if he was okay, so she just touched his arm. "Let's just get home?"

"Yeah, of course, sorry," he shook himself.

"No need to apologise Tom, what a day it's been for you, I can't imagine how you are feeling but let's get home and we can talk about it, or not, if that's what you want?"

"What a day for *me*? What about you?"

"Hmm yes fair point, let's just get home, I am fine."

He frowned, "Should we maybe take you to the hospital for a check-up?"

"I don't think so, I haven't even seen a doctor yet so I will organise that as soon as I can. There's no sign that anything is wrong at all and it's probably too early for a scan, so I don't think we need to. Being sick is normal too, in fact I read it's a good sign."

"Ok then, if you're sure," he smiled at her and started the engine.

When they arrived home Iliana flopped herself down on the sofa, suddenly feeling quite tired.

"I'll get you something to eat, are you ok if I have a beer?"

"Of course, I am. I don't expect you to stop drinking just because I can't. I think after the day you've had then you deserve a beer or two."

"Well as I said, it's not just me." He paused for a second and took a sip of his beer, "I really thought I had lost you when I saw you lying on the ground. I had all sorts of awful scenarios going through my mind in that split second before you moved."

His voice wobbled, and he looked down, she stood up and walked over to him. She put her arms around his neck and held him tight. He put his beer down on the kitchen worktop and put his arms around her waist to pull her closer.

"But you didn't lose me, I am here, we are here."

She put his hand on her tummy. He grinned.

"I still can't believe it; you said it could take months or years?"

"I know that's what I was told but here we are, it's early days yet though, a lot can happen."

"Really?"

"Yeah, but don't worry, the sickness is a good sign as I said." She led him by the hand over to the sofa. "I was sitting on the bench in mum's garden thinking of a way I could tell you, make it fun, can't believe I left the test in the trash so you could see it. That's not what I had in mind at all."

He sat next to her, "Well, I am glad you did, otherwise I might not have gone early to get you," he shivered at the thought of what might have been.

"Are you ok?"

"Yeah, I just got that same weird sensation as last time when you were talking about your necklace, and an image in my head." He shook his head.

"What kind of image?"

"Never mind. Anyway, it doesn't matter now, maybe you can do that with the next one?" he chuckled, and she laughed with him.

"Steady."

"So, how do you feel about the wedding now then? I know I said before that I wanted to be married first but it doesn't really matter now, unless ..."

"Unless what?"

One More Try (Book 1)

"Unless we get married soon, like next month or something?"

"Where would we be able to get married at short notice like that though?"

"Well, I did have a thought, not sure how you would feel about it, or if you wanted a big church wedding like Brad and Jane." He paused and gazed at her; she couldn't figure out what he was trying to say. "I could ask Mom tomorrow about getting married at Harrow Falls. We could have the service and meal there and all we would have to arrange is caterers and someone qualified to marry us."

"Hmm that sounds like a really good idea actually, I like the idea of being married to you as soon as possible." She reached over and kissed him on the lips.

"Yeah, me too," he suddenly frowned and looked away.

"What's wrong?"

"I just had a thought, we haven't talked about this yet, but do you really want to have the surname of Anderson after what happened today? Come to think of it, I don't think I want that surname either!"

"Hmm, I hadn't thought of that."

"I'll talk to Mom about it tomorrow, maybe I could change mine to her maiden name, I'll ask her more about my real father too of course but then I wouldn't want his name if he abandoned her."

He frowned and she reached over for his free hand again.

"Yeah, that sounds like a good plan, talk to your mom more first. I am happy with whatever you decide, as long as we have the same name."

"Thanks Illy, but I'll talk to her, and we'll decide together as it affects you too."

They enjoyed a nice meal together and then chilled out on the sofa for the rest of the night.

Chapter 41

Iliana was getting ready for the best day of her life, she had gone for a subtle sparkly two-piece outfit so that she wasn't conscious about her tummy, not that she had a bump yet as she was only eight weeks along, but she felt better about it this way. It was quite plain with a strapless top and she had her hair tied up. Liz had put a little light make up on her face too. They had talked it over with Tom's Mum and she was delighted that they wanted to get married at Harrow Falls. They would have the ceremony outside near the beach then there would be a reception, also outside, with the option of a covered area in case of rain. Tom and Iliana would stay over in one of the chalets, the 'honeymoon' chalet they called it as it was a bit bigger and extra special.

Tom had changed his name after the events of last month, his Mum and the rest of his family understood of course, and he had gone with his Mum's maiden name of Williams since that was his grandfather's surname. She couldn't wait to see Tom in his suit again, she was lost in thought when she heard Liz speak, "That's you done my lovely. You look beautiful."

"Thanks, but you have to say that." They giggled.

Her Mum was giving her away today and she waited in the corner dressed in a lovely light blue skirt suit, with a small fascinator and sandals in matching colours.

"Ok I am ready, are we fashionably late or really late?"

"We are fashionably late so don't worry, "Liz replied, she was her bridesmaid and was wearing a long burgundy satin dress, with thin straps, and fitted at the waist then straight down to her ankles. There was a split in the back so that she could at least walk without waddling, which was one of her main concerns; she looked amazing, as always.

Her Mum took Iliana's arm and Liz walked behind them; they left the chalet, and Liz helped her down the stairs then they slowly walked towards the ceremony area. It was beautiful, with rows of seats on each side and a small arch where the minister stood, with Tom and his best man Brad standing next to him.

As they made their way slowly towards the makeshift aisle adorned with a long piece of red carpet, the music started up. She saw a few people turn around and felt a surge of what could only be described as pure love. This was everyone she loved all in one place, here to help celebrate her marriage to the love of her life. She felt a bit overwhelmed suddenly. Then she saw Tom watching her walk down the aisle. He smiled at her, just as he had at Brad's wedding, she smiled back and couldn't take her eyes off him. She didn't think it was possible, but he looked even more handsome than he had that day, maybe it was just because today he was all hers. When she reached the altar, her Mum stood to the side and Liz stood behind her.

Tom gazed at her in his own way that she loved, the one that made her feel like she was the only person there with him. "You look so beautiful," he whispered and gently brushed her hand. She could see tears in his eyes and was fighting hard to stop them herself, she really didn't want to look like a panda if her make up all ran.

"Hey handsome," was all she could manage to say with a smile and a slight squeeze of his hand.

The ceremony was a bit of a blur for her, she just spent it gazing at Tom and was vaguely aware of the minister talking until he finally said, "You may kiss your bride," Iliana moved closer to Tom, she couldn't stop smiling at him and he appeared to be the same. He lifted his hand and gently touched her jaw, much like he had done when he gave her the necklace all those years ago and kissed her lightly on the lips. He then put out his arm for her to take as they turned to walk back down the aisle together. She smiled at all the people watching them, her school friends, Becca and Vicky, Tom's school friends and their partners and families.

After the photos they mingled with the guests then sat down for the meal. The tables were simply covered with white cloths and flowers in the middle to add a bit of colour.

One More Try (Book 1)

The chairs were covered in white with a silk burgundy bow. Iliana had wanted the speeches to be before the meal so that Tom could relax but she couldn't help thinking that he seemed really relaxed anyway. When the time came Tom stood up, straightened his jacket a bit and tapped the glass with his fork.

"I would just like to start as I mean to go on. My wife has asked me to do something, so I had better get it done and done now, just in case." There was a lot of laughter at this. "Seriously though, we wanted to make a special toast before I start with all of my thank yous and my own toast. This one is extra special because it is for someone who couldn't be here today and would have loved to have been," he looked around and at Iliana who could feel the tears coming already. "Andrew McCoy sadly passed away suddenly when Iliana was only nine years old, so Mary walked her down the aisle today. We wanted everyone to raise a glass for the man who should also be at the top table with us." He raised his glass and everyone else stood up, "Andrew McCoy." Iliana lifted her glass of sparkling water but could feel the tears streaming down her face. Everyone sat back down again, and Tom composed himself to carry on. "Thanks. Ok some special thank yous now from both of us. We would like to thank my brother Brad, sister Elizabeth, my mom Patricia and Iliana's mom Mary for all their help with organising the wedding. All of this," he gestured around him, "beautiful setting was their doing mostly. Iliana told them what she wanted, and they made it happen, it looks amazing too so thank you all," he raised his glass, and they all nodded in acknowledgement. "OK, now the most important part," he smiled, "I would like to talk about my wife for a bit if you don't mind," everyone 'Aawww-ed', and he beamed. "Where do I start?" He paused again, he seemed to be in his element, Iliana smiled to herself, feeling so proud of her husband, "Iliana used to describe herself to me as 'plain', does anyone here think she looks plain?" he gestured towards her with his arm and shook his head. Everyone did the same, Iliana could feel herself blushing profusely. "No, definitely not plain, we all agree." He smiled at her. "She used to say that when she walked into a room, no one would notice, unlike her beautiful best friend who would turn every head in the place," he glanced at her and at Liz. "My answer to that is, *IF* that is the case, and that's a big IF, then you bring something extra to that room, you can work it like no one else I know. You can talk to everyone and anyone in that place and no matter how different they are you can find something in common with them and make friends, so, if the people in that room didn't notice you enter, again big IF, then they would most certainly notice by the time you left that room. Then of course, when you came back in, they would notice too." Everyone' Aawww-ed' again as he paused and smiled at her, "Okay, nearly done then we can eat don't worry." He got another laugh at that comment. "Leading on from Iliana's ability to talk to people, she is now qualified for teaching as you all know. It's something she has always wanted to do and something I understand she is very good at. I know that she has most definitely taught me a lot, about friendship, love, family ..." he gazed at her, and she could feel the tears building up again at the word family, she touched her tummy under the table in an involuntary movement. "I know that she will continue to teach me as well, as we start out in our journey of married life together." He appeared to swallow then continued, "Iliana, thank you for making me the happiest man in the world, I promise to do my best to be a great husband to you." He paused again as his voice wobbled, "My final toast is for the *beautiful* bride" he raised his glass, and everyone stood up and repeated. Goodness she wasn't prepared for how emotional this was. "Thanks everyone, enjoy your meal."

 Tom sat down and looked over at her with tears in his eyes, she couldn't form any words at all. She moved her seat closer to his, leaned into him and put her head on his shoulder. He put his arm around her and held her, "Okay?"

One More Try (Book 1)

"Yes, thank you. Just when I thought I couldn't love you more." She smiled at him, and he gave her a kiss.

"Well, that's pretty much how I feel most of the time, welcome to my world."

She chuckled.

After the first dance they both went to mingle, Iliana went to the toilet and on her way back she passed Billy at the bar, he had just ordered drinks and waved her over.

"Hey Iliana. What a lovely wedding, you look amazing. Do you want a drink?"

"Thanks Billy, I have a drink somewhere. I am so glad you guys could come."

"You are kidding, we wouldn't have missed it for anything."

"I know you worried about me at first, you know, but here we are," she couldn't help but remember their conversation before Prom.

"Hey that was a long time ago, I am so happy for you Iliana. It's quite clear how much he loves you, really, if I had known that then I wouldn't have said what I did."

"Oh thanks, I know you were just being a good friend. If it makes you feel any better, he said he would have done the same."

"What? You told him?"

"Ah, oops, yeah maybe, only because we were talking about his reputation. Sorry, it was ages ago though, when we first started going out, he probably won't even remember."

"Yeah right, oh well it's been a nice day I'll be heading off now," he laughed nervously.

"Really, don't worry about it."

"Hey, Billy, isn't it?" Tom appeared from around the corner just at that moment, put his arm around Iliana, then reached out his other hand to shake Billy's.

"Ah yeah, congratulations to you both. Great speech it was really touching, and true."

"Thanks," Iliana was desperately trying to think of something to say and hoping Tom wouldn't say anything about the reputation comment.

"Did I see you come out of Benny's pool hall the other week?" Tom added.

"Yeah, you might have, I go there quite often. Do you play?"

"Yeah, and I go there a fair bit, surprised I haven't bumped into you. We should go sometime get a few games in?"

Iliana tried not to look shocked. She did a better job than Billy as he looked flabbergasted.

"Yeah, that would be great, I'd like that. I'll give you my number, just give me a call sometime?"

"Great, sounds good."

Billy tapped his pockets and looked around, "I'll get a pen and paper and hand it over to you later."

"Great, I'm off to mingle some more, talk soon," And with that, Tom walked off.

Iliana just looked at Billy and shrugged, "Told you, he is pretty wonderful actually."

"Yeah, it seems that way," Billy smiled at her, a very genuine smile. "See you later." He took his drinks from the bar then went to find Becca.

Iliana moved away from the bar and wondered if there was anyone she hadn't talked to yet. She also thought she should get some water and sit down as she was starting to feel quite tired. She saw Jane carrying Helena with Ethan trailing behind. Jane's parents arrived to take the kids away then Jane flopped down on a seat, Iliana went to join her.

"How are you doing Iliana?"

"Good, really good."

"What a lovely wedding, and what about Tom's speech?"

"Oh, I know, I couldn't say anything for about fifteen minutes after it."

"Yeah, I saw that, it was so special, you guys are so amazing together. I'll never forget what you were like at our wedding, it was so sweet. Even Brad, who probably knows him the best, was shocked at the change in him, you just make him so happy. It's lovely to see."

"Thanks Jane, I am so excited about what's ahead. I'll need your help though of course, but I can't wait."

"Of course, you know where I am, us sisters-in-law have to stick together."

Iliana laughed, she really liked Jane and felt quite blessed to have her as a sister-in-law.

"Okay, I am off to mingle some more, I might even find my husband for a dance."

"Yes, good idea, I might do the same now that we are child free," Jane laughed, and they walked back into the main area.

Iliana then bumped into Lisa who was on her way to the toilets, this was the first time that she had met Robert's partner, and she thought she seemed very nice. They chatted for a bit before Iliana continued to search for Tom. She spotted him talking with Brad in an animated fashion and stopped to admire him for a bit. He did look very happy; she just couldn't believe how lucky she was. She walked towards him, and he glanced over, then smiled at her. He nodded at her,

"One more try?"

"Yes, that sounds good."

He walked over to the DJ, said a few words to him then came back over and held out his hands. The DJ mentioned something about a special request and that he would get back to the dance music after, but she wasn't really listening. She put her arms around Tom's neck, and he held her waist as they snuggled in, other couples joined them on the dance floor, and she just relaxed.

"You think we could have picked a happier song?" she chuckled.

"I am not sure how it became our song though, are you? I remember we heard it in the car when I was driving you home and you said something about the teacher being someone who showed you about life."

"Yeah, I remember that too."

"It was also playing in the cab the night of Brad's bachelor party when we first made love?"

"Oh yeah, so it was," he smiled. "You are my teacher, Illy, as I said in my speech."

"Oh, my goodness Tom your speech was so touching, everyone has commented on it."

"Have they? Well, it's all true."

They snuggled in together and enjoyed the moment.

One More Try (Book 1)

Chapter 42

They enjoyed the rest of the evening, mingling with guests, and the buffet happened about halfway through the night; by about eleven o'clock people started leaving. They said their good nights to everyone and then walked to their chalet. When they arrived Tom picked her up and carried her over the threshold which was supposed to be good luck. Someone, they suspected Liz, had left a small tray with a snack and a half bottle of champagne for them to share together and had decorated the room with flowers. It was a nice touch and they both appreciated it. Iliana sat down on the sofa and took off her sandals.

"What an amazing day, Jane did warn me it goes by so fast, and it really did."

"Yeah, it did. Do you want half a small glass of champagne to finish off the day?"

"Yes, that would be nice, I have had sparkling water all day," she smiled at him as he opened the small bottle of champagne and poured two half glasses. He sat down next to her on the sofa and handed her the smaller glass.

"Here's to us."

"To us," she sipped the champagne and felt the bubbles go to her head right away.

"Did you meet Robert's girlfriend Lisa?" Tom asked after a sip.

"Yes, I did, she seems nice."

"Well, as I said in my speech, you think everyone is nice because you are nice to everyone."

"Hmm, so what did you think then?"

"Actually, yes, she is nice. Too nice for him."

She nudged him with her elbow. "He has been a different person since that day," she didn't have to say any more than that. "I am happy for them."

"Yeah, that's true, she must be good for him. It's amazing what a good woman can do for a man," he laughed.

One More Try (Book 1)

They finished their drinks and snack then Tom went to the bathroom. Iliana thought she would sit on the bed and wait for him. Next thing she knew she woke up lying on the bed still in her wedding dress and next to her, already in bed, was Tom fast asleep. He was lying with his chest bare, the sheets were around his waist and his hands were behind his head. She shook him.

"Tom, did I fall asleep, I am so sorry?" He grumbled a bit but didn't open his eyes. "Tom, wake up?"

"What is it?"

"Did I fall asleep?"

"Yeah, but it's ok, you looked so happy sleeping I didn't want to disturb you, and I didn't want to try and take your dress off as it looked really complicated."

"Oh no, I am so sorry."

"It's ok, don't worry."

"I'm awake now?"

"Hmm," he still had his eyes closed.

She took off her dress and hung it up then removed all her underwear including the blue garter, then joined him in bed. She snuggled next to him, but he didn't stir.

"It's still strictly our wedding night; we can still get naked and have some fun?"

He opened one eye. "Really? Are you not tired?"

"No, not now, I am re energised," she giggled, and climbed on top of him, he opened the other eye and grinned at her.

*

They awoke the next morning feeling very content. Since they were special guests, they didn't have to check out at the normal time, so they planned on chilling out for most of the morning and recovering from a very busy day. They slept quite late; it was just about 10am when Iliana heard a faint knock at the door. She looked at Tom who was still asleep so got up, put her dressing gown on, then went to the door. There was no one there, but when she looked down there was a tray on the floor with a little note. The tray had tea,

One More Try (Book 1)

coffee, bagels, and some scrambled eggs. She lifted the tray and brought it inside the chalet. The note said, 'Good morning, Mr and Mrs Williams, enjoy your breakfast and chill out, love Liz.' She went over to the bed where Tom was still fast asleep and shook him awake.

"Breakfast is served," she whispered.

"Huh?" He stirred and sat up to see what was going on.

Iliana went over to the sofa and poured a coffee and a tea. He stretched and got out of bed, put boxers on, rubbed his hair sleepily and joined her on the sofa.

"What's all this then?"

"From Liz, and I suspect your Mum had a lot to do with it."

"Aw that's nice."

She handed him a bagel on a plate with some eggs.

"Thanks. Are we allowed to go back to bed after this?"

"Oh yes, I need more rest for sure."

He smiled at her. "Can we just stay in bed all day then?"

"Well, I need to eat every two hours so maybe not?"

"I am sure Liz and Mum have that covered," he chuckled.

"Have you thought any more about names for the baby?" she asked him.

"A bit, have you?"

"Yeah, a bit."

He raised his eyebrow. "And?"

"Well, I like Zac for a boy, what do you think of that?"

"I like it, a lot. It's a good name."

"Really? That's good."

"What about Amy if it's a girl?" he said, surprising her.

"Ooh yes, I like that too. Wow, well that was easy enough."

They both giggled.

"It seems so far away but I am sure it will all just fly by."

"Yeah definitely."

*

One More Try (Book 1)

Iliana sat up in the hospital bed looking at her son in her arms, all wrapped up in a light blue blanket. Tom was looking at her with tears in his eyes, she was worried she was going to cry too and drop big wet tears all over their baby boy's beautiful face.

"You did so well. I can't believe what you ladies go through." He had been with her through the whole birth, pulling her hair out of her face and holding her hand.

"It's worth it," she smiled at him.

"Do you think he looks like a Zac then?"

"Yes, I do, Zac really suits him."

"Yeah, I agree. Can I hold him or is it too soon?"

"Of course, you can. He wants to wish you a Happy Birthday."

He chuckled. She reached over with Zac as Tom stood up and held out his arms. He took the baby then carefully sat back down again, cradling him in his arms.

"He is just perfect." He was smiling down at Zac, and she could feel happy tears again.

"He is, isn't he?"

"Perfect," he appeared to swallow a lump in his throat. "He is just so small, look at his tiny little hands and fingers."

She chuckled.

"He won't stay tiny for long I am sure of it."

He smiled at her.

"Zac, I promise to try and be a good Dad to you, help look after you and protect you."

"You will make a wonderful father Tom; I just know it."

"I hope so."

"You've looked after your siblings for so long, even taught them to ride a bike, you'll be great."

He smiled back at her, neither of them wanted to say that he would be a far better father than his stepdad. They didn't talk about him anymore and they wouldn't ruin a lovely moment like this by mentioning him. No one had heard from him since their Mum threw him out of the house, she had packed all his clothes and put them in a charity shop.

"Your mom will be desperate to see him, shall I go and get her?"

"Ok, but you enjoy your cuddle first then she can see him. He will likely want to be fed soon anyway."

He nodded.

"I think he looks like you."

"How can you tell when he is so tiny?"

"Just his features I guess."

"He has blue eyes."

"All babies have blue eyes when they are born. They change colour later, can't remember exactly when. They are a very dark blue so I think they will change colour."

One More Try (Book 1)

Epilogue

Dear Dad,

Mum suggested it might be a good idea to write this letter to you since it's now twenty-three years since we lost you and so much has happened in my life that I wanted to tell you about. It seemed strange at the time but now that I am writing it doesn't feel that way at all.

There isn't a day that goes by that I don't think of you really, my wedding day was wonderful but tough as Mum and I knew you would have loved to be there to give me away. We at least made a toast to you which was nice, albeit emotional. I would have loved for you to meet my husband, Tom; I think you would like him. He is a wonderful husband and father to our three children, Zac who is eight, Ryan who is nearly five and Amy who is three. As I am writing this, I am looking out at them all playing soccer in the yard. Well, it's mostly Tom and Zac really and the others are just running around after them, but they are all having fun. Zac is keen on soccer for some reason, Mum said you used to like it so maybe that's where he gets it. He is also interested in what Tom does around this place and often insists on following him around, it's very sweet. He can already ride his bike so rides around with him and runs errands for him. Tom is so great with our children, we haven't talked about having any more yet, but I think it might happen, he has also mentioned getting a dog which we all like the idea of, so we'll see. He doesn't have favourites of course but I can't help but feel like there is such a special bond between him and Zac, they are so close and very alike too, especially their green eyes.

We now live in Tom's Mum's old house. She said it was far too big for her now and it needed a lot of work so Tom, with help from all his brothers, renovated it and we moved in not long after we had Zac. He also renovated the chalets and runs the business, with help from his Mum of course, she lives in his old place and often comes over along with Mum to help with the kids. I am teaching part time and have also done some private tutoring which I really enjoy.

One More Try (Book 1)

We have hosted Thanksgiving quite a few times as well which has been great, sometimes it's the whole family which is a lot of people but it's a wonderful occasion and one I know Mum and Tom's Mum really enjoy as all the kids are together in one place. Liz doesn't have any kids yet, but she is very happy with her partner John and focussing on her career for now, Robert and Lisa have a little girl who is close in age with our youngest.

Anyway, I do feel like we have had a chat of sorts so I may write again Dad. I just wanted to let you know how happy we are, I hope that we have made you proud.

Your loving daughter, Iliana.

THE END ... for this reality ... but what else could have been different? Is anyone else impacted by Tom and Iliana's decisions?

Read book two to find out what happened when Iliana returned eight years later to find Tom in a relationship with someone familiar. Or, what would happen if she told him about her pregnancy?

One More Try (Book 1)

Acknowledgements

I had so much help and encouragement for this book that I almost don't know where to start! I guess I should start at the beginning, thanks to Laurie and Jackie for being the first ones to read it (and a very raw version if I remember correctly) and provide initial feedback. Then latterly my fabulous beta readers Catrina and Valerie, for indulging me and going a step further with regular meet ups and detailed feedback. I wouldn't have gotten here without your support and encouragement so thank you from the bottom of my heart!

Now for the lovely Karen, who runs Mabel and Stanley Publishing, and has led me through the whole process with help, encouragement and always a smile along the way. This book would not be in front of you right now if it weren't for her. Of course, I can't thank Karen without thanking all the members of the Mabel and Stanley Writing & Publishing Community group, we meet every month, and I always come away from the calls feeling inspired, motivated and thoroughly supported so thank you all. Latterly of course Sam has helped me a lot, as she did me the good deed of publishing her first book a few months before me, so has helped immensely and most of all put up with my barrage of constant questions!

In the lead up to launch date, Danii Butler, of Build the Buzz, has provided me with some very much needed support for marketing and social media, as soon as we had our initial meeting I instantly felt better and very much safe in her expert hands.

One More Try (Book 1)

Lastly, for my husband Paul, who has helped, encouraged, supported and listened to me for the last several years. He has also put up with me disappearing for entire or part days to the library or whichever coffee shop I choose to take my laptop to so that I can immerse myself in writing or editing to my heart's content.

Hopefully I haven't missed anyone but apologies in advance if I have, but it's a series so I'll catch them next time if that's the case!

About the Author

Paula Russell lives in the beautiful city of Edinburgh with her husband, son and two cats.

She has a BEng in Information Technology and Electronics and currently works as a Business Analyst/Project Manager.

Apart from reading of course, she enjoys walks, exercise and watching Tennis and Football.

You can find out more about Paula on her website ...

www.paulacrussellwriter.com

and social media accounts on Facebook and Instagram - @paulacrussell

Printed in Great Britain
by Amazon